Marion Lenno... dairy farm. She moved on, because the cows just weren't interested in her stories! Married to a 'very special doctor', she has also written under the name Trisha David. She's now stepped back from her 'other' career teaching statistics. Finally, she's figured what's important and discovered the joys of baths, romance and chocolate. Preferably all at the same time! Marion is an international award winning author.

New Zealander **Alison Roberts** has written more than eighty romance novels for Mills & Boon. She has also worked as a primary school teacher, a cardiology research technician and a paramedic. Currently, she is living her dream of living – and writing – in a gorgeous village in the south of France.

Fiona McArthur is an Australian midwife who lives in the country and loves to dream. Writing Medical Romance gives Fiona the scope to write about all the wonderful aspects of romance, adventure, medicine and the midwifery she feels so passionate about. When not writing, Fiona's either at home on the farm with her husband or off to meet new people, see new places and have wonderful adventures. Drop in and say hi at Fiona's website www.fionamcarthurauthor.com

Midwives' Miracles

Midwives' Miracles:
Healing Hearts

MARION LENNOX

ALISON ROBERTS

FIONA McARTHUR

MILLS & BOON

First Published in Great Britain 2022
By Mills & Boon, an imprint of HarperCollins*Publishers,* Ltd
1 London Bridge Street, London, SE1 9GF

www.harpercollins.co.uk

HarperCollins*Publishers*
1st Floor, Watermarque Building,
Ringsend Road, Dublin 4, Ireland

MIDWIVES MIRACLES: HEALING HEARTS © 2022 Harlequin Books S.A.

Meant-to-be Family © 2015 Harlequin Books S.A.
Always the Midwife © 2015 Harlequin Books S.A.
Healed by the Midwife's Kiss © 2018 Fiona McArthur

Special thanks and acknowledgement are given to Marion Lennox for her contribution to the *Midwives On-Call* series

Special thanks and acknowledgement are given to Alison Roberts for her contribution to the *Midwives On-Call* series

ISBN: 978-0-263-30401-5

MEANT-TO-BE FAMILY

MARION LENNOX

With thanks to my fellow authors, who've helped make this Midwives On-Call series fabulous. A special thank-you to Alison Roberts, for her friendship, her knowledge and her generosity in sharing, and to Fiona McArthur, whose midwife skills leave me awed.

CHAPTER ONE

LATE. LATE, LATE, LATE. This was the third morning this week. Her boss would have kittens.

Not that Isla was in the mood to be angry, Em thought, as she swiped her pass at the car-park entry. The head midwife for Melbourne's Victoria Hospital had hardly stopped smiling since becoming engaged. She and her fiancé had been wafting around the hospital in a rosy glow that made Em wince.

Marriage. 'Who needs it?' she demanded out loud, as she swung her family wagon through the boom gates and headed for her parking spot on the fifth floor. She should apply for a lower spot—she always seemed to be running late—but her family wagon needed more space than the normal bays. One of the Victoria's obstetricians rode a bike. He was happy to park his Harley to one side of his bay, so this was the perfect arrangement.

Except it was on the fifth floor—and she was late again.

The car in front of her was slow going up the ramp. *Come on...* She should have been on the wards fifteen minutes ago. But Gretta had been sick. Again.

Things were moving too fast. She needed to take the little girl back to the cardiologist, but the last time she'd taken her, he'd said...

No. Don't go there. *There* was unthinkable. She raked

her fingers through her unruly curls, trying for distraction. She'd need to pin her hair up before she got to the ward. Had she remembered pins?

It didn't work. Her mind refused to be distracted, and the cardiologist's warning was still ringing in her ears.

'Emily, I'm sorry, but we're running out of time.'

Was Gretta's heart condition worsening, or was this just a tummy bug? The little girl had hugged her tight as she'd left, and it had been all she could do to leave her. If her mum hadn't been there… But Adrianna adored being a gran. 'Get into work, girl, and leave Gretta to me. Toby and I will watch *Play School* while Gretta has a nap. I'll ring you if she's not better by lunchtime. Meanwhile, go!'

She'd practically shoved her out the door.

But there *was* something wrong—and she knew what it was. The cardiologist had been blunt and she remembered his assessment word for word.

It was all very well, hearing it, she thought bleakly, but seeing it… At the weekend she'd taken both kids to their favourite place in the world, the children's playground at the Botanic Gardens. There was a water rill there that Gretta adored. She'd crawled over it as soon as she could crawl, and then she'd toddled and walked.

Six months ago she'd stood upright on the rill and laughed with delight as the water had splashed over her toes. At the weekend she hadn't even been able to crawl. Em had sat on the rill with her, trying to make her smile, but the little girl had sobbed. She knew what she was losing.

Don't! Don't think about it! Move on. Or she'd move on if she could.

'Come on.' She was inwardly yelling at the car in front. The car turned the corner ponderously then—praise be!— turned into a park on Level Four. Em sighed with relief, zoomed up the last ramp and hauled the steering wheel left, as she'd done hundreds of times in the past to turn into her parking space.

And...um...stopped.

There was a car where Harry's bike should be. A vintage sports car, burgundy, gleaming with care and polish.

Wider than a bike.

Instead of a seamless, silent transition to park, there was the appalling sound of metal on metal.

Her wagon had a bull bar on the front, designed to deflect stray bulls—or other cars during minor bingles. It meant her wagon was as tough as old boots. It'd withstand anything short of a road train.

The thing she'd hit wasn't quite as tough.

She'd ripped the side off the sports car.

Oliver Evans, gynaecologist, obstetrician and in-utero surgeon, was gathering his briefcase and his suit jacket from the passenger seat. He'd be meeting the hospital bigwigs today so he needed to be formal. He was also taking a moment to glance through the notes he had on who he had to meet, who he needed to see.

He vaguely heard the sound of a car behind him. He heard it turning from the ramp...

The next moment the passenger side of his car was practically ripped from the rest.

It was a measure of Em's fiercely practised calm that she didn't scream. She didn't burst into tears. She didn't even swear.

She simply stared straight ahead. Count to ten, she told herself. When that didn't work, she tried twenty.

She figured it out, quite quickly. Her parking spot was supposed to be wider but that was because she shared the two parking bays with Harry the obstetrician's bike and Harry had left. Of course. She'd even dropped in on his farewell party last Friday night, even though it had only been for five minutes because the kids had been waiting.

So Harry had left. This car, then, would belong to the doctor who'd taken his place.

She'd just welcomed him by trashing his car.

'I have insurance. I have insurance. I have insurance.' It was supposed to be her mantra. Saying things three times helped, only it didn't help enough. She put her head on the steering wheel and felt a wash of exhaustion so profound she felt like she was about to melt.

His car was trashed.

He climbed from the driver's seat and stared at his beloved Morgan in disbelief. The Morgan was low slung, gorgeous—and fragile. He'd parked her right in the centre of the bay to avoid the normal perils of parking lots—people opening doors and scratching his paintwork.

But the offending wagon had a bull bar attached and it hadn't just scratched his paintwork. While the wagon looked to be almost unscathed, the passenger-side panels of the Morgan had been sheared off completely.

He loved this baby. He'd bought her five years ago, a post-marriage toy to make him feel better about the world. He'd cherished her, spent a small fortune on her and then put her into very expensive storage while he'd been overseas.

His qualms about returning to Australia had been tempered by his joy on being reunited with Betsy. But now… some idiot with a huge lump of a wagon—and a bull bar…

'What the hell did you think you were doing?' He couldn't see the driver of the wagon yet, but he was venting his spleen on the wagon itself. Of all the ugly, lumbering excuses for a car…

And it was intact. Yeah, it'd have a few extra scratches

but there were scratches all over it already. It was a battered, dilapidated brute and the driver'd be able to keep driving like the crash had never happened.

He wanted to kick it. Of all the stupid, careless...

Um...why hadn't the driver moved?

And suddenly medical mode kicked in, overriding rage. Maybe the driver had had a heart attack. A faint. Maybe this was a medical incident rather than sheer stupidity. He took a deep breath, switching roles in an instant. Infuriated driver became doctor. The wagon's driver's door was jammed hard against where his passenger door used to be, so he headed for its passenger side.

The wagon's engine died. Someone was alive in there, then. Good. Or sort of good.

He hauled the door open and he hadn't quite managed the transition. Rage was still paramount.

'You'd better be having a heart attack.' It was impossible to keep the fury from his voice. 'You'd better have a really good excuse as to why you ploughed this heap of scrap metal into my car! You want to get out and explain?'

No!

Things were already appalling—but things just got a whole lot worse.

This was a voice she knew. A voice from her past.

Surely not.

She *had* to be imagining it, she decided, but she wasn't opening her eyes. If it really was...

It couldn't be. She was tired, she was frantically worried about Gretta, she was late and she'd just crashed her car. No wonder she was hearing things.

'You're going to have to open your eyes and face things.' She said it to herself, under her breath. Then she repeated it in her head twice more but her three-times mantra still didn't seem to be working.

The silence outside the car was ominous. Toe-tappingly threatening.

Maybe it'd go away if she just stayed…

'Hey, are you okay?' The gravelly voice, angry at first, was now concerned.

But it was the same voice and this wasn't her imagination. This was horrendously, appallingly real.

Voices could be the same, she told herself, feeling herself veering towards hysteria. There had to be more than one voice in the world that sounded like his.

She'd stay just one moment longer with her eyes closed.

Her passenger door opened and someone slid inside. Large. Male.

Him.

His hand landed on hers on the steering wheel. 'Miss? Are you hurt? Can I help?' And as the anger in his voice gave way to caring she knew, unmistakably, who this was.

Oliver. The man she'd loved with all her heart. The man who'd walked away five years ago to give her the chance of a new life.

So many emotions were slamming through her head… anger, bewilderment, grief… She'd had five years to move on but, crazy or not, this man still felt a part of her.

She'd crashed his car. He was right here.

There was no help for it. She took a deep, deep breath. She braced herself.

She raised her head, and she turned to face her husband.

Emily.

He was seeing her but his mind wasn't taking her in. Emily!

For one wild moment he thought he must be mistaken. This was a different woman, older, a bit…worn round the edges. Weary? Faded jeans and stained windcheater. Unkempt curls.

But still Emily.

His wife? She still was, he thought stupidly. His Em.

But she wasn't his Em. He'd walked away five years ago. He'd left her to her new life, and she had nothing to do with him.

Except she was here. She was staring up at him, her eyes reflecting his disbelief. Horror?

Shock held him rigid.

She'd wrecked his car. He loved this car. He should be feeling…

No. There was no *should*, or if there was he hadn't read that particular handbook.

Should he feel grief? Should he feel guilt?

He felt neither. All he felt was numb.

She'd had a minute's warning. He'd had none.

'Em?' He looked…incredulous. He looked more shocked than she was—bewildered beyond words.

What were you supposed to say to a husband you hadn't seen or spoken to for five years? There was no handbook for this.

'H-hi?' she managed.

'You've just crashed my car,' he said, stupidly.

'You were supposed to be a bike.' Okay, maybe that was just as stupid. This conversation was going exactly nowhere. They'd established, what, that he wasn't a bike?

He was her husband—and he was right beside her. Looking completely dumbfounded.

'You have a milk stain on your shoulder.'

That would be the first thing he'd notice, she thought. Her uniform was in her bag. She never put it on at home— her chances of getting out of the house clean were about zero—so she was still wearing jeans and the baggy wind-cheater she'd worn at breakfast.

Gretta had had a milky drink before being ill. Em had picked her up and cuddled her before she'd left.

Strangely, the stain left her feeling exposed. She didn't want this man to see…her.

'There are child seats in your wagon.'

He still sounded incredulous. Milk stains? Family wagon? He'd be seeing a very different woman from the one he'd seen five years ago.

But he looked…just the same. Same tall, lean, gorgeous. Same deep brown eyes that crinkled at the edges when he smiled, and Oliver smiled a lot. Same wide mouth and strong bone structure. Same dark, wavy hair, close cropped to try and get rid of the curl, only that never worked. It was so thick. She remembered running her fingers through that hair…

Um, no. Not appropriate. Regardless of formalities, this was her husband. Or ex-husband? They hadn't bothered with divorce yet but she'd moved on.

She'd just crashed his car.

'You're using Harry's car park,' she said, pointing accusingly at…um…one slightly bent sports car. It was beautiful—at least some of it still was. An open sports car. Vintage. It wasn't the sort of car that you might be able to pop down to the car parts place in your lunch hour and buy a new panel.

He'd always loved cars. She remembered the day they'd sold his last sports car.

His last? No. Who knew how many cars he'd been through since? Anyway, she remembered the day they'd sold the sleek little roadster both of them had loved, trading it in for a family wagon. Smaller than this but just as sensible. They'd gone straight from the car showroom to the nursery suppliers, and had had the baby seat fitted there and then.

She'd been six months pregnant. They'd driven home with identical smug looks on their faces.

He'd wanted a family as much as she had. Or she'd thought he did. What had happened then had proved she hadn't known him at all.

'I've been allocated this car park,' he was saying, and she had to force herself back to here, to now. 'Level Five, Bay Eleven. That's mine.'

'You're visiting?'

'I'm employed here, as of today.'

'You can't be.'

He didn't reply. He climbed out of the wagon, dug his hands deep in his pockets, glanced back at his wreck of a car and looked at her again.

'Why can't I, Em?' The wreck of the car faded to secondary importance. This was suddenly all about them.

'Because I work here.'

'It's the most specialised neonatal service in Melbourne. You know that's what I do.'

'You went to the States.' She felt numb. Stupid. Out of control. She'd been sure her ex-husband had been on the other side of world. She didn't want him to be here.

'I did specialist training in in-utero surgery in the States.' This was a dumb conversation. He was out of the car, leaning back on one of the concrete columns, watching her as she clung to the steering wheel like she was drowning. 'I've accepted a job back here. And before you say anything, no, I didn't know you were working here. I thought you were still at Hemmingway Private. I knew when I came back that there was a chance we might meet, but Melbourne's a big place. I'm not stalking you.'

'I never meant...'

'No?'

'No,' she managed. 'And I'm sorry I crashed into your car.'

Finally things were starting to return to normal. Like

her heart rate. Her pulse had gone through the roof when the cars had hit. She'd been subconsciously trying to get it down, practising the deep-breathing techniques she used when she was pacing the floor with Gretta, frightened for herself, frightened for the future. The techniques came to her aid instinctively now when she was frightened. Or discombobulated.

Discombobulated was how she felt, she conceded. Stalking? That sounded as if he thought she might be frightened of him, and she'd never been frightened of Oliver.

'Can we exchange details?' she managed, trying desperately to sound normal. Like this was a chance meeting of old acquaintants, but they needed to talk about car insurance. 'Oliver, it's really nice to see you again...' Was it? Um, no, but it sounded the right thing to say. 'But I'm late as it is.'

'Which was why you crashed.'

'Okay, it was my fault,' she snapped. 'But, believe it or not, there are extenuating circumstances. That's not your business.' She clambered out of the car and dug for her licence in her shabby holdall. She pulled out two disposable diapers and a packet of baby wipes before she found her purse, and she was so flustered she dropped them. Oliver gathered them without a word, and handed them back. She flushed and handed him her licence instead.

He took it wordlessly, and studied it.

'You still call yourself Emily Evans?'

'You know we haven't divorced. That's irrelevant. You're supposed to take down my address.'

'You're living at your mother's house?'

'I am.' She grabbed her licence back. 'Finished?'

'Aren't you supposed to take mine?'

'You can sue me. I can't sue you. We both know the fault was mine. If you're working here then I'll send you my insurance details via interdepartmental memo. I don't carry them with me.'

'You seem to carry everything else.' Once more he was looking into the car, taking in the jumble of kids' paraphernalia that filled it.

'I do, don't I?' she said, as cordially as she could manage. 'Oliver, it's good to see you again. I'm sorry I wrecked your car but I'm running really, really late.'

'You never run late.' He was right: punctuality used to be her god.

'I'm not the Emily you used to know,' she managed. 'I'm a whole lot different but this isn't the time or the place to discuss it.' She looked again at his car and winced. She really had made an appalling mess. 'You want me to organise some sort of tow?'

'Your car's hardly dented. I'll handle mine.'

'I'm…sorry.' She took a deep breath. 'Oliver, I really am sorry but I really do need to go. If there's nothing I can do…'

He was peering into her wagon. 'I doubt your lock's still working,' he told her. 'Once my car's towed free…'

'Locks are the least of my worries.' She slung her bag over her shoulder, knowing she had to move. She knew Isla was short-staffed this morning and the night staff would be aching to leave. 'Look at the stains,' she told him. 'No villain in their right mind would steal my wagon and, right now, I don't have time to care. I'm sorry to leave you with this mess, Oliver, but I need to go. Welcome to Victoria Hospital. See you around.'

CHAPTER TWO

Ruby Dowell was seventeen years old, twenty-two weeks pregnant and terrified. She was Oliver's first patient at the Victoria.

She was also the reason he'd started so soon. He'd been recruited to replace Harry Eichmann, an obstetrician with an interest in in-utero procedures. Oliver had started the same way, but for him in-utero surgery was more than a side interest. For the last five years he'd been based in the States but he'd travelled the world learning the latest techniques.

The phone call he'd had from Charles Delamere, Victoria's CEO, had been persuasive, to say the least. 'Harry's following a girlfriend to Europe. There's no one here with your expertise and there's more and more demand.

'It's time you came home. Oliver, right now we have a kid here with a twenty-one-week foetus, and her scans are showing spina bifida. Heinz Zigler, our paediatric neurologist, says the operation has to be done now. He can do the spinal stuff but he doesn't have the skills to stop the foetus aborting. Oliver, there are more and more of these cases, and we're offering you a full-time job. If you get here fast, we might save this kid shunts, possible brain damage, a life with limited movement below the waist. Short term, I want you to fight to give this kid a happy ending. Long term we're happy to fund your research. We'll cover the costs of whatever extra training you want, any staff you need. We want the best, Oliver, and we're prepared to pay, but we want you now.'

The offer had been great, but he'd had serious reservations about returning to Melbourne. He'd walked away from his marriage five years ago, and he'd thought he'd stay away. Em had deserved a new life, a chance to start again with someone who'd give her what she needed.

And it seemed his decision had been justified. Seeing her this morning, driving a family wagon, with milk stains on her shoulder, with every sign of being a frazzled young working mum, he'd thought…

Actually, he hadn't thought. The sight had knocked him sideways and he was still knocked sideways. But he needed to focus on something other than his marriage. After a brief introduction with Charles, he was in the examination room with Ruby Dowell. Teenage mother, pregnant with a baby with spina bifida.

'At twenty-two weeks we need to get on with this fast,' Charles had told him. 'There's such a short window for meaningful intervention.'

Ruby was lying on the examination couch in a cubicle in the antenatal clinic and, as with all his patients, he took a moment at the start to assess the whole package. Her notes said she was seventeen. She'd been attending clinics in the Victoria's Teenage Mums-To-Be programme. When the spina bifida had been detected on the scans she'd been offered termination but had declined, although the notes said she intended to give the baby up for adoption after birth. Right now she was dressed in shorts and an oversized T-shirt. Her mouse-blonde, shoulder-length hair was in need of a wash and a good cut. Apart from the bump of her pregnancy she was waif thin, and her eyes were red-rimmed and wide with fear.

She looked like a wild creature trapped in a cage, he thought. Hell, why was she alone? Her notes said she was a single mum, but she should have her mother with her, or a sister, or at least a friend.

It was unthinkable that such a kid was alone. Charles had said that Isla, his daughter and also the Victoria's head midwife, was in charge of the Teenage Mums-To-Be programme. Why hadn't she organised to be here, or at least sent a midwife in her place?

But now wasn't the time to head to the nurses' station and blast the powers that be for leaving her like this. Now was the time for reassurance.

'Hey,' he said, walking into the cubicle but deliberately leaving the screens open. He didn't need to do a physical examination yet, and he didn't want that trapped look to stay a moment longer. 'I'm the baby surgeon, Oliver Evans. I'm an obstetrician who's specially trained in operating on babies when they're still needing to stay inside their mums. And you're Ruby Dowell?'

He hauled a chair up to the bedside and summoned his best reassuring manner. 'Ruby, I'm here to get to know you, that's all. Nothing's happening right now. I'm just here to talk.'

But the terrified look stayed. She actually cringed back on the bed, fear radiating off her in waves. 'I'm... I'm scared of operations,' she stuttered. 'I don't want to be here.'

But then the screen was pulled back still further. A woman in nursing uniform, baggy tunic over loose pants, was fastening the screen so Ruby could see the nurses' station at the end of the corridor.

Emily. His wife.

His ex-wife? She'd never asked for a divorce but it had been simply a matter of signing the papers, any time these last five years.

'I'm scared of operations, too,' Em said, matter-of-factly, as if she'd been involved in the conversation from the start. 'I think everyone is. But Dr Evans here is the best baby surgeon in the known universe, I promise. I've known him for ever. If it was my baby there'd be no one else I'd want. Dr Evans is great, Ruby. He's kind, he's skilled and he'll give your baby the best chance of survival she can possibly have.'

'But I told you…I don't want her.' Ruby was sobbing now, swiping away tears with the back of her hand. 'My mum said I should have had an abortion. She would have paid. I don't know why I didn't. And now you're operating on a baby I don't even want. I just want you all to go away.'

In-utero surgery was fraught at the best of times. It was full of potential dangers for both mother and baby. To operate on a mother who didn't want her baby to survive…

He didn't know where to start—but he didn't need to, because Em simply walked forward, tugged the girl into her arms and held her.

Ruby stiffened. She held herself rigid, but Em's fingers stroked her hair.

'Hey, it's okay, Ruby. We all know how hard this is. Pregnancy's the pits. You feel so on your own, and you're especially on your own. You decided not to go ahead with an abortion, going against what your family wanted you to do. That took courage, but there's only so much courage a girl can be expected to show. That's why Isla's been helping you and it's why I'm here now. I'm *your* midwife, Ruby. I'll be with you every step of the way. All the decisions will be yours but I'm right with you. Right now, if you want Dr Evans to go away and come back later, he will. Just say the word.'

She met Oliver's gaze over Ruby's shoulder and her message was unmistakable. Back me up.

So Em was this girl's midwife? Then where the hell had she been when he'd walked in?

Coping with her crashed car, that's where, and then changing out of her mum clothes into nursing gear. Still, surely she could have made it earlier.

'We've had a drama with a prem birth I had to help with,' she said, as if he'd voiced his question out loud. She was still holding, still hugging, as Ruby's sobs went on. 'That's why I'm late, Ruby, and I'm sorry. I wanted to be here when you arrived. But I'm here now, and if you decide to proceed with this operation then you're my number one priority. Do you need some tissues? Dr Evans, hand me some tissues.'

'You helped with an earlier birth?' he asked, before he could help himself, and she had the temerity to glare at him.

'Yep. I had to step in and help the moment I hit the wards. Plus I crashed my car this morning. I crashed my wagon, Ruby, and guess whose gorgeous car I drove into? None other than Dr Evans. It's his first day on the job and I hit him. It's a wonder he hasn't tossed me out of the room already.'

And Ruby's sobs hiccupped to a halt. She pulled back and looked at Em, then turned and stared at Oliver.

'She hit your car?'

'Yes,' he said. He wouldn't normally impart personal information to a patient but he guessed what Em was doing, and he could only agree. What Ruby needed was space to settle. He could help with that—even though he had to get personal to give it to her.

'I have a sixty-four Morgan Plus-4 sports car,' he said, mournfully, like the end of the world was nigh, which was about how he'd felt when he'd seen the damage—before he'd realised the driver of the other car had been Em. 'It's two-tone burgundy with black interior, a gorgeous two-seater. It's fitted with super sports upgrades, including twin Weber carbs, a Derrington header and a bonnet scoop. It also has chrome wire wheels, a badge bar with twin Lucas fog lamps and a tonneau cover. Oh, and it's retrofitted with overdrive transmission. Now it's also fitted with one smashed side—courtesy of your midwife.'

'Yikes,' Em said, but she didn't sound in the least subdued. 'Twin Weber carbs and a Derrington header, hey? Did I damage all that?'

'And if you knew how long it took to get those fog lamps…'

'Whoops. Sorry. But you scratched my car, too.' But Em was talking at Ruby rather than at him and she still sounded cheerful. Chirpy even.

'Scratched…' he muttered, and she grinned.

'That's okay. I forgive you. And they're cars. They're just things. That's what insurance is for. Whereas babies aren't things at all,' Em continued, leading seamlessly back to the reason they were all there. 'Ruby, your little girl is a person, not a thing, and she's far, far more precious. You made the decision to go ahead with this pregnancy. You made the decision early not to choose abortion and you chose it again when the scan showed spina bifida. But you've been telling me you think you might have her adopted when she's born…'

'I can't…deal with it.'

'You don't have to deal with it,' Em said soundly. 'There are lots of parents out there who'll give their eye teeth to have a baby like yours to love. That's right, isn't it, Dr Evans?'

'I… Yes.' But her words were like a punch in the gut. That last night… He'd tried to make her see one last time. *'Em, I can't. I know adoption's the only way, but I can't do it. I can't guarantee to love a child who's not our own.'*

'It will be our own.'

'*Em, no.*'

It had been their last conversation. He'd turned and walked away from the only woman he'd ever loved and it had nearly killed him. But she'd deserved the family she'd wanted so much. He'd had to give her that chance, and from the evidence he'd seen today, she'd taken it.

But now wasn't about him. It was all about Ruby. The kid's terror had been put aside. He had to take advantage of it.

Which meant putting thoughts of Em aside. Putting aside the knowledge that his wife, his ex-wife, presumably—did you need to formally sign papers to accept a marriage was over?—was in the same room.

'Ruby, you created this little girl,' he said, as Em continued to hold her. 'You can have her adopted at birth, but until then you need to look after her. And the staff here have already explained to you—to look after her means an operation now.'

'But why?' Ruby demanded, suddenly belligerent. 'I don't understand. The kid's got spina bifida—Dr Zigler showed me on the scans. What difference does it make whether you operate now or operate when it's born?'

There was fear behind the question. Oliver recognised it. He'd done many in-utero procedures by now, and sometimes one of the hardest things was having the mum understand that the tiny child inside her was an independent being already. Something totally separate from her. This was a child who could be shifted in her uterus, who even at twenty-two weeks could cope with complex surgery and then be resettled, because, no matter how amazing the technology, the womb was still the safest place for her to be.

'Ruby, you know your baby has spina bifida,' he said now, gently. Em still had her arm around the girl. He was talking to them both, as he'd normally talk to a woman and her partner, or a woman and her mum or support person. Em had slid naturally into that role. A good midwife sometimes had to, he thought, and Em had always been brilliant at her job. Efficient, kind, skilled and empathic. He'd worked with her once and he'd loved it.

It was totally disconcerting to be working with her again, but he needed to focus on Ruby.

'You know we've picked up the spina bifida on the ultrasound,' Oliver said matter-of-factly, trying to take the emotion out of the situation. 'You've seen it?'

'It just looked blurry. I couldn't figure it out.'

So she didn't understand. 'Heinz Zigler's a great paediatric neurologist,' Charles had told him. 'He's technically brilliant, but communication's not his strong suit. He'll do the spinal surgery but everything else—including explanations to the mum—we're leaving to you.'

So now he needed to explain from the ground up. 'The scans do look blurry,' he admitted. 'I have trouble reading them myself. Fine detail like the nerve exposure around vertebrae needs incredibly specialised knowledge to see, but the radiologists here are superb. They've double-checked each other's work, and Dr Zigler agrees. Everyone's sure. But would you like me to explain what I think is happening? I don't talk in fine detail, Ruby. I just see the overview. That's actually what I do, total patient care, looking after you as well as your baby. I'm an obstetrician and a surgeon who specialises in looking after mums and bubs if bub needs an operation before it's time for her to be born.'

Silence. Ruby cast him a scared look and subsided. He waited, while Ruby pulled herself together a bit more, while Em handed her a wad of tissues, while both women readied themselves to front what was coming.

'Heinz says he told you the fine detail,' he said at last, when he thought Ruby was as ready as she was going to be. 'But here's the broad outline. The bones of your baby's spine—the vertebrae—haven't formed properly to protect your baby's spinal cord. The spinal cord holds the nerves that control your baby's movements. Because those nerves run right through the body, if the cord gets damaged then long term, your baby might not be able to walk. She might not have control of her bladder and bowel. If she has a severe problem she can also end up with a build-up of fluid in her brain. Then she'll need a shunt, all her life, to drain the excess fluid and relieve pressure.'

Ruby was crying again now, but not sobbing. Em's arm was around her, holding her close, but Ruby's attention was held. Her distress was taking second place to her need to know, and she seemed to be taking it in.

'So,' she whispered. 'So?'

'So the good thing is,' he said, still gently, 'that many problems of spina bifida aren't directly caused by the spina bifida itself. Doctors cleverer than me, like Heinz—did you know he's top in his field in research?—have worked out that the exposure of the spinal cord to the normal fluid in your womb, the amniotic fluid, is what progressively destroys the exposed nerves during pregnancy. If we can operate now, really early, and cover the exposed cord, then we prevent much of the damage. Your baby's much more likely to be able to live a normal, happy life.'

'But not with me,' Ruby whispered.

That was another issue altogether. Adoption. This was a single mum, a teenager, facing a life apart from the baby she was carrying.

'You haven't decided definitely on adoption,' Em murmured, and the girl shook her head.

'I can't think…'

'And you don't need to think.' Em's hold on her tightened. 'There's too much happening now for you to think past what you need to face right now. But, Ruby, regardless of what you decide to do when your baby's born, regardless of whether you decide you can care for her yourself or if you want to give her to parents who need a baby to love, she'll still be your daughter. You have the choice now to make a huge difference in your daughter's life.'

'You're…sure she has to have this operation?' Ruby whispered. 'I mean…really sure?'

'We're sure,' Oliver told her, suddenly immensely grateful for Em's presence. Without Em he doubted whether he'd have been able to get past the fear. 'But the operation's not without risks.' He had to say that. There was no way he could let this kid agree to surgery without warning her. 'Ruby, there are risks to you and risks to your baby. I believe those risks are small but they're still there.'

'But…I will make a difference.'

'Heinz tells me that because the spinal cord exposure is relatively high and very obvious on the ultrasound, then if we leave the operation undone, your daughter will probably spend her life in a wheelchair,' he said bluntly. 'And with the amount of exposure…there will be fluid build-up in the brain. She'll need a shunt and there may even be brain damage.'

'That's why Dr Evans has arrived here so fast,' Em went on smoothly. 'We haven't had a specialist in-utero surgeon on staff, but when we saw your ultrasound Dr Zigler knew we had to get the best obstetrician here as fast as we could. That's who Dr Evans is. The best. So now it's up to you, Ruby, love. Will you let us operate on your baby?'

'Heinz and I can close the gap over the cord,' Oliver told her. 'There's probably already a little damage done, but it's so early that damage should be minimal. What we'll do is put you to sleep, cut the smallest incision in your tummy as possible—you'll be left with a scar but I'm very neat.' He grinned at the girl, knowing a bit of pseudo modesty often worked, and he got a shaky smile in return. 'Then we'll

gently turn your baby over where she's lying—with luck
we won't have to take her out. Once her back is exposed
Heinz will check everything, tweak things to where they
should be, then we'll close the gap over her spinal cord.
We'll settle her back down again and tuck her in, stitch
you up and leave you both to get on with your pregnancy.
You'll need to stay in hospital for about a week, maybe a bit
longer, until we're sure we haven't pressured bub into coming early, but then everything should proceed as normal.'

'And she won't have to be in a wheelchair?'

'Ruby, we can't make any promises.' He caught her
hand and held it. Em was still hugging her, and Oliver
thought, not for the first time, Em was a wonderful midwife. She knew when to intervene and she knew when to
shut up. She also exuded a quiet calm that was a tranquil-
liser all by itself.

He'd met her ten years ago. He'd been a barely qualified doctor, she'd been a student nurse, but already the
confidence she'd engendered in the patients he'd worked
with had been impressive. He'd seen her with some terrified teenage mums.

There was no nurse he'd rather have by his side and
by the time they'd dated twice he'd known there was no
woman he'd rather have with him for ever. Their attraction
had been instant, their marriage inevitable.

It was only babies…or lack of babies…that had driven
them apart.

The night their son had been stillborn had been the
worst night of his life. He'd watched Em's face contort
with an anguish so deep it had seemed endless, and there
had been nothing he could do to stop it. He'd been unable
to help her. He'd been unable to reach her.

But it was hardly the time to be thinking of that now.
It was hardly the time to be thinking of it ever. After five
years, they'd moved on.

'I can't make any promises,' he repeated, hauling himself back to the here and now, to the needs of the teenage kid in front of him. 'The procedure Heinz and I are trained to perform usually has an excellent outcome but there are exceptions. I won't hide that from you, Ruby. There are risks. There's a chance of infection, for you as well as your baby. We'll take every care in the world...'

'But no guarantees.'

'No guarantees,' he agreed. 'So it's up to you. This is your daughter, Ruby. It's up to you to make the choice.'

'I'm too young to have a daughter.' It was a wail and Em's arm tightened around her.

'That's where I come in,' she said solidly, a blanket of comfort and reassurance. 'You want advice, I'm full of advice. You want a hug, that's what I'm here for, too.'

'You can't be here with me all the time.'

'I can't,' Em agreed. 'I have my own son and daughter to look after. But I'm here every day during the week, and if I'm needed, I can come in at other times. My mum lives with me so I can usually drop everything and come. I don't do that for all my mums, but I'll try for you.'

'Why?' Ruby demanded, suspicious.

'Because you're special,' she said soundly. 'Isn't that right, Dr Evans? You're one special woman, and you're about to have one special daughter.'

But Oliver was hardly listening. Somehow he managed to make a grunt of acquiescence but his mind felt like it was exploding.

I have my own son and daughter to look after.

Somehow...a part of his brain had hoped—assumed?—that she'd stayed...as Em. The Em he'd left five years ago.

She hadn't. She'd moved on. She was a different woman.

I have my own son and daughter to look after...

'What do you think, Ruby?' Em was saying gently. 'Do

you want to go ahead with the operation? Do you want time to think about it?'

'I don't have a choice,' Ruby whispered. 'My baby… It's the best thing…'

It was. Oliver watched Ruby's hand drop to cover the faint bulge of her tummy, the instinctive gesture of protection that was as old as time itself.

And the gesture brought back the wedge that had been driven so deep within his marriage that it had finished it. Em had wanted to adopt, and he'd known he couldn't love like parents were supposed to love. He was right, he thought bleakly. He'd always been right. What was between Ruby and her baby was what her baby needed. Ruby was this baby's mum. Adoption was great if there was no choice, but how could an adoptive parent ever love a child as much as this?

He knew he couldn't and that knowledge had torn his marriage apart.

But Em was watching him now, with those eyes he'd once thought he could drown in. He'd loved her so much, and yet he'd walked away.

And she'd walked, as well.

I have my own son and daughter to look after.

It was nothing to do with him. He'd made his choice five years ago, and Em had obviously made choices, too.

He needed to know what those choices had been.

But now wasn't the time or the place to ask. All he could do was turn his attention back to Ruby, reassure her as much as possible and then set about working out times and details of the forthcoming surgery.

As they finished, a woman who introduced herself as one of the hospital social workers arrived. It seemed Ruby needed help with housing—as well as everything else, she'd been kicked out of her parents' house. She was staying in a boarding house near the hospital but she wouldn't be able to stay there when the baby was born.

There'd be more talk of adoption. More talk of options.

Ruby's surgery was scheduled for the day after tomorrow, but for now he was redundant. He was free to head to the next mum Charles had asked him to see.

He left, but his head was spinning.

Em was still sitting on the bed, still hugging Ruby. *I have my own son and daughter to look after.*

Whatever she'd done, it had been her choice. He'd walked away so she'd have that choice.

Why did it hurt so much that she'd taken it?

CHAPTER THREE

EM GOT ON with her day, too.

One of the wonderful things about being a midwife was that it took all her care, all her attention. She had little head-space for anything else. What was the saying? Find a job you love and you'll never have to work again? She'd felt that the first time she'd helped deliver a baby and she'd never looked back.

She sometimes…okay, she often…felt guilty about working when her mum was home with the kids, but the decision to foster had been a shared one. Her mum loved Gretta and Toby as much as she did. They had the big old house, but they needed Em's salary to keep them going.

Sometimes when Em got home her mother was more tired than she was, but whenever she protested she was cut off at the pass.

'So which baby are we giving back? Don't be ridiculous, Em. We can do this.'

They could, and knowing the kids were at home, waiting…it felt great, Em thought as she hauled off her uniform at the end of her shift and tugged on her civvies. Right, supermarket, pharmacy—Gretta's medications were running low—then home. She'd rung her mum at lunchtime and Adrianna had been reassuring. 'She's looking much better.' But, still, there was no way she was risking running out of Gretta's drugs.

'Big day?' Sophia Toulson, one of the more recent arrivals to the Victoria's midwifery staff, was hauling her uniform off, too, but instead of pulling on sensible clothes like Em's—yikes, where had that milk stain come from?—she was putting on clothes that said she was heading out clubbing or to a bar—to a life Em had left behind years ago.

Not that she missed it—much. Though there were times...

'It has been a big day,' she agreed, thinking of the night to come. Em had had three sleepless nights in a row. Gretta needed to be checked all the time. What she'd give for a solid eight-hour sleep...

'But have you met the new obstetrician? You must have—he's been fast-tracked here to operate on your Ruby. Em, he's gorgeous. No wedding ring, either. Not that that tells you anything with surgeons—they hardly ever wear them. It's not fair. Just because rings can hold infection it gives them carte blanche to disguise their marital state. But he's come from the States and fast, so that hints at single status. Em, you'll be working with him. How about giving it a shot?'

Yeah, right. Propositioning Oliver? If Sophia only knew... But somehow she managed to grimace as if this conversation were completely normal, an anonymous, gorgeous obstetrician arriving in the midst of midwives whose first love was their job, and whose second love was dissecting the love lives of those around them.

She turned to face the full-length mirror at the end of the change room. What she saw there made her grimace. Faded jeans, with a rip at the knee. Trainers with odd shoelaces. A windcheater with a milk stain running down the shoulder—why hadn't she noticed that before she'd left the house?

Her hair needed a cut. Oliver had loved her hair. She'd had it longer then and the dull brown had been shiny. It had bounced—she'd spent time with decent shampoo and conditioner, and she'd used a curling wand to give it body.

Now she bought her shampoo and conditioner in bulk at the discount store and her curling wand was rusting under the sink.

Oliver had never seen her like this—until today.

Sophia was suggesting she make a play for him?

'Can you see Oliver Evans with someone like me?' she asked incredulously. 'Sophia, get real.'

'You could try,' Sophia said, coming up behind her friend and staring over her shoulder at the reflection. 'Em, you're really pretty. With a bit of effort...'

'All my effort goes into the kids.'

'You're burying yourself.'

'I'm giving them a chance.' She glanced at her watch and grimaced again. 'Ouch. I need to go. Have a great time tonight.'

'I wish I could say the same for you. Home with your mum and two kids...' She bit her lip and Em knew why. Sophia had the same problem she did—she'd barely worked with her for a month before she'd winkled out of her the reason for the gravity behind what somehow seemed a forced gaity.

Did all women who couldn't have children feel like this? Maybe they did, but Em's solution horrified Sophia.

'I love it,' she said soundly, even defiantly, because she did. Of course she did. 'And you have fun at... Where are you going?'

'The Rooftop Bar. Madeleine just happened to mention to your Dr Evans that we might be there.' She grinned and started searching her bag for her lipstick. 'If you're not interested...'

'He's all yours,' Em said tightly. 'Best of luck. The

supermarket's waiting for me. Whoo-hoo, a fabulous night for both of us.'

'Right,' Sophia said dryly. 'Em, I wish...'

'Well, don't wish,' Em said, more sharply than she'd intended. 'Don't even think about it. This is the life I chose for myself, and I'm happy. Dr Oliver Evans might be at the bar and I guess that's the life he's chosen, too. We're all where we want to be, and we can't ask for more than that.'

Oliver's day wasn't supposed to be frantic. Weren't new staff supposed to have an orientation day, a shift where they spent the time acquainting themselves with ward and theatre staff, meeting everyone in the canteen, arranging stuff in their office? Not so much. Harry, it seemed, had left in a hurry. His lady had been enticing; he'd left without giving proper notice and the work had backed up.

Apart from that, Harry hadn't had specialist in-utero surgical training. It seemed that word of Oliver's arrival had flown around Melbourne before he arrived. He had three consultations lined up for the afternoon and more for the next day.

Ruby's case was probably the most complex. No, it *was* the most complex, he thought, mostly because the scans showing the extent of the problem had made him wince.

Plus she was alone. His next mum, Lucy, arrived with a support cast, husband, parents, an entourage of six. Her baby had a congenital heart malfunction. The little boy in utero was a twenty-four-weeker. He needed an aortic valvuloplasty—opening the aortic foetal heart valves to allow blood flow. It was one of the most common reasons for in-utero surgery, the one that Oliver was most comfortable with—as long as he had the backup of decent cardiac surgeons.

Oliver had already met Tristan Hamilton, the Victoria's neonatal cardiothoracic surgeon—in fact, they'd gone to university together. Tristan had backed up Charles's calls, pressuring him to come, and he had been one of the inducements. Tristan was incredibly skilled, and if he could work side by side with him, for this mum, things were likely to be fine.

But what seemed wrong was that Lucy and her little boy had huge family backup—and Ruby had no one.

But Ruby had Em.

That had to be compensation. Em would be terrific.

If indeed she was with her. She'd been running late that morning. She'd looked harassed, like she had one too many balls in the air.

She'd come flying into Ruby's room half an hour after she'd hit his car, burbling about an early delivery. Really? Or had she spent the half hour on the phone to her insurance people?

It was none of his business.

Still, it was a niggle…

Isla Delamere was the Victoria's head midwife—plus she was the daughter of the CEO. Apparently she'd also just become engaged to the hospital's neonatal intensive care specialist. Isla was not a person to mess with, he'd decided. He'd been introduced to her by Charles, and as he was about to leave he saw her again.

'You have how many in-utero procedures lined up for me?' he said, half joking. 'You guys believe in throwing me in at the deep end.'

'You just do the surgery,' she said, smiling. 'My midwives will keep everything running smoothly. I have the best team…'

'My midwife this morning was running late.' He shouldn't have said it. He knew it the moment he'd opened his mouth. The last thing he wanted was to get Em into trouble and this woman had power at her fingertips, but Isla didn't seem bothered.

'I'm sorry about that. We had three births within fifteen minutes of each other just as Em came on duty. I know her care of Ruby's a priority, but one of the births was prem, the mum was out of her tree, and there's no one better at calming a frantic mum than Em. I only used her for the final fifteen minutes but it made a difference. You did cope by yourself until then?'

She raised her beautifully formed eyebrows quizzically...head midwife wondering if surgeon could cope without a little assistance...

Right. He'd got his answer but now Isla thought he was a wimp. Great start.

'Some of the staff are going to the Rooftop Bar after work,' Isla told him. 'Have you been invited? You're welcome to join us.'

'Thanks but I have a problem to sort.'

'Your car?' She was still smiling and, he thought, that was just the sort of thing that hospital staff the world over enjoyed. Specialist's car being trashed, especially since most staff here could never afford to run a car like Betsy.

He loved that car and now she was a mess. But...

'Em's promised to sort it,' Isla told him. 'She's not the sort of woman to let her insurance lapse.'

'It's not the insurance...'

'And she's really sorry. She was stricken when she first came in this morning. She's been so busy all day I suspect she hadn't had time to apologise but—'

'Will she be at the bar now?'

'Em? Heavens, no. She has two kids waiting for her at home.'

'Two?'

'Gretta's four and Toby's two. They're special kids but, wow, they're demanding.'

'I guess...' And then he asked because he couldn't help himself. Had a miracle happened? *Gretta's four*...She must have moved like the wind. 'Her partner...' He knew there couldn't have been a marriage because there'd never been a divorce but...there must be someone. 'Is he a medic? Does she have help?'

But Isla's eyebrows hit her hairline. Her face closed, midwife protecting her own. 'I guess that's for you to ask Em if it's important for you to know,' she said shortly, clearing her desk, making signals she was out of there. Off to the Rooftop Bar to join her colleagues? 'She doesn't talk about her private life. Is there anything else you need?'

More information, he thought, and he'd bet Isla knew everything he wanted to know. But he couldn't push without opening a can of worms. Evans was a common name. Em had clearly not told anyone there was a connection.

Better to leave it that way, maybe.

'Thanks, no.'

'Goodnight, then. And good luck with the car. You might let Em know when you have it sorted. She's beating herself up over it. She's a great midwife and I don't like my midwives stressed. I'd appreciate it if you could fix it.'

'I'll try,' he said, but it was too late. Isla had gone.

He headed down to the car park. He hadn't been back to assess the damage during the day—he hadn't had time.

The park next to his was empty. Em was gone.

Her wagon had still been drivable. Her doors had been bent, but the wheels were still okay, whereas his... One of the wheels was far from okay and he wasn't driving anywhere. He stooped and examined it and thought of the hassle it had been to find the right parts for his little beauty. Where was he going to find another wheel rim? And the panels were a mess.

Strangely, it didn't upset him as much as he'd thought it might. He checked the damage elsewhere and knew he'd have to get her towed—actually, carried, as there was no way she could be towed like this. And then he'd go searching for the parts he needed.

He kind of liked searching the internet for car parts. It was something to do at three in the morning when he couldn't sleep.

Which was often.

He rounded the front of the car and there he saw a note in his windshield. Em?

Oliver, I really am sorry about this. I've put my hand up, it was all my fault, and I've told my insurance company to pay without arguing. I photocopied my driver's licence and my insurance company details—they're attached. One of the girls on the ward knows of a great repair place that specialises in vintage cars—the details are here, too. See you when you next see Ruby.
Em

It was all about the car. There was nothing personal at all.

Well, what did he expect? A *mea culpa* with extras? This was more than generous, admitting total culpability. Her insurance company would hate her. As well as that, she'd probably have to pay the first few hundred dollars, plus she'd lose her no-claim bonus.

He could afford it. Could she?

He re-read the note. What was he hoping for? Personal details?

Her driver's licence told him all he was going to get. Emily Louise Evans. She was still using his name, then. So…single mother? How? Had she gone ahead and adopted by herself? He checked again, making sure he was right—she was living at her mother's address.

He liked Adrianna. Or he had liked her. He hadn't seen his mother-in-law for years.

He could drop in…

Why?

'Because she shouldn't accept full responsibility,' he said out loud. 'If she's supporting kids…'

She'd said she'd already phoned her insurance company and confessed, but maybe he could reverse it. Maybe he could take some of the load.

The independent Em of five years ago would tell him to shove it.

Yeah? He thought back to the Em of five years ago, shattered, gutted, looking towards the future with a bleakness that broke his heart.

'If you won't do it with me then I'll do it alone. If you think I can go back to the life we led… I'm over nightclubs, Oliver. I'm over living just for me.'

'Isn't there an us in there?'

'I thought there was, but I thought we wanted a family. I hadn't realised it came with conditions.'

'Em, I can't.'

'So you're leaving?'

'You're not giving me any choice.'

'I guess I'm not. I'm sorry, Oliver.'

Five years…

Okay, their marriage was long over but somehow she still seemed…partly his responsibility. And the cost of this repair would make her insurance company's eyes water.

It behoved him…

'Just to see,' he told himself. He'd thought he'd drop in to visit Adrianna when he'd come to Melbourne anyway, to see how she was.

And talk to Adrianna about Em?

Yeah, but he was over it. He'd had a couple of relationships in the last five years, even if they had been fleeting. He'd moved on.

'So let's be practical,' he told himself, and hit his phone and organised a tow truck, and a hire car, and half an hour later he was on the freeway, heading to the suburb where his ex-mother-in-law lived. With his wife and her two children, and her new life without him.

'You hit who?'

'Oliver.' Em was feeding Toby, which was a messy joy. Toby was two years old and loved his dinner. Adrianna had made his favourite animal noodles in a tomato sauce. Toby was torn between inspecting every animal on his spoon and hoovering in the next three spoonfuls as if there was no tomorrow.

Adrianna was sitting by the big old fire stove, cuddling Gretta. The little girl's breathing was very laboured.

Soon…

No. It hurt like hot knives to have to think about it. Much better to concentrate on distractions, and Oliver was surely a distraction.

'He's working at the Victoria?'

'Yep. Starting today.'

'Oh, Em… Can you stay there?'

'I can't walk away. We need the money. Besides, it's the best midwifery job in Melbourne. I love working with Isla and her team.'

'So tell him to leave. You were there first.'

'I don't think you can tell a man like Oliver Evans to leave. Besides, the hospital needs him. I read his CV on the internet during lunch break. His credentials are even more awesome than when I knew him. He's operating on Ruby's baby and there's no one better to do it.'

And that had Adrianna distracted. 'How is Ruby?'

Em wasn't supposed to bring work home. She wasn't

supposed to talk about patients outside work, but Adrianna spent her days minding the kids so Em could work. Adrianna had to feel like she was a part of it, and in a way she was. If it wasn't for her mum, she'd never be able to do this.

This. Chaos. Animal noodles. Mess on the kitchen floor. Fuzzy, a dopey half-poodle, half something no one could guess at, was currently lurking under Toby's highchair on the off-chance the odd giraffe or elephant would drop from on high.

'Hey, it's all done.' There was a triumphant bang from the laundry and Mike appeared in the doorway, waving his spanner. 'That's that mother fixed. I'd defy any drop to leak anywhere now. Anything else I can do for you ladies?'

'Oh, Mike, that's fabulous. But I wish you'd let us pay—'

'You've got free plumbing for life,' Mike said fiercely. Mike was their big, burly, almost scary-looking next-door neighbour. His ginger hair was cropped to almost nothing. He wore his jeans a bit too low, he routinely ripped the sleeves out of his T-shirts because sleeves annoyed him, and in his spare time he built his body. If you met Mike on a dark night you might turn the other way. Fast.

Em had met Mike on a dark night. He'd crashed into their kitchen, banging the back door so hard it had broken.

'Em, the wife... My Katy... The baby... There's blood, oh, my God, there's blood... You're a midwife. Please...'

Katy had had a fast, fierce delivery of their third child, and she'd haemorrhaged. Mike had got home to find her in the laundry, her baby safely delivered, but she'd been bleeding out.

She'd stopped breathing twice before the ambulance had arrived. Em had got her back.

Mike and Katy were now the parents of three boys who promised to grow up looking just like their dad, and Mike was Em's slave for ever. He'd taken Em and her household under his wing, and a powerful wing it was. There were usually motorbikes parked outside Mike and Katy's place—multiple bikes—but no matter what the pressure of his family, his job or his biker mates, Mike dropped in every night—just to check.

Now, as Toby finished the last mouthful of his noodles, Mike hefted him out of his highchair and whirled him round and hugged him in a manner that made Em worry the noodles might come back up again. But Toby crowed in glee.

'Can I take him next door for a few minutes?' he asked. 'We've got a new swing, a double-seater. My boys'll be outside and Henry and Tobes'll look a treat on it. Give you a bit of peace with Gretta, like.'

He glanced at Gretta but he didn't say any more. What was happening was obvious. Gretta was more and more dependent on oxygen, but more and more it wasn't enough.

If Mike took Toby, Em could sit by the fire and cuddle Gretta while Adrianna put her feet up and watched the telly. Toby was already lighting up with excitement.

'That'd be great, Mike, thank you,' Em told him. 'I'll pop over and pick him up in an hour.'

'Bring Gretta with you,' Mike said. 'Give her a go on the swing. If she's up for it.'

But she wasn't up for it. They all knew it, and that knowledge hung over the house, a shadow edging closer.

Today Oliver's presence had pushed that shadow back a little, made Em's thoughts fly sideways, but, Oliver or not, the shadows were there to stay.

CHAPTER FOUR

THE LAST TIME Oliver had visited his ex-mother-in-law, her house had looked immaculate. Adrianna was devoted to her garden. At this time of year her roses had always looked glorious, her herbaceous borders had been clipped to perfect symmetry and her lawns had always been lush and green, courtesy of the tanks she'd installed specifically so she could be proud of her garden the year round.

Not now.

The grass on the lawn was a bit long and there were bare patches, spots where things had been left for a while. Where once an elegant table setting had stood under the shade of a Manchurian pear, there was now a sandpit and a paddling pool.

A beach ball lay on the front path. He had to push it aside to reach the front door.

It took him less than a minute to reach the door but by the time he had, the last conversation he'd had with Em had played itself out more than a dozen times in his head.

'Em, I can't adopt. I'm sorry, but I can't guarantee I can love kids who aren't my own.'

'They would be your own,' she'd said. She'd been emotional, distraught, but underneath she'd been sure. *'I want kids, Oliver. I want a family. There are children out there*

who need us. If we can't have our own...to not take them is selfish.'

'To take them when we can't love them is selfish.'

'I can love them. I will.'

'But I can't.' He'd said it gently but inexorably, a truth he'd learned by fire.

'You're saying I need to do it alone?'

'Em, think about it,' he'd said fiercely. *'We love each other. We've gone through so much...'*

'I want a family.'

'Then I can't give it to you. If this is the route you're determined to take, then you'll need to find someone who can.'

He'd walked away, sure that when she'd settled she'd agree with him. After all, their love was absolute. But she'd never contacted him. She hadn't answered his calls.

Adrianna had spoken to him. 'Oliver, she's gutted. She knows your position. Please, leave her be to work things out for herself.'

It had gutted him, too, that she'd walked away from their marriage without a backward glance. And here was evidence that she'd moved on. She'd found herself the life she wanted—without him.

He reached the door, lifted his hand to the bell but as he did the door swung inwards.

The guy opening the door was about the same age as Oliver. Oliver was tall, but this guy was taller and he was big in every sense of the word. He was wearing jeans, a ripped T-shirt and big working boots. His hands were clean but there was grease on his forearms. And on his tatts.

He was holding a child, a little boy of about two. The child was African, Oliver guessed, Somalian maybe, as dark as night, with huge eyes. One side of his face was badly scarred. He was cradled in the guy's arms, but he was looking outwards, brightly interested in this new arrival into his world.

Another kid came flying through the gate behind Oliver, hurtling up the path towards them. Another little boy. Four? Ginger-haired. He looked like the guy in front of him.

'Daddy, Daddy, it's my turn on the swing,' he yelled. 'Come and make them give me a turn.'

The guy scooped him up, as well, then stood, a kid tucked under each arm. He looked Oliver up and down, like a pit bull, bristling, assessing whether to attack.

'Life insurance?' he drawled. 'Funeral-home plans? Not interested, mate.'

'I'm here to see Emily.'

'She's not interested, either.'

He was still wearing his suit. Maybe he should have changed. Maybe a tatt or two was necessary to get into this new version of his mother-in-law's home.

'I'm a friend of Em's from the hospital.' Who was this guy? 'Can you tell her I'm here, please?'

'She's stuffed. She doesn't need visitors.' He was blocking the doorway, a great, belligerent bull of a man.

'Can you ask her?'

'She only has an hour at most with Gretta before the kid goes to sleep. You want to intrude on that?'

Who was Gretta? Who was this guy?

'Mike?' Thankfully it was Em, calling from inside the house. 'Who is it?'

'Guy who says he's a friend of yours.' Mike didn't take his eyes off Oliver. His meaning was clear—he didn't trust him an inch. 'Says he's from the hospital. Looks like an undertaker.'

'Mike?'

'Yeah?'

'It'll be Oliver,' she called, and Mike might be right

about the 'stuffed' adjective, Oliver conceded. Her voice sounded past weariness.

'Oliver?'

'He's the guy I was married to.' *Was?*

'Your ex is an undertaker? Sheesh, Em…'

'He's not an undertaker. He's a surgeon.'

'That's one step before the undertaker.'

'Mike?'

'Yeah?'

'Let him in.'

Why didn't Em come to the door? But Mike gave him a last long stare and stepped aside.

'Right,' he called back to Em. 'But we're on the swings. One yell and I'll be here in seconds. Watch it, mate,' he growled at Oliver, as he pushed past him and headed down the veranda with his load of kids. 'You upset Em and you upset me—and you wouldn't want to do that. You upset Em and you'll be very, very sorry.'

He knew this house. He'd been here often with Em. He'd stayed here for weeks on end when, just after they were married, Em's dad had been diagnosed with inoperable lung cancer.

It had taken the combined skill of all of them—his medical input, Em's nursing skill and Adrianna's unfailing devotion—to keep Kev comfortable until the end, but at the funeral, as well as sadness there had also been a feeling that it had been the best death Kev could have asked for. Surrounded by his family, no pain, knowing he was loved…

'This is how I want us to go out when we have to,' Em had whispered to him at the graveside. 'Thank you for being here.'

Yeah, well, that was years ago and he hadn't been with her for a long time now. She was a different woman.

He walked into the kitchen and stopped dead.

Different woman? What an understatement.

She was sitting by Adrianna's old kitchen range, settled in a faded rocker. Her hair was once more loose, her curls cascading to her shoulders. She had on that baggy wind-cheater and jeans and her feet were bare.

She was cuddling a child. A three- or four-year-old?

A sick child. There was an oxygen concentrator humming on the floor beside them. The child's face was buried in Em's shoulder, but Oliver could see the thin tube connected to the nasal cannula.

A child this small, needing oxygen… His heart lurched. This was no ordinary domestic scene. A child this sick…

The expression on Em's face…

Already he was focusing forward. Already he was feeling gutted for Em. She gave her heart…

Once upon a time she'd given it to him, and he'd hurt her. That she be hurt again…

This surely couldn't be her child.

And who was Mike?

He'd paused in the doorway and for some reason it took courage to step forward. He had no place in this tableau. He'd walked away five years ago so this woman could have the life she wanted, and he had no right to walk back into her life now.

But he wasn't walking into her life. He was here to talk to her about paying for the crash.

Right. His head could tell him that all it liked, but his gut was telling him something else entirely. Em… He'd loved her with all his heart.

He looked at her now, tired, vulnerable, holding a child who must be desperately ill, and all he wanted was to pick her up and carry her away from hurt.

From loving a child who wasn't hers?

Maybe she was hers. Maybe the in-vitro procedures had finally produced a successful outcome. But if this was her child…

His gut was still churning, and when she turned and gave him a tiny half-smile, a tired acknowledgement that he was there, a sort of welcome, the lurch became almost sickening.

'Ollie.'

No one had called him Ollie for five years. No one dared. He'd hated the diminutive—Brett, his sort of brother, had mocked him with it. *'Get out of our lives, Pond Scum Ollie. You're a cuckoo. You don't belong here.'*

Only Em had whispered it to him in the night, in his arms, when their loving had wrapped them in their own cocoon of bliss. Only Em's tongue had made it a blessing.

'Hey,' he said softly, crossing to where she sat, and, because he couldn't help himself, he touched her hair. Just lightly. He had no right, but he had to…touch.

It was probably a mistake. It hauled him into the intimate tableau. Em looked up at him and smiled, and it was no longer a half-smile. It was a smile of welcome. Acceptance.

A welcome home? It was no such thing. But it was a welcome to *her* home, to the home she'd created. Without him.

'Gretta, we have a visitor,' she murmured, and she turned slightly so the child in her arms could see if she wanted.

And she did. The little girl stirred and opened her eyes and Oliver's gut lurched all over again.

Isla had said Em had a two- and a four-year-old. This little one was older than two, but if she was four she was tiny. She was dressed in a fuzzy pink dressing gown that almost enveloped her.

She was a poppet of a child, with a mop of dark, straight hair, and with huge eyes, almost black.

Her lips were tinged blue. The oxygen wasn't enough, then.

She had Down's syndrome.

Oh, Em… What have you got yourself into?

But he couldn't say it. He hauled a kitchen chair up beside them both, and took Gretta's little hand in his.

'I'm pleased to meet you, Gretta.' He smiled at the little girl, giving her all his attention. 'I'm Oliver. I'm a friend of your…' And he couldn't go on.

'He's Mummy's friend,' Em finished for him, and there was that lurch again. 'He's the man in the picture next to Grandma and Grandpa.'

'Ollie,' the little girl whispered, and there was no outsider implication in that word. She was simply accepting him as part of whatever this household was.

There was a sudden woof from under the table, a scramble, another woof and a dog's head appeared on his knee. It was a great, boofy, curly brown head, attached to a body that was disproportionly small. It woofed again but its tail wagged like a flag in a gale.

'This is Fuzzy,' Em said, still smiling at him. His presence here didn't seem to be disconcerting her. It was as if he was simply an old friend, dropping by. To be welcomed and then given a farewell? 'Mike gave us Fuzzy to act as a watchdog. He sort of does, but he's always a bit late on the scene.'

'Oliver!' And here was the last part of the tableau. Adrianna was standing in the door through to the lounge and her eyes weren't welcoming at all. 'What are you doing here?'

Here was the welcome he'd expected. Coldness and accusation…

'Mum…' Em said warningly, but Adrianna was never one who could be put off with a mere warning.

'You hit Em's car.'

'Mum, I told you. I hit his.'

'Then he shouldn't have been parked where you could hit him. What are you doing here?'

'Offering to pay for the damage.'

Her eyes narrowed. 'Really?'

'Really.'

'Mum, it was my fault,' Em protested, but Adrianna shook her head.

'It's your no-claim bonus that's at risk. Oliver's a specialist obstetric surgeon, and I'm betting he has no mortgage and no kids. He can afford it.'

'Mum, it's my debt.'

'You take on the world,' her mother muttered. 'Oliver owes you, big time. My advice is to take his money and run. Or rather take his money and say goodbye. Oliver, you broke my daughter's heart. I won't have you upsetting her all over again. Raking up old wounds…'

'He's not,' Em said, still gently, and Oliver was aware that her biggest priority was not Em or the emotions his presence must be causing, but rather on not upsetting the little girl in her arms. 'Mum, he's welcome. He's a friend and a colleague and he's here to do the honourable thing. Even if I won't let him. I can afford to pay, Oliver.'

'I won't let you,' he told her.

'I'll make you a cup of tea, then,' Adrianna said, slightly mollified. She humphed across to the kettle, made tea—and, yep, she remembered how he liked it. She plonked two mugs on the table, one for Em, one for him. Then she hoisted Fuzzy into one arm, took her own mug in the other hand and headed back to the sitting room. 'Semi-final of *Boss of My Kitchen*,' she said briefly over her shoulder. 'Shall the croquembouche disintegrate into a puddle? The tension's a killer. Nice to see you, Oliver—sort of—but don't you dare upset Em. Goodbye.'

And she disappeared, using a foot to shove the door closed behind her.

Her message couldn't be clearer. My daughter wants me to be polite so I will be, but not one inch more than I must.

He was left with Em, and the little girl in her arms. Sitting in Adrianna's kitchen.

It was a great kitchen.

He'd always loved this house, he thought, inconsequentially. Kevin and Adrianna had built it forty years ago, hoping for a huge family. They'd had four boys, and then the tail-ender, Emily. Adrianna's parents had moved in, as well, into a bungalow out the back. Em had said her childhood had been filled with her brothers and their mates, visiting relations, cousins, friends, anyone Adrianna's famous hospitality could drag in.

Oliver and Em had built a house closer to the hospital they both worked in. They'd built four bedrooms, as well, furnishing them with hope.

Hope hadn't happened. The IVF procedures had worn them down and Josh's death had been the final nail in the coffin of their marriage. He'd walked out and left it to her.

'You're not living in our house?' He'd signed it over to her before going overseas, asking their lawyer to let her know.

'It's better here,' she said simply. 'My brothers are all overseas or interstate now, but I have Mum, and Mike and Katy nearby. The kids are happy here. I've leased our house out. When I emailed you, you said I could do what I like. I use half the rent to help with expenses here. The other half is in an interest-bearing deposit for you. I told you that in the email. You didn't answer.'

He hadn't. He'd blocked it out. The idea of strangers living in the gorgeous house he and Em had had built with such hopes…

'I couldn't live there,' Em said, conversationally. 'It doesn't have heart. Not like here. Not like home.'

Yeah, well, that was another kick in the guts, but he was over it by now. Or almost over it. He concentrated on his tea for a bit, while Em juggled Gretta and cannula and her mug of tea. He could offer to help but he knew he'd be knocked back.

She no longer needed him. This was her life now.

Gretta was watching him, her great brown eyes carefully assessing. Judging? Who knew? The IQs of kids with Down's syndrome covered an amazingly broad spectrum.

He touched the cannula lightly. 'Hey, Gretta,' he said softly. 'Why do you need this?'

'For breeving,' she lisped, but it was as if even saying the words was too much for her. She sank back against Em and her eyes half closed.

'Gretta has an atrioventricular septal defect,' Em said matter-of-factly, as if it was a perfectly normal thing for a kid to have. No problem at all.

But those three words told Oliver all he needed to know about the little girl's condition.

An atrioventricular septal defect… Common term— hole in the heart.

A large percentage of babies with Down's syndrome were born with congenital heart defects. The most common problem was atrioventricular septal defects, or holes in the heart. That this little one was at home with oxygen, with a cannula helping her breathe, told Oliver there was more than one hole. It must be inoperable.

And he had to ask.

'Em, is she yours?'

The words echoed around the kitchen, and as soon as they came out he knew it was the wrong thing to ask.

The arms holding Gretta tightened, and so did the look on Em's face.

'Of course she's mine,' she whispered, but the friendliness was gone. 'Gretta's my daughter. Oliver, I think you should leave.'

'I meant—'

'You meant is she adopted?' Her face was still bleak. 'No, she's not adopted. I'm Gretta's foster-mum, but her birth mother has given all responsibility to me. That means I can love her as much as I want, and that's what I do. I love her and love her and love her. Gretta's my daughter, Oliver, in every sense of the word.'

'You have another...son?'

'You'll have met Toby on the way out with Mike, and he's my foster-child, too. He has spinal kyphoscoliosis. He's the bravest kid. I'm so proud of my kids. Mum's so proud of her grandkids.'

He got it. Or sort of. These were fostered kids. That's what Em had wanted him to share.

But that's what he'd been, he thought bleakly. Someone else's reject. Much as he approved of the idea in theory, in practice he knew it didn't work.

But what Em did was no longer his business, he reminded himself. This was what she'd decided to do with her life. He had no business asking...

How could he not?

'Who's Mike?' he asked, and he hadn't known he was going to ask until he did.

'My lover?' Her lips twitched a little at the expression on his face. 'Can you see it? Nope, Mike's our next-door neighbour, our friend, our man about the house. He and Katy have three kids, we have two, and they mix and mingle at will. You like going to Katy's, don't you, Gretta?'

There was a faint nod from Gretta, and a smile.

And the medical part of Oliver was caught. If Gretta

was responding now, as ill as she was, her IQ must be at the higher end of the Down's spectrum.

He watched Em hold her tight, and he thought, She's given her heart…

And he never could have. He'd never doubted Em's ability to adopt; it was only his reluctance…his fear…

'Is there anything I can do to help?' he found himself saying. 'Now that I'm here?'

'But you don't want to be here.' Em shifted a little, making herself more comfortable. 'You've moved on. At least, I hope you have. I'd have thought you'd have asked for a divorce, found a new partner and had kids by now. You wanted kids. What's stopping you?'

And there was a facer. He had wanted children, they both had, but after a stillbirth and so many attempts at IVF it had worn them—and their marriage—into the ground. Em had told him to leave.

No. She hadn't. She'd simply said she wanted to adopt a child, and that was a deal-breaker.

'I haven't found the right person,' he said, trying to make it sound flippant, but there was no way he could make anything about what had happened to them flippant. The last year or so of their marriage had been unswervingly grey. He looked at Em now and he thought some of the grey remained.

A lot of the grey?

He glanced around the kitchen, once sparkling and ordered, if a bit cluttered with Adrianna's bits and pieces from the past. But now it was all about the present. It was filled with the detritus of a day with kids—or a life with kids.

But this was what Em wanted. And he hadn't?

No, he thought fiercely. It had been what he'd wanted more than anything, and that's why he'd walked away.

So why hadn't he found it?

There was the sound of feet pounding up the veranda, a perfunctory thump on the door and two little boys of about six and four burst in. They were followed by Mike, carrying the toddlers. The six-year-old was carrying a bunch of tattered kangaroo paws, flowers Oliver had seen in the next-door front garden. Tough as nails, Australian perennials, they hardly made good cut flowers but these were tied with a gaudy red bow and presented with pride.

'These are for Gran Adrianna,' the urchin said. And when she obviously wasn't in the kitchen, he headed through the living-room door and yelled for her. 'Gran? Gran Adrianna, we've got you a present. Mum says happy birthday. She was coming over to say it but she's got a cold and she says she wants to give you flowers for your birthday and not a cold.'

And Em turned white.

CHAPTER FIVE

EVERYONE ELSE WAS looking at the kid with the flowers, and then at Adrianna, who reappeared and stooped to give the kids a hug. Only Oliver saw the absolute mortification that crossed Em's face.

She'd forgotten, he thought. Of course she had. Even if she'd remembered this morning, after crashing her car, doing a huge day on the wards, then coming home to such a sick kid, forgetting was almost inevitable.

Think. Think! he told himself. He used to live in this town. Cake. St Kilda. Ackland Street. Cake heaven. It wasn't so far, and the shops there stayed open late.

'Are you guys staying for the cake?' he asked, glancing at his watch, his voice not rising, speaking like this was a pre-ordained plan. 'It'll be here in about twenty minutes. Em asked me to order it but it's running a bit late. Adrianna, is it okay if I stay for the celebration? Em thought it might be okay, but if you'd rather I didn't… Mike, can you and the kids show me the swing while we wait? I'm good at pushing.'

'Em asked you to order a cake?' Adrianna demanded, puzzled, and Oliver spread his hands.

'I crashed into her car this morning. She's been run off her legs all day and I asked if there was anything I could do. Therefore, in twenty minutes there'll be cake. Swing? Kids?'

'Oliver…' Em started, but Oliver put up his hand as if to stop her in mid-sentence. Which was exactly what he intended.

'She always wants to pay,' he told his ex-mother-in-law, grinning. 'She's stubborn as an ox, your Em, but you'd know that, Adrianna. We seem to have been arguing about money all day. I told you, Em, I'm doing the cake, you're on the balloons. Sorry I've mistimed it, though. I'll pay ten percent of the balloons to compensate. Any questions?'

'N-no,' Em said weakly, and his grin widened.

'How about that? No problems at all. Prepare for cake, Adrianna, and prepare for Birthday.'

And suddenly he was being towed outside by kids who realised bedtime was being set back and birthday cake was in the offing. Leaving an open-mouthed Em and Adrianna in the kitchen.

Two minutes later, Mike was onside. They were pushing kids on swings and Oliver was on the phone. And it worked. His backup plan had been a fast trip to the supermarket for an off-the-shelf cake and blow-them-up-yourself balloons but, yes, the shop he remembered had decorated ice cream cakes. They were usually pre-ordered but if he was prepared to pay more… How fast could they pipe Adrianna's name on top? Candles included? Could they order a taxi to deliver it and charge his card? Did they do balloons? Next door did? Was it still open? How much to bung some of those in the taxi as well? He'd pay twice the price for their trouble.

'You're a fast mover,' Mike said, assessing him with a long, slow look as they pushed the double swing together. And then he said, not quite casually, 'Should I worry? If Em gets hurt I might just be tempted to do a damage.'

So Em had a protector. Good. Unless that protector

was threatening to pick him up by the collar and hurl him off the property. He sighed and raked his hair and tried to figure how to respond.

'Mate, I'm not a fast mover,' he said at last. 'For five years I haven't moved at all. I'm not sure even what's happening here, but I'm sure as hell not moving fast.'

'Oh, Em, you remembered.' The moment the boys were out of the house Adrianna stooped and enveloped Em—and Gretta—in a bear hug. 'I've been thinking all day that no one's remembered and… Oh, sweetheart, I'm sorry.'

'You're sorry!' Em struggled to her feet, still cradling Gretta. She should confess, she thought, but as she looked at her mum's face she thought, no. Confession might make her feel better, but right now Adrianna was happy because her daughter had remembered. Oliver had given her that gift and she'd accept, because to do anything else would be cruel. Her mum did so much…

Oliver had rescued her. It'd be dumb to spoil his efforts with more than Adrianna had to know.

But she wasn't going to be dishonest. Not entirely. 'Mum, I remembered when I woke up this morning,' she said. 'But when Gretta was sick I forgot to say it. It was such a rush all day and there's been nothing I could do. But when I met Oliver—'

'You knew he was coming?'

'He ordered the cake. And you know he's always loved you.' And that at least was the truth.

'Oh, Em…'

'And I've bought you a half-day spa voucher.' Yeah, she was lying about that but she could order and get it printed tonight. 'And if we can, I'll do it with you.' That's what Adrianna would like most in the world, she knew, but how would she manage that? But she looked at her mum's tired face and thought she had to do it. It might have to wait until Gretta was better, but she would do it.

If Gretta got better.

'Oh, but, Em…Gretta…'

'It can't be all about Gretta,' Em said gently, and that, too, was true. No matter how much attention Gretta needed, there were others who needed her, as well. It'd be a wrench to spend one of her precious free days…

But, no. This was her mum.

Oliver had saved the situation for now. The least she could do was take it forward.

The cake was amazing, an over-the-top confection that made the kids gasp with wonder. The taxi driver brought it in with a flourish then directed the kids to bring in the balloons. Whatever Oliver had paid, Em thought numbly, it must have been well and truly over the top, as the balloons were already filled, multi-coloured balls of floating air, bursting from the cab as soon as the doors were open, secured only by ribbons tied to the cab doors.

The kids brought them in, bunch upon bunch, and the kitchen was an instant party.

Katy arrived from next door, summoned by her kids. She wouldn't come right in—her flushed face verified her self-diagnosis of a streaming head cold and she declared there was no way she was risking Gretta catching anything—but she stood in the doorway and sang 'Happy Birthday' with the rest of them and watched while Adrianna blew out the candles and sliced the creamy caramel and chocolate and strawberry confection into slices that were almost cake-sized each.

'I can't believe it,' Adrianna said mistily, between mouthfuls of cake. 'Thank you all so much.'

And Em looked across at Oliver, who was sitting with Toby on his knee, one spoonful for Oliver, one spoonful for Toby, and she caught his gaze and tried to smile. But it didn't come off.

This was how it could have been, she thought. This was what she'd dreamed of.

But she'd pushed too hard, too fast. Josh's death had gutted her. She remembered sobbing, 'I can't do IVF any more, I'm too tired. There are babies out there who need us. We'll adopt. You're adopted, Oliver, you know it can work.'

But: 'It doesn't work,' he'd said, not angrily, just flatly, dully, stating immutable facts. 'It's second best and you know it.'

His reaction had shocked her. She'd been in no mood to compromise, and suddenly everything had escalated. The tension of five years of trying for a family had suddenly exploded. Leaving them with nothing.

What had he been doing for five years? Building his career, by the look of his CV. Turning into a wonderful doctor.

A caring doctor… His patience with two-year-old Toby, not the easiest kid to feed, was wonderful. The way he responded to the kids around the table, the mess, the laughter…

The way he smiled up at Adrianna and told her he was so sorry he'd missed her last five birthdays, she'd have to have five slices of cake to make up for it…

He was wonderful.

She wanted to weep.

She wanted to set Gretta down, walk around the table and hug him. Hold him.

Claim him again as her husband?

Right, like that was about to happen. The past was the past. They'd made their decisions and they'd moved on.

'Em's given me an afternoon at the day spa,' Adrianna said happily, cutting across her thoughts. Or almost. Her thoughts were pretty intense right now, pretty much cen-

tred on the gorgeous guy with the toddler, right across
the table from her. She was watching his hands. She'd
loved those hands—surgeon's hands. She remembered
what those hands had been able to do.

She remembered…

'That's gorgeous,' Katy was saying from the doorway.
'But, Em, you still haven't had that colour and cut Mike
and I gave you for Christmas. Right, Adrianna, this time
it's going to work. As soon as I get over my snuffles I'm
taking all five kids and you two are having your Christmas
and birthday treats combined. This weekend?'

Once again, right. As if. Em gave her a smile, and then
went to hug Adrianna, but she thought Katy would still be
recovering by this weekend and her boys would probably
catch her cold after her and Gretta was still so weak…

Adrianna should—and would—have her day spa but
there'd be no day spas or colour and cuts for Em until…
until…

The *until* was unthinkable. She hugged Gretta and her
mind closed.

'What about this Saturday and using me?' Oliver asked,
and she blinked. Had she misheard?

'You?'

'Anyone can see you've got the cold from hell,' he told
Katy. 'Even if you're not still contagious you'll be wiped
out, and you have three of your own to look after. Whereas
I've just moved to Melbourne and my job hasn't geared up
yet. There's nothing to stop me coming by and taking care
of a couple of kids for a few hours.' He spooned chocolate
ice-cream cake into Toby's waiting mouth and grinned at
the little boy. 'Piece of cake, really. We'll have fun.' And
then he smiled across at Gretta, focusing entirely on the
little girl. 'How about it, Gretta? Will you let me take care
of you and Toby?'

Gretta gazed back at him, clearly not understanding

what was happening, but Oliver was smiling and she responded to the smile. She tried a tentative one of her own.

She was one brave kid, Oliver thought. But she looked so vulnerable… Her colour… Oxygen wasn't getting through.

'That'd be fantastic,' Adrianna breathed. 'Em worries about Gretta's breathing, but with you being a doctor…'

'Is he a doctor?' Katy demanded.

'He's Em's ex,' Mike growled, throwing a suspicious, hard stare at Oliver.

'But I'm still reliable,' Oliver said—hopefully—and Katy laughed.

'Hey, I hooked with some weirdos in my time,' she told the still-glowering Mike. 'But a couple of them turned into your mates. Just because they didn't come up to my high standards doesn't mean they're total failures as human beings. What do you say, Em? Trust your kids for a few hours with your ex? And him a doctor and all. It sounds an offer too good to refuse to me.'

And they were all looking at her. From what had started as a quiet night she was suddenly surrounded by birthday, kids, mess, chaos, and here was Oliver, threatening to walk into her life again.

No. Not threatening. Offering.

She'd been feeling like she was being bulldozed. Now… She looked at Oliver and he returned her gaze, calmly, placidly, like he was no threat at all. Whatever he'd been doing for the last five years it was nothing to do with her, but she knew one thing. He was a good man. She might not know him any more, but she could trust him, and if a specialist obstetrician and surgeon couldn't look after her Gretta, who could?

Her mind was racing. Gretta and Toby were both accustomed to strangers minding them—too many stays in hospital had seen to that. Oliver was currently feeding Toby like a pro.

She *could* take Adrianna for an afternoon out. She glanced again at her mum and saw the telltale flicker of hope in her eyes. She was so good… Without Adrianna, Em couldn't have these kids.

The fact that she'd once hoped to have them with Oliver…

No. Don't go there. She hauled herself back from the brink, from the emotions of five years ago, and she managed a smile at Oliver.

'Thank you, then,' she said simply. 'Thank you for offering. Mum and I would love it. Two p.m. on Saturday? We'll be back by five.'

'I'll be here at one.'

Four hours… Did she trust him that long?

Of course she did, she told herself. She did trust him. It was only… She needed to trust herself, as well. She needed to figure out the new way of the world, where Oliver Evans was no longer a lover or a husband.

It seemed Oliver Evans was offering to be a friend.

An hour later she was walking him out to his car. Amazingly, he'd helped put the kids to bed. 'If I'm to care for them on Saturday, they should see me as familiar.' The children had responded to his inherent gentleness, his teasing, his smile, and Em was struggling not to respond, as well.

But she was responding. Of course she was. How could she not? She'd fallen in love with this man a decade ago and the traces of that love remained. Life had battered them, pushed them apart, but it was impossible to think of him other than a friend.

Just a friend? He had to be. She'd made the decision five years ago—Oliver or children. She'd wanted children so much that she'd made her choice but it had been like chopping a part of herself out. Even now... The decision had been made in the aftermath of a stillbirth, when her emotions had been all over the place. If she was asked to make such a decision again...

She'd make it, she thought, thinking of the children in the house behind her. Gretta and Toby. Where would they be without her?

Someone else might have helped them, she thought, but now they were hers, and she loved them so fiercely it hurt.

If she'd stayed with Oliver she would have had...nothing.

'Tell me about the kids,' he said, politely almost, leaning back on the driver's door of his car. His rental car.

It had been a lovely car she'd destroyed. That's what Oliver must have decided, she thought. He'd have a gorgeous car instead of kids—and now she'd smashed it.

'I'm sorry about your car,' she managed.

He made an exasperated gesture—leave it, not important. But it was important. She'd seen his face when he'd looked at the damage.

'Tell me about the kids,' he said again. 'You're fostering?'

'Mum and I decided...when you left...'

'To have kids?'

'You know I can't,' she said, evenly now, getting herself back together. 'For the year after you left I wasn't... very happy. I had my work as a midwife. I love my work, but you know that was never enough. And then one of my mums had Gretta.'

'One of your mums.'

'I know... Not very professional, is it, to get so personally involved? But Gretta was Miriam's third child. Miriam's a single mum who hadn't bothered to have any prenatal checks so missed the scans. From the moment the doctors told her Gretta had Down's she hadn't wanted any-thing to do with her. Normally, Social Services can find adoptive parents for a newborn, even if it has Down's, but Miriam simply checked herself out of hospital and disap-peared. We think she's in Western Australia with a new partner.'

'So you've taken her baby…'

'I didn't take her baby,' she said, thinking suddenly of the way he'd reacted to her suggestion of adoption all those years ago. It had been like adoption was a dirty word.

'I wasn't accusing…'

'No,' she said and stared down at her feet. She needed new shoes, she thought inconsequentially. She wore lace-up trainers—they were the most practical for the running she had to do—and a hole was starting to appear at her left big toe. Not this pay, she thought. Maybe next? Or maybe she could stick a plaster over the toe and pretend it was a new fashion. One of the kids' plasters with frogs on.

'What do you know about Miriam?' Oliver asked, and she hauled her attention back to him. Actually, it had never really strayed. But distractions were good. Distractions were necessary.

'We…we don't hear from Miriam,' she told him. 'But it's not for want of trying. Her two older children are in foster care together on a farm up near Kyneton—they're great kids and Harold and Eve are a wonderful foster-mum and dad—but Gretta couldn't go with them. Her heart problems have meant constant hospitalisation. We knew from the start that her life would be short. We knew it'd be a fight to keep her alive, so there was a choice. She could stay in hospital, institutionalised until she died, or I could take her home. She stayed in hospital for two months and then I couldn't bear it. Mum and I reorganised our lives and brought her home.'

'But she will die.' He said it gently, as if he was making sure she knew, and she flushed.

'You think we don't know that? But look at her tonight. She loved it. She loves…us.'

'I guess…'

'And don't you dare bring out your "Well, if she's adopted you can't possibly love her like your own" argument to say when she dies it won't hurt,' she snapped, suddenly unable to prevent the well of bitterness left from an appalling scene five years ago. 'We couldn't possibly love her more.'

'I never said that you couldn't love an adopted child.'

'Yes, you did.'

'I just said it's different and I hold by that. It's not the same love as from birth parents and you know it.'

'As Miriam's love? No, it's not and isn't Gretta lucky that it's not?'

'Em…'

'What?' She had her hands on her hips now, glaring. He'd shocked her so much, all those years ago. She'd been totally gutted when Josh had been stillborn, devastated beyond belief. She'd curled into a tight ball of misery, she'd hardly been able to function, but when finally daylight had begun to filter through the blackness, she'd clung to what had seemed her only hope.

Oliver, let's stop with the in-vitro stuff. It's tearing me apart—it's tearing us apart. Let's try instead for adoption.

But his reaction had stunned her.

Em, no. He'd said it gently but the words had been implacable. *I can't guarantee to love a child who's not my own. I won't do that to a child.*

It had been a divide neither of them could cross. She had been so desperate for a child that she couldn't accept his refusal to consider adoption—and Oliver had walked away rather than concede.

'I love Gretta and so does Adrianna,' she said now, forcing herself to stay calm. Forcing herself to put the hurt of years ago on the back burner. 'So, moving on…'

'Toby?'

And mentioning her son's name was a sure way to defuse anger. Even saying his name made her smile.

'Adrianna found Toby,' she told him. 'Or rather Adrianna helped Toby find us.'

'Would you like to tell me about him?'

She'd prefer not to, actually. She was finding it disturbing on all sorts of levels to stand outside in the dusk with this man who'd once been her husband. But he had offered to take the children on Saturday, and she did need help. These last few months, with Gretta's health deteriorating, had been taking their toll on Adrianna. This Saturday would be gold for both of them, she knew, and Oliver had offered.

Therefore she had to be courteous. She had to share.

She had to stand outside with him a moment longer, even though a part of her wanted to turn around and run.

Why?

It was how he made her feel. It was the way her body was responding. He'd been her husband. She'd thought she knew this man at the deepest, most primeval level—yet here he was, standing in the dusk asking polite questions about children he knew nothing about.

Her children.

'Toby has multiple problems.' Somehow she'd pulled herself together…sort of. 'He's African, as you can probably guess. He has scoliosis of the spine; his spine was so bent he looked deformed even when he was born, and his family abandoned him. One of the poorest families in the village took him in. His pseudo-mum did the best she could for him but he hadn't been fed properly and he was already suffering from noma—a facial bacterial infection.

She walked for three days to the nearest hospital to get him help—can you imagine that? But then, of course, she had to go back to her own family. But she'd fought for him first. One of the international aid agencies took on his case and brought him over here for facial reconstruction. So far he's been through six operations. He's doing great but...'

'But you can't keep him.'

She stilled. 'Why not? The hospital social worker in charge of his case knew Adrianna and I were already fostering Gretta, and she took a chance, asking us if we'd be willing to take him on. Adrianna did all the paperwork. Mum drove this, but we both want it. Theoretically he's supposed to go home when he's been treated. We're still in touch with his African foster-mum but she's so poor and she's very happy that he stays here. So in practice we're fighting tooth and nail to keep him.'

'Em, for heaven's sake...' He sounded appalled. 'You can't look after the world's waifs and strays. There are too many.'

'I can look after the ones I love,' she threw back at him, and tilted her chin. Defiant. She knew this argument—and here it came.

'You can't love him.'

'Why not?'

'He's not your kid.'

'Then whose kid is he? The woman who bore him? The woman who walked for three days to save him but can't afford to feed him? Or Mum and me, who'll do our damnedest to keep him healthy and safe?'

'Em...' He raked his hair, a gesture she knew all too well. 'To take two kids like Gretta and Toby... A kid who'll die and a kid you might lose. They'll break your heart.'

'You just said I can't love them. You can't have it both ways, Oliver.'

'Is this what you wanted me to do? Adopt the kids the world's abandoned?'

'I don't think I expected anything of you,' she managed, and was inordinately proud of how calm she sounded. 'At the end of our marriage all I could see was what I needed. I know that sounds selfish, and maybe it is, but it's what I desperately wanted. Despite loving you I couldn't stop that wanting. You always knew I wanted a family. I'm a midwife, and I'm a midwife because watching babies come into the world is what I love most. I'd dreamed we could have our own family...'

'And when that didn't happen you walked away.'

'As I remember it, you walked.'

'Because it's not fair for me to adopt. These kids need their own parents.'

'They don't have them. Are you saying second best is worse than nothing?'

'They'll know...that they're second best.'

'Oliver, just because that happened to you...'

And she watched his face close, just like that.

He didn't talk about it, she thought. He'd never talked about it but she'd guessed.

She thought, fleetingly, of her in-laws, of Oliver's adoptive parents. But she had to think fleetingly because thinking any more made her so angry she could spit.

She only knew the bare bones but it was enough. She could infer the rest. They'd had trouble conceiving so they'd adopted Oliver. Then, five years later, they'd conceived naturally and their own son had been born.

Oliver never talked about it—never would talk about it—but she'd seen the family in action. Brett was five years younger than Oliver, a spoiled brat when Em had first met him and now an obnoxious, conceited young man who thought the world owed him a living.

But his parents thought the sun shone from him, and

it seemed to Em that they'd spent their lives comparing their two sons, finding fault with Oliver and setting Brett on a pedestal.

Even at their wedding…

'He's done very well for himself,' Em had overheard his adoptive mother tell an aunt. *'Considering where he comes from. We've done what we could, but still… I know he's managed to get himself qualified as a doctor but… His mother was a whore, you know, and we can never forget that. Thank God we have Brett.'*

It had been as much as Em could do not to front the woman and slap her. It wouldn't have been a good look on her wedding day—bride smacks mother-in-law—but she'd come awfully close. But Oliver had never talked of it.

It was only when the adoption thing had come up when Josh had died that the ghosts had come from nowhere. And she couldn't fight them, for Oliver wouldn't speak of them.

'Oliver, we're doing our best,' she told him now, gentling, reminding herself that it was his ghosts talking, not him. She knew it was his ghosts, but she'd never been allowed close enough to fight them. 'Mum and I are loving these kids to bits. We're doing all we possibly can…'

'It won't be enough.'

'Maybe it won't.' She was suddenly bone weary again. Understanding could only go so far. 'But we're trying the best that we can. We'll give these kids our hearts, and if that's not enough to let them thrive then we'll be incredibly sad but we won't be regretful. We have love to give and we're giving it. We're trying, whereas you… You lacked courage to even think about it. "No adoptions," you said, end of story. I know your background. I know how hard it was for you to be raised with Brett but your parents were dumb and cruel. The whole world doesn't have to be like that.'

'And if you ever had a child of your own?'

'You're saying I shouldn't go near Gretta or Toby because I might, conceivably, still have a child biologically?'

'I didn't mean that.' He raked his hair again, in that gesture she'd known and loved. She had a sudden urge to rake it herself, settle it, touch his face, take away the pain.

Because there was pain. She could see it. This man was torn.

But she couldn't help him if he wouldn't talk about it. To be helped you had to admit you needed help. He'd simply closed off, shut her out, and there was nothing she could do about it.

She'd moved on, but he was still hurting. She couldn't help him.

'Go home,' she said, gently again. 'I'm sorry, Oliver, I have no right to bring up the past, but neither do you have a right to question what I'm doing. Our marriage is over and we need to remember it. We need to finalise our divorce. Meanwhile, thank you for tonight, for Adrianna's birthday. I'm deeply appreciative, but if you want to pull out of Saturday's childminding, I understand.'

'I'll be here.'

'You don't need to...'

'I will be here.'

'Fine, then,' she said, and took a step back in the face of his sudden blaze of anger. 'That's good. That's great. I'll see you then.'

'I'll see you at the hospital tomorrow,' he said. 'With Ruby.'

And her heart sank. Of course. She was going to see this man, often. She needed to work with him.

She needed to ignore the pain she still saw in his eyes. She needed to tell herself, over and over, that it had nothing to do with her.

The problem was, that wasn't Em's skill. Ignoring pain.

But he didn't want her interference. He never had.

He didn't want her.

Moving on…

'Goodnight, then,' she managed, and she couldn't help herself. She touched his face with her hand and then stood on tiptoe and lightly kissed him—a feather touch, the faintest brush of lips against lips. 'Goodnight, Oliver. I'm sorry for your demons but your demons aren't mine. I give my heart for always, non-negotiable, adoption, fostering, marriage… Ollie, I can no more change myself than fly. I'm just sorry you can't share.'

And she couldn't say another word. She was suddenly so close to tears that she pushed away and would have stumbled.

Oliver's hand came out to catch her. She steadied and then brushed him off. She did it more roughly than she'd intended but she was out of her depth.

'Thank you,' she whispered, and turned away. 'Goodnight.' And she turned and fled into the house.

Oliver was left standing in the shadows, watching the lights inside the house, knowing he should leave, knowing he had to.

'I give my heart for always.'

What sort of statement was that?

She'd been talking about the kids, he told himself, but still…

She'd included marriage in the statement, and it was a statement to give a man pause.

CHAPTER SIX

EM HARDLY SAW Oliver the next day. The maternity ward was busy, and when she wasn't wanted in the birthing suites, she mostly stayed with Ruby.

The kid was so alone. Today was full of fill-in-the-blanks medical forms and last-minute checks, ready for surgery the next day. The ultrasounds, the visit and check by the anaesthetist, the constant checking and rechecking that the baby hadn't moved, that the scans that had shown the problem a week ago were correct, that they had little choice but to operate... Everything was necessary but by the end of the day Ruby was ready to get up and run.

She needed her mum, a sister, a mate, anyone, Em thought. That she was so alone was frightening. Isla dropped in for a while. Ruby was part of Isla's teen mums programme and Ruby relaxed with her, but she was Ruby's only visitor.

'Isn't there anyone I can call?' Em asked as the day wore on and Ruby grew more and more tense.

'No one'll come near me,' Ruby said tersely. 'Mum said if I didn't have an abortion she'd wash her hands of me. She said if I stayed near her I'd expect her to keep the kid and she wasn't having a thing to do with it. And she told my sisters they could stay away, too.'

'And your baby's father?'

'I told you before, the minute I told him about it, he was off. Couldn't see him for dust.'

'Oh, Ruby, there must be someone.'

'I'll be okay,' Ruby said with bravado that was patently false. 'I'll get this kid adopted and then I'll get a job in a shop or something. I just wish it was over now.'

'We all wish that.'

And it was Oliver again. He moved around the wards like a great prowling cat, Em thought crossly. He should wear a bell.

'What?' he demanded, as she turned towards him, and she thought she really had to learn to stop showing her feelings on her face.

'Knock!'

'Sorry. If I'm intruding I'll go away.'

'You might as well come in and poke me, too,' Ruby sighed. 'Everyone else has. I'm still here. Bub's still here. Why is everyone acting like we're about to go up in smoke before tomorrow? Why do I need to stay in bed?'

'Because we need your baby to stay exactly where she is,' Oliver told her, coming further into the room. He had a bag under his arm and Ruby eyed it with suspicion. 'Right now she's in the perfect position to operate on her spine, and, no, Ruby, there's not a single thing in this bag that will prod, poke or pry. But I would like to feel your baby for myself.'

Ruby sighed with a theatrical flourish and tugged up her nightie.

'Go ahead. Half the world already has.'

'Has she moved?'

'Nah.' She gave a sheepish grin. 'I feel her myself. I'm not stupid, you know.' And she popped her hand on her tummy and cradled it.

There was that gesture again. Protective. *'Mine.'*

Oliver sat down on the bed and felt the rounded bump

himself, and Em looked at the way he was examining the baby and thought this was a skill. Ruby had been poked and prodded until she was tired of it. Oliver was doing the same thing but very gently, as if he was cradling Ruby's unborn child.

'She's perfect,' he said at last, tugging Ruby's nightie back down. 'Like her mother.'

'She's not perfect. That's why I'm here.'

'She's pretty much perfect. Would you like to see a slide show of what we're about to do?' He grinned at Ruby's scared expression. 'There's not many gory bits and I can fast-forward through them.'

'I'll shut my eyes,' Ruby said, but he'd caught her, Em thought. She wasn't dissociated from this baby. Once again she saw Ruby's hand move surreptitiously to her tummy.

He flicked open his laptop. Fascinated, Em perched on the far side of the bed and watched, too.

'This is one we prepared earlier,' Oliver said, in the tone TV cooks used as they pulled a perfect bake from the oven. 'This is Rufus. He's six months old now, a lovely, healthy baby, but at the start of this he was still inside his mum, a twenty-two-weeker. This is the procedure your little one will have.'

The screen opened to an operating theatre, the patient's face hidden, the film obviously taken for teaching purposes as identities weren't shown. But the sound was on, and Em could hear Oliver's voice, calmly directive, and she knew that it was Oliver who was in charge.

She was fascinated—and so was Ruby. Squeamishness was forgotten. They watched in awe as the scalpel carefully, carefully negotiated the layers between the outside world and the baby within. It would be an intricate balance, Em knew, trying to give the baby minimal exposure to the outside world, keeping infection out, disturbing the baby as little as possible yet giving the surgeons space to work.

There were many doctors present—she could hear their voices. This was cutting-edge surgery.

'I can see its back,' Ruby breathed. 'Oh…is that the same as my baby?'

'They're all different,' Oliver said. 'Your daughter is tilted at a better angle.'

'Oh…' Ruby's eyes weren't leaving the screen.

They could definitely see the baby now, and they could see how the baby was slightly tilted to the side. Carefully, carefully Oliver manoeuvred him within the uterus, making no sudden movements, making sure the move was no more dramatic than if the baby himself had wriggled.

And now they could see the spine exposed. The tell-tale bulge…

'Is that the problem? The same as mine?' Ruby whispered, and Oliver nodded.

'Rufus's problem was slightly lower, but it's very similar.'

Silence again. They were totally focused, all of them. Oliver must have seen this many times before, Em thought—and he'd been there in person—but he was still watching it as if it was a miracle.

It was a miracle.

'This is where I step back and let the neurosurgeon take over,' Oliver said. 'My job is to take care of the whole package, you and your baby, but Dr Zigler will be doing this bit. He's the best, Ruby. You're in the best of hands.'

They watched on. The surgery was painstaking. It was like microsurgery, Em thought, where fingers were reattached, where surgeons fought hard to save nerves. And in a way it was. They were carefully working around and then through the bulge. There'd be so many things to work around. The spinal cord was so fragile, so tiny. The task was to repair the damage already done, as far as possible, and then close, protecting the cord and peripheral nerves from the amniotic fluid until the baby was born.

'Is…is it hurting?' Ruby breathed, as the first incision was made into the tiny back.

'Is *he* hurting? No. Rufus is anaesthetised, as well as his mum. Did you see the anaesthetist working as soon as we had exposure? The jury's out on whether unborn babies can feel pain. There are those who say they're in a state similar to an induced coma, but they certainly react to a painful touch. It makes the procedure a little more risky—balancing anaesthetic with what he's receiving via his mum's blood supply—but the last thing we want is to stress him. Luckily the Victoria has some of the best anaesthetists in the world. Vera Harty will be doing your anaesthetic and your daughter's. I'd trust her with a baby of my own.'

Ruby was satisfied. She went back to watching the screen.

Em watched, too, but Oliver's last statement kept reverberating.

I'd trust her with a baby of my own.

The sadness was flooding back. Oliver had been unable to have a baby of his own—because of her. She had fertility problems, not Oliver.

He'd left her years ago. He could have found someone by now.

Maybe he had. Maybe he just wasn't saying.

But he hadn't. She knew him well, this man.

There'd been an undercurrent of longing in the statement.

They'd both wanted children. She'd released him so he could have them. Why hadn't he moved on?

Watch the screen, she told herself. Some things were none of her business. Oliver was none of her business—except he was the obstetrician treating her patient.

She went back to being professional—sort of. She went back to watching Rufus, as Oliver and Ruby were doing.

The procedure was delicate and it took time but it seemed Oliver was in no hurry to finish watching, and neither was Ruby. Em couldn't be, either. Her job was to keep Ruby calm for tomorrow's operation, and that's what was happening now. The more familiar the girl was about what lay ahead, the more relaxed she'd be.

And not for the first time, Em blessed this place, this job. The Victoria considered its midwives some of the most important members of its staff. The mothers' needs came first and if a mum needed her midwife then Isla would somehow juggle the rest of her staff to cover.

Unless there was major drama Em wouldn't be interrupted now, she thought, and she wasn't. They made an intimate trio, midwife and doctor, with Ruby sandwiched between. Protected? That's what it felt like to Em, and she suspected that's how Ruby felt. Had Oliver set this up with just this goal? She glanced at him and knew her suspicion was right.

The first time she'd met him she'd been awed by his medical skills. Right now, watching him operate on screen, feeling Ruby's trust growing by the second, that awe was escalating into the stratosphere.

He might not make it as a husband, but he surely made it as a surgeon.

Back on screen, the neurosurgeon was suturing, using careful, painstakingly applied, tiny stitches, while Oliver was carefully monitoring the levels of amniotic fluid. This baby would be born already scarred, Em thought. He'd have a scar running down his lower back—but with luck that was all he'd have. Please...

'It worked a treat,' Oliver said, sounding as pleased as if the operation had happened yesterday, and on screen the neurosurgeon stood back and Oliver took over. The final stitches went in, closing the mum's uterus, making the incision across the mum's tummy as neat as the baby's. 'Rufus was born by Caesarean section at thirty-three weeks,' Oliver told them. 'He spent four weeks in hospital as a prem baby but would you like to see him now?'

'I... Yes.' Ruby sounded as if she could scarcely breathe.

'We have his parents' permission to show him to other parents facing the same procedure,' Oliver told her. 'Here goes.'

He fiddled with the computer and suddenly they were transported to a suburban backyard, to a rug thrown on a lawn, to a baby, about six months old, lying on his back in the sun, kicking his legs, admiring his toes.

There was a dog at the edge of the frame, a dopey-looking cocker spaniel. As they watched, the dog edged forward and licked the baby's toes. Rufus crowed with laughter and his toes went wild.

'He doesn't...he doesn't look like there's anything wrong with him,' Ruby breathed.

'He still has some issues he needs help with.' Oliver was matter-of-fact now, surgeon telling it like it was. 'He'll need physiotherapy to help him walk, and he might need professional help to learn how to control his bladder and bowels, but the early signs are that he'll be able to lead a perfectly normal life.'

'He looks...perfect already.' Ruby was riveted and so was Em. She was watching Ruby's face. She was watching Ruby's hand, cradling her bump. 'My little one...my little girl...she could be perfect, too?'

'I think she already is.' Oliver was smiling down at her. 'She has a great mum who's taking the best care of her. And you have the best midwife...'

Em flashed him a look of surprise. There was no need to make this personal.

But for Ruby, this was nothing but personal. 'Em says

she'll stay with me,' Ruby told him. 'At the operation and again when my baby's born. There's a chance that she can't—she says no one's ever totally sure because babies are unpredictable—but she's promised to try. I hope she can, but if she's not then she's introduced me to Sophia, or Isla will take over. But you'll look after...' Her hand cradled the bump again as she looked anxiously at Oliver. 'You'll look after us both?'

'I will.' And it was a vow.

'Tell me again why I need a Caesarean later—when my baby's born properly?'

He nodded, closed his laptop and sat back in a visitor's chair, to all appearances prepared to chat for as long as Ruby wanted. He was busy, Em knew. As well as the promises he'd made her to childmind on Saturday, she knew he already had a full caseload of patients. But right now Ruby was being given the impression that he had all the time in the world, and that time was Ruby's.

He was...gorgeous. She knew it, she'd always known it, but suddenly the thought almost blindsided her.

And it was more than him being gorgeous, she thought, feeling dazed. She was remembering why she'd loved this man.

And she was thinking—idiotically—that she loved him still.

Concentrate on medicine, on your patient, on anything other than Oliver, she told herself fiercely. Concentrating on Oliver was just too scary.

What had Ruby asked? Why she needed a Caesarean?

'You see the incision we just cut in Rufus's mum's uterus?' Oliver was saying, flicking back to the screen, where they could see the now closed incision in the abdomen. 'I've stitched it with care, as I'll stitch you with care, but when your bub comes out, she'll push. You have no idea how hard a baby can push. She wants to get out to meet you, and nothing's going to stop her. So maybe she'll push against that scar, and if she pushes hard enough on very new scar tissue she might cause you to bleed. I have two people I care about, Ruby. I care about your daughter but my absolute priority is to keep you safe. That means a Caesarean birth, because, much as I want to meet your baby, we'll need to deliver her before she even thinks about pushing.'

'But if you wanted to keep me really safe you wouldn't operate in the first place,' Ruby muttered, a trace of the old resentment resurfacing. But it didn't mess with Oliver's composure.

'That's right,' he agreed, his tone not changing. 'I believe we *will* keep you safe but there are risks. They're minor but they're real. That's why it's your choice. You can still pull out. Right up to the time we give you the anaesthetic, you can pull out, and no one will think the worse of you. That's your right.'

The room fell silent. It was such a hard decision to make, Em thought, and once again she thought, Where was this kid's mum?

But, surprisingly, when Ruby spoke again it seemed that worry about the operation was being supplanted by something deeper.

'If I had her...' Ruby said, and then amended her statement. '*When* I have her...after she's born, she'll have a scar, too.'

'She will,' Oliver told her, as watchful as Em, waiting to know where Ruby was going with this.

'And she'll have it for ever?'

'Yes.'

'She might hate it—as a teenager,' Ruby whispered. 'I know I would.'

'I'll do my best to make it as inconspicuous as possible—and cosmetic touch-ups when she's older might help even more. It shouldn't be obvious.'

'But teenagers freak out about stuff like that. I know I would,' Ruby whispered. 'And she won't have a mum to tell her it's okay.'

'If she's adopted, she'll have a mum,' Em ventured. 'Ruby, we've gone through what happens. Adoption is your choice all the way. You'll get to meet the adoptive parents. You'll know she goes to parents who'll love her.'

'But...I'll love her more. She's *my* baby.'

And suddenly Ruby was crying, great fat tears slipping down her face, and Em shifted so she could take her into her arms. And as she did so, Oliver's laptop slid off the bed and landed with a crash on the floor.

Uh-oh. But Em didn't move. For now she couldn't afford to think of computers. For now holding this girl was the most important thing in the world.

But still... A car and then a laptop...

She was starting to be an expensive ex-wife, she thought ruefully, and she almost smiled—but, of course, she didn't. She simply held Ruby until the sobs receded, until Ruby tugged away and grabbed a handful of tissues. That was a bit late. Em's shoulder was soaked, but who cared? How many times had Em ever finished a shift clean? She could count them on one hand. She always got her hands dirty, one way or another.

And it seemed, so did Oliver, for he was still there. Most consultants would have fled at the first sign of tears, Em thought. As a breed, surgeons weren't known for their empathy.

He'd risen, but he was standing by the door, watching, and there was definitely sympathy. Definitely caring.

He was holding the two halves of his laptop. The screen had completely split from the keyboard. And the screen itself...smashed.

'Whoops,' she said, as Ruby blew her nose.

He glanced down at the ruined machine. 'As you say, whoops.'

And as Ruby realised what he was holding, the teenager choked on something that was almost a laugh. 'Em's smashed your computer,' she said, awed. 'Do you mind?'

'I can't afford to mind.'

'Why not?' She was caught, pulled out of her misery by a smashed computer.

'Priorities,' he said. 'You. Baby. Computer. In that order.'

'What about Em?' she asked, a touch of cheekiness emerging. 'Is she a priority?'

'Don't you dare answer,' Em told him. 'Not until you've checked that your computer is covered by insurance. Ruby, if you're rethinking your plans to adopt…'

'I think…I might be.'

'Then let's not make any decisions yet,' she said, hurriedly. Surely now wasn't the time to make such an emotional decision? 'Let's get this operation over with first.'

Ruby took a deep breath and looked from Oliver to Emily and back again. 'Maybe I do need a bit of time,' she conceded. 'Maybe a sleep…time to think.'

'Of course you do.' She pulled up her covers and tucked her in. 'Ruby, nothing's urgent. No decisions need to be made now. Just sleep.'

'Thank you. And, Dr Evans…'

'Mmm?' Oliver was about to leave but turned back.

'I hope your computer's all right.'

'It will be,' he said. But it wouldn't. Em could see the smashed screen from where she stood. 'But even if it's not, it's not your problem,' he said, gently now, almost as a blessing. 'From here on, Ruby, we don't want you to worry about a thing. You've put yourself in our hands and we'll keep you safe. Em and I are a great team. You and your baby are safe with us.'

His lovely, gentle bedside manner lasted until they were ten feet from Ruby's door. Em closed the door behind her, looked ahead—and Oliver was staring straight at her. Vibrating with anger.

'You're planning on talking her out of keeping her baby?'

The turnabout from empathy to anger was shocking. The gentleness had completely gone from his voice. What she saw now was fury.

She faced him directly, puzzled. 'What are you saying? I didn't. I'm not.'

'You are. She'd decided on adoption but now she's changing her mind. But you stopped her.'

'I didn't stop her. I'd never do that.' She thought back to the scene she'd just left, trying to replay her words. 'I just said she had time…'

'You told her not to make a decision now. Why not? Right now she's thinking of keeping her baby. You don't think it's important to encourage her?'

'I don't think it's my right to direct her one way or another.' She felt herself getting angry in response. 'All I saw in there was a frightened, tired kid who's facing major surgery tomorrow. Who needs to stay calm and focused. Who doesn't need to be making life-changing decisions right now. She's already decided enough.'

'But maybe when you're emotional, that's the time to make the decision. When she knows she loves her baby.'

'She'll always love her baby.' Em was struggling to stay calm in the face of his anger—in the face of his accusation? 'Ruby is a seventeen-year-old, terrified kid with no family support at all. If she decides to keep this baby, it'll change her life for ever. As it will if she gives it up for adoption. What I did in there—and, yes, I interceded—was give her space. If she wants to keep her baby, she'll need every ounce of strength and then some.'

'She'll get support.'

'And she can never be a kid again. But, then, after this, maybe being a kid is no longer an option. But I agree, that's none of my business. Oliver, is this discussion going anywhere? I've been away from the birthing suites for over an hour and I don't know what's going on. I may well be needed.'

'You won't influence her?'

'Why would I influence her?'

'Because you believe in adoption.'

'And you don't? Because of what happened to you when you were a kid?' Anger was washing over her now. Yes, she should get back to the birthing suites but what was it he was accusing her of? 'Get over it, Oliver. Move on. Not every adoptive mother is like yours, and not every birth mother is capable of loving. There's a whole lot of grey in between the black and white, and it's about time you saw it.'

'So you won't encourage her to adopt?'

'What are you expecting me to do?' She was confused now, as well as angry. She put her hands on her hips and glared. 'Are you thinking I might pop in there, offer to adopt it myself and get myself another baby? Is that what you're thinking?'

'I would never—'

'You'd better not. A midwife influencing a mother's decision is totally unethical. How much more so is a midwife offering to adopt? I'll do neither. I have my kids, Oliver, and I love them to bits. I have no wish for more.'

'But Gretta's going to die.'

Why had he said it? It had just come out, and he could

have bitten his tongue from his head. Em's face bleached white and she leaned back against the wall for support.

Dear heaven… What sort of emotional drop kick was he? Suggesting one kid was going to die so she was lining up for another? Where had the thought come from?

It was confusion, he thought. Maybe it was even anger that she'd got on with her life without him.

Or maybe it was sheer power of testosterone washing through him—because the woman who should be his wife was looking at him as if he was a piece of dirt.

Where to start with apologies? He'd better haul himself back under control, and fast. 'Hell, Em, I'm sorry. I didn't mean that the way it came out, truly.' He reached out and touched her stricken face, and the way he felt… sick didn't begin to describe it. 'Can you forget I said it? Of all the insensitive oafs…I know Gretta's health has nothing to do with…anything. I'm so sorry. Can you wipe it? I know you love Gretta…'

'Are you talking about Emily's little girl?'

They both turned to face the newcomer, and it was a relief to turn away from each other. The tension between them was so tight it was threatening to break, to fly back and hit both of them.

Oliver recognised the young man heading towards them. Oliver had been introduced to Noah Jackson earlier in the week. He was a surgical registrar, almost at the end of his training. 'Technically brilliant,' Tristan, the paediatric cardiologist, had told him. 'But his people skills leave a whole lot to be desired.'

And now he proceeded to display just that.

'Hi, Em,' he called, walking up to them with breezy insouciance. 'Are you discussing Gretta's progress? How's she going?'

'She's…okay,' Em said, and by the way she said it Oliver knew there was baggage behind the question.

'You ought to meet Gretta,' Noah told Oliver, seemingly oblivious to the way Em's face had shuttered. 'She's worth a look. She has Down's, with atrioventricular septal defects, massive heart problems, so much deformity that even Tristan felt he couldn't treat her. Yet she's survived. I've collated her case notes from birth as part of my final-year research work. I'd love to write her up for the med journals. It'd give me a great publication. Em's care has been nothing short of heroic.'

'I've met her,' Oliver said shortly, glancing again at Em. Gretta—a research project? He could see Em's distress. 'Now's not...' he started.

But the young almost-surgeon wouldn't be stopped. 'Gretta wasn't expected to live for more than a year,' he said, with enthusiasm that wouldn't be interrupted. 'It'll make a brilliant article—the extent of the damage, the moral dilemma facing her birth mother, her decision to walk away—Em's decision to intervene and now the medical resources and the effort to keep her alive this far. Em, please agree to publication. You still haven't signed. But Tristan says she's pretty close to the end. If I could examine her one last time...'

And Oliver saw the wash of anger and revulsion on Em's face—and finally he moved.

He put his body between the registrar and Em. Noah was tall but right now Oliver felt a good foot taller. Anger did that. Of all the insensitive...

'You come near Em again with your requests for information about her daughter—her *daughter*, Noah, not her patient—and I'll ram every page of your case notes down your throat. Don't you realise that Em loves Gretta? Don't you realize she's breaking in two, and you're treating her daughter like a bug under a microscope?'

'Hey, Em's a medical colleague,' Noah said, still not

getting it. 'She knows the score—she knew it when she took Gretta home. She can be professional.'

'Is that what you're being—professional?'

'If we can learn anything from this, then, yes…'

Enough. Em looked close to fainting.

The lift was open behind them. Oliver grabbed Noah by the collar of his white jacket, twisted him round and practically kicked him into the lift.

'What…?' Noah seemed speechless. 'What did I say?'

'You might be nearing the end of your surgical training,' Oliver snapped. 'But you sure aren't at the end of your training to be a decent doctor. You need to learn some people skills, fast. I assume you did a term in family medicine during your general training, but whether you did or not, you're about to do another. And another after that if you still don't get it. I want you hands-on, treating people at the coal face, before you're ever in charge of patients in a surgical setting.'

'You don't have that authority.' The young doctor even had the temerity to sound smug.

'You can believe that,' Oliver growled. 'You're welcome—for all the good it'll do you. Now get out of here while I see if I can fix the mess you've made.'

'I haven't made a mess.'

'Oh, yes, you have,' Oliver snapped, hitting the 'Close' button on the lift with as much force as he'd like to use on Noah. 'And you've messed with someone who spends her life trying to fix messes. Get out of my sight.'

The lift closed. Oliver turned back to Em. She hadn't moved. She was still slumped on the wall, her face devoid of colour. A couple of tears were tracking down her face.

'It's okay,' she managed. 'Oliver, it's okay. He's just saying it like it is.'

'He has no right to say anything at all,' Oliver snapped,

and he couldn't help himself. She was so bereft. She was so gutted.

She was…his wife?

She wasn't. Their long separation to all intents and purposes constituted a divorce, but right now that was irrelevant.

His Em was in trouble. *His Em*.

He walked forward and took her into his arms.

She shouldn't let him hold her. She had no right to be in his arms.

She had no right to want to be in his arms.

Besides, his words had upset her as much as Noah's had. His implication that she could replace Gretta…

But she knew this man. She'd figured it out—the hurt he'd gone through as a kid, the rejection, the knowledge that he'd been replaced by his adoptive parents' 'real' son.

Noah was just plain insensitive. He was arrogant and intelligent but he was lacking emotional depth. Oliver's comments came from a deep, long-ago hurt that had never been resolved.

And even if it hadn't, she thought helplessly, even if he was as insensitive as Noah, even if she shouldn't have anything to do with him, for now she wanted to be here.

To be held. By her husband.

For he still felt like her husband. They'd been married for five years. They'd lain in each other's arms for five years.

For five years she'd thought she had the perfect marriage.

But she hadn't. Of course she hadn't. There had been ghosts she'd been unable to expunge, and those ghosts were with him still. He couldn't see…

Stop thinking, she told herself fiercely, almost desperately. Stop thinking and just be. Just let his arms hold me. Just feel his heart beat against mine. Just pretend…

'Em, I'm sorry,' he whispered into her hair.

'For?'

'For what I said. Even before Noah, you were hurt. I can't begin to think how I could have said such a thing.'

'It doesn't matter.' But it did. It was the crux of what had driven them apart. For Oliver, adoption was simply a transaction. Hearts couldn't be held…

As theirs hadn't. Their marriage was over.

But still she held. Still she took comfort, where she had no right to take comfort. They'd been separated for five years!

So why did he still feel like…home? Why did everything about him feel as if here was her place in the world?

'Hey!' A hospital corridor was hardly the place to hold one's ex-husband—to hold anyone. It was busy and bustling and their sliver of intimacy couldn't last.

It was Isla, hurrying along the corridor, smiling—as Isla mostly smiled right now. The sapphire on her finger seemed to have changed Em's boss's personality. 'You know I'm all for romance,' she said as she approached. 'But the corridor's not the place.' She glanced down at the sapphire on her finger and her smile widened. 'Alessi and I find the tea room's useful. No one's in there right now…'

'Oh, Isla…' Em broke away, flushing. 'Sorry. It's not… Dr Evans was just…just…'

But Isla had reached them now and was seeing Em's distress for herself. 'Nothing's wrong with Ruby, is there?' she asked sharply.

'No.' Oliver didn't break his composure. 'But you have a problem with Dr Noah Jackson. He seems to think Em's Gretta is a research experiment.'

'Noah's been upsetting my midwife?' Isla's concern switched to anger, just like that. 'Let me at him.'

'I don't think there's any need,' Em managed. 'Oliver practically threw him into the lift.'

'Well, good for you,' Isla said, smiling again. 'I do like an obstetrician who knows when to act, and one who knows the value of a good cuddle is worth his weight in gold.' She glanced again at her ring. 'I should know. But, Em, love, if you've finished being cuddled, I would like you back in the birthing suite.'

'Of course,' Em said, and fled.

There was a moment's silence. Then...

'Don't you mess with my midwives,' Isla said, and Oliver looked at her and thought she saw a whole lot more than she let on.

'I won't.'

She eyed him some more. 'You two have baggage? Your name's the same.'

'We don't have...baggage.'

'I don't believe it.' She was still thoughtful. 'But I'll let it lie. All I'll say is to repeat—don't mess with my midwives.'

Thursday night was blessedly uneventful. Gretta seemed to have settled. Em should have had a good night's sleep.

She didn't but the fact that she stared into the dark and thought of Oliver was no fault of...anyone.

Oliver was no business of hers.

But he'd held her and he felt all her business.

Oliver...

Why had he come here to work? Of all the unlucky coincidences...

But it wasn't a simple coincidence, she conceded. The Victoria had one of Australia's busiest birthing units. It was also right near her mother's home so it had made sense that she get a job here after the loss of Josh.

And after the loss of Oliver.

Don't go there, she told herself. Think of practicalities.

It made sense that Oliver was back here, she told herself. Charles Delamere head-hunted the best, and he'd have known Oliver had links to Melbourne.

So she should leave?

Leave the Victoria? Because Oliver had…cuddled her?

It's not going to happen again, she told herself fiercely. And I won't leave because of him. There's no need to leave.

He could be a friend. Like Isla. Like Sophia.

Yeah, right, she told herself, punching her pillow in frustration. Oliver Evans, just a friend?

Not in a million years.

But she had no choice. She could do this. Bring on tomorrow, she told herself.

Bring on a way she could treat Oliver as a medical colleague and nothing else.

CHAPTER SEVEN

FRIDAY. EM'S DAY was cleared so she could focus on Ruby. Isla was aware of the situation. 'If she really has no one, then you'd better be with her all the way.'

So she stayed with Ruby in the hour before she was taken to Theatre. She spent their time discussing—of all things—Ruby's passion for sewing. Ruby had shyly shown her her handiwork the day before, so Em had brought in one of Toby's sweaters. Ruby was showing her how to darn a hole in the elbow.

'Darning's a dying art,' she'd told Em, so Em had found the sweater and brought a darning mushroom—Adrianna had one her grandmother had used!—and needle and thread and asked for help.

Ruby took exquisite care with the intricate patch. When she was finished Em could scarcely see where the hole had been, and darning and the concentration involved worked a charm. When the orderlies came to take Ruby to Theatre, Ruby was shocked that the time had already arrived.

She squeezed Em's hand. 'Th-thank you. Will I see you later?'

'I'm coming with you,' Em declared, packing up the darning equipment. 'Isla's told me if I'm to help deliver your baby at term then I should introduce myself to her now. So I'm to stay in the background, not faint, and admire Dr Evans's handiwork.'

'You'd never faint.'

'Don't you believe it,' Em told her, and proceeded to give her some fairly gross examples. She kept right up with the narrative while Ruby was pushed through to Theatre, while pre-meds were given, while they waited for the theatre to be readied. Finally, as Ruby was wheeled into Theatre, they were both giggling.

Oliver was waiting, gowned and ready. So, it seemed, was a cast of thousands. This was surgery at its most cutting edge. They were operating on two patients, not one, but one of those patients was a foetus that was not yet viable outside her mother. The logistics were mind-bending and it would take the combined skills of the Victoria's finest to see it succeed.

Shock to the foetus could cause abortion. Therefore the anaesthetic had to be just right—they had not only the Victoria's top anaesthetist, but also the anaesthetic registrar. Heinz Zigler was gowned and ready. Tristan Hamilton, paediatric cardiologist, was there to check on the baby's heart every step of the way. There were so many possible complications.

The surgery itself was demanding but everything else had to be perfect, as well. If amniotic fluid was lost it had to be replaced. If the baby bled, that blood had to be replaced, swiftly but so smoothly the loss couldn't be noticed. Everything had to be done with an eye to keeping the trauma to the baby at the absolute minimum.

'Hey, Ruby.' Oliver welcomed the girl warmly as she was wheeled in, and if he was tense he certainly wasn't showing it. 'What's funny?'

'Em's been telling me—' Ruby was almost asleep from the pre-meds but she was still smiling '—about muddles. About her work.'

'Did she tell you about the time she helped deliver twins and the team messed up their bracelets?' Oliver was smiling with his patient, but he found a chance to glance—and smile—at Em. 'So Mathew Riley was wrapped in a pink rug and Amanda Riley was wrapped in a blue rug. It could have scarred them for life.'

Em thought back all those years. She'd just qualified, and it had been one of the first prem births where she'd been midwife in charge. Twins, a complex delivery, and the number of people in the birthing room had made her flustered. Afterwards Oliver had come to the prem nursery to check on his handiwork. The nurse in charge—a dragon of a woman who shot first and asked questions later—had been in the background, as Oliver had unwrapped the blue bundle.

Em had been by his side. She'd gasped and lost colour but Oliver hadn't said a word; hadn't given away by the slightest intake of breath that he'd become aware she'd made a blunder that could have put her job at risk. But the mistake was obvious—the incubators had been brought straight from the birthing suite and were side by side. There was no question who each baby was. Without saying a word, somehow Oliver helped her swap blankets and wristbands and the charge nurse was unaware to this day.

That one action had left her...smitten.

But it hadn't just been his action, she conceded. It had also been the way he'd smiled at her, and then as she'd tried to thank him afterwards, it had been the way he'd laughed it off and told her about dumb things he'd done as a student...and then asked her to have dinner with him...

'I reckon I might like to be a nurse,' Ruby said sleepily. 'You reckon I might?'

'I reckon you're awesome,' Oliver told her. 'I reckon you can do anything you want.'

And then Ruby's eyes flickered closed. The chief

anaesthetist gave Oliver a nod—and the operation was under way.

Lightness was put aside.

Oliver had outlined the risks to Ruby—and there were risks. Exposing this tiny baby to the outside world when she was nowhere near ready for birth was so dangerous. Em had no idea how many times it had been done in the past, how successful it had been, but all she knew as she watched was that if it was her baby there was no one she'd rather have behind the scalpel than Oliver.

He was working side by side with Heinz. They were talking through the procedure together, glancing up every so often at the scans on the screens above their heads, checking positions. They wanted no more of the baby exposed than absolutely necessary.

Another screen showed what they were doing. To Em in the background she could see little of the procedural site but this was being recorded—to be used as Rufus's operation had been—to reassure another frantic mum?

Please let it have the same result, she pleaded. She was acting as gofer, moving equipment back and forth within reach of the theatre nurse as needed, but she still had plenty of time to watch the screen.

And then the final incision was made. Gently, gently, the baby was rotated within the uterus—and she could see the bulge that was the unsealed spine.

There was a momentary pause as everyone saw it. A collective intake of breath.

'The poor little tacker,' Tristan breathed. 'To be born like that…she'd have had no chance of living a normal life.'

'Then let's see if we can fix it,' Oliver said in a voice Em had never heard before. And she knew that every nerve was on edge, every last ounce of his skill and Heinz's were at play here.

Please…

The complexity, the minuscule size, the need for accuracy, it was astounding.

Oliver was sweating. Not only was the intensity of his work mind-blowing, but the theatre itself had to be set at a high enough temperature to stop foetal shock.

'Em.' Chris, the chief theatre nurse, called back to her. 'Take over the swabs.'

All hands were needed. Em saw where she, too, was needed. She moved seamlessly into position and acted to stop Oliver's sweat obscuring his vision.

He wasn't aware of her. He wasn't aware of anything.

They were using cameras to blow up the images of the area he and Heinz were working on. Every person there was totally focused on the job or on the screens. Two people at once—two hearts, two lives...

She forgot to breathe. She forgot everything but keeping Oliver's vision clear so he could do what had to be a miracle.

And finally they were closing. Oliver was stitching—maybe his hands were steadier than Heinz's because he was working under instruction. He was inserting what seemed almost microstitches, carefully, carefully manoeuvring the spinal wound closed. Covering the spinal cord and the peripheral nerves. Stopping future damage.

The spine was closed. They were replacing the amniotic fluid. Oliver was closing the uterus, conferring with Heinz, seemingly relaxing a little.

The outer wound was being closed.

The thing was done.

Emily felt like sagging.

She wouldn't. She wiped Oliver's forehead for the final time and at last he had space to turn and give her a smile. To give the whole team a smile. But his smile ended with Em.

'We've done it,' he said with quiet triumph. 'As long as

we can keep her on board for another few weeks, we've saved your baby.'

'Your baby'...

Where had that come from?

And then she thought back to the teasing he'd given her when they'd first met, when they'd been working together, she as a brand-new nurse, he as a paediatric surgeon still in training.

'Em, the way you expose your heart... You seem to greet every baby you help deliver as if it's your own,' he'd told her. *'By the end of your career, you'll be like Old Mother Hubbard—or the Pied Piper of Hamelin. Kids everywhere.'*

And wouldn't she just love that! She thought fleetingly of the two she was allowed to love. Gretta and Toby.

She did love them, fiercely, wonderfully, but she looked down at Ruby now and she knew that she had love to spare. Heart on her sleeve or not, she loved this teenage mum, and she loved the little life that was now securely tucked back inside her.

The heart swelled to fit all comers...

She thought back to Oliver's appalling adoptive mother and she thought he'd never known that.

He still didn't know it and they'd gone their separate ways because of it.

She stood back from the table. Her work there was done. She'd wait for Ruby in the recovery ward.

The team had another patient waiting for surgery. Oliver was moving on.

Em already had moved on. She just had to keep moving.

'Well done.' Out at the sinks the mood was one of quiet but deep satisfaction. There'd be no high fives, not yet— everyone knew the next few days would be critical—but the procedure had gone so smoothly surely they'd avoided embryo shock.

Tristan hitched himself up on the sinks and regarded his friend with satisfaction. He and Oliver had done their general surgical training together. They'd split as Oliver had headed into specialist surgical obstetrics and Tristan into paediatric cardiology, but their friendship was deep and longstanding.

Tristan alone knew the association between Em and Oliver. They'd had one heated discussion about it already...

'The hospital grapevine will find out. Why keep it secret?'

'It's not a secret. It's just a long time ago. Moving on...'

But now...

'Are you telling me you and Em have really moved on?' Tristan demanded as he watched his friend ditch his theatre garb. 'Because, sure, Em's your patient's midwife and she was in Theatre as an observer in that capacity, but the contact you and she had... You might not have been aware how often you flicked her a glance but every time you were about to start something risky, it was like you were looking to her for strength.'

'What the...?' Where had this come from? As if he needed Em for strength? He'd been operating without Em for years.

He'd never depended on her.

'You might say it's in the past,' Tristan went on, inexorably. 'But she's still using your name, and as of today, as an onlooker, it seems to me that the marriage isn't completely over.'

'Will you keep your voice down?' There were nurses and orderlies everywhere.

'You think you can keep this to yourself?'

'It's not obvious.'

'It's obvious,' Tristan said, grinning. 'Midwife Evans and Surgeon Evans. Sparks. The grapevine will go nuts.'

'You're not helping.'

'I'm just observing.' Tristan pushed down from the bench. He and Oliver both had patients waiting. Always there were patients waiting.

'All I'm saying is that I'm interested,' Tristan said, heading for the door. 'Me and the rest of staff of the Victoria. And some of us are even more interested than others.'

Trained theatre staff were rostered to watch over patients in Recovery, but Isla had cleared the way for Em to stay with Ruby. With no family support, the need to keep Ruby calm was paramount. So Em sat by her bedside and watched. Ruby was drifting lightly towards consciousness, seeming to ease from sedation to natural sleep.

Which might have something to do with the way Em was holding her hand and talking to her.

'It's great, Ruby. You were awesome. Your baby was awesome. It's done, all fixed. Your baby will have the best of chances because of your decision.'

She doubted Ruby could hear her but she said it anyway, over and over, until she was interrupted.

'Hey.' She looked up and Sophia was watching her. Sophia was a partnering midwife, a friend, a woman who had the same fertility issues she did. If there was anyone in this huge staff she was close to, it was Sophia. 'Isla sent me down to see how the op went,' she said, pulling up a chair to sit beside Em. 'All's quiet on the Western Front. We had three nice, normal babies in quick succession this morning and not a sniff of a contraction this arvo. Isla says you can stay here as needed; take as long as you want.'

'We're happy, aren't we, Ruby?' Em said gently, squeezing Ruby's hand, but there was no response. Ruby's natural sleep had grown deeper. 'The operation went brilliantly.'

And then, because she couldn't help herself, she added a rider. 'Oliver was brilliant.'

'Yeah, I'd like to talk to you about that,' Sophia said, diffidently now, assessing Ruby as she spoke and realising, as Em had, that there was little chance of Ruby taking in anything she said. 'Rumours are flying. Someone heard Tristan and Oliver talking at the sinks. Evans and Evans. No one's put them together until now. It's a common name. But...Evans isn't your maiden name, is it? Evans is your married name. And according to the rumours, that marriage would be between you and Oliver.'

Whoa. Em flinched. But then...it had to come out sooner or later, she thought. She might as well grit her teeth and confess.

'It was a long time ago,' she murmured. 'We split five years ago but changing my name didn't seem worth the complications. I was Emily Green before. I kind of like Emily Evans better.' She didn't want to say that going to a lawyer, asking for a divorce, had seemed...impossibly final.

'As you kind of like Oliver Evans?' Sophia wiggled down further in her chair, her eyes alight with interest. 'The theatre staff say there were all sorts of sparks between you during the op.'

'Ruby's in my care. Oliver was...keeping me reassured.' But she'd said it too fast, too defensively, and Sophia's eyebrows were hiking.

Drat hospitals and their grapevines, she thought. Actually, they were more than grapevines—they were like Jack's beanstalk. Let one tiny bean out of the can and it exploded to the heavens.

What had Oliver and Tristan been talking about to start this?

And...how was she to stop Sophia's eyebrows hitting the roof?

'You going to tell Aunty Sophia?' she demanded, settling down further in a manner that suggested she was going nowhere until Em did.

'You knew I was married.'

'Yeah, but not to Oliver. Oliver! Em, he's a hunk. And he's already getting a reputation for being one of those rarest of species—a surgeon who can talk to his patients. Honest, Em, he smiled at one of my mums on the ward this morning and my heart flipped. Why on earth…?'

'A smile doesn't make a marriage.' But it did, Em thought miserably. She'd loved that smile. What they'd had…

'So will you tell Aunty Sophia why you split?'

'Kids,' she said brusquely. She'd told Sophia she was infertile but only when Sophia had told her of her own problems. She hadn't elaborated.

'He left you because you couldn't have babies?'

'We…well, I already told you we went through IVF. Cycle upon cycle. What I didn't tell you was that finally I got pregnant. Josh was delivered stillborn at twenty-eight weeks.'

'Oh, Em…' Sophia stared at her in horror. 'You've kept that to yourself, all this time?'

'I don't…talk about it. It hurts.'

'Yeah, well, I can see that,' Sophia said, hopping up to give her friend a resounding hug. 'They say IVF can destroy a marriage—it's so hard. It split you up?'

'The IVF didn't.' Em was remembering the weeks after she'd lost Josh, how close she and Oliver had been, a couple gutted but totally united in their grief. If it hadn't been for Oliver then, she might have gone crazy.

Which had made what had come next even more devastating.

'So what…?'

'I couldn't…do IVF any more,' Em whispered.

Silence.

Ruby seemed soundly asleep. She was still holding the girl's hand. She could feel the strength of Ruby's heartbeat, and the monitors around her told her Ruby's baby was doing fine, as well. The world went on, she thought bleakly, remembering coming out of hospital after losing Josh, seeing all those mums, all those babies…

'Earth to Em,' Sophia said gently at last, and Em hauled herself together and gave her a bleak little smile.

'I wanted a family,' she whispered. 'I think…I was a bit manic after the loss but I was suddenly desperate. Maybe it was an obsession, I don't know, but I told Oliver I wanted to adopt, whatever the cost. And in the end, the cost was him.'

'He didn't want to adopt?'

'He's adopted himself. It wasn't happy, and he wouldn't concede there was another side. He wouldn't risk adoption because he didn't think he could love an adopted kid. And I wasn't prepared to give, either. We were two implacable forces, and there was nowhere to go but to turn away from each other. So there you have it, Sophia. No baby, no marriage. Can I ask you not to talk about it?'

'You don't have to ask,' Sophia said roundly. 'Of course I won't. But this hospital…the walls have ears and what it doesn't know it makes up. Now everyone knows you were married…'

'It'll be a one-day wonder,' Em told her, and then Ruby stirred faintly and her eyes flickered open.

'Well, hi,' Em said, her attention totally now on Ruby. 'Welcome to the other side, Ruby, love. The operation was a complete success. Now all we need to do is let you sleep and let your baby sleep until we're sure you're settled into nice, normal pregnancy again.'

CHAPTER EIGHT

Saturday.

Oliver did a morning ward round, walked into Ruby's room—and found Em there.

According to his calculations—and he'd made a few—Em should be off duty. Why was she sitting by Ruby's bedside?

She was darning…a sock?

Both women looked up as he walked in and both women smiled.

'Hey,' Ruby said. 'Is it true? Were you two married?'

'How…?' Em gasped.

'I just heard,' Ruby said blithely. 'It's true, isn't it?'

Em bundled up her needlework and rose—fast. 'Yes,' she managed. 'But it was a long time ago. Sorry, Oliver, I'll be out of your way.'

'Why are you here?' Damn, that had sounded accusatory and he hadn't meant to be.

'I'm off duty but Ruby's teaching me how to darn.'

'That's…important?'

'It is, as a matter of fact,' she said, tossing him a look that might well be described as a glower. And also a warning to keep things light. 'The whole world seems to toss socks away as soon as they get holes. Ruby and I are doing our bit to prevent landfill.'

'Good for you.' He still sounded stiff but he couldn't help it. 'Are you going home now?'

'Yes.'

'So why did you two split?' Ruby was under orders for complete bed rest but she was recovering fast, the bed rest was more for her baby's sake than for hers, and she was obviously aching for diversion.

'Incompatibility,' Em said, trying for lightness, stooping to give Ruby a swift kiss. 'He used to pinch all the bed-covers. He's a huncher—you know the type? He hunches all the covers round him and then rolls in his sleep. I even tried pinning the covers to my side of the bed but I was left with ripped covers and a doomed marriage. I'll pop in to-morrow, Ruby, but meanwhile is there anything you need?'

'More socks?' Ruby said shyly, and Em grinned.

'Ask Dr Evans. I'll bet he has a drawer full. I need to go, Ruby, love. Byee.'

And she was gone.

It had been an informal visit. She'd been wearing jeans and a colourful shirt and her hair was down. She had so much to do at home—he knew she did.

Why was she here on a day off?

Because she cared?

She couldn't stop caring. That had been one of the things he'd loved about her.

He still loved?

'You're still dotty about her,' Ruby said, and he realised he'd been staring at the corridor where she'd disappeared.

'Um…no. Just thinking I've never walked in on a darn-ing lesson before. How's bub?'

'Still kicking.'

'Not too hard?'

'N-no.' And once again he copped that zing of fear.

This was why Em had 'popped in', he thought. This kid was far too alone.

That was Em. She carried her heart on her sleeve.

If it was up to Em they would have adopted, he thought, and, despite the things he'd said to her after Josh had died, he was beginning to accept she was capable of it. *It?* Of loving a child who wasn't her own. The way she'd held Gretta… The way she'd laughed at Toby… Okay, Em was as different from his adoptive mother as it was possible to be, and it had been cruel of him to suggest otherwise.

It had taken him a huge leap of faith to accept that he'd loved Em. Even though he'd supported her through IVF, even though he'd been overjoyed when she'd finally conceived, when Josh had died…

Had a small part of him been relieved? Had a part of him thought he could never extend his heart to all comers?

He would have loved Josh. He did. The morning when they'd sat looking down at the promise that had been their little son had been one of the worst of his life. But the pain that had gone with it…the pain of watching Em's face…

And then for Em to say let's adopt, let's put ourselves up for this kind of pain again for a child he didn't know…

'Let's check your tummy,' he told Ruby, but she was still watching him.

'You are still sweet on her.'

'She's an amazing woman. But as she said, I'm a huncher.'

'Is it because you couldn't have children?'

How…? 'No!'

'It's just, one of the nurses told me Em's got two foster-kids she looks after with her mum. If you and she were married, why didn't you have your own?'

'Ruby, I think you have quite enough to think about with your own baby, without worrying about other people's,' he said, mock sternly.

'You're saying butt out?'

'And let me examine you. Yes.'

'Yes, Doctor,' she said, mock meekly, but she managed the beginnings of a cheeky grin. 'But you can't tell me to butt out completely. It seemed no one in this hospital knew you guys have been married. So now everyone in this hospital is really, really interested. Me, too.'

After that he was really ambivalent about the babysitting he'd promised. Actually, he'd been pretty ambivalent in the first place. Work was zooming to speed with an intensity that was staggering. He could easily ring and say he was needed at the hospital and it wouldn't have been a lie.

But he'd promised, so he put his head down and worked and by a quarter to one he was pulling up outside the place Em called home.

Em was in the front yard, holding Toby on a push-along tricycle. When she saw him she swung Toby up into her arms and waved.

Toby hesitated a moment—and then waved, too.

The sight took him aback. He paused before getting out of the car. He knew Em was waiting for him, but he needed a pause to catch his breath.

This was the dream. They'd gone into their marriage expecting this—love, togetherness, family.

He'd walked away so that Em could still have it. The fact that she'd chosen to do it alone…

But she wasn't alone. She had her mum. She had Mike next door and his brood. She had great friends at the hospital.

The only one missing from the picture was him, and the decision to walk away had been his.

If he'd stayed, though, they wouldn't have had any of this. They'd be a professional couple, absorbed in their work and their social life.

How selfish was that? The certainties of five years ago were starting to seem just a little bit wobbly.

'Hey, are you stuck to the seat?' Em was carrying Toby towards him, laughing at him. She looked younger today, he thought. Maybe it was the idea that she was about to have some free time. An afternoon with her mum.

She was about to have some time off from kids who weren't her own.

But they were her own. Toby had his arms wrapped around her, snuggling into her shoulder.

He had bare feet. Em was tickling his toes as she walked, making him giggle.

She loved these kids.

He'd thought… Okay, he'd thought he was being self-less, walking away five years ago. He'd been giving up his marriage so Em could have what she wanted. Now… Why was he now feeling the opposite? Completely, utterly selfish?

Get a grip, he told himself. He was here to work.

'Your babysitter's here, ma'am,' he said, finally climbing from the car. 'All present and correct.'

She was looking ruefully at the car. 'Still the hire car? Can't you get parts?'

'They're hard to come by.' He'd spent hours on the internet tracking down the parts he needed.

'Oh, Ollie…'

No one called him Ollie.

Em did.

She put her hand on his arm and he thought, She's comforting me because of a wrecked car. And she's coping with kids with wrecked lives…

How to make a rat feel an even bigger rat.

But her sympathy was real. Everything about her was real, he thought. Em… He'd loved this woman.

He loved this woman?

'Hey, will you go with Uncle Ollie?' Em was saying,

moving on, prising Toby away from his neck-hugging. 'I bet he knows how to tickle toes, too.'

'I can tickle toes.' He was a paediatric surgeon. He could keep a kid entertained.

But Toby caught him unawares. He twisted in Em's arms and launched himself across, so fast Oliver almost didn't catch him. Em grabbed, Oliver grabbed and suddenly they were in a sandwich hug, with Toby sandwiched in the middle.

Toby gave a muffled chortle, like things had gone exactly to plan. Which, maybe in Toby's world, they had.

But he had so much wrong with him. His tiny spine was bent; he'd have operation after operation in front of him, years in a brace...

He'd have Em.

He should pull away, but Em wasn't pulling away. For this moment she was holding, hugging, as if she needed it. As if his hug was giving her something...

Something that, as his wife, had once been her right?

'Em...'

But the sound of his voice broke the moment. She tugged away, flipped an errant curl behind her ear, tried to smile.

'Sorry. I should expect him to do that—he does it all the time with Mike. He has an absolute conviction that the grown-ups in his life are to be trusted never, ever to drop him, and so far it's paid off. One day, though, Toby, lad, you'll find out what the real world's like.'

'But you'll shield him as long as you can.'

'With every ounce of power I possess,' she said simply. 'But, meanwhile, Mum's ready to go. She's so excited she didn't sleep last night. Gretta's fed. Everything's ready, all I need to do is put on clean jeans and comb my hair.'

'Why don't you put on a dress?' he asked, feeling... weird. Out of kilter. This was none of his business, but he was starting to realise just how important this afternoon was to Em and her mum. And how rare. 'Make it a special occasion.'

'Goodness, Oliver, I don't think I've worn a dress for five years,' she flung at him over her shoulder as she headed into the house. 'Why would the likes of me need a dress?'

And he thought of the social life they'd once had. Did she miss it? he wondered, but he tickled Toby's toes, the little boy giggled and he knew that she didn't.

They left fifteen minutes later, like a pair of jail escapees, except that they were escapees making sure all home bases were covered. Their 'jail' was precious.

'Mike might come over later to collect Toby,' Em told him. 'Toby loves Mike, so if he does that's fine by us. That'll mean you only have Gretta so you should cope easily. You have both our cellphone numbers? You know where everything is? And Gretta needs Kanga…if she gets upset, Kanga can fix her. But don't let her get tired. If she has trouble breathing you can raise her oxygen…'

'Em, trust me, I'm a doctor,' he said, almost pushing them out the door.

'And you have how much experience with kids?'

'I'm an obstetrician and a surgeon.'

'My point exactly. Here they're outside their mum, not inside, and you don't have an anaesthetist to put them to sleep. There's a stack of movies ready to play. You can use the sandpit, too. Gretta loves it, but you need to keep her equipment sand-free…'

'Em, go,' he said, exasperated. 'Adrianna, take Em's arm and pull. Em, trust me. You can, you know.'

'I do know that,' Em told him, and suddenly she darted back across the kitchen and gave him a swift kiss on the cheek. It was a thank-you kiss, a perfunctory kiss, and why it had the power to burn… 'I always have,' she said simply. 'You're a very nice man, Oliver Evans. I would have trusted you to be a great dad, even if you couldn't trust yourself. That's water under the bridge now, but I still trust you, even if it's only for an afternoon.'

And she blinked a couple of times—surely they weren't tears?—then ducked back and kissed Gretta once again—and she was gone.

And Oliver was left with two kids.

And silence.

The kids were watching him. Toby was in his arms, leaning back to gaze into his eyes. Cautiously assessing? Gretta was sitting in an oversized pushchair, surrounded by cushions.

To trust or not to trust?

Toby's eyes were suddenly tear-filled. A couple of fat tears tracked down his face.

Gretta just stared at him, her face expressionless. Waiting to see what happened next?

Both were silent.

These were damaged kids, he thought. Rejects. They'd be used to a life where they were left. They'd come from parents who couldn't or wouldn't care for them and they had significant medical problems. They'd be used to a life where hospital stays were the norm. They weren't kids who opened their mouths and screamed whenever they were left.

Could you be stoic at two and at four? That's how they seemed. Stoic.

It was a bit…gut-wrenching.

Kanga—it must be Kanga: a chewed, bedraggled, once blue stuffed thing with long back paws and a huge tail—was lying on the table. He picked it—him?—up and handed him to Toby. Gretta watched with huge eyes. This wasn't what was supposed to happen, her eyes said. This was *her* Kanga.

He lifted Gretta out of her chair with his spare arm and carried both kids out into the yard, under the spreading oak at the bottom of the garden where the lawn was a bit too long, lushly green.

He set both kids down on the grass. Fuzzy the dog flopped down beside them. He, too, seemed wary.

Toby was still holding Kanga. Warily.

He tugged Gretta's shoes off so both kids had bare feet. Em had made the tickling thing work. Maybe it'd work for him.

He took Kanga from Toby, wriggled him slowly towards Gretta's toes—and ticked Gretta's toes with Kanga's tail.

Then, as both kids looked astonished, he bounced Kanga across to Toby and tickled his.

Toby looked more astonished. He reached out to grab Kanga, but Oliver was too fast. The tickling tail went back to Gretta's toes—and then, as Toby reached further, Kanga bounced sideways and tickled Fuzzy on the nose.

Fuzzy opened his mouth to grab but Kanga boinged back to Gretta, this time going from one foot to the other.

And then, as Gretta finally reacted, Kanga boinged up and touched her nose—and then bounced back to Toby.

Toby stared down in amazement at his toes being tickled and his eyes creased, the corners of his mouth twitched—and he chuckled.

It was a lovely sound but it wasn't enough. Kanga bounced back to Gretta, kissed her nose again, then bounced right on top of Fuzzy's head.

Fuzzy leaped to his feet and barked.

Kanga went back to Toby's toes.

And finally, finally, and it was like a minor miracle all by itself, Gretta's serious little face relaxed. She smiled and reached out her hand.

'Kanga,' she said, and Kanga flew to her hand. She grabbed him and held, gazing dotingly at her beloved blue thing.

'Kanga,' she said again, and she opened her fingers— and held Kanga back out to Oliver.

Her meaning was clear. He's mine but it's okay to play. In fact, she wanted to play.

But that one word had left her breathless. What the…? He'd seen the levels of oxygen she was receiving and she was still breathless? But she was still game.

She was trusting.

He wanted to hug her.

She was four years old. He'd met her twice. He was feeling…feeling…

'Hey!' It was Mike, and thank heaven for Mike. He was getting emotional and how was a man to keep tickling when he was thinking of what was in store for this little girl? He looked across at the gate and smiled at Mike with gratitude.

'Hey, yourself.'

'We're going to the beach,' Mike called. 'You want to come?'

'I'm sitting the kids,' he said, and Mike looked at him like he was a moron.

'Yeah. Kid-sitting. Beach. It's possible to combine them—and your two love the beach. Katy and Drew are staying home—Katy's still under the weather but her mum's here and Drew has a mate over. But we have four kid seats in the wagon—we always seem to have a spare kid—and why not?'

Why not? Because he'd like to stay lying under the tree, tickling toes?

It wouldn't last. His child entertainment range was limited, to say the least, and both kids were looking eager.

But, Gretta… Sand… Maybe he could sort it.

'What if we put one of the car seats into your car,' Mike said, eyeing the rental car parked at the kerb. 'Rental cars always have bolts to hold 'em. That way you can follow me and if Gretta gets tired you can bring her straight home. And we have beach shelters for shade. We have so much beach gear I feel like a pack mule going up and down the access track. Katy's mum's packed afternoon tea. Coming?'

'Yeah,' he said, because there was nothing else he could say. But there was part of him that was thinking as he packed up and prepared to take his charges beachwards, I wouldn't have minded caring for them myself. I wouldn't have minded proving that I could be a...

A father? By minding them for a couple of hours? Would that make him a hero? Could it even disprove what he'd always felt—that you couldn't love a kid who wasn't your own? Of course it couldn't.

It was just that, as the kids had chuckled, he'd felt, for one sliver of a crazy moment, that he could have been completely wrong. That maybe his judgement five years ago had been clouded, distorted by his own miserable childhood.

And an afternoon alone with these kids would prove what? Nothing. He'd made a choice five years ago. It had been the only honest option, and nothing had changed.

Except the way Gretta was smiling at the thought of the beach seemed to be changing things, like it or not. And the knowledge that Em would think giving Gretta an afternoon at the beach was great.

Would it make Em smile?

'You coming, mate, or are you planning on writing a thesis on the pros and cons?' Mike demanded, and he caught himself and took Kanga from Toby and handed him to Gretta.

'We're coming,' he told him. He looked at the muscled

hulk of a tattooed biker standing at the gate and Oliver Evans, specialist obstetric surgeon, admitted his failings. 'But you might need to help me plan what to take. I'm a great obstetrician but as a father I'm the pits.'

'You reckon he'll be okay? You reckon he'll manage?'

'If you're worried, ring Mike.'

Em and her mum were lying on adjoining massage tables. They had five minutes' 'down' time before the massage was to begin. The soft, cushioned tables were gently warmed, the lights were dim, the sound of the sea washed through the high windows and a faint but lovely perfume was floating from the candles in the high-set sconces.

They should almost be asleep already but Em couldn't stop fretting.

'Ring Mike and ask him to check,' Adrianna said again. 'We all want you to enjoy this. I want to enjoy this. Check.'

So she rang. She lay on her gorgeous table and listened to Mike's growl.

'You're not supposed to be worrying. Get back to doing nothing.'

'You've got Toby?'

'Me and Oliver—that's one hell of a name, isn't it?— we're gunna have to think of something shorter—have Toby—and my kids and Gretta. We're at the beach. Want to see? I'm sending a video. Watch it and then shut up, Em. Quit it with your worrying. Me and your Ollie have things in hand.'

He disconnected. She stared at the phone, feeling disconcerted. Strange. That her kids were somewhere else without her... With Oliver. Ollie...

No one called him Ollie except her, but now Mike was doing the same. It was like two parts of her life were merging.

The old and the new?

It was her imagination. Oliver…Ollie?…would do this afternoon of childminding and move on.

A ping announced the arrival of a message. She clicked and sure enough there was a video, filmed on Mike's phone and sent straight through.

There was Toby with Mike's two littlies. They were building a sandcastle—sort of. It was a huge mound of sand, covered with seaweed and shells. Fuzzy was digging a hole on the far side and Mike's bitser dog was barking in excitement.

As Em watched, Toby picked up a bucket of water and spilt it over the castle—and chuckled. Mike laughed off camera.

'If you think I don't have anything better to do than fill buckets for you, young Toby—you're right…'

And then the camera panned away, down to the shore-line—and Em drew in her breath.

For there was Oliver—and Gretta.

They were sitting on the wet sand, where the low, gentle waves were washing in, washing out.

Oliver had rigged a beach chair beside them, wedging it secure with something that looked like sandbags. Wet towels filled with sand?

Gretta's oxygen cylinder was high on the seat, safe from the shallow inrushes of water, but Ollie and Gretta were sitting on the wet sand.

He had Gretta on his knee. They were facing the in-coming waves, waiting for one to reach them.

'Here it comes,' Oliver called, watching as a wave broke far out. 'Here it comes, Gretta, ready or not. One, two, three…'

And he swung Gretta back against his chest, hugging her as the water surrounded them, washing Gretta's legs, swishing around his body.

He was wearing board shorts. He was naked from the waist up.

She'd forgotten his body…

No, she hadn't. Her heart couldn't clench like this if she'd forgotten.

'More,' Gretta whispered, wriggling her toes in the water, twisting so she could see the wave recede. Her eyes were sparkling with delight. She was so close to the other side, this little one, and yet for now she was just a kid having fun.

A kid secure with her… Her what?

Her friend. With Oliver, who couldn't give his heart.

Silently Em handed her phone to her mum and waited until Adrianna had seen the video.

Adrianna sniffed. 'Oh, Em…'

'Yeah.'

'Do you think…?'

'No.'

'It's such a shame.'

'It's the way it is,' Em said bleakly. 'But…but for now, he's making Gretta happy.'

'He's lovely,' Adrianna said stoutly.

'Don't I know it?' Em whispered. 'Don't I wish I didn't?'

'Em…'

The door opened. Their massage ladies entered, silently, expecting their clients to be well on the way on their journey to complete indulgence.

'Are you ready?' the woman due to massage Em asked. 'Can you clear your mind of everything past, of everything future and just let yourself be. For now there should be nothing outside this room.'

But there was, Em thought as skilful hands started their skin-tingling work. There was a vision of her ex-husband holding her little girl. Making Gretta happy.

Massages were wonderful, she decided as her body responded to the skill of the woman working on her.

They might be wonderful but thinking about Oliver was…better?

He sat in the waves and watched—and felt—Gretta enjoy herself. She was a wraith of a child, a fragile imp, dependent on the oxygen that sustained her, totally dependent on the adults who cared for her.

She trusted him. She faced the incoming waves with joy because she was absolutely sure Oliver would lift her just in time, protect the breathing tube, hug her against his body, protect her from all harm.

But harm was coming to this little one, and there was nothing anyone could do about it. He'd mentioned Gretta to Tristan and Tristan had spelt out the prognosis. With so much deformity of the heart, it was a matter of time…

Not very much time.

That he had this time with her today was precious. He didn't know her, she wasn't his kid, but, regardless, it was gold.

If he could somehow take the pain away…

He couldn't. He couldn't protect Gretta.

He couldn't protect Em.

Hell, but he wanted to. And not just for Em, he conceded. For this little one. This little girl who laughed and twisted and buried her face in his shoulder and then turned to face the world again.

Em loved her. *Loved her.*

An adopted child.

He'd thought… Yeah, okay, he knew. If Em was able to have her own child it'd all change. Gretta would take second place.

But did he know? Five years ago he'd been sure. He'd

been totally judgmental and his marriage was over because of it.

Now the sands were shifting. He was shifting.

'More,' Gretta ordered, and he realised two small waves had washed over her feet and he hadn't done the lift and squeal routine. Bad.

'Em wouldn't forget,' he told Gretta as he lifted and she squealed. 'Em loves you.'

But Gretta's face was buried in his shoulder, and that question was surfacing—again. Over and over.

Had he made the mistake of his life?

Could he…?

Focus on Gretta, he told himself. Anything else was far too hard.

Anything else was far too soon.

Or five years too late?

CHAPTER NINE

BY THE TIME Em and Adrianna arrived home, Oliver had the kids squeaky clean. He'd bathed them, dressed them in their PJs, tidied the place as best he could and was feeling extraordinarily smug about his child-minding prowess.

The kids were tired but happy. All Em and Adrianna had to do was feed them and tuck them into bed. He could leave. Job done.

They walked in looking glowing. They both had beautifully styled, shiny hair. They both looked as squeaky clean as the kids—scrubbed? They'd obviously shopped a little.

Em was wearing a new scarf in bright pink and muted greens. It made her look…how Em used to look, he thought. Like a woman who had time to think about her appearance. Free?

And impressed.

'Wow.' Both women were gazing around the kitchen in astonishment. The kids were in their chairs at the table. Oliver had just started making toast to keep them going until dinner. 'Wow,' Adrianna breathed again. 'There's not even a mess.'

'Mike took them all to the beach,' Em reminded her, but she was smiling at Oliver, her eyes thanking him.

'Hey, I had to clean the bathroom,' Oliver said, mock wounded. 'I've had to do some work.'

'Of course you have.' Adrianna flopped onto the nearest chair. 'Hey, if we make some eggs we could turn that toast into soldiers, and the kids' dinner is done. Kids, how about if I eat egg and toast soldiers too, and then I'll flop into bed, as well. I'm pooped.' But then she turned thoughtful. 'But, Em, you aren't ready for bed yet. You look fabulous, the night's still young, the kids are good and Oliver's still here. Why don't you two go out to dinner?'

Em stared at her like she'd lost her mind. 'Dinner...'

'You know, that thing you eat at a restaurant. Or maybe it could be fish and chips overlooking the bay. It's a gorgeous night. Oliver, do you have anything else on?'

'No, but—'

'Then go on, the two of you. You know you want to.'

'Mum, we don't want to.'

'Really?' Adrianna demanded. 'Honestly? Look at me, Em, and say you really don't want to go out to dinner with Oliver. Oliver, you do the same.'

Silence.

'There you go, then,' she said, satisfied. 'Off you go. Shoo.'

What else could they do but follow instructions? The night was warm and still, a combination unusual for Melbourne, where four seasons were often famously represented in one day. But this night the gods were smiling. Even the fish-and-chip kiosk didn't have too long a queue. Oliver ordered, then he and Em walked a block back from the beach to buy a bottle of wine, and returned just as their order was ready.

They used to do this often, Em thought. Once upon a time...

'I still have our picnic rug,' Oliver said ruefully, as they collected their feast. 'But it's in the back of the Morgan.'

'I'm sorry.'

'Don't be. Just be glad your wagon only got scratches—you're the one who's dependent on it. Moving on… Hey, how about this?' A family was just leaving an outside table and it was pretty much in the best position on the beachfront. Oliver swooped on it before a bunch of teenagers reached it, spread his parcels over it and signalled her to come. Fast.

'You're worse than the seagulls,' she retorted, smiling at his smug expression. 'Talk about swoop for the kill…'

'Table-swooping's one of my splinter skills,' he told her. 'Surely you remember.'

'I try…not to.'

'Does that help? Trying not to?'

Silence. She couldn't think of an answer. They unwrapped their fish and chips and ate a few. They watched a couple of windsurfers trying to guide their kites across the bay with not enough breeze, but the question still hung.

How soon could you forget a marriage? Never? It was never for her.

'I… How was America?' she asked at last, because she had to say something, the silence was becoming oppressive.

'Great. I learned so much.'

'You went away an obstetrician and came back…'

'I'm still first and foremost an obstetrician.'

'But you have the skills to save Ruby's baby—and countless others. You must feel it's worth it.'

'Em…'

'And you wouldn't have done that if we'd stayed together.' She was determined to get this onto some sort of normal basis, where they could talk about their marriage as if it was just a blip in their past. It was nothing that could affect their future. 'But I'm surprised you haven't met anyone else.' She hesitated but then ploughed on. She needed to say this. Somehow.

'You ached to be a dad,' she whispered, because somehow saying it aloud seemed wrong. 'I thought… There's nothing wrong with you. It's me who has the fertility problems. I thought you'd have met someone else by now and organised our divorce. Isn't that why we split? I sort of…I sort of wanted to think of you married with a couple of kids.'

'Did you really want that?' His curt response startled her into splashing her wine. She didn't want it anyway, she decided. She put down her glass with care and met his look head-on.

Say it like it is.

'That's what you wanted. That's why I agreed to separate.'

'I thought ending the marriage was all about you needing a partner so you could adopt.'

'It's true I wanted kids,' she managed, and her voice would hardly work for her. It was hard even to whisper. 'But I never wanted another husband than you.'

'You didn't want me.'

'Your terms were too hard, Oliver. Maybe now…maybe given some space it might be different. But we'd lost Josh and I was so raw, so needy. All I wanted was a child to hold…I think maybe I was a little crazy. I demanded too much of you. I hadn't realised quite how badly you'd been wounded.'

'I hadn't been wounded.'

'I've met your adoptive parents, remember? I've met your appalling brother.'

'I'm well over that.'

'Do you ever get over being not wanted? You were adopted, seemingly adored, and then suddenly supplanted by your parents' "real" son. I can't imagine how much that must have hurt.'

'It's past history.'

'It's not,' she said simply. 'Because it affects who you are. It always will. Maybe…' She hesitated but this had been drifting in and out of her mind for five years now. Was it better left unsaid? Maybe it was, but she'd say it anyway. 'Maybe it will affect any child you have, adopted or not. Maybe that's why you haven't moved on. Would you have loved Josh, Oliver, or would you have resented him because he'd have had the love you never had?'

'That's nuts.'

'Yeah? So why not organise a divorce? Why not re-marry?'

'Because of you,' he said, before he could stop himself. 'Because I still love you.'

She stilled. The whole night seemed to still.

There were people on the foreshore, people on the beach. The queue to the fish-and-chip shop was right behind them. Kids were flying by on their skateboards. Mums and dads were pushing strollers.

Because I still love you…

He reached out and touched her hand lightly, his lovely surgeon's fingers tracing her work-worn skin. She spent too much time washing, she thought absently. She should use more moisturiser. She should…

Stop blathering. This was too important.

Five years ago they'd walked away from each other. Had it all been some ghastly mistake? Could they just… start again?

'Em…' He rose and came round to her side of the table. His voice was urgent now. Pressing home a point? He sat down beside her, took both her hands in his and twisted her to face him. 'Do you feel it, too?'

Did she feel it? How could she not? She'd married this

man. She'd loved him with all her heart. She'd borne him a son.

He was holding her, and his hold was strong and compelling. His gaze was on her, and on her alone.

A couple of seagulls, sensing distraction, landed on the far side of the table and edged towards the fish-and-chip parcel. They could take what they liked, she thought. This moment was too important.

Oliver... Her husband...

'Em,' he said again, and his hold turned to a tug. He tugged her as he'd tugged her a thousand times before, as she'd tugged him, as their mutual need meant an almost instinctive coming together of two bodies.

Her face lifted to his—once again instinctively, because this was her husband. She was a part of him, and part of her had never let go. Never thought of letting go.

And his mouth was on hers and he was kissing her and the jolty, nervy, pressurised, outside world faded to absolutely nothing.

There was only Oliver. There was only this moment.

There was only this kiss.

She melted into him—of course she did. Her body had spent five years loving this man and it responded now as if it had once again found its true north. Warmth flooded through her—no, make that heat. Desire, strength and surety.

This man was her home.

This man was her heart.

Except he wasn't. The reasons they'd split were still there, practical, definite, and even though she was surrendering herself to the kiss—how could she not?—there was still a part of her brain that refused to shut down. Even though her body was all his, even though she was returning his kiss with a passion that matched his, even though her hands were holding him as if she still had the right to hold, that tiny part was saying this was make-believe.

This was a memory of times past.

This would hurt even more when it was over. Tug away now.

But she couldn't. He was holding her as if she was truly loved. He was kissing her regardless of the surroundings, regardless of the wolf whistles coming from the teenagers at the next table, regardless of…what was true.

It didn't matter. She needed this kiss. She needed this man.

And then the noise surrounding them suddenly grew. The whistles stopped and became hoots of laughter. There were a couple of warning cries and finally, finally, they broke apart to see…

Their fish…

While they had been otherwise…engaged, seagulls had sneaked forward, grabbing chips from the edge of their unwrapped parcel. Now a couple of braver ones had gone further.

They'd somehow seized the edge of one of their pieces of fish, and dragged it free of the packaging. They'd hauled it out…and up.

There were now five gulls…no, make that six…each holding an edge of the fish fillet. The fish was hovering in the air six feet above them while the gulls fought for ownership. They'd got it, but now they all wanted to go in different directions.

The rest of the flock had risen, too, squawking around them, waiting for the inevitable catastrophe and broken pieces.

Almost every person around them had stopped to look, and laugh, at the flying fish and at the two lovers who'd been so preoccupied that they hadn't even defended their meal.

A couple more gulls moved in for the kill and the fish almost spontaneously exploded. Bits of fish went everywhere.

Oliver grabbed the remaining parcel, scooping it up before the scraps of flying fish hit, and shooed the gulls away. They were now down to half their chips and only one piece of fish, but he'd saved the day. The crowd hooted their delight, and Oliver grinned, but Em wasn't thinking about fish and chips, no matter how funny the drama.

How had that happened? It was like they'd been teenagers again, young lovers, so caught up in each other that the world hadn't existed.

But the world did exist.

'I believe I've saved most of our feast,' Oliver said ruefully, and she smiled, but her smile was forced. The world was steady again, her real world. For just a moment she'd let herself be drawn into history, into fantasy. Time to move on...

'We need to concentrate on what's happening now,' she said.

'We do.' He was watching her, his lovely brown eyes questioning. He always could read her, Em thought, suddenly resentful. He could see things about her she didn't know herself.

But he'd kept himself to himself. She'd been married to him for five years and she hadn't known the depth of feeling he'd had about his childhood until the question of adoption had come up. She'd met his adoptive parents, she'd known they were awful, but Oliver had treated them—and his childhood—with light dismissal.

'They raised me, they gave me a decent start, I got to be a doctor and I'm grateful.'

But he wasn't. In those awful few weeks after losing Josh, when she'd finally raised adoption as an option, his anger and his grief had shocked them both. It had resonated with such depth and fury it had torn them apart.

So, no, she didn't know this man. Not then. Not now.

And kissing him wasn't going to make it one whit better.

He'd said he still loved her. Ten years ago he'd said that, too, and yet he'd walked away, telling her to move on. Telling her to find someone else who could fit in with her dreams.

'Em, I'd like to—'

'Have your fish before it gets cold or gets snaffled by another bird?' She spoke too fast, rushing in before he could say anything serious, anything that matched the look on his face that said his emotions were all over the place. That said the kiss had done something for him that matched the emotions she was feeling. That said their marriage wasn't over?

But it was over, she told herself fiercely. She'd gone through the pain of separation once and there was no way she was going down that path again. Love? The word itself was cheap, she thought. Their love had been tested, and found wanting. 'That's what I need to do,' she added, still too fast, and took a chip and ate it, even though hunger was the last thing on her mind right now. 'I need to eat fast and get back to the kids. Oliver, that kiss was an aberration. We need to forget it and move on.'

'Really?'

'Really. Have a chip before we lose the lot.'

The kids were asleep when she got home, and so was Adrianna. The house was in darkness. Oliver swung out of the driver's seat as if he meant to accompany her to the door, but she practically ran.

'I need my bed, Oliver. Goodnight.'

He was still watching her as she closed the front door. She'd been rude, she admitted as she headed for the children's bedroom. He'd given her a day out, a day off. If he'd been a stranger she would have spent time thanking him.

She should still thank him.

Except…he'd kissed her. He'd said he loved her.

She stood in the kids' bedroom, between the two cots, watching them sleeping in the dim light cast by a Humpty Dumpty figure that glowed a soft pink to blue and then back again.

She had to work with him, she reminded herself. She needed to get things back to a formal footing, fast.

Resolute, she grabbed her phone and texted.

Thank you for today. It was really generous. The kiss was a mistake but I dare say the gulls are grateful. And Mum and I are grateful, too.

That's what was needed, she thought. Make it light. Put the gratitude back to the plural—herself and her mother— and the seagulls? She was thanking someone she'd once known for a generous gesture.

Only…was it more than that? Surely.

He'd kissed her. Her fingers crept involuntarily to her mouth. She could still feel him, she thought. She could still taste him.

After five years, her body hadn't forgotten him.

Her body still wanted him.

He'd said he still loved her.

Had she been crazy to walk away from him all those years ago? Her body said yes, but here in this silent house, listening to the breathing of two children who'd become her own, knowing clearly and bleakly where they'd be if she hadn't taken them in, she could have no regrets. Her mind didn't.

It was only her heart and her body that said something else entirely.

* * *

What he wanted to do was stand outside and watch the house for a while. Why? Because it felt like his family was in there.

That was a dumb thought. He'd laid down his ultimatum five years ago and he'd moved on. He'd had five professionally satisfying years getting the skills he needed to be one of the world's top in-utero surgeons. Babies lived now because of him. He'd never have had that chance if he'd stayed here—if he'd become part of Em's menagerie.

He couldn't stay standing outside the house, like a stalker, like someone creepy. What he'd like was to take his little Morgan for a long drive along the coast. The car was like his balm, his escape.

Em had smashed his car. She'd also smashed…something else.

She'd destroyed the equilibrium he'd built around himself over the last few years. She'd destroyed the fallacy that said he was a loner; that said he didn't need anyone.

He wanted her. Fiercely, he wanted her. He'd kissed her tonight and it would have been worth all the fish.

It had felt right.

It had felt like he'd been coming home.

His phone pinged and he flipped it open. Em's polite thank-you note greeted him, and he snapped it shut.

She was making light of the kiss. Maybe that was wise.

Dammit, he couldn't keep standing here. Any moment now she'd look out the window and see him. Ex-husband loitering…

He headed back to the hire car. He had an apartment at the hospital but he wasn't ready for sleep yet. Instead, he headed back to the beach. He parked, got rid of his shoes and walked along the sand.

The night was still and warm. This evening the beach had been filled with families, kids whooping it up, soaking up the last of Melbourne's summer, but now the beach seemed to be the domain of couples. Couples walking hand in hand in the shallows. Couples lying on rugs on the sand, holding each other.

Young loves?

He walked on and passed a couple who looked to be in their seventies, maybe even older. They were walking slowly. The guy had a limp, a gammy hip? The woman was holding his hand as if she was supporting him.

But the hold wasn't one of pure physical support, he thought. Their body language said they'd been holding each other for fifty years.

He wanted it still. So badly…

Could he take on the kids? Could he take that risk?

Was it a risk? He'd held Gretta today and what he'd felt…

She had Down's syndrome with complications. Tristan said her life expectancy could be measured in months. It was stupid—impossible even—to give your heart to such a kid.

He could still hear his adoptive mother…

'It's not like he's really ours. If we hadn't had Brett then we wouldn't have known what love really is. And now…we're stuck with him. It's like we have a cuckoo in the nest…'

If he ever felt like that…

It was too hard. He didn't know how to feel.

But Em had made the decision for him. She'd moved on, saying he was free to find someone and have kids of his own. Kids who he could truly love.

Hell. He raked his hair and stared out at the moonlit water.

Melbourne's bay was protected. The waves were small, even when the weather was wild, but on a night like this they were practically non-existent. The windsurfers had completely run out of wind. The moonlight was a silver shimmer over the sea and the night seemingly an endless reflection of the starlit sky.

He wanted Em with him.

He wanted her to be...free?

It wasn't going to happen. She had encumbrances. No, he thought, she has people she loves. Kids. Her mother.

Not him.

It's for the best, he thought, shoving his hands deep into his pockets and practically glaring at the moon. I should never have come to the Victoria. I wouldn't have if I'd known Em would be here.

So leave?

Maybe he would, he thought. He'd agreed with Charles Delamere on a three-month trial.

Twelve weeks to go?

CHAPTER TEN

ON MONDAY OLIVER hit the wards early. He'd been in the day before, not because he'd been on duty but because he'd wanted to check on Ruby. But Ruby was doing all the right things and so was her baby, so he didn't check her first. He worked on the things he needed for his embryonic research lab, then decided to check the midwives' roster and choose a time to visit Ruby when he knew Em wouldn't be around.

So he headed—surreptitiously, he thought—to the nurses' station in the birthing centre—just as Isla Delamere came flying down the corridor, looking, for Isla, very harassed indeed.

When she saw Oliver she practically sagged in relief.

'Dr Evans. Oliver. I know your specialty's in-utero stuff and I know Charles has said you can spend the rest of your time on your research but you're an obstetrician first and foremost, yes?'

'Yes.' Of course he was.

'I have four births happening and we're stretched. Two are problems. Emily's coping with one, I have the other. Mine's a bit of a spoilt socialite––she was booked at a private hospital but had hysterics at the first labour pain so her husband's brought her here because we're closer. I can deal with that. But Em's looking after a surrogate mum.

She's carrying her sister's child—her sister's egg, her sister's husband's sperm, all very organised—but the emotion in there seems off the planet. Maggie's a multigravida, four kids of her own, no trouble with any, but now she's slowed right down and her sister's practically hysterical. But we can't kick her out. Oliver, Em needs support. Our registrar's off sick, Darcie's at a conference, Sean's coping with a Caesar so that leaves you. Can you help?'

'Of course.'

'Excellent. Here are the case notes. Suite Four.'

'You're okay with yours?'

'My one wants pethidine, morphine, spinal blocks, amputation at the waist, an immediate airlift to Hawaii and her body back,' Isla said grimly. 'And she's only two centimetres dilated. Heaven help us when it's time to push. But I've coped with worse than this in my time. What Em's coping with seems harder. She needs you, Dr Evans. Go.'

The last time he'd seen her he'd kissed her. Now...

Em seemed to be preparing to do a vaginal examination. She was scrubbed, dressed in theatre gear, looking every inch a midwife. Every inch a professional. And the look she gave him as he slipped into the room had nothing to do with the kiss, nothing to do with what was between them. It was pure, professional relief.

'Here's Dr Evans,' she said briskly to the room in general. 'He's one of our best obstetricians. You're in good hands now, Maggie.'

'She doesn't need to be in good hands.' A woman who looked almost the mirror image of the woman in the bed— except that she was smartly dressed, not a hair out of place, looking like she was about to step into a boardroom—was edging round the end of the bed to see what Em was doing. She ignored Oliver. 'Maggie, you just need to push. Thirty-six hours... You can do this. It's taking too long. Just push.'

Em cast him a beseeching look—and he got it in one. The whole set-up.

A guy who was presumably Maggie's husband was sitting beside her, holding her hand. He looked almost as stressed as his labouring wife.

The other woman had a guy with her, as well, presumably her husband, too? He was dressed in casual chinos and a cashmere sweater. Expensive. Smooth.

Both he and his wife seemed focused on where the action should be taking place. Where their child would be born. Even though the woman had been talking to Maggie, she'd been looking at the wrong end of the bed.

Surrogate parenthood... Oliver had been present for a couple of those before, and he'd found the emotion involved was unbelievable. Surrogacy for payment was illegal in this country. It had to be a gift, and what a gift! To carry a child for your sister...

But Maggie wasn't looking as if she was thinking of gifts. She was looking beyond exhaustion.

Thirty-six hours...

'Can't you push?' Maggie's sister said again, fretfully. 'Come on, Maggie, with all of yours it was over in less than twelve hours. The book says it should be faster for later pregnancies. You can do it. You have to try.'

'Maggie needs to go at her own pace,' Em said, in a tone that told him she'd said it before, possibly a lot more than once. 'This baby will come when she's ready.'

'But all she needs to do is push...'

He'd seen enough. He'd heard enough. Oliver looked at Maggie's face, and that of her husband. He looked at Em and saw sheer frustration and he moved.

'Tell me your names,' he said, firmly, cutting off the woman who looked about to issue another order. 'Maggie, I already know yours. Who are the rest of you?'

'I'm Rob,' said the man holding Maggie's hand, sounding weary to the bone. 'I'm Maggie's husband. And this is Leonie, Maggie's sister, and her husband, Connor. This is Leonie and Connor's baby.'

'Maybe we need to get something straight,' Oliver said, gently but still firmly. He was focusing on Maggie, talking to the room in general but holding the exhausted woman's gaze with his. 'This baby may well be Leonie and Connor's when it's born, but right now it has to be Maggie's. Maggie needs to own this baby if she's going to give birth successfully. And I'm looking at Maggie's exhaustion level and I'm thinking we need to clear the room. She needs some space.'

'But it's our baby.' Leonie looked horrified. 'Maggie's agreed—'

'To bear a baby for you,' he finished for her. Em was watching him, warily now, waiting to see where he was going. 'But right now Maggie's body's saying it's hers and her body needs that belief if she's to have a strong labour. I'm sorry, Leonie and Connor, but unless you want your sister to have a Caesarean, I need you to leave.'

'We can't leave,' Leonie gasped. 'We need to see her born.'

'You may well—if it's okay with Maggie.' They were in one of the teaching suites, geared to help train students. It had a mirror to one side. 'Maggie, that's an observation window, with one-way glass. Is it okay if your sister and her husband move into there?'

'No.' Leonie frowned at Oliver but the look on both Maggie and Rob's faces was one of relief.

'I just…need…to go at my own pace,' Maggie whispered.

'But I want to be the first one to hold our baby,' Leonie snapped, and Oliver bit his tongue to stop himself snapping back. This situation was fraught. He could understand that sisterly love was being put on the back burner in the face of the enormity of their baby's birth, but his responsibility was for Maggie and her baby's health. Anything else had to come second.

'What Maggie is doing for you is one of the most generous gifts one woman can ever give another,' he said, forcing himself to stay gentle. 'She's bearing your baby, but for now every single hormone, every ounce of energy she has, needs to believe it's her baby. You need to get things into perspective. Maggie will bear this baby in her own time. Her body will dictate that, and there's nothing you or Connor can say or do to alter it. If Maggie wants to, she'll hold her when she's born. That's her right. Then and only then, when she's ready and not before, she'll make the decision to let her baby go. Emily, do you agree?'

'I agree,' she said.

Em had been silent, watching not him but Maggie. She was a wonderful midwife, Oliver thought. There was no midwife he'd rather have on his team, and by the look on her face what he was suggesting was exactly what she wanted. The problem, though, was that the biological parents exuded authority. He wouldn't mind betting Leonie was older than Maggie and that both she and her husband held positions of corporate power. Here they looked like they'd been using their authority to push Maggie, and they wouldn't have listened to Em.

Isla had sent him in for a reason. If this had been a normal delivery then Em could have coped alone, but with the level of Maggie's exhaustion it was getting less likely to be a normal delivery.

Sometimes there were advantages to having the word *Doctor* in front of his name. Sometimes there were advantages to being a surgeon, to having given lectures to some of the most competent doctors in the world, to have the gravitas of professional clout behind him.

Sometimes it behoved a doctor to invoke his power, too.

'Maggie, would you like to have a break from too many people?' he asked now.

And Maggie looked up at him, her eyes brimming with gratitude. 'I... Yes. I mean, I always said that Leonie could be here but—'

'But your body needs peace,' Oliver said. He walked to the door and pulled it wide. 'Leonie, Connor, please take seats in the observation room. If it's okay with Maggie you can stay watching. However, the mirror is actually an electric screen. Emily's about to do a pelvic examination so we'll shut the screen for that so you can't see, but we'll turn it back on again as soon as Maggie says it's okay. Is that what you want, Maggie?'

'Y-yes.'

'But she promised...' Leonie gasped.

'Your sister promised you a baby,' Oliver told her, still gently but with steel in every word. 'To my mind, that gift needs something in return. If Maggie needs privacy in this last stage of her labour, then surely you can grant it to her.'

And Leonie's face crumpled. 'It's just... It's just... Maggie, I'm sorry...'

She'd just forgotten, Oliver thought, watching as Leonie swiped away tears. This was a decent woman who was totally focused on the fact that she was about to become a mother. She'd simply forgotten her sister. Like every other mother in the world, all she wanted was her baby.

She'd have to wait.

He held the door open. Leonie cast a wild, beseeching look at Maggie but Em moved fast, cutting off Maggie's view of her sister's distress. Maggie didn't need anyone else's emotion. She couldn't handle it—all her body needed to focus on was this baby.

'We'll call you in when Maggie's ready to receive you,' Oliver said cheerfully, as if this was something that happened every day. 'There's a coffee machine down the hall.

Go make yourself comfortable while Maggie lets us help her bring your baby into the world.'

And he stood at the door, calm but undeniably authoritative. This was his world, his body language said, and he knew it. Not theirs.

They had no choice.

They left.

Em felt so grateful she could have thrown herself on his chest and wept.

The last couple of hours had been a nightmare, with every suggestion she made being overridden or simply talked over by Leonie, who knew everything. But Maggie had made a promise and Maggie hadn't been standing up to her. Em had had to respect that promise, but now Oliver had taken control and turned the situation around.

Now there were only four of them in the birthing suite. Oliver flicked the two switches at the window.

'I've turned off sight and sound for the moment,' he told Maggie. 'If you want, we'll turn on sight when you're ready, but I suggest we don't turn on sound. That way you can say whatever you want, yell whatever you want, and only we will hear you.'

'She wants to be here...' Maggie whispered, holding her husband's hand like she was drowning.

'She does, but right now this is all about you and your baby.' He put the emphasis on the *your*. 'Emily, you were about to do an examination. Maggie, would you like me to leave while she does?'

Em blinked. An obstetrician, offering to leave while the midwife did the pelvic exam? Talk about trust...

'But you're a doctor,' Maggie whispered.

'Yes,'

'Then stay. I sort of...I mean...I need...'

'You need Oliver's clout with your sister,' Em finished

for her. 'You need a guy who can boss people round with the best of them. You've got the right doctor for that here. Oliver knows what he wants and he knows how to get it. Right now Oliver wants a safe delivery for your baby and there's no one more likely than Oliver to help you achieve it.'

He stayed. Maggie's labour had eased right off. She lay back exhausted and Em offered to give her a gentle massage.

He watched as Em's hands did magical things to Maggie's body, easing pain, easing stress.

Once upon a time she'd massaged him. He'd loved…

He loved…

Peace descended on the little room. At Maggie's request Oliver flicked the window switch again so Leonie and Connor could watch, but she agreed with Oliver about the sound.

As far as Leonie and Connor were concerned, there was no audio link. Any noise Maggie made, anything they said, stayed in the room.

Maggie's relief was almost palpable, and as Em's gentle fingers worked their magic, as Maggie relaxed, the contractions started again. Good and strong. Stage two was on them almost before they knew it.

'She's coming,' Maggie gasped. 'Oh, I want to see.'

And Oliver supported her on one side and Rob supported her on the other, while Em gently encouraged.

'She's almost here. One more push… One more push, Maggie, and you'll have a daughter.'

And finally, finally, a tiny scrap of humanity slithered into the world. And Em did as she did with every delivery. She slid the baby up onto Maggie's tummy, so Maggie could touch, could feel, could savour the knowledge that she'd safely delivered a daughter.

The look on Maggie's face…

Oliver watched her hand touch her tiny baby, he watched her face crumple—and he made a fast decision. He deliberately glanced at the end of the bed and carefully frowned—as if he was seeing something that could be a problem—and then he flicked the window to black again.

He put his head out the door as he did.

'It's great,' he told Leonie and Connor, whose noses were hard against the glass, who turned as he opened the door as if to rush in, but his body blocked them. 'You can see we have a lovely, healthy baby girl, but there's been a small bleed. We need to do a bit of patching before you come in.'

'Can we take her? Can we hold her?'

'Maggie needs to hold her. The sensation of holding her, maybe letting her suckle, will help the delivery of the placenta; it'll keep things normal. Maggie's needs come first right now. I assume you agree?'

'I… Yes,' Leonie whispered. 'But we agreed she wouldn't feed her. I just so want to hold her.'

'I suspect you'll have all the time in the world to hold her,' Oliver told her. 'But the feeding is part of the birthing process and it's important. I'm sorry but, promises or not, right now my focus is on Maggie.'

Em's focus was also on Maggie. She watched while Maggie savoured the sight of her little daughter, while she watched, awed, as the little girl found her breast and suckled fiercely.

Her husband sat beside her, silent, his hand on her arm. He, too, was watching the baby.

Without words Em and Oliver had changed places— Oliver was coping with the delivery of the placenta, checking everything was intact, doing the medical stuff. This was a normal delivery—there was no need for him to be here—but still there was pressure from outside the room and he knew that once he left Leonie and Connor would be in here.

'You know,' he said mildly, to the room in general, 'there's never been a law that says a surrogate mother has to give away her baby. No matter how this baby was conceived, Maggie, you're still legally her birth mother. If you want to pull back now...'

But Maggie was smiling. She was cradling her little one with love and with awe, and tears were slipping down her face, but the smile stayed there.

'This little one's Leonie's,' she whispered. 'You've seen Leonie at her worst—she's been frantic about her baby and it was no wonder she was over the top at the end. But I can't tell you how grateful I am that you've given us space to say goodbye. To send her on with love.'

How could she do this? Oliver wondered, stunned. She'd gently changed sides now so the baby was sucking from the other breast. The bonding seemed complete; perfect.

'It's not like we're losing her,' Rob ventured, touching the little one's cheek. 'She'll be our niece and our goddaughter.'

'And probably a bit more than that,' Maggie said, still smiling. 'Our kids will have a cousin. My sister will have a baby. To be able to do this... She's not ours, you can see. She has Connor's hair. None of ours ever looked like this. But, oh, it's been good to have this time.' She looked up at them and smiled, her eyes misty with tears. 'Em, would you like to ask them to come in now?'

'You're sure?' Em asked, with all the gentleness in the world. 'Maggie, this is your decision. As Oliver says, it's not too late to change your mind.'

'My mind never changed,' Maggie said, serene now, seemingly at peace. 'While I was having her she felt all mine and that was how I wanted to feel. Thank you for realising that. But now…now it's time for my sister to meet her baby.'

'How could she do that?'

With medical necessities out of the way, Oliver and Em were able to back out of the room. Leonie was holding her daughter now, her face crumpled, tears tracking unchecked. Connor, too, seemed awed.

Rob was still holding Maggie but the two of them were watching Leonie and Connor with quiet satisfaction.

'Love,' Em said softly, as they headed to the sinks. 'I don't know how surrogacy can work without it.'

'Do you seriously think Leonie can make a good mother?'

'I do. I've seen her lots of times during Maggie's pregnancy—she's been with her all the way. Yeah, she's a corporate bigwig, but her life has been prescribed because she and Connor couldn't have children. Maggie seems the ultimate earth mother—and she is—but she and Leonie love each other to bits. I suspect the over-the-top reaction we saw from Leonie in there—and which you saved us from—was simply too much emotion. It felt like her baby was being born. She wanted what was best for her baby and everything else got ignored. Mums are like that,' she said simply. 'And thank God for it.'

'You really think she can look after the baby as well as Maggie could?'

'I have no idea. I do know, though, that this baby will be loved to bits, and that's all that counts.'

'She can love it as much as Maggie?'

'That's right, you don't think it's possible.' She lowered her voice to almost a whisper. 'It's a bleak belief, Ollie, caused by your own grief. Have you ever thought about counselling?'

'Counselling?' In the quiet corridor it was almost a shout. He stood back and looked at her as if she was out of her mind.

'Counselling,' she said, serenely. 'It's available here. We have the best people...'

'I don't need counselling.'

'I think you do. You have so much unresolved anger from your childhood.'

'I'm over it.'

'It destroyed our marriage,' she said simply. 'And you haven't moved on. I expected you to have a wife and a couple of your own kids by now. You were scared of adoption—are you worried about your reaction to any child?'

'This is nuts.'

'Yeah, it is,' she said amiably, tossing her stained robes into the waiting bins. 'And it's none of my business. It's just... I've got on with my life, Oliver. You kissed me on Saturday and I found myself wondering how many women you'd kissed since our split. And part of me thinks...not many? Why not?'

Silence.

She was watching him like a pert sparrow, he thought, as the rest of his brain headed off on tangents he didn't understand. She was interested. Clinically interested. She was a fine nurse, a midwife, a woman used to dealing with babies and new parents all the time. Maybe she had insights...

Maybe she didn't have any insights. Maybe she was just Em, his ex-wife.

Maybe that kiss had been a huge mistake.

Step away, he told himself. He didn't need her or anyone else's analysis. But...

'Em, I would like to see Gretta and Toby again.'

Where had that come from? His mouth? He hadn't meant to say it, surely he hadn't.

But...but...

On Saturday he'd sat on the beach and he'd held Gretta, a little girl who had very little life left to her. He should have felt...what? Professional detachment? No, never that, for once an obstetrician felt removed from the joy of children he might as well hand in his ticket and become an accountant. Grief, then, for a life so short?

Not that, either.

He'd felt peace. He acknowledged it now. He'd sat in the waves and he'd felt Gretta's joy as the water had washed her feet. And he'd also felt Em's love.

Em made Gretta smile. He was under no illusions—with Gretta's myriad medical problems and her rejection by her birth mother, she'd faced spending her short life in institutions.

And watching Em now, as she looked at him in astonishment, he thought, what a gift she's given her children.

It was his cowardice that had made that possible. He'd walked away from Em, so Em had turned to fostering.

If he'd stayed with her maybe they could have adopted a newborn, a child with no medical baggage, a child Em could love with all her heart. Only he'd thought it wasn't possible, to love a child who wasn't his own. He'd walked away because such a love wasn't possible, and yet here was Em, loving with all her heart when Gretta's life would be so short...

Had he been mistaken? Suddenly, fiercely, he wanted that to be true. For he wanted to be part of this—part of Em's loving?

Part of her hotchpotch family.

'Oliver, there's no need—'

'I'd love to spend more time with Gretta.' He was wise enough to know that pushing things further at this stage would drive her away. The way he felt about Em...it was so complicated. So fraught. He'd hurt her so much… Make it about her children, he thought, and even that thought hurt.

Her children.

'What time do you finish tonight?' he asked.

'Six.'

'I'm still reasonably quiet and I started early.' He glanced at his watch. 'I should be finished by five. What say I head over there and give Adrianna a break for an hour?'

'Mum'd love that.' She hesitated. 'You could…stay for tea?'

'I won't do that.' And it was too much. He couldn't stop his finger coming up and tracing the fine lines of her cheek. She looked exhausted. She looked like she wasn't eating enough. He wanted to pick her up, take her somewhere great, Hawaii maybe, put her in a resort, make her eat, make her sleep…

Take her to his bed…

Right. In his dreams. She was looking at him now, confused, and there was no way he was pushing that confusion.

'I have a meeting back here at the hospital at seven,' he lied. 'So I'll be leaving as you get home.'

'You're sure you want to?'

'I want to. And if I can…for what time Gretta has left, if you'll allow me, it would be my privilege to share.'

'I don't—'

'This is nothing to do with you and me,' he said, urgently now. 'It's simply that I have time on my hands—and I've fallen for your daughter.'

CHAPTER ELEVEN

SHE SHOULD HAVE said no. The thought of Oliver being with the kids when she wasn't there was disconcerting, to say the least. She rang Adrianna and warned her and Adrianna's pleasure disconcerted her even more.

'I always said he was a lovely man. I was so sorry when you two split. It was just that awful time—it would have split up any couple.'

'We're incompatible, Mum,' she said, and she heard Adrianna smile down the phone.

'You had differences. Maybe those differences aren't as great as they once seemed.'

'Mum…'

'I'm just saying. But, okay, sweetheart, I won't interfere. I'll say nothing.'

Which didn't mean she was thinking nothing, Em decided as she headed to her next case. Luckily, it was a lovely, normal delivery, a little girl born to an Italian couple. Their fourth baby—and their fourth daughter—was greeted like the miracle all babies were.

She left them professing huge gratitude, and Em thought: How come the cases where all I do is catch are the ones where I get the most thanks? But it cheered her immeasurably and by the time she went to see Ruby, her complications with Oliver seemed almost trifling.

Ruby was about to bring those complications front and centre. The teenager was lying propped up on pillows, surrounded by glossy magazines. She had the television on, but she looked bored. And fretful. She lightened up when Em came in, and before Em could even ask her how she was, she put in a question of her own.

'Emily, I've been thinking. You and Dr Evans split because you couldn't have a baby. That's what I guessed, but it's true, I know it is.'

Whoa! Hospital grapevine? Surely not. Sophia was the only one she'd told. Surely Sophia wouldn't break a confidence and even if she had, surely no member of staff would tell a patient things that were personal.

'How—'

'I'm sure I heard it.' Ruby's eyes were alight with interest, a detective tracking vital clues. 'When I was asleep. After Theatre. You and that other nurse were talking.'

Sophia. Em did a frantic rethink of what they'd talked about. Uh-oh.

'So I've been thinking. I've got a baby I don't want,' Ruby said, and suddenly the detective Ruby had given way to a scared kid. 'Maybe you could have mine.'

There was an offer. It took her breath away.

She plonked down on the bed and gazed at Ruby in stupefaction. 'Ruby,' she said at last. 'How can you think such a thing?'

'I can't keep it,' she said fretfully. 'Dr Evans says I have to stay in bed so I don't go into labour and it's driving me nuts, but it's giving me time to think. Ever since I got pregnant…first Jason said he didn't want anything to do with it, or me. Then Mum said she'd kick me out if I kept it. And I was pig stubborn—it just seemed so wrong. I thought I was in love with Jason, and when I realised I was pregnant I was happy. I wasn't even scared. I even thought I might make a good mum. It was only after that... the complications came in.'

'Most of those complications are over,' Em said gently. 'Your daughter has every chance of being born healthy.'

'Yeah, but I've been couch-surfing since Mum found out,' she said fretfully. 'I had to leave school because I had nowhere to stay, and how can I couch-surf with a kid—no one's going to want me.'

'Then this isn't about adoption,' Em told her, forcing herself to sound upbeat and cheerful. 'This is all about plans for the future. We have a couple of excellent social workers. I'll get one of them to pop in and talk to you. She can help you sort things out.'

'But there are so many things...and if the baby's prem, which Dr Evans says is even probable, how can I cope with a baby? If she had a good home...if you and Dr Evans could look after her...'

'Ruby, leave this.' The girl's eyes had filled with tears and Em moved to hug her. 'Things will work out. You won't have to give away your baby, I promise.'

'But you need her. It could save your marriage.'

'My marriage was over a long time ago,' she said, still hugging. 'It doesn't need your daughter to try and mend it. Ruby, I want you to stop worrying about me and my love life. I want you to only think about yourself.'

Oliver arrived at Em's house right on five. Adrianna greeted him with unalloyed pleasure—and promptly declared her intention of taking a nap.

'When Em rang, that's what I decided I'd do,' she told him. 'The tea hour's the hell hour. If I can have a nap first it'll take the pressure off both of us when Em comes home.' She smiled and suddenly he found himself being hugged. 'It's great to have you back, Oliver,' she told him. 'And it's great that you arrived just when we need you most.'

He was left with the kids.

He carried them out into the soft autumn evening, stupidly grateful that Mike from next door was nowhere to be seen. Both kids seemed a bit subdued, pleased to see him, relaxed but tired.

The end of a long day? He touched Toby's forehead and worried that he might have a slight fever.

Katy next door had a cold. Had she or her kids spread it?

Maybe he was imagining things. He was like a worried parent, he thought, mocking himself.

He wasn't a parent. Not even close.

He had these kids for an hour.

He set them on the grass under the tree. Fuzzy the dog came out and loped herself over Gretta's legs. Gretta's oxygen cylinder sat beside her, a harsh reminder of reality, but for now there was no threat. A balmy evening. Warm, soft grass.

'Look up through the trees and tell me what you see,' he said, and both kids looked up obediently.

'Tree,' Gretta said.

'Tree,' Toby agreed, and he found himself smiling. Gretta and her parrot.

Together they were family, he thought. They were a fragile family at best, but for today, well, for today this was okay.

'I'm seeing a bear,' he said, and both kids looked at him in alarm.

'Up there,' he reassured them. 'See that big cloud? It has a nose on the side. See its mouth? It's smiling.'

Neither kid seemed capable of seeing what he was seeing but they looked at each other and seemed to decide mutually to humour him.

'Bear,' Gretta said.

'Bear,' Toby agreed.

'He must live up there in the clouds,' Oliver decreed.

'I think he might be the bear from "Goldilocks". Do you guys know that story?'

Toby was two, a tiny African toddler suffering the effects of early malnutrition as well as the scoliosis and scarring on his face from infection. Gretta was a damaged kid with Down's. 'Goldilocks' was way out of their sphere.

'Well,' Oliver said serenely, settling himself down. The kids edged nearer, sensing a story. 'Once upon a time there were three bears and they lived up in the clouds. Baby Bear had a lovely soft little cloud because he was the smallest. Mumma Bear had a middly sort of cloud, a bit squishy but with a nice high back because sometimes her back hurt, what with carrying Baby Bear all the time.'

'Back,' said Toby.

'Back,' Gretta agreed, obviously deeply satisfied with the way this story was progressing.

'But Papa Bear had the biggest cloud of all. It was a ginormous cloud. It had great big footprints all over it because Papa Bear wore great big boots and, no matter what Mumma Bear said, he never took them off before he climbed onto his cloud. Mumma Bear should have said no porridge for Papa Bear but Mumma Bear is really kind…'

'My Emmy,' Gretta murmured, and he wondered how much this kid knew. How much did she understand?

My Emmy…

It had been a soft murmur, a statement that Gretta had her own Mumma Bear and all was right with that arrangement.

'Porridge,' Toby said, and Oliver had to force his thoughts away from Em, away from the little girl who was pressed into his side, and onto a story where porridge was made in the clouds.

And life was fantasy.

And the real world could be kept at bay.

* * *

Em arrived home soon after six, walked in and Adrianna was in the kitchen, starting dinner. She was singing.

Oliver's hire car was parked out the front.

'Where's Oliver?' she asked cautiously, and then gazed around. 'Where are the kids?' Had he taken them out? It was late. They'd be tired. Maybe they'd gone next door. But Katy had passed her cold on to her youngest. She didn't want them there, not with Gretta's breathing so fragile.

'Hey, don't look so worried.' Her mum was beaming and signalling out the window. 'Look.'

She looked.

The two kids were lying under the spreading oak in the backyard. Oliver was sandwiched between them. He had an arm round each of them and they were snuggled against him.

Fuzzy was draped over his stomach.

'You can hardly see him,' Adrianna said with satisfaction. 'It's an Oliver sandwich. He's been telling them stories. I went for a nap but I left my window open. He's an excellent storyteller. He makes them giggle.'

'They can't understand.'

'They can understand enough to know when to giggle. Cloud Bears. Porridge stealing. High drama. Lots of pouncing, with Fuzzy being the pouncee.'

'You're kidding.'

'He's adorable,' Adrianna said. 'He always was. He always is.'

'Mum…'

'I know.' Her mother held up her hands as if in surrender. 'It's none of my business and I understand the grief that drove you apart.'

'It wasn't the grief. It was…'

'Irreconcilable differences,' Adrianna said sagely. She looked out the window again. 'But from this angle they don't look so irreconcilable to me. You want to go tell him dinner is ready?'

'I... No.'

'Don't be a coward.'

'Mum, don't.' She swiped a stray curl from her tired eyes and thought she should have had more cut off. She needed to be practical. She wanted...

She didn't want.

'I don't want to fall in love with him again,' she whispered. 'Mum...'

And her mother turned and hugged her.

'It's okay, baby,' she told her as she held her close. 'There's no fear of that, because you've never stopped loving him anyway.'

She came out to tell the kids dinner was ready. She was looking tired and worried. She stood back a bit and called, as if she was afraid of coming further.

Fuzzy raced across to her, barking. The kids looked round and saw her and Toby started beetling across the lawn to her. The scoliosis meant he couldn't walk yet, but he could crawl, and crawl he did, a power crawl, his stiff legs making him look like a weird little bug. He was a bug who squealed with joy as Em swung him up in her arms.

Gretta couldn't crawl. She lay and smiled, waiting for Em to come and fetch her, and Oliver thought that, combined, these kids weighed heaps and Em was slight and...

And it was the life she'd chosen. The life she'd wanted as an alternative to staying married to him.

He rose, lifted Gretta and her oxygen cylinder and carried her across to Em. Gretta reached out her arms to be hugged. Oliver tried for a kid swap in midair and suddenly they were all squeezed together. Kids in the middle. Him on one side, Em on the other, Fuzzy bouncing around in the middle of all their feet.

It was a sandwich squeeze, he thought, a group hug, but he was holding Em. They were the wagons circling the kids. Keeping them safe?

Nothing could keep Gretta safe.

And then Toby coughed and Em tugged away with quick concern. 'Oh, no,' she whispered as she took in Toby's flushed face. 'Katy's bug…'

'I've had them lying on either side of me, and that's the first cough. In the fresh air it should be okay. Should we try and isolate them?'

'It'll be too late, if indeed it's Katy's cold. And besides…' Her voice fell away.

'Besides?'

'We made a decision, Mum and I. The first couple of years of Gretta's life were practically all spent in hospital. She was growing so institutionalised she was starting to not respond at all. Tristan's been her doctor from the beginning. After the last bout of surgery—it was a huge gamble but it didn't pay off—he told us to take her home and love her. And that's what we're doing. We'll be a family until the end.'

Her voice broke a little as she finished but her eyes were still resolute. 'She's Toby's sister,' she said. 'We know there are risks, but the fact that she's family overrides everything.'

'So you'll let her catch—'

'I'll do as much as I can to not let her catch whatever this is,' she said. 'Toby can sleep with Mum and I'll sleep with Gretta so they're not sharing a room. We'll wash and we'll disinfect. But that's all we'll do.'

'That alone will take a power of work.'

'So what's the alternative?' she demanded, lifting her chin. 'Gretta's my daughter, Oliver. The decision is mine.'

Toby's cold was minor, a sniffle and a cough, no big deal. He was quieter than usual, but that was okay because it meant he was supremely happy to lie under the oak tree every evening and listen to Oliver's stories.

Because Oliver kept coming every evening.

'Why?' Em demanded on the third evening. 'Oliver, you don't need to. You owe me nothing.'

'This is little to do with you,' he said, and was surprised into acknowledging that he spoke the truth. For at first these kids had seemed like Em's kids, the kids he'd refused her, a part of Em. And at first he'd agreed to take care of them because of Em. It had been a way to get to know her again—and there was a hefty dose of guilt thrown in for good measure.

But now… He lay under the oak and the bears became tortoises or heffalumps or antigowobblers—that one took a bit of explaining—and he found he was taking as much pleasure as he was giving. And as much quiet satisfaction.

The last five years had been hectic, frantic, building up a career to the point where he knew he was one of the best in-utero surgeons in the world. It hadn't been easy. He'd had little time for anything else, and in truth he hadn't wanted time.

If he'd had free time he'd have thought about Em.

But now, with his career back in Australia yet to build up, he did have that time. And he wasn't thinking about Em—or not all the time, he conceded. He was thinking of two kids.

Of what story he could tell them tonight to make them laugh.

Of how to lessen the burden on Em's shoulders while acknowledging her right to love these two.

How had he ever thought she couldn't love an adopted child?

And as time went on, he thought…How could he have thought that of himself? These kids were somehow wrapping themselves around his heart like two tiny worms. They were two brave, damaged kids who, without Em's big heart, would be institutionalised and isolated.

These were kids who could well break her heart. Gretta's prognosis was grim. Once Toby's medical condition improved, the paperwork to keep him in the country would be mind-blowing.

It didn't seem to matter. Em just…loved. Her courage took his breath away.

Her love made him rethink his life.

What sort of dumb, cruel mistake have I made? he demanded of himself after his first week of childminding. What have I thrown away?

For he had thrown it. Em was always happy to see him, always grateful for the help he gave, always bubbly with the kids when he was around. But as soon as possible she withdrew. What would she say if he asked her to reconsider their relationship? He had no right to ask, he thought. And besides… How could he cope with the pain she was opening herself up to? To adopt these kids…

Except he didn't seem to have a choice. He might not be able to adopt them but, lying under the tree evening after evening, he knew he was beginning to love them.

As he'd always loved their mother?

Every night Em got home from work and he was there. Unbidden, Adrianna pushed mealtime back a little. So instead of coming home to chaos, sometimes Em had time to lie under the tree with them.

It became a routine—they greeted her with quiet pleasure, shifted a little to make room for her on the lushest part of the lawn, Fuzzy stretching so he managed to drape over everyone.

Oliver never tried to talk to her. There was no 'How was your day, dear?' He simply kept on with his stories, but he included her in them.

He found an Emily-shaped cloud and demanded the kids acknowledge it had the same shaped nose, and the same smile. And then he made up a story about Emily and the beanstalk.

It was better than any massage, Em conceded, lying back, looking up through the trees, listening to Oliver making her kids happy.

For he did make them happy. They adored this story time. Gretta probably understood little, but she knew this was story time. Lying on the grass, she was totally relaxed. Her breathing wasn't under pressure, she wriggled closer to Oliver and Em felt her heart twist with the pleasure she was so obviously feeling.

And Toby… The scarring on his face had left the side of his mouth twisted. He had trouble forming words, but with Oliver's gentle stories he was trying more and more.

'And here comes the giant…' Oliver intoned, and Toby's scarred little face contorted with delight.

'S-stomp…stomp…stomp…' he managed.

And Em thought, How smart is my little son? And she watched Oliver give the toddler a high five and then they all said, 'Stomp, stomp, stomp,' and they all convulsed into giggles.

And Em thought…Em thought…

Maybe she'd better not think, she decided. Maybe it was dangerous to think.

What had her mum said? She'd never stopped loving him?

She had, she told herself fiercely. She'd thrown all her love into her children. She had none left over for Oliver.

But she lay and listened to giants stomping, she lay and listened to her children chuckling, and she knew that she was lying.

And she couldn't get away from him. The next morning she walked into Ruby's room and Oliver was there. Of course he was.

It seemed the man had slipped back into her world and was there to stay. He was an obstetrician, and a good one, so of course he was on the wards. He'd offered to help with Gretta and Toby, so of course he was at her house every night when she got home. He was the doctor in charge of making sure Ruby's baby stayed exactly where she was, so of course he was in Ruby's room.

It was just… Why did he take her breath away? Every time she saw him she lost her breath all over again.

She couldn't still love him, she told herself, more and more fiercely as time went on. Her marriage was five years past. She'd moved on. Oliver was now a colleague and a friend, so she should be able to treat him as such.

There was no reason for her heart to beat hard against her ribs every time she saw him.

There was no reason for her fingers to move automatically to her lips, remembering a kiss by the bay…

'Hey,' she managed now as she saw Ruby and Oliver together. She was hauling her professional cheer around her like a cloak. 'I hope Dr Evans is telling you how fantastic you've been,' she told Ruby. 'Because she has been fantastic, Dr Evans. She's been so still, she's healing beautifully and she's giving her baby every chance and more. I can't believe your courage, Ruby, love. I can't believe your strength.'

'She'll be okay,' Ruby said in quiet satisfaction, and her hand curved around her belly.

'We're going to let you go home,' Oliver told her. He'd

been examining her, and now he was tucking her bed-clothes around her again. 'As long as you keep behaving. Do you have somewhere to go?'

And Em blinked again. This was a surgeon—*a surgeon*—tucking in bedclothes and worrying about where his patient would go after hospital.

'Wendy, the social worker, has organised me a place at a hostel near here,' she told them. 'Mum won't let me home but Wendy's organised welfare payments. She's given me the name of a place that'll give me free furniture and stuff for the baby. It's all good.'

'You'll be alone.' Oliver was frowning. 'I'm not sure—'

'Wendy says the lady who runs the hostel has had other pregnant girls there. If I'm in trouble she'll bring me to the hospital. It sounds okay.' She hesitated. 'But there is something I wanted to talk to you about.'

She was speaking to Oliver. Em backed away a little. 'You want me to come back later?'

'No,' Ruby said, firmly now, looking from one to the other. 'I wanted you both here. I've been thinking and thinking and I've decided. I want you to adopt my baby.'

For Em, who'd heard this proposition before, it wasn't a complete shock. For Oliver, though… He looked like he'd been slapped in the face by a wet fish. How many times in his professional career had he been offered a baby? Em wondered. Possibly never.

Probably never.

'What are you talking about?' he asked at last. 'Ruby, I'm sorry, but your baby has nothing to do with us.'

'But she could have everything to do with you.' Ruby pushed herself up on her pillows and looked at them with eagerness. More, with determination. 'I've been think-ing and thinking, and the more I think about it the more

I know I can't care for her. Not like she should be cared for. I didn't even finish school. All my friends are doing uni entrance exams this year and I can't even get my Year Twelve. I don't have anyone to care for my baby. I don't have any money. I'll be stuck on welfare and I can't see me getting off it for years and years. I can't give my baby... what she needs.'

'She needs you,' Em said gently. 'She needs her mum.'

'Yes, but she needs more. What if she wants to be a doctor—how could someone like me ever afford that sort of education? And there'll be operations for the spina bifida—Dr Zigler's already told me there'll be more operations. She'll need special things and now I don't even have enough to buy her nappies. And the choice is adoption but how will I know someone will love her as much as I do? But I know you will. I heard...when I was asleep... It was like it was a dream but I know it's true. You two need a baby to love. You split up because you couldn't have one. What if you have my baby? I could...I dunno...visit her... You'd let me do that, wouldn't you? Mum probably still won't let me go home but I could go back to school. I'd find a way. And I could make something of myself, have enough to buy her presents, maybe even be someone she can be proud of.'

'Ruby...' Doctors didn't sit on patients' beds. That was Medical Training 101, instilled in each and every trainee nurse and doctor. Oliver sat on Ruby's bed and he took her shoulders in his hands. 'Ruby, you don't want to give away your baby.'

Em could hardly hear him. Look up, she told herself fiercely. If you look up you can't cry.

What sort of stupid edict was that? Tears were slipping down her face regardless.

'I want my baby to be loved.' Ruby was crying, too, and

her tears were fierce. 'And you two could love her. I know you could. And you love each other. Anyone can see that. And I know Em's got two already, but Sophia says you're round there every night, helping, and Em's mum helps, too, and she has a great big house…'

'Where did you hear all this?' Em managed.

'I asked,' she said simply. 'There are so many nurses in this hospital and they all know you, Em. They all say you're a fantastic mum. And you should be married again. And it'd be awesome for my baby. I'd let you adopt her properly. She'd be yours.' She took another breath, and it seemed to hurt. She pulled back from Oliver and held her tummy again, then looked from Oliver to Em and back again.

'I'd even let you choose her name,' she managed. 'She'd be your daughter. I know you'd love her. You could be Mum and Dad to her. You could be married again. You could be a family.'

There was a long silence in the room. So many elephants… So much baggage.

Oliver was still sitting on the bed. He didn't move, but he put a hand out to Em. She took a step forward and sat beside him. Midwife and doctor on patient's bed… No matter. Rules were made to be broken.

Some rules. Not others. Other rules were made to protect patients. Ethics were inviolate. No matter what happened between Em and himself, the ethics here were clear-cut and absolute.

But somehow he needed to hold Em's hand while he said it. Somehow it seemed important to say it as a couple.

'Ruby, we can't,' he said gently, and Em swiped a handful of tissues from the bedside table and handed them to Ruby, and then swiped a handful for herself.

The way Oliver was feeling he wouldn't mind a handful for himself, too.

Get a grip, he told himself fiercely, and imperceptibly his grip on Em's hand tightened.

Say it together. Think it together.

'Ruby, what you've just offered us,' he said gently but firmly—he had to be firm even if he was feeling like jelly inside—'it's the greatest compliment anyone has ever given me, and I'm sure that goes for Em, too. You'd trust us with your baby. It takes our breath away. It's the most awesome gift a woman could ever give.'

He thought back to the birth he'd attended less than a week ago, a sister, a surrogate mother. A gift.

And he thought suddenly of his own birth mother. He'd never tried to find her. He'd always felt anger that she'd handed him over to parents who didn't know what it was to love. But he looked at Ruby now and he knew that there was no black and white. Ruby was trying her best to hand her daughter to people she knew would love her, but they couldn't accept.

Would it be Ruby's fault if the adoptive parents turned out...not to love?

His world was twisting. So many assumptions were being turned on their heads.

He saw Em glance at him and he was pathetically grateful that she spoke. He was almost past it.

'Ruby, we're your treating midwife and obstetrician,' she said, gently, as well, but just as firmly. 'That puts us in a position of power. It's like a teacher dating a student—there's no way the student can divorce herself from the authority of the teacher. That authority might well be what attracted the student to the teacher in the first place.'

'I don't know what you mean.'

'I mean we're caring for you,' Em went on. 'And you're seeing that we're caring. It's influencing you, whether you know it or not. Ruby, we couldn't adopt your baby, even if we wanted to. It's just not right.'

'But you need a baby. You said…it'll heal your marriage.'

'I'm not sure what you heard,' Em told her. 'But no baby heals a marriage. We don't need a baby. Your offer is awesome, gorgeous, loving, but, Ruby, whatever decision you make, you need to take us out of it. We're your midwife and your obstetrician. We look after you while your baby's born and then you go back to the real world.'

'But I don't want to go back to the real world,' Ruby wailed. 'I'm scared. And I don't want to give my baby to someone I don't know.'

'Do you want to give your baby to anyone?' Oliver asked, recovering a little now. Em had put this back on a professional basis. Surely he could follow.

'No!' And it was a wail from the heart, a deep, gut-wrenching howl of loss.

And Em moved, gathering the girl into her arms, letting her sob and sob and sob.

He should leave, Oliver thought. He wasn't needed. He was this girl's obstetrician, nothing else.

But the offer had been made to him and to Em. Ruby had treated them as a couple.

Ruby had offered them her baby to bind them together, and even though the offer couldn't be accepted, he felt… bound.

So he sat while Ruby sobbed and Em held her—and somehow, some way, he felt more deeply in love with his wife than he'd ever felt.

His wife. Em…

They'd been apart for almost five years.

She still felt…like part of him.

Em was pulling back a bit now, mopping Ruby's eyes, smiling down at her, pushing her to respond.

'Hey,' she said softly. 'Hey… You want to hear an alternative plan?'

An alternative? What was this? Surely alternatives should be left to the social workers?

If Em was offering to foster on her own he'd have to step in. Ethics again, but they had to be considered, no matter how big Em's heart was.

But she wasn't offering to foster. She had something bigger…

'My mum and I have been talking about you,' she told Ruby, tilting her chin so she could mop some more. 'I know that's not the thing to do, to talk about a patient at home, but I did anyway. My mum lives with me, she helps care for my two kids and she's awesome. She also has a huge house.'

What…what?

'Not that we're offering to share,' Em said, diffidently now, as if she was treading on shifting sand. 'But we have a wee bungalow at the bottom of the garden. It's a studio, a bed/sitting room with its own bathroom. It has a little veranda that looks out over the garden. It's self-contained and it's neat.'

Ruby's tears had stopped. She looked at Em, caught, fascinated.

As was Oliver. He knew that bungalow. He and Em had stayed in it in the past when they'd visited Adrianna for some family celebration and hadn't wanted to drive home.

Josh had been conceived in that bungalow.

'Anyway, Mum and I have been talking,' Em repeated. 'And we're throwing you an option. It's just one option, mind, Ruby, so you can take it or leave it and we won't be the least offended. But if you wanted to take it…you could have it for a peppercorn rent, something you could well afford on your welfare payments. You'd have to put up with our kids whooping round the backyard and I can't promise they'd give you privacy. But in return we could help you.

'The school down the road is one of the few in the state that has child care attached—mostly for staff but they take students' children at need. They have two young mums doing Year Twelve now, so if you wanted to, you could go back. Mum and I could help out, too. It would be hard, Ruby, because your daughter would be your responsibility. But you decided against all pressure not to have an abortion. You've faced everything that's been thrown at you with courage and with determination. Mum and I think you can make it, Ruby, so we'd like to help. It's an option. Think about it.'

What the...?

But they couldn't take it further.

Heinz Zigler arrived then, with an entourage of medical students, ostensibly to talk through the success of the operation with Ruby but in reality to do a spot of teaching to his trainees.

They left Ruby surrounded by young doctors, smiling again, actually lapping up the attention. Turning again into a seventeen-year-old?

They emerged into the corridor and Oliver took Em's arm.

'What the hell...'

The words had been running through his head, over and over, and finally he found space to say them out loud.

'Problem?' Em turned and faced him.

'You'd take them on?'

'Mum and I talked about it. It won't be "taking them on". Ruby's lovely. She'll be a great little mum, but she's a kid herself. She made the bravest decision when she chose not to terminate. It's becoming increasingly obvious that she loves this baby to bits and this way...we could maybe help her be a kid again. Occasionally. Go back to school. Have a bit of fun but have her baby, as well.'

'She offered it to you.' He hesitated. 'To us. I know that's not possible.' He was struggling with what he was feeling; what he was thinking. 'But if it was possible... would you want that?'

'To take Ruby's baby? No!'

'I was watching your face. It's not possible to accept her offer but if it was it'd be your own baby. A baby you could love without complications. Is this offer to Ruby a second-best option?'

'Is that what you think?' She was leaning back against the wall, her hands behind her back, watching him. And what he saw suddenly in her gaze...*was it sympathy?*

'You still don't get it, do you?' she said, gently now. This was a busy hospital corridor. Isla and Sophia were at the nurses' station. They were glancing at Em and Oliver, and Oliver thought how much of what had just gone on would spin around the hospital. How much of what he said now?

He should leave. He should walk away now, but Em was tilting her chin, in the way he knew so well, her lecture mode, her 'Let's tell Oliver what we really think of him'. Uh-oh.

'You scale it, don't you?' Her voice was still soft but there was a note that spoke of years of experience, years of pain. 'You scale love.'

'I don't know what you mean.'

'You think you couldn't love a baby because it's not yours. That's your scale—all or nothing. Your scale reads ten or zero. But me...you've got it figured that my scale has a few more numbers. You're thinking maybe ten for my own baby, but I can't have that. So then—and this is how I think your mind is working—you've conceded that I can love a little bit, so I've taken in Gretta and Toby.

'But according to your logic I can't love them at ten.

Maybe it's a six for Toby because he'll live, but he's damaged and I might not be able to keep him anyway so maybe we'd better make it a five. And Gretta? Well, she's going to die so make that a four or a three, or maybe she'll die really soon so I'd better back off and even make it a two or a one.

'But Ruby's baby…now, if she could give her to me then she'd be a gorgeous newborn and I'd have her from the start and she'll only be a little bit imperfect so maybe she'd score an eight. Only of course, I can't adopt her at all, so you're thinking now why am I bothering to care when according to you she's right off the bottom of the caring scale? Baby I can't even foster—zero? So why are we offering her the bungalow? Is that what you don't understand?'

He stared at her, dumbfounded. 'This is nonsense. That's not what I meant.'

'But it's what you think.' She was angry now, and she'd forgotten or maybe she just didn't care that they were in a hospital corridor and half the world could hear. 'Yes, your adoptive parents were awful but it's them that should be tossed off the scale, Oliver, not every child who comes after that. I work on no scale. I love my kids to bits, really love them, and there's no way I could love them more even if I'd given birth to them. And I'll love Ruby's baby, and Mum and I will love Ruby, too, because she's a kid herself.

'And it won't kill us to do it—it'll make us live. The heart expands to fit all comers—it does, Oliver. You can love and you can love and you can love, and you know what? All that loving means is that you can love some more.'

'Em—'

'Let me finish.' She put up her hands as if to ward off his protests. 'I almost have. All I want to say is that you've put yourself in some harsh, protective cage and you're staying there because of this stupid, stupid scale. You can't have what you deem worthy of ten, so you'll stick to zero. And I'm sorry.'

She took a deep breath, closed her eyes, regrouped. When she opened them again she looked resolute. Only someone who knew her well—as well as he did—could see the pain.

'I loved you, Oliver,' she said, gently again. 'You were my ten, no, more than ten, you were my life. But that love doesn't mean there can't be others. There are tens all over the place if you open yourself to them. If you got out of your cage you'd see, but you won't and that has to be okay with me.' She pushed herself off the wall and turned to go. She had work to do and so did he.

'That's all I wanted to say,' she managed, and she headed off down the corridor, fast, throwing her last words back over her shoulder as she went.

'That's all,' she said again as she went. 'We agreed five years ago and nothing's changed. You keep inside your nice safe cage, and I'll just keep on loving without you.'

CHAPTER TWELVE

SHE SPENT THE rest of the day feeling shaken. Feeling ill. She should never have spoken like she had, especially in such a public place. She was aware of silences, of odd looks, and she knew the grapevine was going nuts behind her back.

Let it, she thought, but as the day wore on she started feeling bad for the guy she'd yelled at.

Oliver kept himself to himself. He was a loner. His one foray out of his loner state had been to marry her. Now he'd withdrawn again.

But now she'd put private information into the public domain. He might quit, she thought. He could move on. He hadn't expected her to be here when he'd taken the job. Would the emotional baggage be enough to make him leave?

She'd lose him again.

She'd told him it didn't matter. She'd told him she had plenty of love to make up for it.

She'd lied.

That was problem with tens, she thought as the long day continued. If you had a heap of tens it shouldn't matter if one dropped off.

It did matter. It mattered especially when the one she was losing was the man who still felt a part of her.

Her mother was right.

She still loved Oliver Evans.

He was kept busy for the rest of the day, but her words stayed with him. Of course they did. Tens and zeroes. It shouldn't make sense.

Only it did.

Luckily, he had no complex procedures or consultations during the day—or maybe unluckily, because his mind was free to mull over what Em had said. Every expectant mum he saw during the day's consultations…he'd look at them and think ten.

He wasn't so sure about a couple of the fathers, he decided. He saw ambivalence. He also saw nerves. Six, he thought, or seven. But in the afternoon he helped with a delivery. In the early stages the father looked terrified to be there, totally out of his comfort zone, swearing as he went in… 'This wasn't my idea, babe. I dunno why you want me here…'

But 'Babe' clung and clung and the father hung in there with her and when finally a tiny, crumpled little boy slipped seamlessly into the world the man's face changed.

What had looked like a three on Em's scale became a fourteen, just like that.

Because the baby really was his? Maybe, yes, Oliver thought, watching them, but now…with Emily's words ringing in his ears he conceded, not necessarily.

Afterwards he scrubbed and made his way back to the nursery. There was a premmie he'd helped deliver. He wanted to check…

He didn't make it.

A baby was lying under the lights used to treat jaundice. Two women were there, seated on either side. Maggie and Leonie. Surrogate mum and biological mum.

They didn't see him, and he paused at the door and let himself watch.

Leonie's hand was on her baby's cheek, stroking it with a tenderness that took his breath away. Where was the tough, commanding woman of the birth scene? Gone.

Maggie had been expressing milk, the staff had told him. Leonie had paid to stay in with the baby, as his mum.

She looked a bit dishevelled. Sleep-deprived? He'd seen this look on the faces of so many new mums, a combination of awe, love and exhaustion.

Maggie, though, looked different. She'd gone home to her family, he knew, just popping back in to bring her expressed milk, and to see her sister—and her daughter?

Not her daughter. Her sister's daughter.

Because while Leonie was watching her baby, with every ounce of concentration focused on this scrap of an infant, Maggie was watching her. She was watching her sister, and the look on her face...

Here it was again, Oliver thought. Love off the Richter Scale.

Love.

Zero or ten? Em was right, it came in all shapes and sizes, in little bits, in humungous chunks, unasked for, involuntarily given, just there.

And he thought again of his adoptive parents, of the tiny amount of affection they'd grudgingly given. He thought of Em and her Gretta and her Toby. He thought of Adrianna, quietly behind the scenes, loving and loving and loving.

He stood at the door and it was like a series of hammer blows, powering down at his brain. Stupid, stupid, stupid... He'd been judging the world by two people who were incapable of love outside their own rigid parameters.

He'd walked away from Em because he'd feared he'd be like them.

His thoughts were flying everywhere. Em was there,

front and foremost, but suddenly he found himself thinking of the woman who'd given him up for adoption all those years ago. He'd never wanted to find her—he'd blamed her.

There were no black and whites. Maybe he could... Maybe Em could help...

'Can I help you?' It was Isla, bustling in, wheeling a humidicrib. 'If you have nothing to do I could use some help. I'm a man short and Patrick James needs a feed. Can you handle an orogastric tube?'

Patrick James was the baby he'd come to see. He'd been delivered by emergency Caesarean the day before when his mother had shown signs of pre-eclampsia. Dianne wasn't out of the woods yet, her young and scared husband was spending most of his time with her, and their baby son was left to the care of the nursery staff.

He was a thirty-four-weeker. He'd do okay.

It wasn't an obstetrician's job to feed a newborn. He had things to do.

None of them were urgent.

So somehow he found himself accepting. He settled by the humidicrib, he monitored the orogastric tube, he noted with satisfaction all the signs that said Patrick James would be feeding by himself any day now. For a thirty-four-weeker, he was amazing.

All babies were amazing.

Involuntarily, he found himself stroking the tiny, fuzz-covered cheek. Smiling. Thinking that given half a chance, he could love...

Love. Once upon a time he'd thought he'd had it with Emily. He'd walked away.

If he walked back now, that love would need to embrace so much more.

Black and white. Zero or ten. Em was right, there were no boundaries.

He watched Patrick James feed. He watched Leonie love her baby and he watched Maggie love her sister.

He thought about love, and its infinite variations, and every moment he did, he fell deeper and deeper in love with his wife.

She arrived home that night and Oliver's car was parked out the front. His proper car. His gorgeous Morgan. Gleaming, immaculate, all fixed. It made her smile to see it. And it made her feel even more like smiling that she'd yelled at Oliver this morning and here he was again. Gretta and Toby would miss his visits if they ended.

When they ended?

The thought made her smile fade. She walked into the kitchen. The smell of baking filled the house—fresh bread! Oliver's nightly visits were spurring Adrianna on to culinary quests. Her mum was loving him coming.

She was loving him coming.

'Mumma,' Toby crowed in satisfaction, and she scooped him out of his highchair and hugged him. Then, finally, she let herself look at Oliver.

He was sitting by the stove, holding Gretta in his arms. Gretta wasn't smiling at her. She looked intent, a bit distressed.

Her breathing…

The world stood still for a moment. Still hugging Toby, she walked forward to see.

'It's probably nothing,' Adrianna faltered. 'It's probably—'

'It's probably Katy's cold,' Oliver finished for her. 'It's not urgent but I was waiting… Now you're here, maybe we should pop her back to the Victoria so Tristan can check.'

Congestive heart failure. Of course. She'd been expecting it—Tristan had warned her it would happen.

'You won't have her for very long,' he'd told Em, gently but firmly. 'Love her while you can.'

One cold… She should never…

'You can't protect her from everything,' Oliver murmured during that long night when Gretta's breathing grew more and more labored. 'You've given her a home, you've given her love. You know that. It was your decision and it was the right one. If she'd stayed in a protective isolette then maybe she'd survive longer, but not lived.'

'Oh, but—'

'I know,' he said gently, as Gretta's breathing faltered, faltered again and then resumed, even weaker. 'You love, and love doesn't let go.' And then he said…

'Em, I'm so sorry I let you go,' he said softly into the ominous stillness of the night. 'I was dumb beyond belief. Em, if you'll have me back…'

'Ollie…'

'No, now's not the time to say it,' he said grimly. 'But I love you, Em, and for what it's worth, I love Gretta, too. Thank you for letting me be here now. Thank you for letting me love.'

She was past exhaustion. She held and she held, but her body was betraying her.

Gretta was in her arms, seemingly asleep, but imperceptibly slipping closer to that invisible, appalling edge.

'You need to sleep yourself,' Oliver said at last. 'Em, curl up on the bed with her. I promise I'll watch her and love her, and I'll wake you the moment she wakes, the moment she's conscious.'

They both knew such a moment might not happen. The end was so near…

But, then, define *near*. Who could predict how long these last precious hours would take? Death had its own way of deciding where and when, and sometimes, Oliver thought, death was decided because of absence rather than presence.

Even at the time of death, loved ones were to be protected. How many times had a child slipped away as a parent had turned from a bed—as if solitude gave permission for release? Who knew? Who understood? All he knew was that Em was past deciding.

'I'll take your chair,' he told her, laying his hand on her shoulder, holding. 'Snuggle onto the bed.'

'How can I sleep?'

'How can you not?' He kissed her softly on her hair and held her, letting his body touch hers, willing his strength into her. This woman… She gave and she gave and she gave…

How could he possibly have thought her love could be conditional? How could he possibly have thought adoption for Em could be anything but the real thing?

And how could he ever have walked away from this woman, his Em, who was capable of so much love and who'd loved him?

Who still loved him, and who'd shown him that he, too, was capable of such love.

'I'll wake you if there's any change. I promise.'

'You do…love her?'

'Ten,' he said, and he smiled at her and then looked down at the little girl they were watching over. 'Maybe even more.'

She nodded, settled Gretta on the bed, then rose and stumbled a little. He rose, too, and caught her. He could feel her warmth, her strength, the beating of her heart against his. The love he felt for this woman was threatening to overwhelm him, and yet for this moment another love was stronger.

Together they looked down at this tiny child, slipping away, each breath one breath closer…

Em choked back an involuntary sob, just the one, and then she had herself under control again. There would be no deathbed wailing, not with this woman. But, oh, it didn't mean she didn't care.

'Slip in beside her,' he said, and numbly she allowed him to tug off her windcheater, help her off with her jeans.

She slid down beside Gretta in her knickers and bra, then carefully, with all the tenderness in the world, she held Gretta, so the little girl's body was spooned against hers.

Gretta stirred, ever so slightly, her small frame seeming to relax into that of her mother's.

Her mother. Em.

Somewhere out there was a birth mother, the woman who'd given Gretta up because it had all been too hard. Down's syndrome and an inoperable heart condition that would kill her had seemed insurmountable. But Em hadn't seen any of that when she'd decided to foster her, Oliver thought. She'd only seen Gretta.

She'd only loved Gretta.

'Sleep,' he ordered as he pulled up the covers, and she gave him a wondering look in the shadows of the pale nightlight.

'You'll watch?'

'I swear.'

She smiled, a faint, tremulous smile, and closed her eyes.

She was asleep in moments.

The quiet of the night was almost absolute. The only sound was the faint in-drawing of breath through the oxygen tube. Gretta's tiny body was almost insignificant on the pillows. Em's arms were holding her, mother and child ensconced in their private world of love.

Mother and child... That's what these two were, Oliver thought as he kept his long night-time vigil. Mother and child.

In the next room, Adrianna had Toby in bed with her. Whether Toby needed comfort—who knew what the little boy sensed?—or Adrianna herself needed comfort and was taking it as parents and grandparents had taken and given comfort since the beginning of time—who knew?

Adrianna's love for Toby was almost as strong as Em's.

Grandmother, mother, child.

He wanted to be in that equation, and sitting there in the stillness of the night, he knew he wanted it more than anything else in the world. What a gift he'd had. What a gift he'd thrown away.

But Em had let him into her life again. She'd allowed him to love…

Gretta shifted, a tiny movement that he might not have noticed if all his senses weren't tuned to her breathing, to her chest rising and falling. There was a fraction of a grimace across her face? Pain? He touched her face, and she moved again, just slightly, responding to his touch as he'd seen newborns do.

On impulse he slid his hands under her body and gathered her to him. Em stirred, as well, but momentarily. Her need for sleep was absolute.

'I'm cuddling her for a bit,' he whispered to Em. 'Do you mind?'

She gave a half-asleep nod, the vestige of a smile and slept again.

He gathered Gretta against his chest and held.

Just held.

The night enfolded them. This was a time of peace. A time of blessing?

Gretta was snuggled in his arms, against his heart, and she fitted there. Em slept on beside them.

His family.

Gretta's breathing was growing more shallow. There

was no longer any trace of movement. No pain. Her face was peaceful, her body totally relaxed against his.

He loved her.

He'd known this little girl for only weeks, and her courage, her strength, her own little self had wrapped her around his heart with chains of iron. She was slipping away and his chest felt as if it was being crushed.

Her breathing faltered. Dear God…

'Em?'

She was instantly awake, pushing her tumbled curls from her hair, swinging her legs over the side of the bed, her fingers touching her daughter's face almost instantly.

She just touched.

The breathing grew shallower still.

'Would you like to hold her?' How hard was it to say that? How hard, to hand her over to the woman who loved her?

But he loved her, too.

'I'm here,' Em whispered. 'Keep holding her. She loves you, Oliver. You've lit up our lives in these last weeks.'

'Do you want to call Adrianna?'

'She says she couldn't bear it. If it's okay with you… just us.'

Her fingers stayed on her daughter's face as Gretta's breathing faltered and faltered again. Gretta's frail body was insubstantial, almost transient, but Oliver thought there was nothing insubstantial about the power around them.

A man and a woman and their child.

'I wish I'd been here,' he said fiercely, though he still whispered. 'I wish I'd had the whole four years of her.'

'You're here now,' Em whispered as her daughter's breathing faltered yet again. 'That's all that matters.'

And then the breathing stopped.

They didn't move. It was like a tableau set in stone.

'Stop all the clocks…' Who had said that? Auden, Oliver thought, remembering the power of the poem, and somehow, some way it helped. That others had been here. That others had felt this grief.

Grief for parents, for lovers, for children. Grief for those who were loved.

Gretta had been loved, absolutely. That his own parents had doled out their love according to some weird formula of their own making—this much love for an adopted child; this much love for a child of their own making—it was nothing to do with now, or what he and Em decided to do in the future.

Their loving was so strong it would hold this little girl in their hearts for ever.

It would let them go on.

And Em was moving on. She was removing Gretta's oxygen cannula. She was adjusting Gretta's pink, beribboned pyjamas. She was wiping Gretta's face.

And finally she was gathering her daughter's body into her own arms, holding her, hugging her, loving her. And then, finally, finally the tears came.

'Go call Mum,' she managed, as Oliver stood, helpless in his grief as well as hers. 'She needs to be here now. And Toby… You need to bring him in, Oliver. For now, for this moment, we need to be together. Our family.'

They buried Gretta with a private service three days later. It was a tiny service. Only those who loved Gretta most were there to share.

Gretta's birth mother, contacted with difficulty, chose not to come. 'I don't want to get upset. You take care of her.'

'We will,' Em promised, and they did, the best they could. They stood by the tiny graveside, Oliver at one side of Em, Adrianna at the other, and they said goodbye to a part of themselves.

Such a little time, Oliver thought. How could you love someone so deeply after such a little time?

But he did. Years couldn't have made this love deeper.

He gathered Em into his arms afterwards and there were no words needed for the promises that were being made.

She knew and he knew. Here was where they belonged.

Katy had looked after Toby during the service—there were some things a two-year-old could never remember and couldn't hope to understand—but afterwards she brought him to them. 'Let's go to the Children's Garden,' Mike had suggested. 'The Botanic Gardens is a great place to play. That's where I think we all need to be.'

And it wasn't just Katy and Mike and the kids who arrived at the Gardens. Their hospital friends met them there, appearing unbidden, as if they sensed that now was the time they were needed. Isla and Alessi, Sophia, Charles, Tristan, even the obnoxious Noah—so many people who loved Em and knew the depths of Em's grief.

Heaven knew who was looking after midwifery and neonates at the Victoria, for at two o'clock on this beautiful autumn afternoon it seemed half the staff were here.

And suddenly, as if by magic, pink balloons were everywhere. They wafted upwards through the treetops and spread out. It seemed that each balloon contained a tiny packet of seeds—kangaroo paws, Gretta's favourite—with instructions for planting. Who knew who'd organised it, and who knew how many kangaroo paws would spring up over Melbourne because of Gretta? It didn't matter. All that mattered was that the love was spreading outwards, onwards. Gretta's life would go on.

There were blessings here, Oliver thought as he gazed around at the friends he'd made in such a short time, the friends that had been Em's supports while he'd been away, the friends who'd stand by them for ever.

For ever sounded okay to him.

Their friends drifted away, one by one, hugging and leaving, knowing that while friends were needed, alone was okay, as well. Sophia and Isla took Adrianna by an arm apiece. 'Rooftop Bar?' they queried, and Adrianna cast an apologetic glance at her daughter.

'If it's okay…I'd kill for a brandy.'

'If anyone deserves a brandy or three, it's you. I… We'll meet you there,' Em said, holding back, watching Oliver hugging Toby.

'Do you want me to take Toby?' her mum asked.

'I need Toby right now,' Oliver said, and Em blinked. Of all the admissions…

But no more was said. She stood silent until Sophia and Isla and Adrianna disappeared through the trees and they were alone. With her son. With…*their* son?

Then Oliver tugged her down so they were in their favourite place in the world, lying under a massive tree, staring up through the branches.

Toby, who'd submitted manfully to being hugged all afternoon, took off like a clockwork beetle, crawling round and round the tree, gathering leaves, giggling to himself. Death held no lasting impression for a two-year-old and Em was grateful for it.

'I think that's Gretta's nose,' Oliver said, pointing upwards at a cloud. 'I think she's up there, deciding whose porridge is hers.'

And to her amazement Em heard herself chuckle. She rolled over so her head lay on his chest, and his lovely fingers raked her hair.

'I love you, Em,' he said, softly into the stillness. 'I

love you more than life itself. Will you let me be part of your family?'

She didn't speak. She couldn't.

She could feel his heart beneath her. His fingers were drifting through her hair, over and over. Toby crawled around them once and then again before she found her voice. Before she trusted herself to speak.

'You've always been my family, Oliver,' she said, slowly, hardly trusting herself to speak. 'Five years ago I was too shocked, too bereft, too gutted to see your needs. So many times since, I've rerun that time in my head, trying to see it as you saw it. I put a gun to your head, Ollie. Black or white. Adoption or nothing. It wasn't fair.'

'Even if your way was right? Even if your way *is* right?'

She could feel his heart but she could no longer feel hers. There'd been so many emotions this day... Her world was spinning...

No, she thought. Her world had settled on its right axis. It had found its true north.

'I'm so glad I came back in time to meet Gretta,' Oliver said softly, still stroking her hair. 'I'm so glad I was able to be a tiny part of her life. If I hadn't... She's a part of you, now, Em, and, believe it or not, she's a part of me. A part of us. Like Toby is. Like Adrianna. Like everyone is who released a pink balloon today. You're right, there is no scale. Loving is just loving. But most of all, Em, I love you. Will you take me on again, you and all your fantastic menagerie? Toby and Adrianna and Fuzzy and Mike and Katy and the kids, and Ruby and her baby when she's born? Will you let me love them with you? Will you let me love you?'

Enough. Tears had been sliding down her cheeks all day and it was time to stop. She swiped them away and tugged herself up so she was looking into his face. She gazed into his eyes and what she saw made her heart twist with love. She saw grief. She saw love.

She saw hope.

And hope was all they needed, she thought. Heaven knew how their family would end up. Heaven knew what crazy complications life would send them.

All she knew for now was that somehow, some way, this man had been miraculously restored to her.

Her husband. Her life.

'I can't stop you loving me,' she managed, swiping yet more tears away. 'And why would I want to? Oh, Oliver, I'd never want to. I love you with all my heart and that it's returned...well, Gretta's up there making miracles for us; I know she is.'

There was a crow of laughter from right beside them. They turned and Toby had a handful of leaves. He threw them at both their faces and then giggled with delight.

Oliver tugged Em to lie hard by his side, and then picked Toby up and swung him up so he was chortling down at them.

'You're a scamp,' he told him. 'We love you.'

And Toby beamed down at both of them. God was in his heaven, all was right in Toby's world.

He had his Em and now he had his Oliver. His Gretta would stay with him in the love they shared, in the love they carried forward.

Toby was with his family.

And two weeks later they went back to the gardens, for a ceremony they both decreed was important. For the things they had to say needed to be said before witnesses. Their friends who'd been with them in the tough times now deserved to see their joy, and they were all here. Even Ruby was here this time, carefully cosseted by Isla and Sophia but increasingly sure of herself, increasingly confident of what lay ahead.

Oliver had asked Charles Delamere to conduct this unconventional ceremony—Charles, the man who'd recruited him—Charles, the reason Oliver had finally come home.

Charles, the head of the Victoria Hospital. The man who seemed aloof, a powerful business tycoon but who'd released balloons for Gretta two weeks before. Who'd promised all his support, whatever they needed. Who'd also promised to move heaven and earth to cut bureaucratic red tape, so Toby could stay with them for ever.

But the successful bureaucratic wrangling was for later. This day was not official, it was just for love.

They chose a beautiful part of the garden, wild, free, a part they both loved. They stood under a tangled arch, surrounded by greenery. They held hands and faced Charles together, knowing this was right.

'Welcome,' Charles said, smiling, because what he was to do now was all about joy. 'Today Em and Oliver have asked me if I'll help them do something they need to do, and they wish to do it before all those who love them. Ten years ago, Emily and Oliver made their wedding vows. Circumstances, grief, life, drove them apart but when the time was right fate brought them together again. They've decided to renew their vows, and they've also decided that here, the gardens that are—and have been—loved by the whole family, are the place they'd like to do it. So if I could ask for your attention...'

He had it in spades. There was laughter and applause as their friends watched them stand before Charles, like two young lovers with their lives ahead of them.

'Emily,' Charles said seriously. 'What would you like to say?'

They'd rehearsed this, but privately and separately.

Oliver stood before Emily and he didn't know what she'd say but he didn't care. He loved her so much.

But then the words came, and they were perfect.

'Just that I love him,' Em said, mistily, lovingly. 'That I married Oliver ten years ago with all my heart and he has my heart still. What drove us apart five years ago was a grief that's still raw, but it's a part of us. It'll always be a part of us, but I don't want to face life's griefs and life's joys without him.'

She turned and faced Oliver full on. 'Oliver, I love you,' she told him, her voice clear and true. 'I love you, I love you, I love you, and I always will. For better and for worse. In sickness and in health. In joy and in sorrow, but mostly in joy. I take you, Oliver Evans, back to be my husband, and I promise to love you now and for evermore.'

He'd thought he had it together. He hadn't, quite. When he tried to speak it came out as a croak and he had to stop and try again.

But when he did, he got it right.

'I love you, too, Em,' he told her, taking her hands in his, holding her gaze, caressing her with his eyes. 'Those missing years are gone. We can't get them back, but for now this is all about the future. We have Toby, our little son, and with the help of our friends we'll fight heaven and earth to keep him. As well as that, we have the memory of a baby we once lost, our Josh, and we have so many wonderful memories of our beloved Gretta. And we have all our friends, and especially we have Adrianna, to love us and support us.'

He turned and glanced at Adrianna, who was smiling and smiling, and he smiled back, with all the love in his heart. And then he turned back to his wife.

'But for now...' he said softly but surely. 'For now I'm holding your hands and I'm loving you. I love you, Emily Louise, as surely as night follows day. I love you deeply, strongly, surely, and I swear I'll never let you down again. From this day forth I'll be your husband. You hold my heart in the palm of your hand. For richer, for poorer, in sickness and in health, we're a family. But maybe…not a complete family. I'm hoping there'll be more children. More friends, more dogs, more chaos. I'm hoping we can move forward with love and with hope. Emily Louise, will you marry me again?'

'Of course I will,' Em breathed, as Toby wriggled down from Adrianna's arms and beetled his way between legs to join them. Oliver scooped him up and held and they stood, mother, father and son, a family portrait as every camera in Melbourne seemed to be trained on them.

'Of course I will,' Em whispered again, and the cameras seemed to disappear, as their surroundings seemed to disappear. There was only this moment. There was only each other.

'Of course I will,' Em whispered for the third time, as they held each other and they knew these vows were true and would hold for all time. 'I'm marrying you again right now, my Oliver. I'm marrying you for ever.'

* * * * *

ALWAYS THE
MIDWIFE

ALISON ROBERTS

For Annie, Carol and Linda—who will always
make Melbourne a very special place to
visit for me.

Love you all xxx

CHAPTER ONE

THE BLIP OF the foetal heart monitor had definitely slowed down. Her decision might be a no-brainer but Sophia knew it wasn't going to be popular.

'I'm sorry,' she told her patient, 'but I'm not happy with the way things are going. We need to get you to hospital.'

'No-o-o…' First-time mother Claire Robinson had her heart set on a home birth. 'You said I'm almost fully dilated. It can't be much longer.'

'You're exhausted, sweetheart. Every contraction is harder for you and things are slowing down.' She still had the hand-held Doppler against the distended abdomen of the pregnant woman. 'Can you hear that the baby's heartbeat has slowed down, too? It's a sign that baby is getting distressed.'

'What does that mean?' Claire's husband, Greg, was looking pale and anxious. 'Is the baby in danger? Is *Claire* in danger?'

'No.' Sophia hastened to reassure them both. 'But that's what I want to make sure isn't going to happen. The labour hasn't progressed quite the way we wanted and…' How could she tell these parents-to-be, without scaring them, that it was her instinct that something wasn't right that was making the transfer seem urgent? 'Let me make a call and see how far away an ambulance might be.'

The call was answered instantly.

'My name is Sophia Toulson,' Sophia said. 'I'm a midwife with the Melbourne Maternity Unit at the Victoria. I'm at a planned home birth…' She moved away from the young couple, lowering her voice as she gave the address details and then voiced her concerns.

'An ambulance is probably fifteen minutes away,' the dispatcher told her. 'But we do have a SPRINT guy in your locality.'

'SPRINT?'

'Single Paramedic Response and Intervention. An intensive care paramedic on a motorbike.'

'I think we just need the transport,' Sophia said. 'It's not an emergency…' But she could hear the note of doubt in her own voice. An exhausted first-time mother and a stalled labour. The potential for an emergency was there. Was that why alarm bells had started ringing?

'I'll change the plan,' Claire offered desperately, as Sophia ended the call. 'I'll have more pain relief than the gas. You can rupture the membranes. Whatever it takes…' She was sobbing now. 'We don't want to have our baby in a hospital…'

'I know.' Sophia smoothed damp strands of hair back from Claire's face. 'But you know what the really important thing here is?'

She didn't wait for a response. Greg was perched on

the end of the bed, holding Claire in his arms as she lay back against him. She caught his gaze and then Claire's.

'My job is to keep both you and baby safe. At the end of the day, the only thing that matters is that you get to hold your healthy baby in your arms. I promise that where the delivery happens is not going to take away even the tiniest bit of joy that moment's going to give you.'

A joy that Sophia might never be able to experience herself but that didn't mean she couldn't share it happening for others. It was precisely why she'd chosen this profession. Why she loved it so much. And why she was so passionate about doing whatever it took to ensure a happy outcome.

'That's all I want,' Greg said, his voice cracking. 'For you both to be okay. We always said that we'd go to the hospital the minute we were worried about anything.'

'But I'm not worried. I'm just so tired… Oohhh…' Claire's face scrunched into lines of pain.

'Another contraction?' Sophia reached for the Entonox mouthpiece. 'Here you go. Deep breaths…'

The loud rap on the door made her jump. Surely the ambulance hadn't arrived this quickly?

'Shall I go?' Greg asked.

Claire spat out the mouthpiece. '*No*—don't leave me… It's…. *Ahhh…*'

Sophia wasn't going anywhere either. The contraction had produced a rush of fluid. Claire's membranes had finally broken. It was a sign that her labour was progressing again but Sophia wasn't feeling relieved. Quite the opposite.

The fluid soaking into the pad beneath Claire's hips had the stain of meconium that meant the baby could be in trouble. And…

Oh, dear Lord…yes…that was a loop of umbilical cord showing.

'G'day…' The rich, deep voice came from behind her. 'I let myself in. Hope that's okay.'

Sophia looked up. The man was wearing a high-vis heavy-duty jacket. He had a motorbike helmet on his head with the red, white and blue colours of Melbourne's ambulance service and the title 'Paramedic' emblazoned across the front. The chin-guard and visor were flipped up so that she could see his face but she barely registered what he looked like. There was relief to be felt now— that she had professional help in what had just become an obstetric emergency.

'Claire's waters just broke,' she said quietly. 'We've got a cord prolapse.'

'What's that?' Greg was leaning in, trying to see what was happening. 'What's going on? And who are you?'

The paramedic's helmet was off by the time he'd taken two steps closer. 'I'm Aiden Harrison,' he told Greg. 'Here to help.' He was right beside Sophia now. 'Modified Sims position?'

'Knees to chest, I think. Claire? We're going to get you to turn over, I want you on your knees with your bottom up in the air. Greg, can you help?'

'What? *Why?*' Claire was panting, recovering from the contraction. 'I don't want to move.'

'We've got a small problem, guys.' The paramedic had dropped his helmet and leather gloves, along with a rolled-up kit he'd been carrying. He didn't sound stressed. Rather, he made it sound as if whatever the problem was, it was going to be easily remedied. 'Your baby didn't read the rule book and part of the umbilical cord has come out first. We need to take any pressure off it, which is why we're going to let gravity give us a hand. Here…let me help.'

Somehow he managed to make it seem like nothing out of the ordinary to be getting a woman in labour to get into what seemed a very unnatural position, on her knees with her head lowered. Sophia was ready with the Doppler to check the baby's heart rate again.

Aiden listened, his gaze on his watch. 'Ninety-eight,' he said. 'What was the last recorded rate?'

'One-forty.' Sophia ripped open a packet of sterile gloves. In a blink of time, this had become a potential disaster. The baby's oxygen supply was being cut off. 'I'm going to try and ease the pressure.'

'Oh, my God…' Claire wailed. 'What's happening?'

'You're going to feel me inside,' Sophia warned her. 'I'm going to be pushing on baby's head to take the pressure off the cord.'

Greg's face was as white as a sheet. 'How are you going to take her to hospital if she has to stay in that position?' He glanced sideways to where the paramedic had discarded his bike helmet. 'You're not even driving an ambulance, are you?'

'No, mate. I ride a bike. Gets me where I'm needed faster.' Aiden reached for the radio clipped to his shoulder. 'SPRINT One to Base. How far away is our back-up?'

They could all hear the woman's voice on the other end. 'Should be with you in less than ten minutes.'

'Copy that. Make it a code one.' He nodded at Greg. 'Hang in there, mate. We're under control.'

'I'm getting another contraction,' Claire groaned. 'Ohhh... I want to *push*...'

'Don't push,' Sophia warned. 'Not yet.'

She looked up to find Aiden's gaze on her face. A steady gaze but she could see he knew exactly what she was trying to decide and the almost crushing responsibility for making the right choice here.

'The cord's pulsatile,' she told him. 'And Claire's fully dilated.'

Aiden nodded. If they were in hospital right now, an assisted delivery with forceps would be the fastest and safest way to get this baby out. With Sophia using two fingers to push on the baby's head, the cord was being protected and the blood and oxygen supply was still adequate. She knew what she was doing, this midwife. Intelligent-looking woman, in fact, which probably explained the anxiety he could see in her eyes. She had to know exactly how dangerous this situation was for the baby.

Her hand was probably already aching, although Aiden couldn't detect any signs of discomfort. Could she keep this up until they arrived at the hospital? The other option was not to slow down a natural delivery but to try and speed it up. To get the baby out fast enough to avoid potentially devastating complications from lack of oxygen. She was still looking at him and he got the feeling she was following his train of thought.

'She's also exhausted,' she added. 'Labour's been a bit protracted. That was why I called for an ambulance in the first place. I'm not sure…' Sophia bit her lip as her words trailed to an inaudible whisper. She hated feeling indecisive and it rarely happened, but a baby's life was at stake here and there was another option. But if they encouraged Claire to push and she was too tired to be effective, they would have to wait for another contraction and they could end up in a much worse position, with the baby's head cutting off any oxygen supply. The baby could end up with severe brain damage. Or it could die.

The weighing-up process was lightning fast but agonising. Sophia found she was holding the gaze of the paramedic. Light brown eyes, a part of her brain noted. Unusual. It was a calm gaze but it was intelligent. He knew what the issues were. It was also confident. Crinkles appeared near the corners, like a smile that didn't involve a mouth. There was a good chance they could pull this off.

It was Aiden who broke the eye contact. He crouched beside the bed so that he could look up at Claire who had her forehead resting on clenched fists.

'How tired are you, Claire?' he asked.

'She's stuffed, mate.' It was Greg who responded. 'We never thought it was going to be this hard, you know?'

But Aiden didn't seem to be listening. He was holding Claire's frightened gaze now.

'The best thing for your baby is going to be getting born as fast as possible,' he said. 'And we can help but you're going to have to do most of the work. Do you think you could do that?'

'I want to push,' Claire said with a sob. 'But I'm scared.'

'We're here with you. How 'bout we give it our best shot with the next contraction?'

'O-okay. I'll try.'

'Good girl.' He was smiling at Claire now and the mix of approval and confidence in his voice was compelling. Sophia could have felt defensive about having someone else make that decision for her, but instead she was as ready as Claire to put every effort into making this work. She believed it was the right decision. It *would* work.

Who was this knight in shining armour who'd ridden up on a motorbike instead of a horse just as things were turning to custard? This paramedic with his warm brown eyes and streaked, golden-blond hair that made him look like a surfer.

When the next contraction was due a couple of minutes later, they turned Claire onto her back again and Sophia released the pressure holding the baby's head away from the cervix and the cord. The clock was ticking from that moment on and the three of them, Aiden, Sophia and even Greg—who couldn't help but catch the urgency—coached Claire into giving everything she had. And then a bit more.

'You can do it,' Aiden told her firmly. 'Push, push, push. Keep going. *Push.*'

'Crowning,' Sophia confirmed. 'Keep going, Claire.'

'You're doing great,' Aiden continued. 'But don't

stop. We can't wait for another contraction. This is it. *Push…*'

'*Can't…*' The groan was agonised.

'Yes, you can. You *are* doing it. You're awesome… One more push, that's all we need.'

Good grief, this man had the most amazing voice. Sophia could feel her own abdominal muscles clenching. *She* wanted to push—how ridiculous was that?

'Oh, my God…' Greg's voice was choked. 'I can see him, Claire. Our baby.'

Sophia could see him, too. Could touch and help him into the world, but she'd lost track of how many minutes it had taken since the blood and oxygen supply had been cut off by the pressure of the baby's head and body on the prolapsed umbilical cord.

The baby was limp and blue. It looked lifeless.

Her heart sank like a stone. This had been the wrong decision, then, to let imminent labour progress instead of stalling it and trying to get Claire to hospital before she delivered. This was her patient and her responsibility. How could she have allowed this man she'd never even met before to come in and take charge the way he had? It would be unthinkable to lose a baby like this.

But the motorbike-riding paramedic was by her side, with a kit unrolled and resuscitation gear at the ready and she hadn't yet lost faith in the calm confidence he displayed.

A tiny bag mask to deliver oxygen. Fingers that looked so large against a fragile chest delivering compressions that were gentle but effective.

'Come on, little guy. You can do it. You're gonna be fine...'

The words sounded incongruously casual but Sophia could see the intense concentration in the paramedic's eyes. The fierce determination to save a tiny life.

And there was movement. A gasp as lungs expanded for the first time. A warbling cry. Skin colour that was changing from a deathly blue to a much healthier pink. Arms and legs beginning to stir.

'Hey...welcome back, little guy.' Aiden's hands cupped the baby to gently lift and place the newborn boy against his mother's skin. Both Claire and Greg had tears streaming down their faces. There was an overpowering sense of both relief and joy but fear hadn't been banished yet.

Sophia was watching anxiously. With the level of resuscitation needed, the baby would have still been under intense monitoring in a clinical setting, not being held and touched like this by his parents.

And then Aiden's gaze shifted away from the infant.

'Apgar score nine at five minutes,' he murmured. She could swear there was a ghost of a wink accompanying the report. He knew how anxious she was and he wanted her to know that he was still doing his job—that the baby was being carefully monitored. Sure enough, she could see him resting a finger lightly on the baby's upper arm, taking a brachial pulse. She could stop worrying and focus on Claire. She could deal with the delivery of the placenta and check for any tissue damage.

The emergency was over, almost as quickly as it had appeared.

The ambulance would be arriving within minutes and then they'd have the bustle of preparations to transfer the new family to the maternity unit, where Claire and the baby could both be checked by specialists, but this was a gift of time.

Private time in their own home—the place they had wanted to be in to welcome their first baby.

Aiden stepped back. He stripped off the gloves he'd put on to work on the baby and moved to one side of the room, where he propped an elbow on a tall chest of drawers. He was due to go off duty and he had his usual visit to make as soon as he was done but he wasn't going to leave until the back-up arrived and he didn't want to crowd the young parents as they had their first minutes with their newborn.

Besides, he could watch the midwife as she dealt competently with the delivery of the placenta, transferring it to a bowl where she inspected it for any damage that could suggest part of it had been retained. She was tiny, he noticed. Only a bit over five feet tall. Funny that he hadn't noticed how small she was before. Maybe that was because she'd given off the impression of being confident. Good at her job and in control.

She hadn't felt so in control at one point, though, had she? He remembered that almost telepathic communication between them as they'd weighed up the option of whether to try and stall the labour or push it forward.

Her eyes were a rich brown, weren't they? A nice match for her hair, which had an auburn tinge to its dark colour. It was pinned up to her head to keep it out of the way and Aiden found himself wondering how long it would be if it was unpinned. How soft it might feel.

Good grief... Okay, she was pretty cute but there was no need to get carried away.

But then she looked up from her work and her smile told him there was nothing to worry about.

He could feel that smile as much as he could see it. Gorgeous was the only word for it.

Sophia hadn't noticed the paramedic moving to the other side of the room. Had he apparently read the vibes in the room in the same way he'd seemed to ever since he'd walked in the door?

He'd done the perfect thing, anyway, so she followed his example. Any more cleaning up of either mother or baby could wait until the ambulance arrived. This was a time these new parents could never have again and it was precious. She wasn't about to leave the room and Aiden had chosen the spot that was far away enough to be unobtrusive while still being available so it was a no-brainer to move quietly until she was standing beside him.

He acknowledged her arrival with a grin.

'Good job,' he said softly. 'Thanks for inviting me.'

Her breath came out in a huff of laughter. How could anyone make a life-threatening emergency sound like a party? But paramedics were like that, weren't they? They lived for the adrenaline rush and a 'good' job was one that other medical professionals dreaded having to face. She'd met paramedics who came across as cowboys—galloping from one callout to the next and over-eager to show off their skills.

This one rode a motorbike, for heaven's sake. A mechanical horse. And he'd had no hesitation in taking command and encouraging management that had had the very real potential to have ended in disaster.

Except it hadn't, had it? Another glance at the bed was enough to bring a lump to Sophia's throat. The baby lay in Claire's arms, tiny eyes open and staring up at his parents. Greg's fingers were touching the tiny starfish hand of the baby and his head was touching Claire's. They were both looking down, aware of nothing but their newborn infant. They were talking softly, too, counting fingers and toes and doing what all new parents did in the first minutes of sharing the miracle of new life.

They had probably forgotten the presence of their medical team and wouldn't even hear the murmur of other voices but Sophia looked away, unconsciously allowing them a little more privacy.

It was somewhat startling to find that the paramedic was still looking at her.

'Babies are my favourite thing,' he said softly. 'It was a treat.'

For the first time since he'd let himself into the house, she realised how good looking he was. Oh, she'd noticed the brown eyes and the way they crinkled at the corners and the streaky blond hair. She'd been aware of the intelligence and intense concentration his features could advertise. But he was still grinning at her and she was distracted enough from her patient to appreciate the way everything came together. And not just his face. He had a presence that she'd appreciated on a professional level. Now she was getting the full force of it on a very personal level. Was it so overpowering because he was so much bigger than she was?

No…everyone was pretty much taller than her when she could only boast five feet three inches in bare feet and he probably seemed broader because of the jacket he was still wearing but he gave the impression of a large man. A powerful man, yet she'd seen how skilful those hands had been, positioning the baby's head and fitting the mask to the tiny face. How carefully controlled and gentle his movements had been.

It felt like something was melting deep inside her belly.

He wasn't just incredibly good at his job. He'd done it with humour. With an ability to defuse a terrifying situation. With a confidence that had given them all the belief that they could do it and maybe that had been the reason why they had been able to do it.

Her smile felt odd. As if she was offering him something that she had never offered anyone before on such short acquaintance. Something that came straight from her heart.

'It's me who should be thanking you,' she whispered. 'I can't believe I told Dispatch that we only needed transport, not a SPRINT paramedic.'

'I was eavesdropping on the radio traffic. I'd just ordered a coffee not far away.' He grinned. 'Don't suppose it'll still be hot when I go back.'

'I owe you one, then.'

The crinkles appeared around his eyes again. 'Might just hold you to that.'

Were the butterflies dancing in Sophia's stomach

embarrassment? Did he think she was flirting with him? Suggesting a date, even?

If he did, he didn't seem put off. Or any less relaxed.

Maybe the butterflies were there for an entirely different reason. How long had it been since she'd met such an attractive man? One who had impressed her on so many levels?

Not in the last six months, that was for sure. Changing cities and throwing herself into a new job had left no time at all to think about expanding her social life to include men. She was only beginning to gather a new circle of girlfriends.

Not that this one would be interested, anyway. She could hear an echo of his voice. *Babies are my favourite thing...*

She could feel herself becoming tense. Trying to squeeze something tight enough to suffocate those damned butterflies.

Could he sense that, too? A flicker of something she couldn't identify passed across his face.

'Might be hard to call in the debt,' he said. 'When I don't even know your name.'

'Oh...' She hadn't introduced herself, had she? How rude was that? He'd have paperwork to fill in for this job. He would need more details about Claire as well. 'I'm Sophia,' she said. 'Sophia Toulson. I'm a midwife.'

His grin widened as an eyebrow lifted. 'I should hope so.'

The information about their patient she'd been gathering mentally to help him with his report evaporated as Sophia laughed.

Those cute eye wrinkles deepened and his eyes

danced. 'Come out with me,' he said softly. 'Sophia Toulson, midwife extraordinaire. Come out with me tonight. I'll take a beer instead of a coffee as payment of that debt.'

Sophia's smile died on her lips.

She wanted to say yes.

She really, *really* wanted to say yes, but she could feel her head beginning to roll from side to side.

'No… I can't… I…' The words followed her smile into oblivion. How could she possibly even begin to explain why she had to say no?

Not that Aiden seemed offended by the rejection. His shrug was casual. 'No worries. Maybe another night.'

And then there was a loud knock on a door outside the room. 'Ambulance,' the call came, along with the rattle of a stretcher's wheels.

The snatch of time was gone and Sophia realised that it would have been better spent starting the enormous amount of paperwork she needed to do to record everything that had happened during the emergency birth.

And then she caught Aiden's glance and, if the same thought had occurred to him, he didn't care—he was happy having spent that time doing exactly what they had been doing. And, suddenly, so was she.

Inexplicably happy, in fact, given that she'd denied herself the pleasure of spending more time in this man's company.

But he'd asked. And, for a blink of time, she'd considered saying yes.

That feeling of connection hadn't been one-sided and that, in itself, was something to feel happy about.

Wasn't it?

CHAPTER TWO

It must have been enough because that happiness stayed with her for the rest of her shift.

In fact, this was turning out to be the best day yet since Sophia had made such big changes in her life, leaving her home town of Canberra to shift to Melbourne.

Word had spread quickly through the Melbourne Maternity Unit about her successful management of an obstetrical emergency in the community. With its international reputation for excellence, the MMU attracted the best in the field but this case was earning her congratulations from every quarter.

Alessandro Manos, who headed the neonatal intensive care unit, had been the specialist called to check the baby and he'd been thorough.

'There's no sign of any complications from oxygen deprivation,' he told Sophia. 'He's a lucky little boy that you were there to manage the birth.'

She fastened the disposable nappy and reached for the soft sleep suit Claire had given her to bring up to the unit.

'It wasn't just me. I probably would have chosen to

try and delay the birth and get her in here if I hadn't had some expert paramedic assistance. He was…' Oh, yes…there was a definite extra buzz to be found in the satisfaction of a job well done. 'He was really amazing.'

'Who was?' Isla Delamere—Alessi's fiancée—had popped into the NICU. Her look suggested that the only amazing man around there was her husband-to-be.

'The paramedic who helped me through an acute cord prolapse this afternoon.'

'Oh, I heard about that. How's the baby?'

'Perfect.' Was Alessi referring to the baby he'd just checked? His gaze was resting adoringly on his wife as he spoke.

Sophia's smile had a poignant edge. They might have wanted to keep Isla's pregnancy secret for a bit longer but the news had slipped out and there was no way these two could hide how they felt about each other. They were so happy. And why wouldn't they be? They'd found love and were on the way to being a family.

That had been her own dream once.

People probably assumed it still was. That—like most women her age—she was simply waiting to find the right person to make that dream come true. Only her best friend, Emily, knew that there was no man on earth who could put the pieces of her dream back together.

That it had been permanently shattered.

Maybe it was just as well that the baby scrunched up his face and started crying at that moment.

'I'd better take this little guy back to his mum. She'll be missing him and he's hungry.'

'I'll come with you,' Isla said. 'I want to hear more about this paramedic. Was he hot? Single?'

Sophia shook her head as she wrapped the baby in a cotton blanket and picked him up. An image of those unusual brown eyes, somewhere between hazel and chocolate, flashed into her head. She could even see the crinkles in the corners—the smile that had seemed intimate because it was only intended for the person who had the eye contact.

'Hot enough, I guess,' she said lightly. 'But I doubt very much that he's single.' Liar, her mind whispered. He wouldn't have asked you out if he wasn't single. Her voice rose in pitch as it tightened. 'And even if he was, I wouldn't be interested.'

'Why not?' Loved up herself, Isla was keen for everybody to share her happiness. And maybe she'd picked up on the fact that Sophia was being less than truthful. 'Work is where most people find their partners, you know.'

'I'm not looking for a partner.' With the baby, who'd stopped crying for the moment, in her arms, Sophia led the way out of the ICU and headed towards the room where Claire had been taken for assessment. 'And I do go out. I'm going out tomorrow.' This was a good opportunity to change the subject. 'You're coming, aren't you? To the gardens?'

'For Em and Oliver's vow renewal ceremony?' Isla smiled. 'Of course. I wouldn't miss it. I think everybody from the MMU is going. It's the perfect way for everyone to move forward, isn't it?' she sighed, probably unaware of the way her hand touched her own belly so protectively. 'Em's very brave, isn't she?'

'She certainly is.' Sophia's arms tightened a little around the precious bundle she was carrying, jiggling him as he started grizzling again. They'd all known that Emily's foster-daughter would only have a short life but her death had been gutting. Only last week they'd all gathered in the children's section of Melbourne's botanical gardens to attend the memorial service for little Gretta. So many tears had been shed as the CEO of the Victoria Hospital—Charles Delamere—had spoken so beautifully about how Gretta's short life had touched the lives of so many others.

They'd all been clutching pink balloons that had been released into the sky at the end of the ceremony. The balloons had all held little packets of seeds—Kangaroo paws—all different colours. Apparently they had been Gretta's favourite and Emily had a vision of new plants growing all over Melbourne. It had been a beautiful ending to a very touching ceremony.

'The plan is that later anyone who can will head for the Rooftop for a drink.'

'I heard that. Did I tell you that Darcie's bringing Flick?'

'The midwifery student?'

'Yes. She's due to start shadowing you next week. We thought it would be a good way for her to get to know everyone a bit better. You don't think Emily will mind, do you?'

'It's an open invitation. We all know Em and Oliver and everyone's thrilled that they're back together. The sad bit's been dealt with and this is about the future. It should be a good party.'

'How formal is it?'

'Not at all. You can wear whatever you like. But I did talk Em into buying a new dress and getting her hair done so I don't plan to turn up in jeans myself.'

Emily Evans had been the first real friend that Sophia had made after moving to Melbourne. They'd clicked instantly and it had been Emily who had helped Sophia settle into her new job and home so happily. An evening with a few wines a couple of months into their friendship had sealed the bond when they'd realised how much they had in common. Their journeys may have been very different but the result was the same—they would never know the joy of holding their own newborn infants in their arms.

Had it been stupid to pick this career? Leaving Isla behind, Sophia had a few moments alone, holding Claire's baby boy. This was the part of her job she loved best. The weight of the tiny body that fitted so snugly against her chest. The joy in the mother's face as she handed it over. Watching a tiny mouth latch onto a breast for that first feed…

It was always there, though…that empty feeling in her own arms. The ache in the corner of her own heart.

Emily's journey had been slower. The hope had still been there for all those attempts at IVF and it must have turned to such joy when she'd finally carried a pregnancy almost to term. How devastating would it have been to experience the stillbirth of her son?

More devastating than it had been to wake from an

emergency surgery to be told that you'd not only lost your baby but that your uterus had had to be sacrificed to save your life? There would never be a transition period of chasing an IVF dream to lead to acceptance for Sophia. She'd only been twenty-one but her life had changed for ever that day.

But it hadn't been stupid to choose this career. Yes, she could have shut herself away from the emotional fall-out by choosing a nursing career that had nothing to do with babies or children, but that would have only made the ache worse in the long run and at least, this way, she got to share the joy every day of her life pretty much.

Love always came with some fine print about what you were risking but if you never took that risk, you shut yourself off from what life had to offer. Nobody had ever promised that life was easy and she'd seen more than her fair share of heartbreak in this job, but she'd seen far more people reaping the rewards of taking risks.

Look at Em. She'd chosen to love two children who weren't even hers, both with medical conditions. She'd been brave enough to risk the heartbreak she'd known was coming right from the start. Sophia had thought she was being brave, becoming a midwife and working with other people's babies every day, but, compared to Em, she was still hiding from life, wasn't she?

The next half-hour was happy enough to banish any personal reflections as Sophia spent time with Claire and Greg and the baby who now had a name—Isaac.

The first breastfeed was no drama and she left the happy parents preparing to go back home for their first night as a family.

Weaving through the busy, inner-city streets to get back to her small, terraced cottage when she finally signed off duty wasn't enough of a distraction, however. The ache was a little heavier today. Not just the empty ache of not having a baby to hold. There was the ache of not having a hand to hold. Having someone in her life who was her special person.

It wasn't that she wasn't making new friends here. Good friends. It was because she was essentially alone. She had no family nearby. Her best friend was back with her husband. Sophia had no one who was always available to share the highs and lows of life. And a best friend could never take the place of a life partner, anyway. She had no one to cuddle up to at night.

How stupid had she been, turning down that offer of a date with Aiden Harrison?

Why couldn't she be a bit braver?

If only she could turn the clock back to that moment. She could see those dancing eyes so clearly. A mix of attraction and humour and…confidence that she would say yes?

He hadn't been upset by her stuttering refusal, though, had he?

Maybe, by now, he was feeling relieved.

Oh, for heaven's sake. Sophia gave herself a mental shake. She needed to get over herself or she wouldn't be contributing anything positive at tomorrow's celebration. Maybe she needed to take a leaf out of Emily's book and convince herself that the risk of loving was always worthwhile.

Maybe she could even go down that track herself one day and think about fostering kids.

'It's only me.' Aiden let himself into the big house in Brunswick—his usual stop on his way home. 'Where is everyone? Nate?'

A dark head popped out from behind a nearby door. 'We'll be out in a sec, Aiden. The other boys are in the lounge.'

The lounge was a large room and, like all the other rooms in this converted house, it had polished wooden floors. Unlike most lounges, it had very little furniture, however, because the residents didn't need sofas or arm-chairs. The four young men who lived here were all quadriplegics who needed a high level of domestic and personal assistance. The youngest lad, Steve, was only eighteen. Nathan, at twenty-four, was the oldest.

Not that his younger brother intended to live here for long. This was a halfway step—a move towards the kind of independence he really wanted. At some point they were going to have to talk about it and maybe tonight would be a good time. While he hadn't said anything yet, Aiden was worried about the idea of Nate living independently. He himself had a demanding job and he wouldn't be able to drop everything and go and help his brother if something happened. At least here there were always carers on hand and it was a lot better than the residential home he'd been in for the last few years.

Or was the anxiety about the future more like a form of guilt? That he hadn't been able to care for his brother himself when the accident had happened because he'd only been a kid himself?

That it was his fault that the accident had happened in the first place?

That, if Nathan was capable of living in a normal house, he'd want it to be with *him* and then he'd have to take full responsibility. Oh, he'd have a carer to come in a couple of times a day to help with the transfers from bed to wheelchair and for the personal type care of showering and toileting, but what about the rest of the day? What would happen if Nate fell out of his chair or something and *he* was in the middle of a job like that obstetric emergency today?

He wanted his brother somewhere he was protected and surely this was as good as it got? This was like a regular blokes' flat, with a sports programme playing on its huge-screen television and guys sitting around, yelling approval at the goal that had just been scored.

And then he saw what they were watching. Murderball. The loud, fast and incredibly aggressive form of wheelchair rugby that Nate was currently passionate about. Two of the other guys in the house were part of a local team and Nate was desperate to make the grade. Physically, he certainly qualified.

Many people thought that quadriplegics—or tetraplegics—were always totally paralysed from the neck down but the repercussions of a cervical injury or illness were as individual as the people who suffered them and they were graded according to whether the impairment was complete or incomplete and by how much sensory and motor function remained.

With the C6 spinal injury Nate had received at the age of ten, he had little movement or sensation in his lower body. Thankfully, the injury had been incomplete so he still had a good range of movement in his upper body and better hand function than many. If he got his strength up, he'd probably be lethal on a Murderball court.

'Hey, Aiden. Wassup?'

'All good, Steve. How 'bout you?'

'This is our game from last week. Wanna watch?'

'Sure. Not for long, though. I promised Nate I'd take him out for a beer tonight.'

The young woman who'd greeted him came into the lounge. With her short, spiky black hair and facial piercings, Samantha was unlike any of the carers he'd come across in the years of Nate's care so far.

'He's out of the bathroom, Aiden. You can help him finish getting dressed if you want.'

Nathan's face lit up as Aiden went into his room.

'Hey, bro…' The hand held up for a fist bump took away any awkwardness of the height difference between the brothers and Nate's lack of hand strength. 'What do you call a quadriplegic on your doorstep?'

Aiden rolled his eyes. 'I thought you'd given up on the quadriplegic jokes.'

'Matt.' Nathan snorted with laughter and then pushed on one wheel of his chair to turn it towards a chest of drawers. 'What do you reckon? Leather jacket or the denim one?'

'Either's good. We're going to a garden bar but it's not cold out. Want a hand?'

'Nah...I'm good.'

Rather than watch Nate's struggle to put the jacket on unaided, Aiden looked around his brother's room. The poster collection was growing. Action shots of Murderball games, with wheelchairs crashing into each other and flipping sideways and the occupants only staying with them because they were strapped in.

He waved a hand at the posters. 'You could get really injured doing that stuff, you know.'

'Nah.' Nathan had one sleeve of his jacket on but it was taking a few attempts to get his other hand into a sleeve hole. 'A cracked rib or a squashed finger, maybe. Wouldn't be calling you out with any lights or sirens. Hey...any good jobs today?'

'Yeah... Last call was the best. This midwife was calling for transport to take a home birth in to the maternity unit in the Victoria because it had been going on too long. I overheard the call and decided to poke my nose in just because it was handy and things were quiet. Thought I'd just be waving the flag but the minute I walk in, the woman has a contraction and, *boof!* Umbilical cord prolapse and it's turned into an emergency.'

'Wow. What did you do?'

Aiden settled himself onto the end of Nathan's bed. This would need a few minutes because Nate always wanted a blow-by-blow account of every interesting job. If he'd been able-bodied, he would have been a paramedic himself, no question about it. You'd think he'd only be reminded of what he'd never be able to do by hearing about it but he never seemed to get enough of hearing about Aiden's professional exploits.

Or anything else about his big brother's life, come to that. He particularly loved to hear about the women he met and those he chose to date. What they looked like, where they'd gone on their dates and whether they'd stayed the night. He'd been careful how much he'd said about the midwife on today's job because Nate would have picked up on that pretty fast and, for some reason, Aiden hadn't wanted to answer the inevitable questions about how cute she was or whether she was single and, if so, why hadn't he asked her out yet?

Nate was so sure that someone was going to come along one day who would make him break his three-dates rule. Aiden was just as sure it would never happen.

If he couldn't take responsibility for his own brother's well-being, why the hell would he make himself responsible for anyone else? He didn't even own a dog, for heaven's sake, and he'd chosen a medical career where he generally never had to see his patients more than once.

Aiden Harrison was only too well aware of his limitations when it came to relationships and he'd found the perfect balance. Life was good. And it would continue to be good as long as Nathan didn't insist on putting himself at risk. Yes...tonight was the night for having a serious talk about the future.

'Let's go.' He matched the invitation with movement, standing up and opening the extra-wide door so that Nathan could manoeuvre his wheelchair into the hallway.

'Is it okay if Sam comes too?'

'Huh?'

'Samantha. You know...my carer? I asked her if she'd

like to come out and have a beer with us and she was keen. There's plenty of staff on tonight so it's no problem.'

'I…ah…' Was he going to be playing gooseberry while his brother was having a *date*?

Surely not.

But *why* not? He knew better than anyone that a disability didn't change who you were and his brother was an awesome guy. Why wouldn't a girl be smart enough to realise that? He had to admit it was a disturbing thought, though. What if Nathan fell in love and got his heart broken? Maybe a man-to-man talk about how well the three-dates rule worked needed to take priority over the talk about how risky independent living could be.

Not that either of those talks was going to happen tonight.

'Sure,' he heard himself saying, as though it was no big deal. 'There's plenty of room in the van. Maybe one of the other guys would like to come too.'

'Nope.' Nathan scooted through the door ahead of him. 'I only invited Sam.'

They were in a very different part of the botanical gardens this time. The guests crowded around the couple who were standing beneath the wrought-iron archway on the steps to the Temple of the Winds. The greenery of overhanging trees shaded them from the hot sun of a stunning autumn afternoon and once again Charles Delamere was in place as the master of ceremonies

'Ten years ago,' he told them, 'Emily and Oliver made their wedding vows. Circumstances, grief, life drove them apart but when the time was right fate brought them together again. They've decided to renew their vows, and they've also decided that here, in the gardens that are—and have been—loved by the whole family, is the place they'd like to do it.'

Emily and Oliver exchanged a look that was tender enough to bring a lump to Sophia's throat. She glanced over at Toby, Em's foster son, who was being held by Em's mother, Adrianna. This was a real family affair.

There had been so many tears at Gretta's farewell in the children's playground and there were probably just as many as the couple exchanged heartfelt vows, declaring their love and promising their commitment, but there was real joy this time. An affirmation that the risk of truly loving was worthwhile.

It was contagious, that hope. Maybe there was someone out there for her, Sophia thought. Someone who could see past the fact that she could never give him children of his own. Maybe she could find what Emily and Oliver had. How good would that be?

Something would have to change, though, if she was going to become as brave as Emily. Not that she knew quite what that something was but she was definitely going to give it some serious thought.

And, in the meantime, she could celebrate her friend's happiness. The Rooftop Bar was a good place to be on a sunny Saturday afternoon. Adrianna took little Toby home after a short time but told Oliver and Emily to stay and celebrate with all their friends. She would sort the final packing that was needed before they all went on their family honeymoon to the Great Barrier Reef the next day.

As often happened, the men gravitated together at one point and Sophia found herself sitting with a group of the women she knew best around a deliciously shaded table. Right beside Emily, she impulsively gave her friend another hug.

'I'm just so happy for you, Em. For you and Oliver. You so deserve every bit of this happiness.'

'It'll be your turn next.' Emily's smile was radiant. 'I'm sure of it.'

Isla overheard the comment. She was smiling as she refilled Sophia's glass with champagne. 'Good timing that she's met that hot paramedic, then, isn't it?'

'What?' Emily's jaw dropped. 'How come I haven't heard about this? Who is he?'

'Nobody,' Sophia muttered. 'Just a guy that turned up for that cord prolapse job yesterday.'

'And he's gorgeous,' Isla added. 'Soph said so.'

'I said he was good at his job, that's all.'

'She couldn't stop talking about him.' Darcie Green had joined them. 'I can vouch for that.'

Emily's sideways glance was significant. 'Just remember what I told you,' she said, raising her glass. 'You don't have to marry the guy. Just get out there and have some fun.'

'Why shouldn't she marry the guy?' Isla asked, between sips of her tall glass of soda water. 'Have you got something against marriage, Soph?'

'Not at all. I'm thrilled for Oliver and Em. And for you and Alessi. And…' Sophia glanced around the table, trying to distract the focus of attention. 'And what's going on with you and Lucas, Darcie? I'm sure I wasn't the only one to notice the sparks flying at the ball.'

Lucas was the super-hot senior midwife at the MMU and, while the husbands of the women about to give birth were less than impressed with his popularity, there was no shortage of expectant mums keen to become his patients. No shortage of women in Melbourne just as keen to fill another potential role in his life either.

Darcie was an English obstetrician, on secondment to the MMR. She was dedicated to her job and professional enough to have made several people sharpen up at work. Lucas didn't seem to be in that number, however, and the antagonism between them had been noted on the grapevine, but the obvious sparks at the ball had not come across as being between two people who didn't like each other. Not at all.

Not that Darcie was about to admit anything. She shrugged. 'We all had a good time at the ball,' she said, carefully avoiding eye contact with any of the other women. 'But if there was anything serious going on, I'd say it was between Flick, here, and Tristan.'

There was a murmur of agreement amongst the women and more than one knowing smile accompanying the nods.

'I'm sure I wasn't the only one to see you two leaving together,' Darcie continued lightly. 'Just what time *did* you get home, young woman?'

Felicia Lawrence, the student midwife, turned bright red. For an awful moment, Sophia was sure she was about to burst into tears.

Whatever had happened that night was really none of their business. Sophia needed to give her an escape route.

'So you two aren't dating or anything interesting like that, then?'

Flick shook her head with more emphasis than was needed. 'I'm not remotely interested in dating,' she claimed. 'My career's the only important thing in my life right now. Like Sophia.'

'I didn't say I wasn't *interested* in dating.' Sophia eyed her glass of champagne suspiciously. Had she had too much? 'I just…haven't met anybody. It takes time, you know—when you move to a new city.'

'But you've met the hot paramedic now.' Darcie was smiling. 'What was his name? Andy?'

'Aiden.' It seemed to be Sophia's turn to blush now. She could feel the warmth in her cheeks as she said his name aloud. 'Aiden Harrison.'

'Is he single? Did he ask for your number?'

'No.' She bit her lip. 'He did ask me for a date, though.'

'And you said *no*? What were you thinking?'

Darcie and Flick seemed very relieved to have the spotlight turned onto someone else's love life and, for Flick's sake, Sophia was happy enough to take centre stage.

'I'm not sure,' she admitted. 'Maybe I thought he was just being nice. I'd said I owed him a coffee because he'd had to abandon one to come to the job. He said he'd take a beer instead. It seemed—I don't know—a bit of a joke, maybe?'

'Nonsense,' the women chorused. She was gorgeous,

they assured her. Intelligent. Fun. Any guy would have to be crazy not to be genuinely interested.

Emily caught her glance in a private moment. She was the only one who might understand that moment of panic. That dip into a whirl of thoughts that had been spinning for so many years now. The issue of meeting someone you really liked and then agonising over when to tell them. On the first date? Did you say something like, 'Yeah, I'd love to go out with you but you should know that if you want to have kids some time in the future then I'm not the woman for you'? Or did you wait until things got serious and then field the repercussions of someone feeling a bit cheated? Deceived, even.

Yes. Emily's glance was sympathetic. But there was something else there, too. Encouragement?

'What does it matter if it did start out as a bit of a joke?' she said. 'Isn't the whole idea to have fun? To let your hair down a bit and enjoy the best of what life has to offer that doesn't have anything to do with work? It doesn't ever have to be anything serious.'

You don't have to marry the guy. Was that code for 'You don't have to even tell him'?

'How many guys do we know who have no intention of getting serious?' she added. 'They're just out to have fun. We could learn something from those guys.'

'Like Alessi.' Darcie nodded. 'Oops...sorry, Isla, but he was a terrible flirt and nobody lasted more than one night. Until you, of course...'

'Not a good example,' Emily chided. 'But you're right. Soph could use a bit of that attitude and just get out there and enjoy herself with some attractive male company.'

Sophia found herself nodding. And hadn't she just made a silent vow that very afternoon that something needed to change in her life? Maybe she wouldn't have to give too much thought to what that something was.

'Maybe I will,' she said aloud. 'Not that there's anyone around who's offering the company.'

'The hot paramedic did. You're probably putting anyone off asking by sending out *I'm not available* vibes. Change your attitude and they'll be around in droves. You might even meet *him* again.'

Sophia laughed. 'I don't think so.' But she reached for her glass of champagne, feeling lighter in spirit than she had for a long time. 'But, hey…I'll give it a go. The next time I get asked out—especially if it's the hot paramedic—I'll say yes.'

'Promise?' Emily raised her glass to clink it against Sophie's. The other women followed her example and the glasses met in a circle over the centre of the table.

'I promise,' Sophie said.

CHAPTER THREE

HE HAD THE best job in the world, no doubt about it.

Aiden was rolling slowly, the red and blue lights on his handlebars flashing as he eased through the crowds on Southbank. The wide, paved area on the south side of the Yarra River offered spectacular views of the river and city from cafés, restaurants and upmarket hotels.

The gorgeous autumn afternoon had tourists and locals enjoying the exercise, food and entertainment. A juggler had attracted a good crowd and so had an old aboriginal man playing a didgeridoo. Aiden could hear the hollow, haunting notes of the music over the bike's engine. He angled his path to avoid smudging the work of a street artist who was working with chalk and then he could see his destination. Another huddle of people, but they weren't there for entertainment. He'd been called to a woman who'd collapsed on one of the riverside benches beneath the trees.

'I've put her in the recovery position,' a man told Aiden as soon as he'd propped the bike up on its stand. 'I did a first-aid course last year.'

'Good work.' He flipped up the chinguard of his helmet. 'Did anyone see what happened?'

'She was walking around, looking weird,' someone else offered. 'Like she was drunk. And then she sat down and just toppled sideways.'

Aiden had reached the unconscious woman. He stripped off his gloves, tilted her head to make sure her airway was open and then felt for a pulse in her neck. It was there. Rapid and faint enough to suggest low blood pressure. Her skin felt cool and clammy. He shook her shoulder.

'Hello? Can you hear me? Open your eyes, love.'

No response. Aiden looked up. 'Does anyone know this woman? Was she with someone?'

There was a general sound of denial and shaking of heads. Aiden checked for a MedicAlert bracelet or necklace as he ran through the possible causes of unconsciousness in his head. He couldn't smell any alcohol and there was no sign of any head trauma. The woman was young, probably in her early thirties. This could be due to epilepsy or drugs or diabetes. At least he could eliminate one of the possible causes easily. Unrolling a kit, he took a small lancet, pricked the woman's finger and eased the drop of blood onto a testing strip for a glucometer. He also reached for his radio to give Dispatch an update. Whatever was going on, here, this young woman would need transport to hospital.

The glucometer beeped and it was a relief to see that the reading was low. Hypoglycaemia certainly fitted with the limited information he'd been given of her appearing drunk and then collapsing. It also fitted the physical signs of the clammy skin, rapid heart rate and a low blood pressure. Back-up was on the way but it would take time to get a stretcher through the crowds from the nearest point an ambulance could park and Aiden had everything he needed to start treatment.

IV access was the first priority and there were plenty of willing hands to hold up the bag with the glucose infusion. He got the small cardiac monitor out of one of the panniers on the back of his bike as well. It had only been a few days ago that he'd read an interesting article suggesting that sudden death in young diabetics could be due to cardiac problems from electrolyte disturbances.

The glucose infusion was working its magic well before he started attaching electrodes. The young woman opened her eyes, blinked a couple of times and then groaned.

'Oh, no…it happened again, didn't it?'

'I'm Aiden, a paramedic. What's your name, love?'

'Hayley. I…' She looked up at the crowd of onlookers. 'Oh…God…this is so embarrassing.'

'You're diabetic?'

'Yeah…I knew I needed to eat. That's why I came along here. I was heading for the food court in Southgate. It came on so suddenly…'

Aiden could see an ambulance crew manoeuvring a stretcher through the crowd. More people were stopping to stare, wondering what was going on. No wonder the poor girl was embarrassed. The sooner they got her into the privacy of the back of an ambulance, the better.

Checking her blood-glucose levels again could wait until then as well. Aiden kick-started his bike and followed the crew, until he could park beside the ambulance. He needed to fill in his paperwork and he had a feeling that Hayley was not going to be keen to be taken to hospital.

'I don't need to go,' she insisted a few minutes later. 'I feel fine now.'

'When was the last time you had a hypo?'

'A couple of weeks ago,' she admitted reluctantly. 'But before that, it hadn't happened for ages. Over a year.'

'That means your control is becoming more challenging. You need a reassessment.'

'I'll go to my doctor. Soon.'

'It could happen again today.'

'I'll eat. I'll go and get a sandwich right now.'

It took time to persuade Hayley that it would be a good idea to go the emergency department at the Victoria but none of the paramedics were happy to let her go when she didn't have someone with her to monitor her condition. And Aiden had something else that was bothering him.

'Have you thought of wearing a MedicAlert bracelet?'

Hayley made a face. 'It's bad enough having to live with something like this, without advertising it. And have you any idea how much harder it makes it to find a job? People look at you like you've got a disability or something.'

Her words stayed with Aiden as he watched the ambulance take his patient away. He stayed where he was, astride his bike, watching the mill of the people he could still see on Southbank. This wasn't a bad place to park up until he got another call. Central city and covering a patch well away from the nearest ambulance station. A young man in a wheelchair went past amongst the crowd.

There was a disability that couldn't be disguised. And he knew what it was like to attract the intrusive attention of people who felt they had the right to ask personal questions. They'd often been directed at him over the years—as if Nathan's brain didn't work any better than his legs did.

'Why's he in a wheelchair, then?'

'Oh, the poor boy. Can he feed himself?'

'How does he go to the toilet?'

The guilt was always there, welded onto his soul, and the curiosity of strangers turned the screws painfully for Aiden, but Nathan had developed a resilience in his teenage years that had astounded him. He could deal with any situation now with a humour that often shocked the nosy people. Like those awful jokes he kept adding to.

'What do you call a quadriplegic under your car? Jack.'

Despite himself, Aiden found his lips quirking. What did it matter what other people thought? Nathan had it sorted. He was happy. In fact, he was happier than he'd ever been right now. The way he'd been looking at Sam the other night… Was something going on already and, if so, how badly could that end? He needed to have a serious talk with his younger brother. Try and get him prepared for something that would hurt more than public scrutiny or pity.

His radio crackled into life.

'Code One,' Dispatch told him, giving him an address

not far away. 'Twenty-four-year-old female with severe abdominal pain.'

'Copy that.' Aiden tilted the bike off its stand and kicked it into life. He activated the lights and then the siren. Traffic was building up but he'd be able to weave through it fast. He loved a code one response and the freedom it allowed. With a bike, he got way more freedom than an ambulance to break a speed limit or use the tramlines. He just had to be a bit more careful. Hitting tram lines at the wrong angle and the ambulance would have to stop for him instead of getting to the job.

It took less than four minutes to arrive on scene. Another thirty seconds and he was in the room with the young woman who was bent over a chair and groaning loudly.

'It's the fish I had last night. Ohhh…. It *really* hurts and I've been sick.'

Aiden blinked. Dispatch hadn't bothered mentioning that his patient was pregnant.

'How far along are you?'

'Thirty-seven weeks.'

'And how far apart are the pains you're getting?'

'I dunno. It's happening every five or ten minutes, I guess. But I'm not in labour. It's that fish… I knew I shouldn't be eating prawns.'

It took very little time to convince his patient that this was, indeed, labour.

'I'm not going to hospital. I'm having a home birth. Can you call my midwife?'

'Sure. What's her name?'

'Sophia Toulson. Her card's on the fridge.'

The phone in his hand seconds later, Aiden found himself smiling again. It was surprising how strong the hope was that Sophia would be available and able to get here fast.

For his patient's benefit, of course...

Flick was excited. This was the first home birth she had been to since starting to shadow Sophia.

'But what if something goes wrong? Like a post-partum haemorrhage or something?'

'We call for back-up. The Melbourne ambulance service is fabulous. And we're not far from the hospital. In most cases, if there's going to be trouble, we get enough warning.'

'You didn't the other day, with that cord prolapse, did you?'

'No.'

And her pager hadn't warned her that the paramedic on scene had been riding a motorbike. She could see it parked outside Gemma's house.

'Nice bike,' Flick murmured.

'Mmm.'

Those butterflies were dancing in her stomach again. How many SPRINT paramedics rode bikes in the city? It didn't mean that she was about to have another encounter with the man her friends were all now referring to as 'the hot paramedic'.

Except it appeared that she was.

'Hey...' Aiden Harrison was grinning. 'We've got to stop meeting like this. Rumours will start.'

Flick gave a huff of laughter and Sophia gave her

a warning glance before letting her gaze shift back to Aiden, her lips curling into a smile.

'You did say that babies were your favourite thing but you don't have to take over my job, you know.' She moved past him. 'Why didn't you call me when the pains started, Gemma?'

'I didn't think it was labour. I thought I had some dodgy prawns last night because I started getting cramps just after I'd eaten. They went away for a while this morning and then one was so painful I screamed and my neighbour called the ambulance.'

'Contractions are four to five minutes apart,' Aiden told her. 'Lasting about ninety seconds. Vital signs all good. Gemma's been happy to keep walking around.'

'Let's get you on your bed for a minute,' Sophia said. 'I want to check how baby's doing and what stage of dilatation you're at. This is Flick, by the way. Our student midwife. Are you happy to have her assisting? It's very valuable experience for her if she can be hands-on.'

Gemma nodded as she let Sophia guide her towards the bedroom.

'I can stay until I get another call,' Aiden said. 'Unless I'm in the way.'

It was entirely unprofessional to get distracted by noticing how much she didn't want him to disappear. Even worse to take another look at him and find it so hard to look away. Those eyes were just as warm and interesting as she'd remembered, and that smile made it impossible not to smile back.

Oh…help. How long had they been staring at each

other? Long enough for Flick and Gemma to exchange a surprised glance and then a complicit grin.

'It's fine by me if you stay,' Gemma said. *You know you want to*, her tone suggested. 'My mum's on her way but I told her not to hurry. This is going to take ages, isn't it?'

'Let's find out. Flick, get some gloves on and you can examine Gemma and find out what her stage of dilatation is.'

Keeping her voice low, it was possible to use this opportunity as a teaching and practical experience session for Flick.

'Tell me how you'll make the assessment.'

'At two centimetres I'll be able to fit one finger loosely through the cervix but not two fingers. Two fingers will be loose at four centimetres. There's two centimetres of cervix palpable on both sides at six centimetres, one at eight and there's only an anterior lip or a bit left laterally at nine centimetres.'

'And what are you feeling?'

'Nothing.' Flick's eyes widened. 'I can't feel any cervix at all. Am I doing something wrong?'

Sophia smiled as she double-checked Flick's findings, shaking her head at her student, who had been correct in her evaluation. 'You're fully dilated, Gemma,' she told their patient. 'Let's check the baby's position and then get set up. What do you need to do now, Flick?'

'The four Leopold's manoeuvres. First one checks the upper abdomen to make sure it's the baby's buttocks and not the head and then the umbilical area to locate the baby's back and—'

'Can I go to the bathroom first?' Gemma pleaded. 'I really need to go.'

Aiden helped Flick set up for the birth while Sophia stayed close to Gemma. They spread waterproof sheets over the bed and one of the armchairs in the living room and gathered some clean towels. Flick opened a kit and checked the resuscitation gear they carried in case it would be needed.

Aiden found himself glancing frequently at the door, waiting for the reappearance of Sophia and Gemma.

The attraction he'd felt the first time he'd met the cute little midwife had come back with a vengeance. Those lovely brown eyes were so warm and that smile made him feel like he'd just done something outstanding. Something that deserved approval because he'd somehow made the world a better place.

Heck…all he'd done was crack a fairly weak joke. Imagine how Sophia would look at him if he really did something to be proud of.

He wasn't going to let his opportunity slip past. He might have made a note of the number he'd used to call her but that was just her pager service. He was going to ask for her personal number as soon as he got the chance—as long as he didn't get called away first. Who knew how long this labour might take? Gemma was taking long enough just to go to the loo.

And she was being noisy about it, too. They heard a cry of pain. And then another.

And then Sophia's calm voice. 'Could you bring a couple of towels, please, Flick? Lean on me, Gemma…

Yes, that's your baby's head you can feel. Deep breath and give me one good push…'

The wail of a healthy newborn could be heard a moment later and Aiden moved to peer in the bathroom door at the crowded scene. Gemma was still sitting on the toilet and Sophia was guiding her hands to help her hold the slippery baby against her skin. Gemma was sobbing and Sophia looked…as if she was blinking back tears?

'She's gorgeous, Gemma. A dear wee girl… Flick, have you got the clamps and scissors? Gemma, would you like to cut the cord?'

'No…' Gemma shook her head.

Somehow, Aiden had moved further into the small space without noticing and he was now blocking Flick's access to the toilet. Some signal passed between Sophia and her student and Aiden found himself holding the clamps in his gloved hands. He attached one a few inches away from the baby and then another to leave an isolated area to cut. He'd done this before and knew to expect how tough it was to cut through the umbilical cord.

He already felt involved in this birthing scene but then Sophia smiled at him again.

'Can we give baby to Aiden for just a minute, Gemma? I'd like to get you cleaned up and comfortable in bed to wait for the placenta.'

Flick gave him a clean towel and Aiden carefully took charge of the tiny infant, with Sophia's assistance. This was the closest he'd been to her and he could smell the fragrance of her hair. Almost feel the warmth of her skin through the gloves as their hands brushed. And then he looked at the tiny scrunched-up face of the baby and got completely distracted.

The miracle of birth never failed to amaze him but he never wanted the responsibility of one of these himself. The enormity of bringing a new person into the world and trying to keep them safe for ever was overwhelming. As he backed away, carrying the precious burden in his arms, he looked up to find Sophia watching him.

He couldn't read the expression in her face but it struck him as poignant and something inside his chest squeezed hard. But then it was gone. She smiled and turned back to her patient.

'Put your arm around my shoulders and we'll take this slowly. You might find your legs are pretty shaky.'

The five-minute Apgar score was a perfect ten and Aiden returned the pink, vigorously crying infant to his mother. There was no reason for him to stay on the job any longer and watch as Sophia guided Flick to help the baby latch onto Gemma's nipple and begin its first breastfeed.

And then Sophia supervised Flick in attending to the delivery of the placenta and checking it for any damage, and it really was time for him to leave. He stripped off his gloves and picked up his helmet and kit.

Flick was giving Gemma a wash with a hot, soapy cloth and Sophia was putting the placenta into a bag. This was it—the best opportunity he was going to get. He stepped closer.

'I know you were busy last time I asked,' he said

casually. 'But are you doing anything special after work today?'

Wide, surprised brown eyes met his gaze. 'Not really,' she said, 'but I won't finish for a while. We usually spend a few hours with a new mother and make sure she's happy before we go.'

'Maybe we could meet up later, then?'

Gemma looked up from watching her baby suckle. 'Are you asking Sophia for a date?' She grinned.

Flick was staring at Sophia and seemed to be stifling laughter. What was going on here?

Sophia tied the bag and stripped off her gloves. Her cheeks had a rosy glow and she seemed to be carefully avoiding meeting his gaze. 'It's not about a date,' she said. 'I happen to owe Aiden a coffee, that's all.'

She made it sound like that was the only reason he might be interested in taking her out. Aiden couldn't let that pass.

'Yeah…' he said slowly. 'I'm asking for a date. Would you like to come out with me this evening, Sophia?'

'Um… I…' Sophia bit her lip. 'Maybe you can call me later. We're both at work and this isn't, you know, very professional.'

'I don't mind,' Gemma said.

'And I'm not going to tell anybody,' Flick added. She looked as if she was trying not to smile. 'Was that a *yes* I heard there, Soph?'

There was definitely an undercurrent here that Aiden had no way of interpreting but right then Sophia met his gaze again and he didn't care about anything other than hearing her say that word.

'Okay. Yes.' He could see her chest rise as she took a deep breath. 'I'd love to go on a date with you, Aiden.'

'Cool. I'll pick you up about seven? Where do you live?'

'How 'bout I meet you somewhere? A nice bar, maybe?'

So she didn't want him to know where she lived? No problem. When you had a three-dates rule, it was probably better not to intrude too far on anyone's personal space. Aiden named a trendy bar that he knew wasn't too far from the Victoria, guessing that Sophia probably lived reasonably close to where she worked.

'I know it.' She nodded. 'I'll meet you there at seven.'

At six-thirty p.m. Sophia was staring at the pile of clothes on her bed.

It might be a cliché but she really *didn't* have anything to wear. Nothing that would project the image she wanted anyway, which was one of a confident young woman who wasn't the least bit desperate. Who was happy to go out and have a bit of fun but wasn't looking for anything remotely serious.

Something frilly? She didn't possess frills. Something low-cut that would show a bit of cleavage? No. That might send entirely the wrong message about the kind of fun she was after.

What *was* she after? And why was she feeling so ridiculously nervous?

'Oh, for heaven's sake.' Wearing only her jeans and bra, Sophia went to rummage in her handbag for her phone. She would text Aiden and tell him she couldn't make it after all. One of her patients had gone into early labour? Yeah…perfect excuse.

And she wasn't really breaking her promise, was she? She had said yes. She just wasn't going to follow through and actually *go* on the date.

A small problem became apparent the moment she picked up her phone. She didn't have Aiden's phone number, did she?

She had absolutely no way of contacting him unless she fronted up at the bar in…oh, help…twenty minutes.

But there was a message on *her* phone. For a hopeful heartbeat Sophia thought that Aiden might have sent her a message to cancel the date.

No such luck. He didn't have her number either, did he?

The message was from Emily. 'I hear you said yes,' it said. 'You go, girl. And have fun.'

So Flick had spread the word. Her friends would demand details and she was a hopeless liar. Her voice always got sort of tight and high. She'd never be able to make something up and sound convincing.

Gritting her teeth, Sophia marched back into her bedroom. She jammed her feet into knee-high boots, threw on a camisole top and covered it with a velvet jacket. Pulling the band from her hair, she raked her fingers through the shoulder-length waves and spent no more than thirty seconds in front of the mirror, putting on a slick of lipstick.

Then she grabbed her bag and slammed the door of the cottage behind her. She had less than ten minutes to get to the bar but having to rush was probably a good thing. It would give her less time for her stupid nerves to grow wings.

There was no sign of Sophia.

Aiden ordered a beer and stayed at the bar, an elbow propped and his posture relaxed enough to suggest he was thoroughly enjoying his view of the women coming in through the doors. Enjoying the appreciative looks he got in return even more.

Normally, he would be doing exactly that.

So why did he feel…good grief…*nervous*?

A little out of control even?

Maybe it was because he was meeting Sophia here, instead of having picked her up first. What if she didn't show up?

Hey…no problem. There were plenty of very attractive women who seemed to be here unaccompanied by any male friends.

But he hadn't come here to randomly score. He'd come here because he really wanted to spend some time with Sophia.

And maybe the strength of that want was why he was feeling a bit weird. Why this was assuming an importance that it wasn't allowed to have.

No problem. Aiden took another fortifying swallow of his beer. This was only a number-one date. No big deal. If it continued to feel weird, he could just pull the plug and there wouldn't be a number two.

Suddenly, he saw her. Looking small and a little bit lost as she stood near the door and scanned the crowded bar. And then she spotted him and smiled.

The noise of the people around him and the background music seemed to fade away.

The people themselves seemed to fade away. Until there was only himself.

And Sophia.

How weird was *that*?

CHAPTER FOUR

HE WAS THERE.

He must have spotted her the moment she walked through the door because he was already looking straight at her when Sophia turned her head. She'd been worried she might not even recognise him out of uniform but even in a crowd of people there was no mistaking Aiden Harrison.

Her relieved smile faded as she threaded her way to the bar, however. He hadn't smiled back. He'd looked a bit stunned even... Had he been surprised that she'd actually turned up? Or maybe he was disappointed that she had. There was no shortage of opportunities in a place like this. She could feel the gaze of other girls on her as she made her way towards the gorgeous guy standing alone at the bar. Envious glances.

'Hi...' He was smiling now. 'Can I get you something to drink?'

'A white wine would be lovely, thank you.'

'Do you want to have it here or find a table out in the garden? They have live music here tonight so there won't be any room to move in here soon.'

So she'd end up dancing or squashed against him at the bar? Sophia sucked in a breath. 'The garden sounds great.'

There were rustic tables and wrought-iron chairs, flickering candles and the greenery of a rampant grape-vine on an overhead pergola. The last unoccupied table they found in a corner with only two chairs was roman-tic enough to make Sophia hesitate. This was supposed to be fun. Nothing serious.

Aiden put their drinks down on the table. 'Don't know about you,' he said, 'but I'm *starving*. Fancy some nachos or a big bowl of fries?'

That was the right note to hit. They were here for a drink and something to eat and it just happened to be with company. They'd be able to hear the music out here without being deafened. A fun night out.

'Sure. Nachos are my absolute favourite.'

'Mine, too.'

They grinned at each other. They were on the same page and suddenly everything seemed easy. Over the cheese and bean-laden tortilla chips, the conversation was just as relaxed.

'It must be a great job, being a SPRINT paramedic.'

'Best job in the world. I love having no idea of what's coming next or where I'm going.'

'I love being out of the hospital environment most of the time, too. You get to connect a lot more with pa-tients when you're in their own home. Even more when they've had a home delivery. I feel like part of the fam-ily sometimes.'

But Aiden shook his head at that. 'It's the opposite

that appeals to me. I get to ride in, do the exciting stuff and then hand the responsibility on to someone else.'

'Don't you ever follow your patients up and see what happened?'

'I'll talk to the crew that transports them. Or, if I've travelled in with them, I might hang around in the emergency department and see how it's handled from there. Some of the docs are great. If I'm ending a shift, they let me go into Theatre or talk over the results of a CT scan or something. If I can learn something that's going to help me manage better next time, I'm in.'

'You should poke your nose into the MMU some time. You're a bit of a hero up there after that cord pro-lapse job the other day.'

Aiden shook off the compliment. 'We were lucky.' He raised his eyebrows. 'How's that baby doing? Do you know?'

Sophia laughed. 'Of course I know. I'm still doing daily visits. His name is Isaac and he's doing extremely well. Claire and Greg are over the moon.'

'Good to know. Did he get a thorough neurological check?'

It was Sophia's turn to raise her eyebrows. 'Are you kidding? We've got the best doctors there are. He passed every test with flying colours. He might turn out to be a brain surgeon himself one day. Or the prime minister or something. You'll see him on television and think about what might have happened if you hadn't been there the day he was born.'

'I might have a bit of trouble recognising him.' But Aiden was smiling and Sophia felt...relieved? He did

have a connection with his patients that wasn't purely
technical. Maybe he didn't want to revel in that connection like she did but it was there—whether he wanted
it to be or not.

And the idea of him being a maverick medic who
rode around the city saving lives and touching those
lives only briefly added to his attraction, didn't it? Gave
him a kind of superhero edge?

Oh, yeah…the attraction was growing for sure and
it didn't seem to be one-sided. Eye contact was becoming more frequent and held for a heartbeat longer. Their
fingers brushed as they shared the platter of food. The
butterflies in Sophia's gut danced up a storm as she
wondered if he would kiss her at the end of this date.

But then what?

She could hear an echo of Em's voice in the back of
her mind. *You don't have to marry the guy. You don't
even have to tell him anything. Just have fun…*

Maybe the connection was even stronger than it felt.
She could see a flicker in Aiden's eyes that had nothing
to do with the candles around them.

'I should warn you,' he said, 'that I'm not looking for
anything serious.'

Good grief…was that shaft of sensation disappointment? Or shame even? Was there something about her
that wasn't attractive enough to warrant any kind of
emotional investment?

His smile suggested otherwise. So did the way his
hand covered hers, touching her skin with the lightness
of a feather—the fingers moving just enough to sound
a deliciously seductive note.

'It's not that you're not absolutely gorgeous,' he murmured. 'But I have rules. One rule, anyway.'

'Oh?' This was confusing. His words were warning her off but his eyes and his touch were inviting her closer. Much closer.

'A three-dates rule.'

'A…*what*?'

'Three dates. I've discovered that's the perfect number.'

'Perfect for what?'

'To get to know someone. To have fun but not to let anything get out of hand. You know…to get…*serious*.'

He made the word sound like some kind of notifiable disease. Sophia's head was spinning. Wasn't this exactly what she was looking for? Fun with a gorgeous guy but within limits. Limits that would mean there was no need to tell him anything about herself that could impinge on the fun. She could pretend there was nothing wrong with her. That she was as desirable as any other young woman who was out there dating. That it was only because of 'the rule' that it wouldn't go any further.

'I love it,' she whispered with a smile.

'Really?' Aiden's eyebrows shot up. His fingers tightened over her hand.

'Really.' Sophia nodded. 'I'm not looking for anything serious either. Three dates sounds like exactly the rule that's been missing from *my* life.'

'Wow…' Aiden's gaze was frankly admiring. 'You're even more amazing than I thought.' He stood up, still holding Sophia's hand, so that she was drawn to her feet as well. 'You do realise that means we'll have to make the most of each and every date, don't you?'

The butterflies had congregated into a cluster that throbbed somewhere deep in Sophia's belly like a drumbeat. She couldn't look away from Aiden's gaze, even when he dropped her hand and raised his to touch her face. A finger on her temple that traced a gentle line around her eye, across her cheek and down to the corner of her mouth. Her lips parted in astonishment at the wave of sensation the touch was creating and it was then that Aiden dipped his head and kissed her.

Right there—in a noisy, crowded garden of a trendy bar. Their corner was secluded enough but it was a long way from being private. Not that the kiss got out of hand or anything. The control of those soft, questioning lips on hers suggested that Aiden was a very experienced kisser. The teasing touch of his tongue hinted at where this kiss could go at any moment. Oh, yeah…it ended far sooner than Sophia would have chosen.

What now?

Would Aiden take her home to his place? Should she suggest that he came to hers?

On a *first* date?

The idea was shocking. Okay, she was doing this to have fun but jumping into bed with someone this fast made it feel wrong. But they only had three dates to play with, didn't they? Did 'making the most of them' imply that they shouldn't waste any time?

But Aiden was smiling again and Sophia had the feeling that he knew the argument she was having with herself.

'Let's plan date number two,' he said. 'And give ourselves something to look forward to.'

'So…how was it, then?'

'What?'

'Date *numero uno* with the cute midwife?'

Aiden shrugged as he looked away from his brother to stare over the veranda railings into the garden of the old house. He upended his bottle to catch a mouthful of his beer. 'Not bad.'

'Score?'

Aiden frowned. Nate loved to hear about his love life as much as his job and he'd always been happy to share the details. He couldn't remember who had come up with the scoring system but it had become a tradition. This was the first time it had occurred to Aiden how degrading it would seem if the women he dated ever knew about it.

Not that he would ever tell them, of course.

But he'd never told any women about the three-dates rule until now, had he? It was a secret, known only to himself and Nate. The astonishment factor of actually sharing the secret with a woman he was on a date with was only surpassed by the totally unexpected way Sophia had embraced the idea.

What was with that? Was there something about him that didn't make him attractive longer term?

The thought shouldn't be disturbing but it was. So was the niggle of doubt that he'd come right out and put a limit on how much time he was going to have with the gorgeous Sophia. How the stupidity of that move had been plaguing him ever since he'd left her at the end of their date with no more than another kiss.

She was…

'That good, huh?' He could hear the grin in Nate's voice. 'Off the scale, was she?'

Aiden merely grunted.

She was perfect, that's what she was. Absolutely gorgeous. Smart. So easy to talk to. And that all too brief taste of her lips…

Man… The way she'd felt in his arms. The way she'd responded to his kisses. He had a fair idea of exactly where their second date was going to end up and he couldn't wait. How, in fact, would he be able to enjoy the day on the beach they now had planned for when their next days off coincided? He would be hanging out to get her somewhere a lot more private. Somewhere they could *really* get to know each other.

But that would mean there was only one date left. And then what?

This had never bothered him before. He'd never even thought ahead like this before.

'Could be the one, then.' Nate was nodding. 'A four-dates woman.'

'No way.'

'Why not?'

'Because I'm not getting into anything serious, that's why.'

'Why not?'

This was getting annoying. Aiden had stopped by after work for his usual visit. He just wanted a quiet beer with his brother, not some kind of interrogation.

'You know why. I'm not interested in getting married or having kids.'

'Doesn't mean you can't have a long-term relationship. Not every woman out there is hanging out to walk down the aisle in a meringue dress or stockpile nappies.'

'They all get to that point at some stage. I know that from painful experience. And the longer it goes on for, the harder it is when you break it off. I'm not going to be responsible for someone else's happiness.'

'Why not?' There was an edge to Nate's voice he hadn't heard before. 'Because you feel you have to be responsible for mine?'

'Whoa…where did that come from?' Aiden glanced over his shoulder as he broke the moment of startled silence. Wasn't it about time for the boys to all roll their chairs into the dining room for their evening meal? Where was everybody else, anyway? In the lounge, watching reruns of Murderball games? If he stepped away from the corner he could probably see through the window and, if there was a game on, he could distract Nate. He had a feeling that he wasn't going to like whatever Nathan was about to unbottle.

'You do, though, don't you?' Nathan swivelled his wheelchair with practised ease and trapped Aiden so that it would look like a deliberate evasion if he tried to step past him. 'You feel responsible for what happened to me and so you think you have to *be* responsible for me for the rest of your life.'

Of course he felt responsible for what had happened. It had been his fault.

Nate was staring at him. He shook his head. 'It wasn't your fault.'

Aiden stared back at him. 'You were too young to remember what it was like. If I hadn't lost my rag and yelled back at Dad, he'd never have come after me. He'd never have knocked you down the stairs and broken your neck.'

The horror of that day as a sixteen-year-old whose life had changed for ever in a heartbeat had never gone. Crouched over the crumpled form of his ten-year-old brother at the bottom of the stairs, his hands had been shaking as he'd tried to hold his phone still enough to call for an ambulance. To stop Nathan moving, even as they'd both heard the dreadful sound of the gunshot that had come from an upstairs room.

Maybe the worst horror had been the relief of knowing that he didn't have to protect Nathan from their father's tyranny any more—the twisted bitterness that had come from blaming an innocent baby for his wife's death.

He'd held Nathan's head still, knowing that moving him could make it worse. And he'd talked to him as he'd crouched there, waiting for help to arrive.

'*I'm here,*' he'd said, over and over again. '*I'll look after you. I'll always look after you.*'

'I remember a lot more than you give me credit for. And you know what? I've had enough of this.'

Nate sounded angry. His clever, brave, determined kid brother was letting his irrepressible good humour go for once. He was angry with him.

Finally. There was a relief to be found in that. He

deserved the anger. He could handle it. He was the one who could still walk. The one who had a job he loved. Who could get out there and kiss gorgeous women. Nate was allowed to be angry about what had happened in his life. The opportunities he would never have.

'It was Dad who pushed me down the stairs. Not you. It's ancient history. Get over it, Aiden. *I* have.'

'How can you say that?' Aiden was shocked. 'You have to live with that accident for the rest of your life. It should never have happened.'

'Oh, get off the guilt train,' Nate snapped. 'Yeah...I have to live with it for the rest of my life. *Me*. And you don't get to feel so guilty about it that you stuff up your own life. I'm not having that put on me, thanks.'

'I'm not—'

'Yeah, you are. You baby me. You're always here, checking up on me. Trying to make life better for me, but guess what? I like my life. I don't need this.'

Aiden stared at his brother. He'd thought he could handle the anger but that was when he'd thought it was going to be about the accident that had wrecked a young life—not about him honouring a vow to look after the only person who'd ever been so important to him.

This hurt, dammit. Enough to make him feel angry right back at Nate.

'I've only ever done what I could to help. You were ten years old.'

'And you're still treating me like I'm ten years old. I'm twenty-four, man. I'm grown up. I've got a *girlfriend*.'

How on earth had this all come out after sharing the news that he'd gone on a date with the cute midwife?

'And there's no way I'm going to play by your stupid three-dates rule.'

So that was it.

'You do know it's stupid, don't you?'

'Works for me.' Aiden's voice was tight. At least, it had.

'I'm going to live by myself one of these days,' Nate continued fiercely. 'I'm going to try out for the Murderball team and if I get in I'll give it everything I've got. I'm going to make the best of my life. I don't want to end up like you.'

'What's that supposed to mean?'

'Shut off. Scared of losing control.'

'People get hurt if you lose control.' Surely Nate knew that better than anyone after what had happened.

'So? That's life.' Nate shook his head. 'Get over it and start having some fun. Like me.' The crooked smile was a plea for understanding. Forgiveness, too, maybe, for saying some hard stuff?

The lump in his throat made it hard to suck in a breath. Okay, he was hurt but, man, his little brother had courage, didn't he? He was so proud of him.

A window got pushed up along the veranda and a dark, spiky head emerged. 'You coming in for dinner, Nate?'

'Sure.'

'You want to stay, Aiden? There's plenty.'

'Nah…I'm good.' He needed some time to think about what had just happened. That his brother had grown up and just let him know in no uncertain terms? Or that he thought he had, anyway. He still needed his big brother, even if he didn't think he did. More than ever, in fact, as he strived for independence. Did he think he could do that without a lot of help? Even if he wasn't welcome, there was no way Aiden could back away from his responsibilities here. He might just have to be a bit cleverer in how he looked after Nate.

'Hey…' Nathan stopped the movement of his chair. He looked back at his brother. He looked a lot younger all of a sudden. Worried. Aiden could see him swallow hard. 'We okay?'

If he'd needed any evidence that his brother still needed him, it was right there in how vulnerable Nate looked right now. Aiden didn't hesitate. 'Sure.'

But it was an awkward moment that could go either way.

Aiden did his best to smile. 'You were right, man. She was off the scale.'

Nate's grin tugged at his heart. 'So she gets a second date, at least?'

'Already sorted. We're going to the beach.'

'Maybe me and Sam can come, too.'

Aiden snorted. 'No way. I only invited Sophia.'

CHAPTER FIVE

MELBOURNE IS FAMED for the ability to produce four seasons in one day with its fickle weather. It was also capable of pulling something astonishing out of its meteorological hat—like a blazingly hot day in April when it could just as easily have been more like winter than summer.

How lucky was it that it was like this for date number two when they had agreed that the beach was a good place to go? Sophia stood on the pavement outside the picket fence of her cottage at the appointed time. She was wearing her bikini as underwear beneath her jeans and shirt and she carried a beach towel in her bag—just in case it was warm enough to swim. The thick jacket she had on over her shirt earned her a few curious looks from passers-by but she was just following the instructions that had come with the plan.

Had her choice regarding the mode of transport been a mistake?

'The van's old and clunky,' Aiden had told her as he walked her home from the bar and they'd planned this date. 'But it does have walls. If you're brave, you can come on the back of my bike.'

'You get to use your work bike at home?'

'No. I've got one of my own. A Ducati. A red one.'

'Red, huh? What colour is the van?'

'White. Boring, boring white.' He wanted her to choose the bike. She wanted to see the approval in his eyes when she made the right choice.

'Then it's no contest, is it? I pick red.'

But her stomach did an odd little flip as she saw the sun glinting on the red metal of the huge bike as it rolled to a halt in front of her.

Or was it Aiden's grin as he lifted the visor of his helmet that was doing it?

He unclipped a second helmet and held it out to her. 'Are you ready?'

Sophia had to suck in a big breath. *Was* she ready? This was about way more than a long bike ride, wasn't it?

Those unusual light brown eyes were doing that dancing thing again. A look that implied mischief. *Fun...*

She reached for the helmet as she nodded and returned the grin. 'I'm ready.'

It was a long ride. Leaving the outskirts of Melbourne behind, they took to the open road, heading south. They bypassed the large town of Geelong and sped towards the point where the harbour met the open sea—the quaint seaside village of Queenscliff.

'It's gorgeous,' Sophia exclaimed as they parked the bike and took off on foot to explore. 'Look at the turrets on that house!'

'We're lucky it's not a weekend. With weather like this, it gets really crowded.'

'You've been here before?'

'It's a great destination when I want to get out on the road and blow a few cobwebs away.'

'It certainly does that.' Sophia made a face as she threaded her fingers into the end of her hair where the waves brushed her shoulders. 'I should have tied this up. I might never get the knots out. I didn't even think to bring a brush. It probably looks like a rat's nest.'

Aiden stopped walking. They were outside the door of a bakery and a woman came out, laden with paper bags. She had to walk around them but Aiden didn't seem to notice because he was only looking at Sophia. He caught her hand and pulled her fingers out of her hair. Then he flattened her hand gently against her head with his still on top of it.

'Forget about it,' he told her. 'You look gorgeous.'

And then he bent his head and kissed her. Right there on the footpath, half blocking the door to the bakery.

Sophia had relived the softness of that first kiss in a bar a hundred times by now. Had conjured up the tingle of anticipation and the curl of desire so many times that she'd been sure she had magnified it out of all connection with reality.

Turned out she hadn't.

This was even better. It still had the restraint that being in a public place required but there was a new depth to it. A familiarity. The knowledge that they both wanted this and it was going to go somewhere else. Very soon.

'*Excuse* me.' The voice sounded annoyed. Breaking apart, they could see why. A young woman with a twin pushchair had no chance of getting past them to the door.

Aiden smiled at the mother as he murmured an apology. He held the door open for her but it was obvious she had already forgiven him.

'No worries,' she said, smiling up at him. 'You have a great day.'

'Oh…' Aiden's glance went over the top of her head, straight to Sophia's. 'I already am.'

The woman turned her head and her smile widened. Her gaze told Sophia exactly how lucky she was. Then she winked and disappeared into the shop. The smell of something hot and delicious wafted out as the door swung shut.

'Hungry?'

'Starving.' Sophia took a step towards the door but Aiden shook his head.

'Bit crowded in there. I've got a better idea.'

He took her across the road to the fish-and-chip shop. A short time later, they were walking down the hill and away from the shops. Aiden held the big white paper parcel in one hand and Sophia's hand in the other. He led her across the railway lines and onto a track that took them to a grassy spot with a view through the trees to the water. The meal was still hot and absolutely delicious. A woman walked past on the track with a dog and then a whole family with a toddler in a pushchair and a small child on a bike, but nobody came to share their patch of grass or even looked their way. It felt as if they were almost invisible.

'This is perfect.' Sophia licked salt off her fingers as she looked away from the pelicans and swans gliding peacefully on water still enough to mimic glass.

'Mmm. I find it pays to put some effort into planning date number two.' Aiden turned away from the view with a smile.

'One of the rules? I'll—um—have to remember that.'

Not that she was likely to remember anything other than the look in Aiden's eyes that she could already recognise as the intention to kiss her. She barely even noticed the colourful cloud of parakeets landing on the fig tree that was shading them as Aiden leaned towards her.

The cloak of invisibility was still around them but Sophia would have forgotten about the rest of the world anyway as soon as Aiden's lips touched hers. Or maybe it was the moment she felt things change as the intensity kicked up several notches. Aiden's hand cradled her head as he pushed her back to lie on the grass. Their tongues danced, the pang of lingering salt a delicious foil to the sweetness of escalating desire. She felt the touch of Aiden's fingers beneath the hem of her shirt, a trail of fire on the delicate skin of her belly, and the heat when it reached her breast was enough to make her gasp into his mouth.

He pulled away with a groan.

'You make me forget where I am,' he murmured.

'You're on date number two,' Sophia whispered back. 'I think it's okay to get distracted. Isn't it?' she added, feeling her eyes widen.

'Yes, but there's a time and place for everything. And

this probably isn't the place for what I'm thinking about right now.'

Sophia's inward breath was audibly ragged as she sat up. She'd been thinking along similar lines and she certainly hadn't wanted him to stop. Anybody could have seen them. Like that woman with her dog, who was coming down the track towards them again, presumably on the homeward stretch of their walk. The dog—a very cute miniature schnauzer—ran towards them and the woman called it back with an apologetic smile.

'I doubt there's enough time anyway.' There was a wicked edge to Aiden's smile as the woman disappeared along the track. 'It'll get cold around here when the sun goes down.'

He wanted a whole night with her? The thought made Sophia's toes curl. But this was a daytime date.

Oh, help… What if there was a rule about not going any further until date number three? What if this three-dates business was just a build-up for a one-night stand?

Hard not to believe that it would be worth waiting for, if that was the case.

'We have options,' Aiden added. 'You get to choose.'

'Oh?' Maybe one of those options included going somewhere really private. Sophia grinned. 'Fire away. I like choosing.'

'Option one: we could take the ferry over to Sorrento to get dessert. There's a shop there that has the best vanilla slices in the world and we might get to see some dolphins on the way.'

Sophia nodded thoughtfully. He really had planned

this date carefully. Or—the thought sent a chill down her spine—was this a standard number-two date?

'Option two is a swim. The water is probably arctic but it's warm enough to dry off on the beach and, by then, it'll be about time to head home.'

Home? To his place? After getting almost naked and lying in the sun for a while? It wasn't hard to make a choice.

'It would be a shame to come to the seaside and not have a swim.'

'I knew you were brave.' The kiss was swift but sweet. 'Let's go.'

The walk made the day seem even warmer and by the time they went down the sandy stairs to the endless white beach with a misty lighthouse far away, they were more than ready to pull off their clothes and brave the curl of the surf. The beach was a popular place to be but most people were sunbathing. Some sat in beach chairs, reading, and others were having picnics or playing ball games. There were children paddling and building sand-castles but there were very few people swimming.

And no wonder. The first splash of water was cold enough to make Sophia shriek but Aiden simply laughed and dived through the next wave. She jumped up and down as she went further out, getting more of her body wet each time, and suddenly it wasn't so bad. And then Aiden surfaced right beside her and his smile made her aware of the silky caress of the sea water over her entire body.

'This is gorgeous,' she called over the sound of the waves. 'I love it.'

'I knew you would,' he called back. 'You're my kind of girl.'

They couldn't stay in the water for long and they were both shivering as they towelled themselves dry but then they lay on their towels on the soft sand and there was enough warmth in the sun for the chill to ebb slowly away.

For the longest time, they lay there, absorbing the warmth. Side by side on their backs, saying nothing. And then Sophia felt the brush of Aiden's fingers and his hand curl itself around hers.

'I really like you, Sophia.'

'I really like you, too, Aiden.' Sophia's eyes were still closed and her smile grew slowly. She couldn't remember the last time she'd felt this happy. Even the noises around them—the roll of the waves and the shouting of children enjoying themselves—only added to this feeling of contentment. 'I think this has been the best second date I've ever been on.'

Aiden tightened his grip on Sophia's hand. This was by far the best second date he'd ever been on as well. The only thing wrong with it was that it would have to end soon. They were almost dry and they needed to get dressed again because the heat of the day would start dropping rapidly before long. They had a long ride to get back to the city as well and by then it would be evening. They both had an early start for work tomorrow but did that really mean that it had to be over? Sophia believed that he'd planned this whole date after they'd agreed to go to a beach. She didn't need to know that he'd kept his options open and hadn't planned it to continue on into the evening, did she?

'It's not over yet.'

He heard the words come out of his mouth and they felt…right. Of course it couldn't be over yet.

'Oh? What else is in the plan?'

He could hear the smile in Sophia's voice. And something more. A willingness to go along with whatever he wanted?

He wanted to take Sophia home. To his bed. Okay, they both needed to get to work early but there were a lot of hours between now and then. Why shouldn't they make the most of every single one of them?

'Well, I was thinking…' Aiden propped himself up on one elbow. Maybe he didn't need to say anything here. He could just kiss her again. And then he could look into her eyes and he'd know whether she was happy with the new plan.

He let his mouth hover over hers for a deliciously long moment. Feeling the tingle of their lips not quite touching. Knowing just how much better it was going to get in a nanosecond.

And then he heard it. Faintly at first but getting steadily louder.

Sophia's lips moved under his. Tickling. 'What *is* that?'

'My phone.' He didn't want to answer it. Dammit… all he wanted to do was kiss Sophia but her lips were moving again. Smiling?

'It's a *siren*?'

'Yeah, I know. Cheesy. My kid brother chose it for me.'

And it could be that kid brother who was calling right now. Highly likely to be, seeing as they hadn't spoken yet today. In fact, they hadn't spoken very often for a few days now. Ever since that tense conversation about Aiden smothering Nate because of his misplaced guilt.

He still wanted to kiss Sophia more than answer it but something else was making his skin prickle and he recognised that sensation.

Guilt. He barely knew this woman and suddenly she was more important than his brother? What was he thinking?

'I'd better get that. Sorry.'

'No problem.'

A soft breeze had sprung up, making it colder. Or maybe he just had more skin exposed as he sat up and rummaged in his coat pocket for his phone. Sure enough, the caller ID said 'Nate'. Aiden swiped the screen.

'Hey… What's up?'

'Guess.'

'I can't. You'll have to tell me.'

'I went for the team trials today.'

'Yeah? How'd that go?'

'I got in, man. I'm in the team.'

'That's…fantastic.' The smile that pulled at his lips was genuine. 'Great news. I reckon it calls for a celebration.'

'Too right. We're having a few beers back at our place. Thought you might want to drop by.'

He was listening to Nate but he was looking at Sophia. She still lay on her back, shading her eyes from the sun with her arm. Her hair was still damp and looked almost

black where it lay against the pale skin of her shoulders.
He couldn't help his gaze travelling further. Over the
rest of that gorgeous, soft-looking skin and the perfect
proportions of her small, slim body.

He'd never wanted anybody this much.

He'd have to take a rain-check on that celebratory
beer with Nate because otherwise he wouldn't get to take
Sophia home and make love to her properly.

Slowly…

Or maybe not so slowly the first time…

His throat suddenly felt dry.

'You still there, man? Where *are* you, anyway?'

Impressions flashed through Aiden's brain with the
speed of light. That note in Nate's voice when he'd made
that suggestion so casually that he 'might' want to drop
by.

Things hadn't been quite right between them since
that conversation the other day. And if he didn't join in
the celebration of Nate making the Murderball team,
it could be interpreted as not being supportive of his
brother as he achieved one of his long-held ambitions and
that could push them further apart. What then? Would
Nate choose not to even tell him when he was moving
out of the house to try living independently?

His brother was trying out his wings and surely that
meant that now—more than ever—he needed support.
Aiden had to be there for him one hundred per cent.

How could he even entertain the idea of letting a
woman get between them? It wasn't as if she'd still be in
his life in a week or two from now but Nate would be. He
would always be in his life and he'd always take priority.

'I'm still here,' he said. 'Bad line. I'm out of the city but I'll be back soon.'

'No worries. You went for a ride? You on a date or something?'

'Yeah…Queenscliff.'

'Oh…of course. This is your number two with Sophia. Hey…hope I'm not interrupting anything.' His laugh made a lie of his words but didn't quite ring true for some reason.

'Not at all. Just went for swim, would you believe?'

'Well, don't hurry back, man. Enjoy yourself. Catch you soon.'

The beeping signalled that Nate had hung up. The note of disappointment in his words was still there, though. And the odd edge to the laughter as he'd tried to make light of things.

Aiden dragged his eyes away from Sophia. Closed them, in fact.

'Not a problem,' he heard himself saying into the silence of a dead line. At least he could sound reluctant now. As though there was something he really had to do even though he didn't want to. 'I'll get there as soon as I can.'

Sophia was already pulling her clothes on by the time he shoved his phone back into his pocket.

'Sorry about that.'

'It's not a problem.' He could hear the note of determined cheerfulness in her voice as she echoed his own words. 'We've had a lovely day. If there's somewhere else you need to be now, it's okay. I understand.'

She might understand but he could see the disappointment in her eyes and he felt like a jerk. He could say it wasn't that important and the only place he needed to be for now was with her.

But Nate was disappointed too. He'd have that in the back of his mind all evening if he stayed with Sophia.

The feeling of being torn was unpleasant. The desire to tell Sophia he only wanted to be with her was strong enough to ring warning bells.

It wasn't supposed to feel like this. It was supposed to be fun.

For both of them.

And it wasn't any more, was it? How could being between a rock and a hard place ever be considered fun?

He pulled his clothes on, feeling the added unpleasantness of the sand in his shoes. He watched Sophia roll up her damp towel and shove it in her beach bag.

'You dry enough? It'll be cold on the bike, otherwise.'

'I'm fine. I've got my coat.'

The coat wasn't enough to make her feel fine.

Not at all.

Maybe it would have helped if they'd been able to talk but there was no way they could do that on a bike. Sophia held onto Aiden's waist and kept her face hidden against his back. Damp tendrils of hair still flicked her face and her skin was cold enough to make them sting.

How had that happened?

One minute she'd been feeling more blissful than she could remember ever feeling and then it had all gone wrong, the atmosphere lost thanks to the intrusion of a phone call. He'd just been about to kiss her. To tell her the plans that meant the date wasn't over yet.

Why hadn't he just ignored the call? Why did he have a stupid siren call tone that made it impossible for anyone to ignore? Just as impossible as it was not to think it was probably another woman who'd been calling him. Was he already lining up the next contender in his three-dates game?

What was so fantastic about the news he'd received? Was whoever she was available? *Tonight?*

It wasn't fair. Their first date hadn't really counted and date number two had just been sabotaged.

So much for getting out there and having some fun.

This wasn't fun at all any more.

Did she even want a third—and last—date?

There was plenty of time on that long, cold ride to turn that question over in her head. As she made her stiff limbs co-operate in climbing off the big, red bike in front of her house and her fingers work well enough to undo her helmet and hand it back, Sophia was sure that this was goodbye and she had decided that she was quite happy about that.

She was, in fact, more angry than disappointed now.

But then Aiden caught her gaze and held it.

'I'm really sorry about this,' he said. 'If I could get out of it, I would.'

There was something in his gaze that told her he was being absolutely sincere. That he wanted to be with her—maybe even more than she'd wanted him to be. And that it *was* something really important that was dragging him away.

She wanted to tell him that it didn't matter. That they still had one date left so everything would be okay. That it was no big deal.

But the words wouldn't come out. She managed half a smile. A shrug that said, Yeah, it sucks but that's life, isn't it?

And then she turned away and went into her house without a backward glance, leaning her forehead against the closed door until she heard the sound of a motor-bike's engine being gunned and then fading into silence.

'What are you doing here?'

Aiden held up the six-pack of beer. 'I heard there was a bit of a celebration going on.'

Nate had been the one who'd come to open the door when Aiden had rung the bell. The wide hallway of the old house was empty behind him.

'You ditched your date to come *here*?'

Aiden's shrug said that it was no big deal but Nate shook his head and his huff of sound was disgusted. 'Man, you're an idiot. How d'you think that made Sophia feel?'

The cardboard handle of the beer pack was cutting into Aiden's hand. He had been an idiot. He'd made Sophia feel bad only to find he wasn't welcome here.

Something was going wrong in his life right now. The wheels were still turning but it felt like they weren't quite on the tracks and he couldn't, for the life of him, figure out why. He looked away from Nate.

'I thought this was more important.' He cleared his throat. 'And…I wanted to…I dunno…put things right,

I guess. Wouldn't want you to think I don't support you in whatever you want to do.'

Nate gave an audible snort this time. 'It's only selection. Miss my first game next week and you'll definitely be in trouble.'

The lightness in his tone didn't match the expression on his face when Aiden turned back. Nate understood what he'd been too clumsy to articulate well and held up his hand, the fingers curled into a fist. 'There's nothing to put right, man. We're brothers. Family.'

Aiden bumped the fist with his own. Nate shook his head but he was grinning as he swivelled the chair on the polished floor. 'Seeing as you're here, you might as well come in for a beer. Hey, what do you call a quadriplegic in a pile of leaves?'

There was relief to be found as he followed Nate towards the lounge. Enough to stop the automatic protest at a joke that would seem so distasteful to people outside this community.

'I dunno. What?'

'Russell.'

There was even more relief in the shared laughter but it still wasn't quite enough to put the wheels completely back on track. Nate had said there was nothing to put right but that wasn't entirely true, was it?

Things had gone unexpectedly wrong with someone else as well. A woman he'd had no desire at all to hurt. Quite the opposite, in fact.

How on earth was he going to put that right?

CHAPTER SIX

'You okay?'

'A bit nervous, I think. I watched a Caesarean before but I've never been actually involved.'

'I won't ask you to do anything you're not ready to cope with, don't worry.'

Flick nodded, pulling her theatre cap over her dark blonde hair. She looked a bit pale, Sophia thought, which was probably nerves on top of the weariness of a long day.

She was feeling weary herself. It didn't help that she'd been feeling as flat as a pancake ever since that date with Aiden had ended on such an unsatisfactory note.

She hadn't heard from him since and the mix of disappointment and—it had to be admitted—frustration had made her wonder if the downside of dating outweighed any of the potential benefits.

She'd brushed off Flick's friendly query about how the date had gone and she'd tried really hard to focus on her work and let the satisfaction her job always gave her chase the blues away, but that hadn't worked very well today either. Not when they were now in a situation none of them had expected—or wanted—to be in.

They should be heading home by now, after the home birth of their patient Kim's second baby, but things hadn't gone according to plan and, after transferring Kim to the MMU hours ago, a Caesarean section had been deemed the best option for an exhausted mother and a now distressed baby.

Kim and her husband, Peter, were in the theatre's anteroom under the care of an anaesthetist as she received an epidural.

'Put some theatre booties on over your shoes.' Sophia pulled the disposable covers from the dispenser on the wall of the changing room. 'And here's a mask.'

'Do we have to scrub in as well?'

'No. We don't go anywhere near the operating site. Our role is to support Kim in getting the best birth experience she can under the circumstances.'

'Like making sure she gets the skin-to-skin contact?'

'Exactly. But only if the baby's well enough, of course. We have to be prepared, though. What's the most important thing to make sure we've sorted?'

'That her gown can be moved without disturbing the theatre drapes?'

'Good.' Sophia smiled at her student. 'Now, let's get moving. We've got a few things to organise. I'm going to liaise with the ward and check that a midwife is available to take transfer of care in the recovery room and I want you to ring the lab and order a bucket of iced water.'

'For the cord blood gas samples?'

'You're onto it. We've also got to check that both the

transport cot and the resuscitation cot are turned on and I want to make sure you know where all the equipment is. Follow me.'

There was a hum of activity in Theatre as the staff prepared for the surgery.

'We'll move the resuscitation cot over to here,' Sophia decided.

'Why?'

'Hopefully, it's not going to be needed, but if it is, we want a line of direct vision for both the parents so they can maintain visual contact with their baby at all times.'

Kim was wheeled in moments later. Lights were shifted and positioned and monitoring equipment attached. An ECG trace blipped into action on an overhead screen and numbers flashed and changed as they displayed heart rate, blood pressure and blood oxygen levels. Sophia showed Peter where he was allowed to stand, checked the function of the foetal monitor and then smiled at Kim.

'All good?'

'I'm scared.'

'I know.' Sophia squeezed her patient's hand, careful not to dislodge the IV line. 'You've got a fantastic team who are here to look after you and you'll be amazed how fast it goes.'

'I'm not sure any more…about…you know…'

'Watching baby come out?' Sophia glanced at the drape screen the theatre nurses were putting up at chest level. The plan had been to lower the screen after the incision to the uterus had been made but another glance showed how pale Peter was looking. A definite contender for fainting.

'You don't have to see that bit,' she told Kim. 'We can still put baby straight onto your chest.' Her gaze caught Flick's. 'Let's put a chair in for Peter. That way he can hold Kim's hand and he doesn't have to see anything he doesn't want to either.'

The surgeon and her registrar came into Theatre and, for a while at least, Sophia could totally forget about her personal life as she got caught up in one of the more dramatic ways to bring a new life into the world.

She made sure Flick could stand close enough to see what was happening as the surgeon and her registrar stood on either side of Kim's swollen abdomen. The only sounds were the beeping of the monitors and the calm requests for instruments as the initial incision was made and then the tissues quickly dissected with gloved fingers in use more often than a scalpel or scissors.

Sophia was sure that Flick was holding her breath— as she always did—when the careful incision into the uterus was made and they could see the dark whorls of wet hair on the baby's head. Forceps were fitted to lift the head far enough for the surgeon to be able to hold it with her hands and then the baby was eased out, pausing long enough for the registrar to suction the infant's airways.

The baby's eyes were open and an arm waving slowly. Sophia breathed a sigh of relief. It started crying as its legs were lifted clear of the uterus and she heard a gasp that was more like a strangled sob of relief from both Peter and Kim. Flick was focused on the registrar clamping and cutting the cord but then her gaze caught Sophia's and she gave a quick nod. She took the baby from the registrar as Flick helped a nurse to move the screen and she could place the newborn on her mother's chest.

The longest part of the surgery came now, with the precise task of repairing all the layers of tissue, but, with the screen back in place, Kim was unaware of what was happening and time ceased to matter as she and Peter touched and marvelled at their new baby.

'Did you note the time and sex of the baby?'

Flick nodded. 'I've got the labels ready for the cord blood gas samples.'

'Good. Now, double-check this with me. We have to make sure that the details on the maternal and neonatal wrist labels match.'

Thirty minutes later, Kim was ready to be transferred to a ward bed and taken into Recovery. The paediatrician had checked their daughter and she was wrapped and warm. Sophia put the small bundle into Peter's arms to be carried into Recovery. The transfer of care to the ward midwife would happen there but Sophia wasn't ready to leave yet. This was her favourite time after the tension of a Caesarean, to help with the first breastfeed and watch the bonding happening between the baby and her parents. Kim's mother was waiting nearby, too, with their three-year-old son, who would be able to come and meet his new sister before they got transferred to the ward.

'That was amazing,' Flick said quietly, when they were finally heading home. 'But I am *so* tired.' She stepped into the lift and leaned against the wall.

'Me too. This is when you really feel it, when the excitement's all over.' Sophia pushed the button to take them to the ground floor. It wasn't just physical weariness either. With the prospect of heading home alone as soon as she stepped out of the Victoria's front doors, she knew that she would end up feeling flatter than ever. 'The café will still be open. Let's go and get a coffee.'

Flick groaned. 'Oh, no…not coffee. Even the thought of it makes me feel ill.'

'Really?' Sophia's head swivelled to take a closer look at her student. 'That's not like you.' She noted the pale skin and dark circles under Flick's eyes. Something clicked into place. 'Wait…you're not pregnant, are you?'

'I think it's just something I ate.'

The lift stopped with a jerk as she spoke and then the doors slid open but was that enough to explain the way Flick was avoiding her gaze?

'I've got to go. See you tomorrow, Soph.'

'Hang on…' She'd put her foot in it, even making the suggestion, hadn't she? It certainly hadn't been her intention to upset her student. 'Hey…I'm sorry, Flick. I didn't—'

Flick raised her hand, without turning. 'It's okay. I'm fine. Really.'

'Sophia?'

The voice from behind made her spin round without thinking. It was so unexpected. So…welcome?

'Aiden… What are you doing here?'

No. It wasn't welcome. She didn't want to talk to him right now. She needed to talk to Flick. Or maybe Flick needed to talk to *her*. Turning her head again, just as quickly, she could see Flick disappearing towards the front doors. She could hardly run away from Aiden.

She didn't want to talk to him. He'd interrupted a conversation she'd been having with her student and she was on the brink of excusing herself and running away.

He didn't want that to happen. Catching sight of her as she'd stepped out of the lift had been like a slap in the face. Enough to bring back the guilt he'd been wrestling with ever since he'd cut their date short to go and see Nathan.

He'd picked up the phone half a dozen times since then, with the intention of trying to contact Sophia, but something had always got in the way. A call to a job made it easy to hang up but it was never enough of an excuse. He'd been…scared? Well, nervous anyway. He hadn't been able to come up with any plausible plan to put things right so he'd known he could well make things worse. And he hadn't wanted to face the potential rejection.

But actually seeing her instead of a faceless phone call brought back all the reasons why he wanted to put things right.

She looked tired. The way she stared after her student had a worried edge to it. And he could sense that her mood was different. More serious. Sad, even? Oh, help…was he flattering himself or could that have something to do with him?

Despite all of that—or maybe because of it—she was still the most gorgeous woman he'd ever met. He wanted to put his arms around her and hold her close. Kiss whatever it was better. But he could only say something and hope that she might choose to stay in his company for just a little longer. Long enough for him to think of something. Some way to put things right.

'I came in to check up on a patient from today,' he heard himself saying. 'Cyclist that got clipped by a tram. I was worried about her.'

'Oh...' A rush of mixed emotions washed through Sophia. The attraction that came from imagining him on the job, weaving through heavy traffic with the lights and siren going on that huge bike. Admiration that came from knowing how calmly he would have taken charge of the emergency. Warmth that came from knowing that he did care about his patients.

And there was more threaded through those feelings. She couldn't pretend that the personal attraction had been quashed by the disappointment of that last date. Maybe the strongest memory right now was the sincerity she'd seen in his eyes when he'd left her on the footpath. She'd been too angry to believe that he wouldn't have been abandoning her unless it had been for something too important to ignore, but that anger had faded into the flatness of the last few days.

She wanted to believe it now.

She wanted...

'Would you like to grab a coffee or something?' Aiden seemed to be watching her carefully, as though he was aware of the struggle she was having, trying to capture a thought that would determine her response to this unexpected meeting.

'I...um...' There was no point looking towards the

main entrance but she turned her head again anyway, despite knowing that Flick was long gone.

'Do you need to catch up with her?'

'No.' Sophia pushed her concern about her student to one side. She would see her soon enough and, if that startling suspicion had any grounds, it would only become more apparent with the passing of time. She sucked in a breath and looked back at Aiden.

'I was planning to get a coffee,' she admitted. 'It's been a long day. We had a case that got complicated and we had to bring her in for a Caesarean. And…' Something she couldn't identify was melting away deep inside her. 'I believe I still owe you a coffee?'

Aiden's smile lit up his face and she saw a flash of what looked like relief in his eyes.

'I believe you do.'

The tension eased as they began walking towards the cafeteria together but now Sophia was aware of how she must look. Her hair had been squashed beneath a cap for too long and she had crumpled scrubs on under her jacket. Any make-up she'd started the day with must have worn off long ago and she was probably tired enough to look years older.

Except that—oddly—she didn't feel that tired any more. And a sideways glance showed that Aiden's uniform was pretty crumpled as well. His boots looked scuffed and he had a big scratch on one hand.

For both of them, their appearance was nothing more than evidence of what they did for a living. A badge of honour even?

Aiden held the door of the cafeteria open for Sophia.

The relief he'd felt when she'd agreed to have a coffee with him should have been a warning but he was going to ignore it. So what if it felt like a major victory? That the wheels were back on exactly the right tracks? It shouldn't feel this good, of course. Not when all he might be winning was the chance for a third—and final—date.

But he was feeling better than he had for days so why shouldn't he make the most of it? Sophia looked happier too. She was smiling as they headed for the machine that provided coffee that was dreadful but free. She put a polystyrene cup under the dispenser.

'What can I get you?' she asked. 'Cappuccino? A latte?'

'I think a long black might be the safest choice.'

'Done.' With the button pushed the machine whirred into life. 'And I think I might push the boat out and have a hot chocolate.'

There would be a rush before too long, when staff on an early dinner break came in, but, for now, the cafeteria was almost completely deserted. They found a table in the corner and sat down. Sophia was at right angles to Aiden. Their knees bumped under the table and the eye contact they made was instantaneous. And intense enough to make her heart skip a beat.

'This doesn't count as a date,' she murmured.

'Of course not.' Aiden nodded, his face serious. 'It wasn't planned so how could it be?'

'Mmm.'

'And besides…we never got to finish date number two, did we?'

'Ah…' The tension was back again. They had to both

be thinking of that moment. Not that any words had been spoken but Sophia could actually feel the impression of that half-smile she'd summoned. The dismissive way she'd shrugged and turned away. 'No…' She had to drop her gaze. 'It didn't feel finished.'

'We should do something about that, then.'

It took courage to meet his gaze. 'Yes. I think maybe we should.'

The intensity humming between them bore no relation to the casual words from Aiden.

'I've got a thing I have to go to tomorrow night. Would you like to come with me?'

'What sort of a thing?'

Not that it mattered. She would have agreed to go anywhere with him.

Or maybe it did matter. A flicker of something in Aiden's face made Sophia realise that, whatever it was, it was important to him. That he was inviting her into a part of his life that might not be something he shared with just anyone. That he was taking a risk?

'A surprise,' he said, after that tiny hesitation. 'If I tell you what it is, that would make it more like a new date and it's not. It's—'

'A half-date?' Sophia suggested.

'Just a thing. Let's not try and define it.'

'Okay.'

'So you'll come?'

'Sure. How could I resist? I've never been to a "thing" before. I'm intrigued.'

'Don't get too excited. It's a bit…different.'

'I'm even more intrigued now. Give me a clue?'

'Uh-uh.' Aiden shook his head but he was smiling. 'I'll pick you up at seven-thirty.'

'Dress code?'

'Definitely casual. And warm.' Aiden took a sip of his coffee and made a face. 'This is awful. I don't even think it deserves to be called coffee.'

A bubble of happiness made Sophia giggle. 'Guess I still owe you one, then.'

Aiden's nod was thoughtful. 'I'll put this in the category of medication. Something to wake me up after a tough day.'

'So what happened? How badly injured was your cyclist?'

'Multi-trauma. She's up in Intensive Care now but I wanted to see what had been found. The head injury made her combative so it was hard to assess her.'

Sophia nodded. She had plenty of questions and was genuinely interested in the responses as Aiden told her more about the case, but there was an undercurrent that made it all so much more enjoyable.

She was going to see him again tomorrow night.

They were going to a *thing*...

Parking outside a suburban gymnasium was a surprise. So the 'thing' was a sporting event of some kind? This was weird but Sophia was prepared to keep an open mind, especially when Aiden took her hand to lead her inside.

And there was another surprise. The seats were crowded and the atmosphere loud and vibrant but the last thing she'd expected to see were the teams on the basketball-style court. They were all young men and they were all in wheelchairs.

'What is this?'

'Murderball.' Aiden waved to a girl with spiky black hair and facial piercings who was in the first row of seats. 'Wheelchair rugby.' He led her towards some empty seats in the third row. 'It's my brother's first game.'

Wow. No wonder she'd got the impression that this was a private part of Aiden's life.

'Your brother is paraplegic?'

'Tetraplegic. You have to have disability in all four limbs to qualify to play.'

'But…' Sophia stared at the activity below as she took her seat. The team members were rolling across the floor with some doing fast spins, looking like they were warming up. They were definitely using their hands and arms.

'There's a scale,' Aiden told her. 'The level of disability is graded from zero point five, which is the greatest restriction, to three point five. If you were able-bodied you'd score five and if you were totally paralysed you'd be a zero. There are four on the court at any one time and they have to have a total score between them of no more than eight points.'

The teams were lining up, face to face in the centre of the court, and then they peeled off, high-fiving each other.

'Which one is your brother?'

'Number three for the Melbourne Mobsters. The red and black team. He's not going to be on in the first quarter. He may not get on at all but I hope he does. This is his first game.'

'Oh…' That made it even more of a big deal to be here. No wonder Aiden was looking tense, with his jaw knotted and his focus intently on the court. Sophia slipped her hand over his to give it a squeeze and found it caught and gripped hard.

'What's his name?' Sophia grinned. 'Just so I can yell when he scores a goal.'

'Nathan. Nate.'

A whistle blew and the referee threw a ball high in the air and then it was all on. A player for the Canberra Cowboys put the ball on his lap and sped away from the others to cross the goal line between cones. A cheer erupted from the crowd but it was nothing on the noise level when one of the local boys scored less than a minute later.

The game was fast and furious and Sophia was hooked well before the first quarter ended. She gasped at the first collision she saw between three players going for the ball that made the chairs tip and her jaw dropped when one player fell backwards with a crash, but the game carried on with a supporter rushing onto the court to right the upturned chair, and within seconds the fall was forgotten.

A hooter sounded to signal the rolling rotation of the players but Nathan wasn't one of the new team members. Sophia tried to figure out the rules but the game was so fast, she was having trouble. This was like a mix of basketball, rugby and bumper cars.

'Why do they bounce the ball sometimes?'

'You have to either bounce it or pass it to someone else within ten seconds.'

'What happened there?'

'Penalty awarded for a foul. That cowboy hit a mobster's chair behind the main axle, which makes it spin out of control.'

Scores jumped quickly but stayed close. The noise level steadily increased until Sophia had to shout to be heard as the final quarter began.

'That's Nathan. He's *on*.'

She'd barely known this game existed before coming here tonight, but suddenly it felt personal. Nathan looked a lot younger than Aiden and he looked a bit nervous. Sophia felt nervous herself. The chairs were clearly designed to cope with the impacts with their metal bumpers and spoke guards. And the players wore gloves and elbow protection but surely there was a huge potential for injury down there?

Aiden obviously thought so too, given the way he winced visibly the first time Nathan's chair got hit. But, moments later, a wide overhead pass from the other side of the court saw Nathan catch the ball and dump it on his lap. He spun his chair on the spot and took off, his arms almost a blur as he powered towards the goal line. Three other chairs converged on his path but he saw them as he looked up to bounce the ball off to one side. With another lightning-fast spin, he changed direction and had a clear line to speed towards the cones.

The cheer was the loudest yet. Maybe because she and Aiden were both on their feet, yelling at the tops of their voices. She saw the girl in the front row, who'd waved at Aiden when they arrived, leaping about and waving two huge pompoms in the red and black team colours.

The Melbourne Mobsters lost by two points but it didn't seem to matter. The crowd was happy to cheer any of the players who came close enough to the spectators to receive a high five or a kiss from a girlfriend. Still holding Sophia's hand, Aiden pulled her towards the front row as a chair rolled directly towards them. Nathan got a kiss from the girl with the spiky black hair and then a fist bump and a one-armed hug from his brother.

'You made it. Didn't see you up there, bro.'

'Wouldn't have missed it for the world. You rocked it, man.'

Sophia nodded her agreement, unable to wipe the grin off her face. 'Most exciting game I've ever watched,' she said. 'Of anything.'

Nathan Harrison's eyes were the same unusual shade of brown as Aiden's and they had the same ability to focus with instant intensity. The slow grin was eerily familiar as well.

'You have to be Sophia,' he said.

She nodded again but didn't miss the glance that flicked between the brothers. Or the disconcerting way Nathan was shaking his head as he looked back, still grinning.

He must have seen her confusion. 'Sorry. It's just that it's the first time I've met one of Aiden's girlfriends. He doesn't usually give me the honour.'

Because a three-dates rule didn't allow for inclusion in a private part of his life? She hadn't imagined that hesitation in inviting her, had she? Or underplayed the significance? But she had no idea whether it meant anything. Or whether she even wanted it to mean anything.

The moment could have been incredibly awkward but it was the girl beside Nathan who saved it.

'There's a first time for everything,' she declared. 'Otherwise nothing would ever change.' She grinned at Sophia. 'I'm Sam,' she said. 'And I'm delighted to meet you—which is what Nate's really trying to say.'

'I knew that.' It was impossible to miss the significance in the glance Sam shared with Nathan. Their love for each other was blindingly obvious.

So was the bond between the brothers. Aiden declined the invitation to join the team and supporters at a local bar, saying he had a horribly early start the next day, but she could hear the fierce pride in his voice when they took their leave.

'You did good, man. Can't wait for the next game.'

Aiden could feel the remnants of a ridiculously proud smile he'd been suppressing as he started up the old van he'd used to collect Sophia that evening. He could also feel the way she was looking at him. The intensity was almost palpable.

'Aiden?'

'Yeah?'

'That call you got at the beach the other day.'

'Yeah?' Oh, help. He'd hoped that had been forgotten by now. That he'd put things right. It had needed something special and inviting her into a part of his life he'd never shared with a woman had seemed like the way to go, but maybe he'd been wrong.

Maybe he was still in the dog box.

'Was it a call from Nathan?'

'Um…yeah…' He turned his head, the query of why she was asking on the tip of his tongue but the word never escaped.

He didn't need to ask why.

She understood.

She might not have any idea why the bond was so strong between him and Nathan but she knew it was there and how important it was.

Weirdly, he could feel something inside his chest crack and something warm seeped out.

Something really nice.

He did have a really early start tomorrow but that hadn't been the real reason for declining the after-game social occasion with the team. He'd known he wanted to take Sophia home and be alone with her.

And the desire to do that had just leapt right off the scale.

CHAPTER SEVEN

THIS WAS THE way the last date should have ended.

Once again, Sophia was pressed against her front door the moment it shut behind her but she wasn't standing there with her head bowed, listening to the sound of a fading engine.

This time, it was her back against the door. And her arms, as she lifted them in a helpless gesture, unable to think of anything else to do with them as she met the intensity of the kiss she was receiving.

Who knew that you could actually *taste* desire? Was it her own or Aiden's or the chemical reaction of mixing them that made this so incredibly delicious?

For the longest time, that was enough. The silky glide of tongue against tongue. The endless variations of pressure in lips that was a conversation all by itself. But then Aiden's hands left her neck, where they'd been cradling her head, and they trailed down to cup her breasts. His lips left hers to touch the soft skin below her ear where she could feel her own pulse pounding and suddenly it wasn't enough.

Not nearly enough.

And she knew what to do with her arms, now, too. She could wrap them around his neck and run her fingers through the softness of that closely cropped hair. Press her lips against that vulnerable spot on his temple.

She couldn't say who started moving first. If it hadn't been her, Aiden didn't seem to have any problem finding her bedroom, but it was a tiny house. The interruption of removing clothes felt like a nuisance and Sophia hastily stripped off her sweater at the same time Aiden peeled off his leather jacket. They both kicked off their shoes but then they looked at each other and abandoned undressing to kiss again.

And time seemed to stop. Taking their clothes off was no longer a nuisance. It was a game to be savoured. A slow reveal of buttons coming undone and zips being separated. Exposed skin that needed exploring. Touching and kissing with murmurs of appreciation and the odd whimper of escalating desire.

Too soon—and not nearly soon enough—they were in her bed and now there were no limits on the touching. No stopping the roller-coaster of sensation that was pushing them towards ecstasy. The interruption of Aiden leaning over the side of the bed to find his discarded jeans and fish in the pocket for a foil packet was unbearable.

There's no need, Sophia wanted to say. *Don't stop.*

But, of course, she didn't say it. And it wasn't entirely true, anyway. Okay, there was no way she could get pregnant but there were other reasons to use protection…

And maybe that was why she found the interruption unbearable. She didn't want to have to think about anything like that—even for the few seconds it took.

Easy to forget about it again, though. To cry out with the pleasure of feeling him inside her and then to simply surrender to the mounting tension that was taking them both to that place like no other. Where the world could stop turning for as long as it took.

It took quite a while for either of them to get their breath back as they lay there, their limbs entangled and the only sound their rapid panting.

'Oh, my God,' Sophia whispered, when words were finally available. 'How did you *do* that?'

'I was going to ask you the same thing.' There was a smile in Aiden's voice as he eased himself free. He didn't let go of Sophia, though, and she found herself rolling onto to her side, with her head cradled against his chest. 'You're amazing. You do know that, don't you?'

She could feel the edge of his nipple against her lips as she smiled. 'I do now. You're pretty amazing yourself.'

He pressed his lips to the top of her head. 'Maybe it was the combination.'

'Mmm.' Post-coital drowsiness was enveloping Sophia. She could feel herself relaxing into sleep and the thought that she would wake in Aiden's arms was blissful.

But he moved, just a little. 'I should go,' he murmured. 'I wasn't kidding about the early start.'

'You don't have to.'

The soft sound was regretful. 'But I know exactly what would happen if I stayed and I only had one condom in my pocket.'

The temptation to say something was even stronger this time. 'You don't need to worry about me getting pregnant.'

He moved enough to break the contact between their bodies. 'Don't take it personally but I've never relied on anyone else for contraception and I'm not about to break that rule.'

'Oh…' Sophia could feel the chill of exposed skin. And then she felt the dip of her mattress as Aiden sat up and swung his legs over the side of the bed.

He turned then but it was too dark to read his expression. 'I'm never going to have kids,' he said quietly. 'I had to be a father to Nate when he was growing up and that was enough. More than enough.'

There was a world of pain behind those words. But there was also a warning note. He'd shared more than his body with her tonight. He'd shared a lot of his personal life but there were limits. This wasn't something he was ready to talk about.

He leaned towards her and gave her a swift kiss. 'I do have to go.'

'Okay.'

Sophia listened to the sounds of him getting dressed again. She sat up, pulling the duvet around her like a shawl.

'It was the best half-date I've ever been on,' she told him. 'Thank you.'

The glimmer of his smile gave her the impression she'd said exactly the right thing. Not pushing him to talk any more about his 'rules' or the reason they were so iron-clad.

He came close and this time the kiss lingered.

'Just as well it was a half-date,' he said. 'That means we still have one left.'

One.

Sophia's heart sank.

'Would it count as a date if we didn't go anywhere? Like—if you came round for dinner one night or something?'

Something like a chuckle rumbled in Aiden's chest. 'I don't reckon it would. Do you?'

'No.' Sophia injected complete authority into her voice. 'I'm quite sure it wouldn't. Give me your phone number and I'll text you when I've had time to go shopping.'

Finding time to go grocery shopping wasn't so hard because there were supermarkets that regularly stayed open until at least midnight.

Finding time to cook something as amazing as Sophia wanted it to be was another matter. With what felt like a blinding flash of inspiration, a couple of days later she remembered the slow cooker tucked away at the back of one of her kitchen cupboards. Perfect. Getting up a little earlier to get ready for work, she had time to sear meat and brown the vegetables and then all she had to do was push the button and let the cooker work its magic while she worked with Flick for another busy day of home visits.

The concern about her student was still there but had been pushed into the background. Flick had dismissed her reaction to coffee after that Caesarean case as being due to a bit of a tummy bug and Sophia had been embarrassed that she'd blurted out the first suspicion that had sprung to mind—that Flick might be pregnant. The fact that she'd been pale and quiet for a few days after that fitted with her having been off colour and if she still seemed on the quiet side now, that could well be due to the extra studying she was doing. Flick seemed determined to learn everything about her chosen career and today was a great one for introducing her to things she hadn't done before.

It was good for her to have her teaching to distract her, as well. If she hadn't had Flick in the car with her as she negotiated the heavy traffic in places, she might have been tempted to wonder about how that meal was progressing as it simmered gently.

Or notice the desire that was simmering a little less gently deep in her belly. Would they go to bed again? Or maybe the real question was when and not if. Before or after dinner?

The car jerked a little with the firm pressure of her foot on the accelerator. 'What do you think is the most important thing about the postnatal care we give for up to six weeks after birth?'

'Support,' Flick answered promptly. 'Help with things like breastfeeding and bathing baby and how to cope with fatigue.'

'And?'

'Monitoring the health of both the baby and the mother. Especially after a Caesarean in case of infection. And making sure they don't think that breastfeeding is a reliable form of contraception.'

Hmm. Expanding on that topic was not going to help her stay focused. 'Good. What else do we do?'

'Watch out for signs of postnatal depression?'

They discussed the kind of signs that could be important as Sophia drove them to their first visit of the day but their first mother—Judith—seemed to be coping extremely well, having had a home birth two days ago.

'I'm lucky I've got Mum staying. I'm getting plenty of sleep between feeds.'

'Looks like baby's getting plenty of sleep, too.' Sophia smiled at the tiny, perfect face peeping from the folds of blanket in Judith's arms.

'I've been a bit worried about today's visit, though. I'm not sure I want her to have the test.' Judith's voice wobbled. 'It's going to hurt her, isn't it?'

'They usually cry,' Sophia said gently. 'But I think it's more about having their foot held still than any pain. It's a tiny prick. And the crying helps. It makes the blood come out faster so the test is over quickly.'

'It's important, Jude.' Their patient's mother was sitting nearby. She looked over at Sophia. 'There's all sorts of diseases it can test for, aren't there? Treatable things?'

'Absolutely. More than twenty different disorders, in fact.'

'Like what?'

'Maybe Flick can tell you about some of them.' Sophia smiled encouragingly at her student.

'There's hypothyroidism,' Flick said. 'And cystic fibrosis. And the enzyme disorders that prevent the normal use of milk.'

'And amino acid disorders,' Sophia added. 'Things

that can lead to something like brain damage if they're not picked up but which can be easily treated by following a special diet.'

'But she's not going to need a special diet for ages. I'm breastfeeding. Can't we put the test off until then?'

'It needs to be done as soon as possible after baby is forty-eight hours old.' Sophia checked her watch. 'And that's right about now.'

'I'll hold her, if you like,' Judith's mother offered. 'Why don't you go and have a quick shower or something?'

'No.' Judith closed her eyes. 'If it has to be done, I want to be the one holding her. Let's just get it over with.'

Flick stored the card with its four blood spots in Judith's file. 'I'd better remember to take that to the lab later,' she told Sophia as they drove to their next appointment. She shook her head. 'Poor Judith. I think she cried more than the baby did. Imagine how hard the six-week vaccinations are going to be for her.'

'Remind me to give her some pamphlets about that on our next visit. And we'll talk to her about how important it is.'

They had a hearing screening test to do on a final visit to a six-week-old baby later that morning and a lesson in hand-expressing breast milk for a young mother in the afternoon.

'I want my partner to share the night feeds,' she told them. 'And he really wants to, don't you, John?'

The young father nodded. The look and smile he gave his partner was exactly what Sophia would want for herself. Overflowing with love and a determination to provide support—even if it meant sacrificing sleep. Un-accountably, an image of Aiden filled her mind. How ridiculous was that? He was so against the idea of ever having a baby that he wouldn't trust anyone else to deal with contraception.

'But I really hate the thought of using one of those breast pumps,' the mother continued. 'It's so...mechani-cal.'

'Hand expression isn't hard. We'll show you how to do it.'

Flick took notes as Sophia provided the instruction. By the end of the day she'd also had plenty of practice taking blood pressures and temperatures on mothers, weighing babies and filling in report forms.

'You're getting very competent,' Sophia told her. 'You'll be doing all this on your own in no time.'

'Thanks. I'm loving it.' Flick opened her mouth as though about to say something else but then she merely smiled. 'See you tomorrow, Soph. Have a good night.'

Sophia smiled back. 'I intend to. You have one too.'

'Oh, man...that has to be the most amazing thing I've ever smelt.'

As an icebreaker, on opening the door to her dinner guest, this was enough to make Sophia smile and stop wondering about what was going to happen before or after they ate.

'Let's hope it tastes as good as it smells.' At least that was something she was pretty sure she didn't need to worry about. She'd been pretty impressed herself to come home to the aroma of those slow-cooked lamb shanks with red wine and mushrooms. The potatoes were cooking now and all she needed to do was mash them and dinner would be ready.

They had time to relax and, seeing as Aiden was holding out a bottle of very nice wine, it would have been rude not to taste it.

'Come in. I've got the fire going. It's pretty cold out there tonight, isn't it?'

'Sure is.' Aiden went straight to the flames of the small gas fire and stood with his back to it, his hand fanned out to catch the heat. He looked around. 'This is really nice.' His grin grew. 'Can't say I really noticed the other night.'

That grin—along with a ghost of a wink—chased away any lingering awkwardness over this date that wasn't a date. Suddenly, Sophia felt completely comfortable in his company. No, it was more than that. Being with him in this small, book-filled room with the smell of hot food and the sound of rain on the roof felt…well, it felt like *home*.

'It is nice, isn't it? Most of this stuff isn't mine, though. I'm house-sitting for a nurse at the Victoria who's gone overseas for a year. Sad to say, the year's half-over now. I'll have to start thinking about finding a place of my own before too long.'

'Where were you before this?' Aiden took the corkscrew Sophia handed him and dealt expertly with opening the wine while she took a couple of steps back into the kitchen to fetch glasses.

'Canberra. It's where I grew up.'

'You've got family there?' Aiden poured the wine.

'Just my parents. Dad's a pharmacist and Mum's a teacher.' Sophia sat down on the sofa and it felt good when Aiden came to sit beside her. 'How 'bout you?'

'No folks. There's just me and Nate. Mum died due to complications with his birth.'

'Oh…that's awful. Do you remember her?'

'Yeah…' For a second, Sophia could see the pain of that loss in his eyes but then his gaze slid sideways, as though he knew he might be revealing too much. 'Not as well as I'd like to, though. I was only six when she died.' He took a huge swallow of his wine.

Sophia's heart ached for the little boy who'd lost his mother. She'd never lost one of her maternity patients but she knew it still happened in rare cases and she could imagine how terrible it would be for the whole family.

'That smell is driving me mad.' Aiden's tone had a forced cheerfulness to it. An attempt to dispel any negative vibe? 'I didn't get time for lunch today.'

'Oh…' Maybe she couldn't do anything to comfort that little boy of years gone by but she could certainly fix this. 'Let's eat. Why don't you choose some music to put on while I mash the potatoes?'

His choice was surprising. 'You went for vinyl?'

'Retro, huh? The girl who owns this place is really into the old stuff.'

Sophia laughed. 'It's more like she's never thrown anything out. Dot's in her early sixties. At least you chose one of my favourites. I adore Cat Stevens.'

'Me, too.' Aiden took the plate from her hands but held her gaze. 'And how did you know that lamb shanks are my all-time favourite food?'

The warmth in that gaze made the pleasure of approval all the more intense and Sophia had to break the eye contact. 'Lucky guess. Or maybe we just have a lot in common.'

The food tasted just as good as it had smelled. The flames on the fake logs of the gas fire danced merrily and the music was the perfect background. All that was missing, Sophia decided, was candlelight.

Except wouldn't that make it too romantic to be a non-date? And what could she talk about that wouldn't take them into ground that might be deemed too personal and put it into the same category?

'You must have had a busy day, if you didn't get time for lunch.'

'Sure did. Two cardiac arrests, one straight after the other, would you believe?'

'Did you get them back?'

'Transported the first one with a viable rhythm but I think the downtime had been too long. The second guy woke up after the third shock and wanted to know what all the fuss was about.'

'No, really?'

'Yeah...' Aiden refilled their glasses and then raised his in a toast. 'Doesn't happen very often but when it does, it makes it all worthwhile. Even missing lunch.' He picked up his fork again. 'Did I tell you how amazing this is? I can't even mash potatoes without leaving lumps in.'

Sophia smiled. 'Tell me about the save. How old was he? Was there bystander CPR happening when you got there?'

Aiden told her about the successful case in so much detail she felt like she'd been standing there, watching the drama.

'You're really good at that.'

'What?'

'Telling a story. You could write a book about your job and people would want to read it.'

Aiden shook his head. 'I've just had practice, that's all. Nathan is a frustrated paramedic, I think. He always wants every gory detail about everything and doesn't let me get away with leaving stuff out. It's become a habit.'

Sophia forgot about any boundaries she might have been watching so that they could keep this time light. And fun. There was such a strong undercurrent to Aiden's words. It had the strength of showing the bond between the brothers in that Aiden was so used to sharing every detail of his life with Nathan, but it had rocks and rapids in it, too. Did Nathan resent that Aiden was out in the world, doing such an exciting and physical job, while he was trapped in a wheelchair? Did Aiden feel guilty about it?

'How did it happen?' she heard herself asking quietly. 'How did Nate become a quadriplegic?'

Aiden stopped chewing his mouthful of food and swallowed. Carefully. He reached for his glass of wine but didn't look at Sophia.

'He got pushed down a set of stairs.' His voice was flat.

'Oh, my God…' If she'd still had any appetite, it evaporated at that moment. 'How old was he?'

'Ten.'

A ten-year-old boy who'd probably loved to ride his bike and play soccer or rugby. A boy who'd already had it tough by having to grow up without his mother.

An echo of those sombre words Aiden had spoken the other night slipped into her head.

I had to be a father to Nate when he was growing up and that was enough. More than enough.

Had he been referring to the growing up before that dreadful accident or the trauma of readjustment that would have come afterwards?

She had so many questions she wanted to ask but didn't dare push further into such personal territory. The silence grew. Aiden was staring at his wineglass.

'Must have been drinking on such an empty stomach that did it,' he mused. 'I never talk about this.'

Then he looked up and caught Sophia's gaze. 'Or maybe it's because I'm with you.'

Something inside her melted into a liquid warmth. Some of it reached her eyes and she knew she'd have to blink a lot to make sure it didn't escape and roll down her cheeks. Her voice came out as a whisper.

'You can tell me anything. Or not. You're safe, either way.' She tried to smile but it didn't quite work.

Aiden wasn't smiling either. He felt like he was drowning in that moisture he could see collecting in Sophia's eyes. The *caring* behind them hit him like an emotional brick and tugged at something long forgotten. Poignant.

Did it remind him of the way his mother had looked at him, maybe?

'It was my father who pushed him down the stairs,' he found himself telling her. 'And it was my fault.'

The shock on her face was all too easy to read and Aiden cringed inwardly. He shouldn't have told her. She would think less of him. As little as he thought of himself?

But then her face changed. She looked like she was backing away even though she didn't move a single muscle.

'I don't believe that,' she said. 'Not one bit.'

How could she say that with such conviction? She barely knew him and she knew nothing of what had happened. A flash of anger made it easy to unchain words.

'My father was an alcoholic. He resented having to raise kids on his own and he blamed Nathan for causing Mum's death. He was a bully and he got really nasty when he was drinking, which was pretty much every day.'

The horror of that childhood was written all over Sophia's face. He could see it that way himself now, with the benefit of hindsight but, at the time, it had just been how things were.

'I knew how to handle him. I learned how to keep Nate safe. But that day? I was sixteen and I'd had enough. Instead of trying to defuse him, I flipped the coin. I started yelling at him and telling him just what a miserable bastard he was. I knew I had to get out of the house before I attacked him physically and I'd almost made it to the front door.' He had to stop for a second. To swallow past the constriction in his throat. 'He came after me but Nate was trying to follow me, too, and he was at the top of the stairs. Dad pushed him to get past and he fell.'

'You *saw* it happen?' Sophia's words were raw. Had she even thought before she reached out and covered his hand with her own? The warmth and pressure of that human contact almost undid Aiden but he couldn't pull his hand away. Instead, he turned it over and threaded his fingers through hers to lock them together.

'That wasn't the worst of it. I didn't know how badly hurt Nate was but I knew not to let him move before the ambulance could get there. So I held his head and kept him still and told him that everything would be okay. And then…and then…'

He could feel the tension in her hand. The terrible anticipation.

'And then we heard it. I didn't even know he had a gun in the house. Just as well, maybe, given how much I hated him that day. But I never had to think about killing him again. He did it himself.'

He choked on those last words. He'd never told anybody this story. Ever. Something was breaking inside his chest. Making him shake. Forcing a kind of horrible, dry sobbing sound to come out of his throat. He had his eyes screwed tightly shut so he didn't see Sophia standing up but he felt the tug on his hand and it was easy to comply with the silent instruction because he had no idea of what to do. How to deal with this awful emotional tidal wave.

How did Sophia know what to do?

She was tiny but he could feel an enormous strength

in the way she wrapped her arms around him and held him so tightly. He had no idea how long they stood there like that but it was long enough for the wave to recede. And now it felt like a huge expanse of sand that had been washed clean.

Deserted. And amazingly peaceful.

He loosened the grip of his arms around Sophia. How had she managed to keep breathing for so long?

'Sorry. I shouldn't have dumped all that on you.'

'I'm glad you did.' She moved a little in his arms so that she could look up at him. 'And, Aiden?'

'Yeah?'

'I was right.'

'What about?'

'It wasn't your fault. Not one bit of it.'

The anger was gone but he could still feel disappointed. Sophia was taking Nathan's side. Was there nobody out there who could understand? See the truth the way he saw it? He stepped back. Could he make some excuse and simply leave?

No. One look at Sophia and he was caught.

'I know why you think that,' she said. 'And when you love someone, it's easy to find a way to take the blame when something bad happens to them, but this wasn't your fault. It was your father's fault.'

'I *provoked* him.'

'And how many times did you *not* provoke him? You'd been living with that for ten years. You'd found every way under the sun to keep your little brother safe. Confronting your father and escaping would have been the only way to make sure of that in the long run and I think you'd finally got old enough to know that, even if it was subconscious. Okay, it went horribly wrong but it was a brave thing to do. How old were you?'

'Sixteen.' Aiden could barely get the word out. He was trying to process what she was saying. Was there any truth in it?

He'd been *brave*?

No way…

'There you go.' Sophia's smile was heartbreakingly tender. 'Just a kid yourself.' She raised her eyebrows. 'Was that when you decided you wanted to be a paramedic?'

'Yeah… They were amazing. I think they looked after me just as much as they looked after Nate. It's something I have in the back of my mind with every job I go to. It's not just the person who's sick or hurt that's your patient. The people who love them are too.'

'And that's part of what makes you so good at your job. No wonder Nate wants to hear your stories.'

That was how this had all started, wasn't it. Aiden jerked his gaze to the table. To the half-eaten meals of that delicious food Sophia had prepared.

'I'm sorry,' he said again. 'I kind of ruined dinner, didn't I?'

'It was my fault,' Sophia said. 'I asked the questions that got you started.'

'I didn't have to tell you. I chose to. Because I wanted to.'

The look he was receiving could only have come from a woman.

'Mmm…okay. I accept that it wasn't my fault.'

In the heartbeat of silence that followed, Aiden made the connection. And found himself smiling, albeit reluctantly.

'How 'bout I zap those plates in the microwave? You still hungry?'

He couldn't look away from her eyes. He was drowning again but this time it came with a lick of fire that would evaporate any moisture.

'Oh, yeah…I'm hungry.'

He caught her hand as she turned towards the table. 'But not for food.'

She gave a tiny gasp as he pulled her into his arms and bent his head to taste her lips. And then she melted against him and he knew, with absolute certainty, that things were going to be all right. He didn't have to leave. Didn't want to.

Things were going to be better than all right, in fact. Life itself seemed to have just become that much better.

CHAPTER EIGHT

THIS WAS NOTHING like last time.

Oh, the desire was the same. That being carried away on a wave of physical sensation that led to ultimate satisfaction, but there was something very different about the way Sophia could feel herself responding.

This physical nakedness had come in the wake of emotional nakedness on Aiden's part. He'd opened his heart to her and made himself vulnerable and it made her want to protect him, even as her own heart broke to think of what his childhood had been like. Weird how it could break but swell at the same time as she saw the depth of the love he had for his brother.

No wonder he shied away from any other responsibilities in his life—like a relationship that lasted more than three dates. Or having a child of his own.

And the guilt he'd carried with him ever since that accident. Was it more than not wanting extra responsibilities? Was he preventing anyone else getting too close as a kind of penance?

She'd told him he was safe to tell her anything and he had. Way more than she'd expected.

He deserved the same kind of honesty from her. To know that he was safe from more than any emotional repercussions of being close, but something stopped her saying anything when he tore open the foil packet of the condom.

It would spoil the moment, she told herself. Bring the rush of escalating desire to a grinding halt and maybe it was more than simply desire for Aiden at the moment. Maybe he needed the intimacy as a kind of reassurance. A reminder that he deserved the good things in life because of who he was.

The good things in life.

Like being loved...

No. Sophia had to shut down the realisation because it was blinding. And terrifying. Far easier to stop thinking and simply feel. To give herself up to the touch of Aiden's hands and mouth. To give in to her own need to feel the closest physical touch possible from another being.

It came back, though, in those quiet minutes of lying there entangled in each other's arms, as heart and breathing rates gradually settled back to normal.

No. This was nothing like last time. Because this had been more than sex. More than having fun. On her part, it had been making love.

Aiden had opened his heart to her and she had fallen into it. Fallen in love with him.

This wasn't supposed to have happened. How could it, when you knew right from the start that it was only going to last for three dates?

* * *

He'd fallen asleep.

He hadn't meant to. He never stayed a whole night because it was one of the rules. He'd learned long ago that it added a depth that made things more difficult when it was time to move on because it gave the impression that he might be happy to stay longer. That it was about more than a bit of fun.

He'd taken the fun element out of the evening himself, though, hadn't he? Spilling his guts like that about Nate. About his father.

Good grief…he'd never told a woman any of that stuff.

But she'd told him it was safe and nobody had ever said that to him before.

And he'd *felt* safe.

He'd even felt…absolved from the guilt for just a heartbeat. The way she'd twisted the idea of being at fault and tipped it towards being someone else's choice.

There was a truth in that. Maybe he'd be able to catch that feeling of absolution again one day. It had been too huge not to push away at the time, though. To shut off everything except the need to take Sophia to bed. To try and thank her for what she'd given him? It wasn't surprising he'd fallen asleep after the roller-coaster of emotions that had been stirred up and then released. Physical release had been the last push into a totally new feeling of being at peace.

Safe.

Such a roller-coaster. Like that extraordinary sensation he'd had when she'd told him he'd been brave.

Brave?

She admired him? Remembering it now gave him that same weird feeling of being…what…special? But she didn't know the truth of it, did she? How scared he'd been so often. The way he'd taken Nathan under his bed sometimes and held the toddler close until he'd known that his father had been drunk enough to be no threat for the rest of the night. How he'd stolen money from their dad's wallet so he could buy a toy for Nate's birthday. How often he'd wagged school or lied about being sick so that he could make sure the housekeeper was taking proper care of his brother.

She wouldn't think he was brave if she'd known the awful relief he'd felt when it had become clear after the accident that Nathan would have to be cared for by people far more qualified than he was. That all he needed to do was visit him every day. That he was free to follow the dream that had been born on that dreadful night and become a paramedic so he could help others.

He'd created exactly the life he'd dreamed of but he had hurt other people along the way, he knew that. Some women in the past had been angry. Had accused him of using them. Others had been upset and the tears had been harder to handle than angry words.

How would Sophia react when they'd had their third—and last—date?

The last thing he wanted was to make her cry.

Even thinking about it made him hold her a little tighter as she lay in his arms, with her head tucked against his chest. The movement made her stir and make a tiny sound, almost like a cat purring.

He loved that sound.

'Mmm.' This was more like a word and it was followed by a slow, deep indrawn breath that was painted into sensation by the small hand that moved across his chest.

'You're still here,' Sophia whispered. 'That's nice.'

'Mmm.' He had to agree. It *was* nice.

'What time is it?'

'I don't know. Close to dawn, I think. The birds are getting noisy.'

'We don't have to get up yet, though.' Her hand was moving again. The soft touch reached his abdomen and Aiden could feel his body coming a lot more awake.

'We don't.' Okay, maybe this wasn't the best idea but how could he resist? 'Just as well I came prepared this time.' His jeans weren't far away. There was another foil packet in the back pocket.

He couldn't miss the way Sophia stilled in his arms, though. The way the fuzzy sense of sleepy peacefulness took on a spiky edge.

'What?' The word was no more than a puzzled murmur. Had he done the wrong thing in being prepared for more than once?

'I…' The hesitation lasted long enough for Sophia to take another deep breath. He could feel the press of her breast against his hand swell and then recede. 'I meant what I said the other night. You don't need it.'

Whoa… This was a step into totally forbidden territory. He didn't care what precautions any woman took. He had to know he was taking responsibility for contraception himself.

The desire for sex was ebbing fast. He needed to escape. Carefully, he started pulling his arm away from where it encircled Sophia but he had no idea what he could say. How he could stop this becoming an unpleasant conversation for both of them.

But he didn't have to find anything to say because Sophia spoke first.

'I can't get pregnant, Aiden. I had a hysterectomy nearly ten years ago.'

'What? *Why?*' Oh, God…had she had cancer? The idea that she'd had to face something so terrible at such a young age was unbearable. Instead of taking his arm away, Aiden found himself pushing it further around her. Pulling her closer, as if he could protect her from something.

'It was an accidental pregnancy.' Her voice was quiet. Matter-of-fact. 'It was ectopic but I ignored the early warning signs. It went on too long and then ruptured really badly. They had to perform a hysterectomy to control the bleeding.'

Aiden swore softly, his eyes tightly shut. He could imagine all too easily the emergency that rupture would have caused. The urgent, major surgery that would have been necessary to save her life. But…

'But why did you ignore the signs?'

It seemed a long time before she spoke again and when she did, her voice was so quiet he barely heard it.

'I wanted the baby,' she said.

That took a few moments to process. 'How old were you?'

'Twenty-one. I was a student midwife. I'd always

loved babies. Maybe because I was an only child and I was so envious when my best friend got a baby sister. My parents both worked full time and it felt like we were…I don't know…less of a family, I guess.'

'But you said the pregnancy was accidental.'

'Of course it was. I wasn't stupid. I was only twenty-one and it wasn't as if the relationship was going anywhere. We were both young. Just out to have a bit of fun.'

Like he was with the women in his life? Aiden had to swallow a nasty pang of guilt. Those women had had every right to be angry or upset, hadn't they? He *had* been using them.

'So he wasn't keen on the idea of being a father?'

'He did his best to be supportive but we both knew it couldn't have worked. I actually went down the track of having a termination but when I went to ring up to make an appointment, I couldn't do it. I realised then that I wanted that baby. I…I already loved it.' There was a wobble in her voice. 'So I ignored the abdominal pain that came and went. I told myself that a bit of bleeding could be perfectly normal in the early stages of some pregnancies. That things would settle down once I got to the end of the first trimester and I'd go and get checked out and have a scan after that. When it was less likely that anyone would try and talk me into getting rid of it.'

'And then it ruptured.'

'I was about fourteen weeks by then. I guess it was lucky it happened while I was at work. I might have bled out pretty fast if I'd been anywhere else.'

'I'm glad you were at work, then. Lucky for me, too.'

A tiny sound that could have been an embryonic sob

came from Sophia but then they were both silent for a long time.

'I'm sorry,' Aiden said, finally, into the light of a new day that was filtering through the gap in the curtains. 'You lost something huge and it must have been devastating.' Not only had she lost the baby she'd already loved but she'd lost the chance of ever having another one.

'Yeah…it was tough but that's just the way it is. I'm not going to let it define me. I'm going to make the best of my life. This isn't a practice run, you know? It's the only life we get.'

She reminded him of Nathan. Totally different things to deal with, of course. Or were they so different? Nathan lived with the loss of mobility. He'd had to come to terms with a different perception of his body and where he was going in life.

Sophia lived with the loss of a dream. Wouldn't being unable to ever be a mother involve the same sort of process in coming to terms with that different perception and direction?

The similarity was there. Perhaps the greatest similarity was in the positive attitude to making the best of his life.

He was so proud of his brother's attitude. He loved him to the point where it made his chest ache.

And right now he was feeling a very similar pride in Sophia.

A similar kind of love?

Oh, man…that was a scary thought. He'd never actually fallen in love with a woman. He'd known to get out as soon as there were any warning signs. Had he ignored them for some reason this time?

He tried to search his memory.

Had it been the first time he'd seen her smile? Or when he'd heard her laugh—way back, when they'd first met and she'd introduced herself as being a midwife and he'd joked that he hoped *she* was, given the emergency cord prolapse she'd just dealt with.

No. That had simply been attraction. No danger signs that could have been spotted there.

What about that first date, though? When he'd seen her at the door of that crowded bar? The way the noise of the people and music had just faded away until it had felt like he and Sophia were the only people on the planet?

Yeah…maybe that should have rung an alarm bell, given that it had never happened before.

And she'd loved his three-dates rule. Maybe that was the problem. She'd made him feel safe.

Or maybe it was the way she'd made him feel safe last night. Safe enough to tell her anything.

He couldn't tell her what he was feeling right now. No way.

She'd said that a three-dates rule was exactly what was missing from *her* life. She didn't want the complications of a long-term relationship. She couldn't have a family so maybe it simply wasn't a part of her life plan now.

She wouldn't want to know how he was feeling. It might make her feel bad when she walked away from him to get on with the life that wasn't a practice run.

He didn't want her to feel bad.

He'd make her feel good instead.

Her lips were easy to find. Soft and deliciously responsive. They still had time, didn't they?

This would be a first for him. Sex without protection, but Sophia had shown him something that made her vulnerable and she deserved at least the reassurance of trust.

And…man, it made things feel different.

Nothing like the last time.

Nothing like any time. Ever.

The text message on Aiden's phone came when he was on the point of leaving her house to go to work.

The atmosphere was a little odd. Sophia thought it was because they'd come out to find the remnants of last night's dinner still on the table and it had been a shock. So much had happened since they'd been sitting there.

So much had changed between them?

Yes. The atmosphere was strange. As if they both realised how huge that change had been and it was making them both nervous.

So much for having fun. A limited amount of time to enjoy each other's company. Some 'no-strings' sex.

'I could help clean up,' Aiden offered.

'No. I've got more time than you. I don't start till eight. You've only got ten minutes if you want to get to the station in time to start at seven.'

'Okay. But next time I'm doing the dishes.'

Next time?

Was that going to be date number three or would it still be a non-date if they didn't go out anywhere? Sophia found herself smiling. On the point of clarifying the 'rules' again when the text message bleeped.

That was even more of a shock than the messy table had been. Not that there was someone else who wanted to make contact so early in the day but the way it made Sophia feel.

Jealous?

'It's only Nate,' Aiden said after a glance at his phone. 'I'll call him when I get to work.'

He kissed her goodbye and once again Sophia found herself listening to the sound of his bike roaring away.

No. That feeling hadn't been jealousy. It was deeper than that. She'd known it was probably his brother rather than another woman who was texting him and that made her remember that he had another part of his life that was more important than any woman could ever be to him.

Another part of his life that would swallow him without a ripple when she was no longer a consideration.

Oh, help… If she could feel this bleak before it had even ended, how bad was it going to be when they said goodbye at the end of date number three?

But did it have to end?

Aiden didn't want to have kids.

She *couldn't* have any.

She'd avoided serious relationships because she had less to offer than most women but Aiden didn't want what she didn't have to offer anyway.

Didn't that make them perfect for each other?

The thought came with a leap of something that felt like hope and Sophia found herself holding it as she took plates to the kitchen sink, scraped off the abandoned food and rinsed them clean.

Who would have thought that she might find a man who could not only accept that she couldn't have a baby but would welcome it?

Except that something didn't feel right about this picture. The pieces didn't quite fit. Or maybe there were some missing that were leaving a hole she couldn't identify.

A wipe down of the table obliterated any reminder of last night's meal and Sophia collected her bag and coat to set off on her walk to the Victoria.

She couldn't shake the feeling that something was wrong, however.

That she was too far along a track for turning around to be possible. That she might be heading for some kind of crash and there was nothing at all she could do to prevent it.

CHAPTER NINE

WHAT WAS A girl to do when she couldn't figure out what it was that was bothering her?

Talk about it, of course. To someone she knew she could trust. Someone who knew more about her than anyone and loved her enough to want to help her figure it out.

Her mum?

Sadly, for Sophia, that couldn't be her first port of call. The love was there but the depth of understanding wasn't. Even after all these years, the relief her mother hadn't been able to hide when she'd lost her baby was hurtful.

'It would have ruined your life, being a single mother,' she'd said. 'Your career would have gone out the window and there aren't many men who really want to take on raising someone else's child.'

But she'd loved that baby. That potential little person to love and be loved by. Her career had seemed far less important in comparison.

'There are worse things than not having children.' Had her mother really thought she was offering comfort? 'You're about to be qualified to do the job you've always wanted to do. Focus on that. It'll make you happy.'

Had it been her mother's job that had made *her* happy? Had it been a mistake to have a child at all? One that would have ruined her life if she'd become pregnant accidentally before she had established her career or found a husband?

If it had been a mistake, her parents hid it well and had done the best job they could in raising their child, but that childhood had been a lonely one. There had clearly never been the possibility of siblings and with both her parents working full time, even a family dog had been ruled out as company.

Which was why it had been such a joy to spend time at home with her best friend, Emily, ever since she'd first arrived in Melbourne. To soak in the chaos of an extended family that included an adorably woolly, brown dog by the name of Fuzzy.

With her next day off coinciding with one of Em's, it was a no-brainer to invite herself for a visit and a chance to talk to the person most likely to be able to identify what it was that was bothering her so much.

They were in the garden of Emily and Oliver's house. Well, the house actually belonged to Em's mother, Adrianna, but it was the family home for them all now. And the family was growing, despite the sadness of losing Emily's foster-daughter, Gretta, a few weeks ago.

'How's it working out, having Ruby here with you?'

'Couldn't be better.' Emily lifted two-year-old Toby from his tricycle and took him to sit under the tree. 'I wish she'd rest a bit more, though. Look—she's over there, pruning roses. It's not that long since the in utero surgery on her baby.'

As if sensing she was being discussed, the waif-like teenager looked across the garden and waved at the two women.

'Am I doing it right?' she called. 'I've never tried this before.'

'You're doing a great job,' Emily called back. 'But you don't have to.'

The shy grin in response came with a shrug that was pure teenager.

'She feels like she has to help out,' Emily told Sophia, 'because we're not charging her any rent for the bunga-low. And Mum wouldn't let her help with any housework this afternoon. Said it could wait till tomorrow because she felt like putting her feet up and reading her book. I'd rather Ruby was reading a book, too. She could be doing a bit of study or something so that she feels ready to go back to school after the baby comes.'

'I'm sure she will, when she gets used to being here. It must be a big thing, feeling like she's part of a family.'

Emily's smile was that of a contented woman as she nodded, watching Toby doing his stiff-legged crawl to-wards Sophia.

'Huge,' she agreed quietly.

Toby stopped and held up his arms. Sophia gladly gathered him onto her lap and let the toddler bury his head against her shoulder as he settled in for a cuddle. The faded blue kangaroo toy in his other hand felt a bit damp against the back of her neck.

'That's Kanga, isn't it? Gretta's toy?'

'Mmm.' Emily's smile grew misty. 'He's barely let it go since we lost her. I don't think he understands that she died but he's missing her.'

Toby's curls were springy and too irresistible not to stroke. An African child, Toby had been brought to Australia so that he could receive treatment for his spinal deformity and the scarring on his face from infection.

'How's it going with the adoption process?'

Emily groaned. 'The paperwork is endless. Ollie's confident that we'll get there, though. He says not getting there simply isn't an option.'

Her smile was proud now. Full of love for the man she 'remarried' so recently.

For a long moment, Sophia focused on the gorgeous cuddle she was receiving. Then her gaze drifted over Toby's head to where Ruby was eyeing up another rose bush, rubbing her back as she straightened.

'Do you remember when Ruby was waking up after the operation on the baby?'

'Of course.'

'What we were talking about?'

'Josh?'

'Mmm.' Josh. The baby Emily had lost at twenty-eight weeks—about the stage that Ruby was in her pregnancy now. The one successful round of all the IVF Emily and Oliver had gone through. 'After that. About why you and Oliver had split up.'

'Because he couldn't face adopting a baby?'

'He'd been adopted himself, hadn't he? And it hadn't been happy?'

'Mmm.'

'But he really wants to adopt Toby now, doesn't he?'

'Even more than I do, I think. Although that's not really possible. Hey, Toby…it's about my turn for a cuddle, isn't it?'

Obligingly, Toby crawled off Sophia's lap and threw himself at Emily with a joyful crow.

'Mumma!'

Even more obligingly, Fuzzy slithered closer and put his head on Sophia's lap so that she still had a head to stroke.

'You wanted kids so much,' she said quietly. 'You weren't going to let infertility stop you. And look what you've got now. A whole family, including a husband who adores you.'

'I'm the luckiest woman in the world,' Emily agreed.

'But you did it anyway, even without Oliver, and you were still happy, weren't you?'

'Ye-es…' Emily peered around Toby's head to give her friend a searching look. 'Where's this coming from, Soph? Is something bothering you?'

Sophia nodded. 'I'm not sure what it is. But I remember being at your vow renewal ceremony and thinking how brave you were. And that I needed to get braver too. Make changes in my life so that I could find something as good as what you've found. I even thought I could maybe try fostering or adopting kids one day, too.'

'You have made changes.' Emily's smile was encouraging. 'It's going well with that gorgeous boyfriend of yours, isn't it?'

'It's almost over,' Sophia told her. 'He has a three-dates rule.'

'A *what*?'

'He only ever goes out on three dates with a woman. That way you can have fun but it doesn't get heavy, you know?'

'No.' Emily shook her head. 'You've been out on more than three dates, haven't you?'

'Hmm. The rules got bent a bit. One of them was finishing off a date that got interrupted. And one wasn't really a date because he came to my place and we didn't go out anywhere.'

Emily laughed. 'Sounds like the rule isn't a real rule at all. I wouldn't worry about it.' She frowned. 'In fact, I don't like it. Sounds like an easy escape route for a commitment-phobe to me.'

'Yeah…well, I told him I liked the rule a lot, the first time we went out. That I was only after a bit of fun, too. Nothing serious.'

'Ohh…' Emily gave her another searching look. 'You've fallen for him, haven't you?'

'Yeah…' The word was a sigh. 'The weird thing is that, on paper, we're perfect for each other. I can't have kids and he doesn't want any.'

'Really? Why not?'

Sophia closed her eyes for a long moment, drawn back instantly to that night when Aiden had bared his soul to her and told her things he'd never told anyone. He'd trusted her.

And, yes, Emily knew all about her own story but that was hers to tell. She couldn't share Aiden's. Couldn't break that trust. But there were parts that weren't as private as an abusive childhood with an alcoholic father. Or the guilt of feeling responsible for a dreadful accident.

'He's got a brother. Nathan. He's a quadriplegic. Aiden's more than a big brother to him. He's like a parent, too, I guess. A whole family. I think he's got an unwritten rule about not letting anything interfere with that responsibility.'

'Wow...' Emily was silent for a minute. 'Does he feel the same way about you?'

'I don't know. I think he's let me into his life more than he ever has with any other woman. I've met Nathan. We went to a Murderball game.'

'Is that the wheelchair rugby?'

'Yes. It's really exciting to watch. And Nathan's cool. I really like him. He lives in sheltered accommodation but he seems to have his life pretty well sorted. He's got a girlfriend who has more facial piercings than I've ever seen and they clearly adore each other.'

Sophia was rubbing Fuzzy's head and pulling gently on his ears. She bent her own head, horrified that she could feel tears gathering. It was great to be talking to Emily but she didn't want to spoil a lovely afternoon by falling to pieces. What was wrong with her?

'Oh, hon...' Emily's voice was full of sympathy. 'You've got it bad, haven't you?'

The nod dislodged a tear. She swiped it away.

'I don't know what I'm so upset about. I knew it was never supposed to last more than three dates and the next one has got to count for number three. We can't keep bending his silly rule for ever.'

'That's not the real problem, though, is it?'

Sophia swallowed. 'Isn't it?'

Emily shook her head. She tickled Toby, making him chortle, and then pulled him closer for another hug. 'I think it goes deeper than that.'

'In what way?'

'You're not really perfect for each other. Paper doesn't count.' Emily's gaze was serious now. 'Aiden doesn't want kids. And maybe he has good reason for that. But you do want them, even if you've tried to convince yourself you didn't for all these years. You probably want that as much as I did. You want a real family and you know it's quite possible to have that, even if you can't give birth to your own babies. Look at me.'

'I know.' Sophia drew in a long, slow breath as she found herself nodding slowly.

Yes. That was it, in a nutshell. What had been niggling away in the back of her mind. Aiden didn't want children. And she did. It could never work.

End of story?

Maybe not.

'But Oliver didn't want to adopt children either and look at him, now—leading the crusade to let you keep Toby in the country.'

'He didn't want to adopt,' Emily agreed, 'but he always wanted to be a father. It's a bit different.' It was her turn to sigh. 'Life's an unfair business sometimes, isn't it?'

Toby had crawled off Emily's lap now and was heading towards Ruby. Fuzzy abandoned Sophia and went after Toby like a sheepdog looking after his charge. Ruby grinned as she saw them coming. She bent to pick Toby up but then froze. Something about her posture made both Emily and Sophia share an alarmed glance.

'Ruby?' Emily was on her feet in a flash. 'What's wrong?'

It was too quiet today.

So much easier to silence an annoyingly persistent voice in the back of your head if you could keep busy. Even better if you had a real challenge to rise to.

What Aiden needed was something dramatic. A cardiac arrest, maybe—one that led to a successful outcome, of course. Or some trauma. A crush injury perhaps, that would need careful management, especially if whatever was doing the crushing was still in place. A prang would do. A mess of two or three vehicles with an unknown number of potential injuries and the chaos of disrupted traffic and impatient onlookers creating difficulty for any emergency personnel to get to the scene. He'd get there first and get to do the scene management and triage, which was always a challenge of unknown quantity.

But no. What he had was an elderly homeless guy in central Melbourne suffering from double pneumonia. He was sitting just under a bridge beside the popular walking track that led to Southbank. Apparently, he'd been sitting there for the last three days so people had eventually noticed that he had barely moved. Finally, a concerned pedestrian had called the police. The police had called the ambulance service for a medical assessment. They knew this man and knew he didn't talk much. Asking questions wasn't going to solve anything.

'His name's Bruce,' they told Aiden. 'But that's all we know about him, other than that he's been living on the streets for years. Him and his dog.'

The dog looked as old and thin and unkempt as his owner and seemed happy to sit just as immobile, with his head on Bruce's lap. It seemed to know that Aiden was trying to help but growled ominously if any of the police came too close.

After an initial assessment, Aiden had called for transport so now he was just keeping Bruce company. He had his patient on oxygen and a foil survival blanket was wrapped around his shoulders. He'd taken a baseline set of vital signs. Blood pressure was too low, temperature too high. The respiration rate was way too high and blood-oxygen level way too low. Even with the mask on and oxygen coming from the small cylinder he carried on the bike, there had been little improvement over the last ten minutes. Bruce's lips were still blue and he could almost hear the crackle in his lungs without using a stethoscope.

Where on earth was the back-up for transport? Had they been diverted to exactly the kind of drama he was desperate for himself? Something that would stop the argument in his head that was gaining momentum—on both sides.

He couldn't even talk to the two police officers who had moved a safe distance away from the dog and seemed to see something on the river that was interesting enough to keep them chatting.

He only had Bruce, who didn't talk. And a sad-looking dog who was going to look even sadder when they had to take his master away in the ambulance. The police had called a pet shelter that was sending a rescue crew to help. Aiden doubted that these two would ever be reunited and that sucked.

'I'm sorry about this,' he told Bruce quietly, crouching beside him and checking that the oxygen saturation probe was still covering a finger. 'But we have to take you somewhere you can be warm and comfortable so the antibiotics have a chance to work.'

He took Bruce's heart and respiration rate again, just for something to do, but it felt wrong to be so silent. The noise of the city was a distant hum. The sound of voices and laughter came occasionally as a pair of joggers or cyclists went past on the track but the snippets of normality vanished as quickly as they came. He had to talk to Bruce even if the old man couldn't respond or possibly didn't even understand. But what could he talk about? He'd only had one thing on his mind for the last couple of days.

'I'd like to go out tonight,' he found himself telling Bruce. Still quietly enough for nobody but the dog to overhear. 'But, at the same time, I don't want to because if I do, it's going to be the last date I have with this girl and that would be a real shame because she's…well… she's perfect, that's what she is.'

The perfect woman for him, at any rate.

He never wanted to have children.

Sophia couldn't ever have children.

And hadn't that vow to never take on the responsibility of a family of his own been the whole basis of the three-dates rule? To get out before he fell in love? Before she fell in love with him and wanted more—like living together or getting married? Before her biological clock started ticking more and more loudly and the desire to have a baby became the priority?

But he'd never been on this side of the equation. Never been the one who didn't want things to end.

Sophia had welcomed the rule. She didn't want anything long term either. And why would she? She wasn't planning on having a family any more than he was so she wouldn't see herself in the role of a mother. Or a wife.

Someone was going to get hurt and Aiden had the horrible feeling it was going to be him.

Could they stay friends, perhaps, after their official dating period was over?

Friends with benefits even?

No. As if that could work.

As if it could ever be enough.

'I didn't get out in time.' The words came out like a sigh of defeat and triggered a move to check his watch. Where on earth was that back-up? He could hear a siren in the distance but that wouldn't be the crew coming to transport his patient because the job wouldn't have been assigned the urgency of needing lights and sirens. It would be well down the list and probably getting bumped repeatedly as calls came in for more serious incidents.

A glance towards the police officers showed them to be in deep conversation now. Maybe they were enjoying the enforced break from their duties. Life still flowed along the track beside them. A young mother was jogging as she pushed a twin stroller that had a toddler on one side and a baby cocoon strapped on the other. Behind her, an older couple walked hand in hand, and as Aiden watched they turned to each other and shared a smile. In his peripheral vision he saw Bruce move, too. A tiny movement of just his hand as it rested on the dog's head. One finger moving to gently rub a floppy ear.

Something inside Aiden twisted painfully. That dog was probably the only living thing that Bruce had a relationship with. Responsibility for. And, any moment now, someone was going to turn up with a van to take the dog away.

'They'll take good care of him,' Aiden said. 'There are families out there who love to foster dogs.'

Was it his imagination or was Bruce's level of consciousness slipping further? He put his hand on the old man's wrist to feel for a pulse. The dog nudged his hand with a cold nose and that twisting sensation in his gut intensified.

It wasn't just about whether or not you could have kids, was it? Responsibility came with any relationship if you wanted to do the best you could and Aiden had never taken anything on without making sure he did his absolute best.

He was the best paramedic he could be.

The best brother.

When you loved somebody enough, their happiness became as important as your own. More important, maybe. Nathan's happiness had always been more important than his own. Right now, it felt like Sophia's happiness was important, too.

He wanted her to be happy.

He wanted to be the one to *make* her happy.

But if he was really honest, he wanted to be happy himself and that was why this was so damned hard.

Sophia didn't want more than three dates so he couldn't throw the rule book away. And that meant that if he wanted to see her again, it would be for the last time.

And *that* meant he would never see her again.

Did that mean he *didn't* want the date even more than he did want it?

Two men were coming along the track now, carrying a wire crate between them. They wore overalls with the logo of the animal rescue service. Not far behind them, an ambulance crew was wheeling a stretcher. The police officers noted the arrival of assistance and started to move closer in case they were needed.

The wait was over.

The speed with which things were sorted seemed almost indecent after the long wait. Surprisingly, the dog didn't protest at being bundled into the crate and Bruce seemed equally defeated—barely conscious as he was lifted to the stretcher and covered with warm blankets. After handing over his paperwork to the ambulance crew, the last thing Aiden needed to do was change the oxygen supply and take his own small cylinder back to the bike.

'All the best, Bruce,' he said. 'I'll keep an eye out for you next time I'm down this way.'

The old man's eyes opened slowly. His lips moved. Aiden lifted the mask.

'Ask her,' Bruce mumbled. 'Tell her…'

Oh, man… It was a cringe-worthy moment to realise

that he'd been heard and understood when he'd been sharing something so decidedly unprofessional. Aiden didn't want to have to think about it and, lucky for him, he didn't have to. He'd barely got his helmet back on his head when a priority call came through to an address in Brunswick.

'Premature labour,' he was told. 'Approximately twenty-eight weeks gestation. Mother seventeen years old. Nearest ambulance is at least ten minutes away.'

Aiden kicked his bike into life and flicked on the beacons. Anticipation was tinged with relief. This was exactly what he needed.

Drama. A life—other than his own—that was hanging in the balance.

'The ambulance is on its way.'

'How long?' Sophia was kneeling behind Ruby, holding the girl in her arms to support her.

'I don't *want* an ambulance,' Ruby sobbed. 'I just want this to *stop*. It *hurts…*'

'I know, sweetheart.' Sophia tightened her hug. 'But sometimes it's baby who decides when things are going to happen.' She turned to catch Emily's gaze and mouthed her question again silently.

Emily held up the fingers of both hands and her look said it all. Ten minutes could well be too long. She tilted her head towards the house with her eyebrows raised but Sophia had to shake her head. They'd already tried to get Ruby inside but she'd been almost hysterical as the first pain had hit and her waters had broken. She'd frozen and then collapsed onto the ground when Emily and Sophia had taken her arms to help her walk.

Emily's mother, Adrianna, came rushing out of the house with an armload of blankets. 'I'll keep Toby in with me,' she said. 'Where on earth is that ambulance? We called them ages ago.'

'It was only a few minutes, Mum,' Emily said. 'And I can hear a siren.'

'Oh…thank goodness.' Adrianna tucked a blanket around Ruby's shoulders. 'You'll be okay now, love. You'll be safely in hospital in no time.'

'I won't,' Ruby sobbed. 'It's too early. I didn't think I wanted this baby but I do…I want it *so* much…'

'I know.' Sophia kept hugging her. She knew how it felt to be faced with the fear of losing an unborn baby you'd already fallen in love with. She also knew that Ruby's fears were justified. This was far too early—especially if this baby was going to arrive before they had the benefit of all the resuscitation gear that the MMU would have on hand. Emily was looking desperately worried and that was enough to pull Sophia even further from the calm, professional space she was trying to hang onto.

And that siren sounded…different?

It wasn't really a surprise to see the big bike pulling in to the side of the road and a helmeted figure opening panniers to grab equipment.

What was surprising was the way her fear seemed to evaporate the moment she saw that it was Aiden who had responded to the call.

'The ambulance isn't far away,' he told Ruby, as he crouched beside her. 'I'm just the advance party.' He looked up to include all of them. 'Tell me what's happening. How far apart are the contractions?'

Emily filled him in on the sudden start of Ruby's labour. She also told him that the baby had had in utero surgery a few weeks ago to correct spina bifida and that Ruby had been kept on complete bed rest until they had been confident she wouldn't go into labour. By the time she finished speaking, the ambulance had arrived.

'We'll get you into the ambulance,' Aiden said. 'But we'll need to check where we're at before we roll.'

'I'm coming too,' Emily said.

There would be no room in the ambulance for Sophia to go as well but she went as far as the ambulance and waited while Aiden and Emily examined Ruby. Everything seemed under control but suddenly Ruby cried out as another contraction hit and then nothing was under control. Within seconds Aiden was holding a tiny scrap of a baby in his hands.

'Soph? Open that kit for me and get the ziplock bag.'

Her hands were shaking as she complied. She knew to wrap preterm infants in bubble wrap but a plastic bag? The baby wasn't making any sound and this was not looking good.

But Aiden seemed to know exactly what he was doing. He cut and clamped the cord and then put the baby into the bag leaving the head outside.

'Dry the head for me,' he told Emily. 'And cover it with a corner of the blanket. Soph—can you bring that airway kit a bit closer, please?'

One of the ambulance crew got there first and Sophia edged further away. The back of the ambulance was crowded now and all Emily could do was hold Ruby's hand and try to reassure her as she watched what was happening with the baby.

Sophia stood pressed against the open back door of the ambulance. She couldn't look away from that fierce concentration on Aiden's face. He was invested in this job a thousand per cent, determined to succeed, and she loved him for that.

And she felt so proud of him. That he knew exactly what to do and that he was doing it with such confidence and skill.

His hands moved so fast. They looked huge against the tiny pieces of equipment, like the smallest ever size of a laryngoscope blade and breathing tube. The ventilation bag was also tiny and he was squeezing it so gently to deliver such small puffs of oxygen.

'Hook up the monitor,' he told one of the crew. 'I need continuous monitoring of end tidal CO_2.'

The baby still wasn't moving but Aiden wasn't starting any chest compressions. His gaze was flicking between the baby and the monitor.

'Heart rate's over sixty,' he said. 'Let's roll. I want to get this little girl into NICU asap.'

Sophia had to step back so that the doors could be slammed shut. Within seconds, the ambulance took off, with its beacons flashing and the siren on. It looked like any other ambulance by the time it got to the end of the street but Sophia knew what was happening inside and she shut her eyes for a moment, sending out a fervent wish that they were going to be successful in saving that tiny life.

Then she opened her eyes and found herself staring at Aiden's bike.

He'd have to come back for that, wouldn't he?

Adrianna would be only too happy if Sophia hung around until Emily got back so that she could hear a first-hand account of how things had gone during transport and what was happening with the baby. It was quite reasonable to also assume that Aiden would come back with her so that he could collect his bike and get back on the road. Sophia picked up his helmet.

For a moment she held it in her arms, close to her chest. It felt like a connection to the man who'd been wearing it a short time ago. It also felt like an insurance policy. He'd have to come in to find it before he could go anywhere else. Like the way her fear had receded when Aiden had arrived at a potentially tragic scene, the knowledge that she would be able to see him again before long made everything feel a bit different.

Better?

Oh, yes… A great deal better.

But would he ask her out on another date when they actually had a chance to talk?

Their last ever date?

Her breath came out in a long, heartfelt sigh.

Maybe she didn't feel better after all.

CHAPTER TEN

MINUTES TURNED INTO hours but still Aiden hadn't come back for his bike.

Sophia helped Adrianna peel a mountain of vegetables that went into the oven to roast, along with a huge leg of lamb.

'Oliver won't be far behind Em and I'm sure they're both starving. Maybe that nice young paramedic will be able to stay and have some dinner as well.'

This household was like that. A real family home where all comers were made to feel welcome.

'Wasn't he marvellous?' Adrianna added. 'It was such a relief when he arrived and even from here I could see how good he was with Ruby. A very impressive young man.'

'Mmm.' Sophia hadn't dared meet the gaze of the older woman. 'He is.'

When the front door finally opened, it was Emily's voice that could be heard.

'We're home. Sorry we were so long.'

Her tone was upbeat enough to suggest that the news was going to be good.

Adrianna came rushing from the kitchen and Sophia dropped the book she'd been reading to Toby as they cuddled on the couch.

It wasn't just Emily. Aiden was right behind her and Oliver was only a step behind them.

'Ollie gave us both a ride back,' Emily said. 'Aiden was going to get an ambulance to drop him back but when he heard that Ollie had a sixty-four Morgan sports car, he couldn't resist the invitation.'

'How did you all fit in?' Adrianna was wiping her hands on her apron.

'Bit of a squeeze,' Emily admitted, 'but we coped.' Her grin in Sophia's direction was accompanied by a ghost of a wink that suggested she hadn't minded the squeeze at all.

'I'm glad.' Adrianna smiled at Aiden. 'I hope you won't resist an invitation to stay for dinner either. I've made enough to feed an army and I want to thank you for helping our Ruby.'

'How *is* Ruby?' Sophia steadied Toby as he tried to stand up on the couch beside her, holding his arms out to his parents.

'Mumma,' he demanded.

Emily scooped him into her arms. 'Ruby's fine. No complications. She's in NICU. We couldn't persuade her to come home and get some sleep. She won't take her eyes off her daughter.'

Sophia couldn't let her breath out. She'd been too scared to ask. Her gaze shifted to Oliver. As the surgeon who'd been in charge of the in utero surgery on Ruby's baby he would be well up to date on what was happening now and he would be able to tell her. But her gaze kept travelling and only stopped when it caught Aiden's. He was smiling.

'She's doing amazingly well,' he said quietly. 'I had the privilege of being allowed to get involved while they got her settled and stable.'

'Of course you did,' Emily said. 'It was you who saved the baby in the first place.' She stepped closer to Sophia. 'You should have heard what they said about Aiden's management. He's brilliant.'

'I knew that.' It felt like her heart was in danger of bursting with pride and an odd lump in her throat made her words a little hoarse. Sophia looked back at Aiden but he seemed to be avoiding her gaze now.

'I learned a lot,' he said. 'It's not often we get to follow on with our patient's treatment like that. Luckily I've got a boss who knows how valuable it is, so I got covered for the rest of my shift.'

'You're off duty?' Adrianna beamed. 'So you can stay for dinner?'

'Well…'

'How 'bout a beer?' Oliver had taken Toby from Emily's arms to get a cuddle but now he put the small boy onto the floor. 'I think we all deserve a bit of wind-down time.'

Toby was doing his stiff-legged crawl towards his new, favourite toy.

'So that's where my helmet got to.'

'I was just looking after it,' Sophia said. 'I knew you'd come back.'

'Of course.' His gaze caught hers. And held. Sophia

could feel Emily and Oliver watching them. She knew they were both smiling and she could feel the colour creeping into her cheeks.

'For the bike,' she added.

A soft chuckle came from Adrianna, who disappeared back into the kitchen.

Aiden cleared his throat. 'I'd better ring HQ and let them know I'll be a bit late dropping it back.'

'And I'll find us a beer. A wine for you, Soph?'

'Thanks, Oliver. I'd love one.'

'Me, too,' Emily said. 'Toby, what are you doing?'

It was Aiden's turn to chuckle. 'I think he fancies riding a bike. Do you want to try that on, Toby?'

The helmet was far too big but Toby whooped with happiness when Aiden held it over his head.

'Where's my phone? I've got to get a picture of this.' Emily was laughing as she went to find it. 'Ollie, come and see. This is priceless.'

It *was* priceless. Aiden sat on the floor with Toby on his lap, wearing the helmet. All you could see was the white grin on the small, dark face. And the smile on the face of the man protecting the toddler's head from too much weight from the enormous helmet.

Something huge caught in Sophia's chest and squeezed so tightly it was hard to breathe.

Maybe it was the way Aiden was holding Toby so protectively. Or that look on his face that revealed that he was enjoying this as much as anybody else.

Or maybe it was just part of the puzzle. Another piece was that expression she'd seen when he'd been working with such determination to save Ruby's baby. How gently he'd done what had needed to be done.

And what about the first time she'd ever met this man? When he'd been holding Claire's baby boy after that emergency delivery. What had he said? Oh, yes...

'Babies are my favourite thing. It was a treat.'

Right now, toddlers seemed to be his favourite thing.

There was no question that he was more than capable of caring for and loving children. Look at the love he had for his younger brother and the way he still took responsibility for Nathan. So much so that he wasn't going to allow anything—or anyone—else to interfere with continuing to make Nathan his priority.

That was why he'd come up with that stupid three dates rule in the first place, wasn't it?

But he'd make such an amazing father.

Did he have any idea how good he would be? Was it really that he never wanted to have his own child or was he denying himself the opportunity to experience the kind of joy it could bring? Did he realise that he was shutting himself away from the chance of having a real family for himself? From having people who could support him instead of it always being the other way around?

It was actually painful to swallow the lump in her throat but Sophia managed. She even kept her tone light.

'I'll go and see if Adrianna needs some help in the kitchen.'

The kid was adorable.

The fun of the helmet wore off but Aiden apparently

had plenty of other attractions. Like the penlight torch clipped to his pocket. He showed Toby how to turn it on and it was dark enough now for the beam to show up and dance along the wall. The dog, Fuzzy, seemed to find this as good a game as Toby did. He bounced from one spot to the next, wagging his tail and barking to announce that he'd found where the light had escaped to, and this never failed to make Toby giggle with delight.

The beer hit the spot and he got the chance to talk about the in utero surgery that that tiny baby had had prior to her birth, while Emily and Sophia took Toby away for his bath. Fascinating stuff and yet his interest seemed to evaporate when the women returned. It was Sophia who was carrying Toby in his fluffy sleep suit, a bedraggled-looking toy kangaroo dangling from one hand. Sophia's cheeks were pink and her hair was a tousled mop of damp curls. And there was something about her expression that made Aiden catch his breath.

Something so tender it actually gave him a lump in his throat. When he saw the way she pressed a kiss onto Toby's head before she handed him to Oliver for a goodnight cuddle, he had to turn away.

How sad was it that she would never be able to have children of her own?

To be a mother?

She'd be…amazing.

It was easy to push that disturbing sense of regret on Sophia's behalf away during the course of the delicious dinner Adrianna served up in the kitchen. There was great conversation and plenty of laughter, a dog sitting under the table in the hope of something falling his way, and an atmosphere of…what was it?

Something Aiden had never really experienced before.

Family, he realised as he reluctantly made his farewells immediately after the meal. He had to get the bike back to HQ and he'd promised Nate he'd drop in this evening so he couldn't stay any longer.

He wanted to, though.

He'd grown up in a house devoid of the kind of warmth this house was full of, and he'd pretty much lived alone ever since then. Nathan's sheltered accommodation had something of this warmth but it was very different. This was a real home—with parents and a child and a dog and even a grandma thrown in for good measure.

A real home. A real family.

Sophia looked different here. She came with him when he went to find his helmet and torch in the lounge and then saw him to the front door. Her hair was still extra-curly and there was a sparkle in her eyes that made her look extra-happy. Totally irresistible. There was nobody to witness their kiss and it was so good it would have been rude not to have another one.

She didn't just look different here. She *felt* different. Softer. More confident?

As if she was in a place where she felt completely at home?

He was even more reluctant to leave now.

'I have to go,' he murmured against her ear as he held her close. 'Nate asked me to drop in on my way home and he'll be wondering why I'm so late.'

Sophia melted out of his arms like a deflating balloon. 'Of course.'

'See you soon?'

She nodded but some of that sparkle had gone. It looked like she was holding herself very still. Holding her breath even?

'This wasn't a date.' Oh, help…why had he said that? Why bring up the fact that they only had one official date left?

Sophia didn't say anything. She smiled but she was turning away at the same time and Aiden was left with the feeling that he'd killed the sparkle completely. Pretty much like he had when he'd ruined their second date by cutting it short to go and visit his brother.

But that was precisely why he *had* to go, wasn't it?

And why he couldn't let how he felt about Sophia go any further.

It was his problem to deal with. His heart that was going to bleed when this was over.

Gunning the powerful engine of his bike gave him a momentary reprieve from the downward spiral of his mood.

He'd survive.

He'd always survived. He'd learned that long ago. Just like he'd learned how to hide how he felt so that nobody knew.

Nate knew.

He took one look at Aiden's face and his eyes narrowed. 'Man—what's up with you? Bad day?'

'No. Great day. Delivered a premmie baby. Twenty-eight-weeker. Not only that, she'd had in-utero surgery to correct spina bifida a few weeks ago, which is probably why the labour came on so early. I got to hang around in NICU while they stabilised her. You wouldn't believe some of the high-tech gear they've got in there.'

But, for once, Nathan didn't want to hear every detail of the interesting job.

'I've got something to tell you,' he said.

His tone suggested that he didn't think it would be something Aiden wanted to hear. Sudden fear made Aiden sink onto the edge of his brother's bed. What had happened? Was there something wrong that he hadn't been told about? Had Nathan's condition worsened in some way? Had he injured himself playing that fierce wheelchair rugby? Was he *sick*?

'What's the matter?' The query came out more tersely than he'd intended. 'You're not sick, are you? I hope it's not another UTI. Have you been—?'

'For God's sake,' Nathan interrupted. 'Will you stop fussing like some mother hen? No. I'm not sick. It's Sam.'

'Sam's sick?'

'*No.*' Nathan gave an exasperated huff of sound. 'She's not sick. She's pregnant.'

The silence fell like a brick.

Nathan shook his head. 'Don't even think about asking that one. Yeah…it's mine.'

Aiden was still too stunned to say anything. This was the last thing he'd expected to hear. Astonishment warred with something else that was even less pleasant. Fear for the challenges Nate was going to have to face? Or was it more than that? Jealousy, maybe, that there were going to be people in his brother's life who would be more important than he was? Sam. A *baby*...

'You're going to be an uncle,' Nathan told him. 'How cool is that?'

It was Aiden's turn to shake his head. 'How did that happen?'

Nathan laughed. 'You mean you don't know?' He tipped his chair, balancing on the back of the wheels. 'And you with all that medical training. Bro...'

A flash of anger surfaced. 'Cut it out, Nate. This is serious. It's not your physical capabilities I'm questioning. It's your level of intelligence in not using any kind of protection. Have you even thought about what happens next?'

The chair came down with a thump. 'What happens next is that I'm going to marry Sam. We've already applied to get a house of our own. We're going to make this work and we're very, very happy about it.' He had an odd expression on his face. 'It'd be nice if you could manage to be happy about it, too.'

'I...' Again, words failed Aiden. It felt like he was being pushed out of Nathan's life. As if the whole foundation of his own life was crumbling.

'It'll work,' Nathan said fiercely. 'I'm going to make sure it works. I can be a good dad, I know I can. And a good husband. I'm going to have a real family, Aiden, and...and I can't wait.'

You've got a family, Aiden wanted to say. *You've got me.*

But he couldn't utter the words. He knew exactly what Nathan was talking about. He'd just spent the evening with a real family, hadn't he? Did he not want that for his brother if it was possible? That kind of security?

That kind of love?

Nathan was watching him.

'It doesn't mean that I don't still need you in my life, you know.'

'I know.' The words were strangled.

But he wasn't enough. He got that but it still hurt.

'You can't make me feel guilty about this.' Nathan's words were raw. 'I know how much you've given up for me. You've felt responsible ever since the accident happened. You decided then and there you were going to be a paramedic, didn't you?'

'I guess...'

'Because you felt guilty about what happened. How many times do you have to be told, bro?' Nathan's glare was fierce. 'It. Was. Not. Your. Fault.'

'Okay...' Aiden held up his hands in a gesture of surrender. Or maybe a signal to stop. He knew that. Sophia had told him the same thing and he had—on some level—accepted it. Now Nathan was making it crystal clear that he had no choice but to let it go. To believe what everybody told him.

Sophia had done more than try to absolve his guilt. She'd thought he'd been *brave...*

'You don't get to feel guilty about me any more,'

Nathan continued. 'And that means I don't get to feel guilty about you either. Is it a deal?'

'Of course you don't get to feel guilty about me. Why would you?'

'Ooh, let me think…' Nathan shook his head. 'Maybe because you also decided you weren't going to let anything get in the way of looking after me. Anything like a pet. Or a partner. Or—heaven forbid—*kids*…'

Surely it hadn't been that obvious? It wasn't as if Aiden had even articulated what lay beneath the decisions about how he lived his life. The boundaries had simply evolved. And strengthened.

Okay, maybe he had articulated the three-dates rule. It had become a joke that was part of the bond between the brothers. He just hadn't expected Nathan to see through it with such clarity. To come to *disapprove* of it with such vehemence…

Was it because he'd fallen in love himself and was determined to make it the best relationship possible? Hurtful words spoken weeks ago drifted into his mind.

Being told that Nathan didn't want to end up like him. Shut off. Scared of losing control.

As if he was reading Aiden's mind, Nathan spoke again. The anger had gone from his voice. It was quiet now. Serious.

'We only get one life, mate, and if we don't make the best of it, we've only got ourselves to blame. You can't keep me safe because I don't want to *be* that kind of safe any more. I want to live. *Really* live. And that's what you should be doing, too.'

He reminded Aiden of Sophia saying that life wasn't

a practice run. Had he missed something along the way? Had he done the wrong thing in trying to be the best brother he could be?

'I wouldn't be where I am if it hadn't been for you,' Nathan said quietly. 'I'll love you for ever for that.'

Aiden tried to swallow the lump in his throat but it wasn't budging.

'You could have that too, you know. You and Sophia. You're perfect for each other.'

'She doesn't want that. She...she can't have kids. Doesn't want a family.'

Except that didn't really ring true, did it? Not after the way she'd looked when she'd been holding a sleepy Toby. How happy she'd been in that family kitchen.

'And you don't want kids. You've always said that being a dad to me was more than enough.'

Aiden swallowed. He had said that. He'd meant it, too. Hadn't he?

'So it's my turn to find out what it's like. You get to be the favourite uncle. Maybe Sophia would like to be an auntie. Hey, can I tell Sam it's okay to come in now? That you're not going to rain on our parade?'

'Sure.'

But Nathan hesitated at the door. 'You've got one date left with Sophia, haven't you?'

Aiden shrugged. What difference did it make?

'Make it count,' Nathan said. 'Tell her that you love her, man. It might change your life.' He grinned and his face lit up with joy. 'It changed mine.'

There were congratulations to be given after that. And plans. Not that Aiden got to say much. Nathan and

Sam seemed to have everything going just the way they wanted it to and they had the support of everybody in the house.

It was impossible not to get captured by the love these two young people had for each other. The hope that shone in their eyes as they looked at each other and shared the plans for their future.

Impossible not to come away without the realisation that he wanted that for himself, too.

That it was something worth fighting for.

It was late but maybe it wasn't *too* late.

The phone rang and rang. Any second now, and it would go to voice-mail and Aiden had no idea what he would say. Somehow he had to tell Sophia how he felt about her but you couldn't do that in a voice-mail, could you?

But then the ringing stopped and he heard Sophia's soft voice.

'Hey, Aiden…what's up?'

'Ah…' He couldn't do it over the phone either. He couldn't tell Sophia how much he loved her when he couldn't see her face. Couldn't touch her. He cleared his throat. 'I just wanted to…to…ask you out.'

'On a date?'

Oh, God…was that reluctance he could hear in her voice? A hint of fear even?

'Yeah…'

He heard what sounded like a slow, indrawn breath. 'Okay. When?'

'Um…I'm not sure. I'll text you.'

'Needs planning, huh?'

'Yeah…' He found a smile. 'The best dates always do.'

'Especially number three?' There was a catch in Sophia's voice. 'Saving the best for last?'

'Something like that. I'll text you as soon as I've got it sorted.'

It wasn't until after he'd put the phone down and started browsing his computer for ideas worthy of the perfect date that it clicked.

That reluctance.

Making it clear that this was date number three and therefore the final one.

Maybe Sophia didn't *want* it to be the final date any more than he did.

He turned back to his browsing with renewed enthusiasm.

Hope even?

The trill of her phone announcing a text came at a truly ungodly hour but Sophia woke instantly and completely as she reached to grab her mobile.

Not that she was expecting any of her women to be going into labour, but a phone call at this time of night could only signal an emergency.

Except it wasn't one of her mums-to-be.

It was an invitation for a date. If she was up for it, a taxi would be arriving to collect her in twenty minutes.

What kind of date started at four a.m.?

Certainly not a kind that Sophia had ever experienced. But, then, she'd never gone on a date knowing that it would be the last either. And she'd certainly never

gone on a date with a man she was so totally and hope-
lessly in love with.

Her fingers were shaking as she entered her response.

Bring it on.

CHAPTER ELEVEN

WITHOUT THE LIGHTS of the city, the night became an inky blackness surrounding the car.

Where on earth was she being taken?

Sophia had rugged up, knowing there could well be a hint of frost with the approaching dawn, but in the heat of the taxi, being wrapped in her puffer jacket and woolly accessories had her feeling drowsy.

Maybe this was all a dream?

Pulling off one woollen glove, she checked her phone. Yes. There were the text messages sent and received so recently. The last one had sent her digging through a drawer to find items of clothing that wouldn't normally make an appearance for a month or two yet.

Dress for something cold! Aiden had instructed.

Real doubt might have surfaced surrounding this date at that point but Aiden had sent another message.

Trust me.

So here she was. Speeding off in the night to an unknown destination. In a car being driven by a total stranger.

Her mother would be horrified. Sophia could almost hear an echo of her voice.

'How could you be so *reckless*, Sophia?'

A smile tilted her lips as she silently answered that voice.

Because it was Aiden who asked me, Mum. That's how.

Maybe she dozed for a while, lulled by the warmth and the rumble of the car's engine, overlaid with some easy listening music on the radio. Any minute now and she'd be hearing a track from Cat Stevens. Not that she needed the cue to think back to that evening with Aiden. To the shock of hearing about his appalling childhood. To the way his vulnerability had stolen her heart. To the understanding she had gained about why he had chosen the career he had and why he felt he had to shut anything out of his life that could get in the way of his devotion to his younger brother.

She loved him enough to know that she would never do that.

Enough to have this final date and let him go?

Yes.

But she was going to make the most of every minute of it. Especially when it had obviously been planned with great care. Like date number two. He'd taken her a long way out of the city that time, too. Was she being taken back there, perhaps? Were they going to watch the sunrise from a lighthouse overlooking one of those gorgeous beaches?

'Where *are* we going?'

'We're here, love.' The taxi driver was slowing his

vehicle, as if he was looking for a signpost. 'In the heart of the Yarra Valley.'

Nowhere near Queenscliff, then. This was pretty much the opposite direction out of Melbourne. Sophia hadn't been in this area yet but she knew it was famous for food and wine and stunning scenery.

A long way to go for a date for breakfast, though.

And the driver wasn't heading for the winery the sign had advertised. He was turning onto a side road that appeared to lead to nothing more than a big paddock beside a small lake.

Well…there was something more. A couple of trucks parked near a group of people. And a motorbike.

And someone breaking away from the group to come and meet her taxi.

Aiden had a big, puffy jacket on, too. And woolly gloves. And a beanie that covered his head and ears, but Sophia would have recognised that smile anywhere.

Her heart recognised it as well. She could feel its joyous squeeze.

'Have you guessed?' His smile widened. 'Have you ever done this before?'

Shaking her head, Sophia took hold of his hand. They were both wearing gloves but she could still feel the warmth and strength of his grip. He led her towards the huddle of people. What looked like a small house made of wicker turned out to be the bottom of a huge basket. On the other side, an enormous puddle of fabric lay on the ground.

A balloon.

This was date number three? A ride in a hot-air

balloon? How scary was this? Sophia's grip on Aiden's hand tightened. In response, he put his arm around her shoulders and pulled her firmly against his side.

You're safe, the gesture told her. *I won't let anything bad happen to you.*

Torchlight showed that the balloon had a background colour of deep gold. Big fans were positioned on either side of the basket and, as Sophia and Aiden watched, people held up the base of the fabric and air began to fill the balloon. And then, with a roar that made Sophia gasp in alarm, a huge flame emerged from the burner as someone turned it on and the air began to heat. Slowly, majestically, the balloon began to rise, tipping the basket into an upright position.

There were openings in the side of the basket and the pilot showed Aiden how to use them as footholds to climb in. Standing inside, he waited only until Sophia had her foot in the first rung and then his hands came under her arms and he lifted her as easily as if she weighed no more than a child.

And there they were, standing inside this huge basket with only the pilot for company.

'This is Jim,' Aiden told her. 'You're in safe hands.'

Sophia shook the pilot's hand. Then she looked at the ground crew, who seemed to be packing up. This was puzzling. She'd seen pictures of balloon rides like this and people were usually crammed into these baskets like human sardines.

'Haven't you got any more passengers?' she asked.

'Not today.' Jim grinned at Aiden. 'This man saved my kid's life a while back. I owed him a favour.'

Another blast of the burner punctuated his sentence and they were lifting off the ground. Aiden led her to the opposite side of the basket and pointed. Far in the distance, over the top of the Dandenong Ranges, the sun was starting to appear—a blindingly brilliant sliver of light that painted the bottoms of nearby clouds deep shades of orange and pink.

Despite the layers of clothing, it was freezing. Sophia was more than happy to be tucked against Aiden's side and each blast of the burner surrounded them with a welcome wave of warmth. It illuminated the balloon, too, and Sophia gasped with delight the first time she looked up. The dark gold of the fabric she'd seen on the ground was now a glowing, rich hue and there were patterns on it. Aboriginal designs of lizards and kangaroos and birds, and there were hand- and footprints and chains of coloured shapes filling other gaps.

'It's gorgeous.' She raised her voice to be heard over the roar of the burner but then it stopped and Aiden's response fell into complete silence.

'So are you,' he said. 'I love you, Sophia.'

Hearing Aiden say those words was like an emotional version of a burner being turned on inside her heart, lighting it up and making it glow.

The silence around them was astonishing. Somewhere down below a rooster was crowing to announce the approaching dawn but Sophia only had to whisper to be heard.

'I love you, too.'

Saying the words out loud was like a seal. The truth was out there now and it would never change. Dawn might be breaking around them to reveal stunning scenery but there was nothing she wanted to see more than what she was seeing in Aiden's eyes right now.

But it was heart-breaking, too. They loved each other but this was the last time they would be together like this. On a date.

The prickle of imminent tears made her wrench her gaze free of Aiden's. She was not going to cry in front of him. Or ruin this spectacular date he had organised. She blinked hard. Gulped in a breath of the icy air. Tried to find something to focus on. There were ponds of ground fog on the patchwork of fields and vineyards below and away in the distance she could see other balloons rising over the misty landscape. One was coloured like a rainbow. She concentrated on that, waiting for its burner to make it glow again, but it wasn't enough. She could feel a tear escape and trickle down the side of her nose.

'Oh, hon...'

Her view of the rainbow balloon vanished as Aiden gathered her into his arms. And when she raised her head all she could see was that look of love in his face. That vanished, too, as his face lowered and he kissed her.

Slowly. So tenderly her heart broke all over again.

A long blast of the burner made them finally break that kiss. Maybe the reminder that they weren't quite alone made them both look out to take in the magic of where they were, floating in the clear air of what was going to be a perfect day. There seemed to Sophia to be nothing more to say but Aiden obviously didn't think so.

'Do you remember our first date?'

'Of course. You kissed me in that garden bar.'

'Do you remember me telling you about my three-dates rule?'

Sophia nodded. How could she have forgotten? She had embraced the idea so enthusiastically. Had she really said that it was exactly the rule that was missing from her own life?

'There's something else you should know about that rule,' Aiden said softly.

'Oh?'

'Mmm.'

Aiden was staring intently at something on the ground. That flock of sheep perhaps?

'It's a load of bull.'

Sophia's jaw dropped. A loud bleating sound came from one of the sheep far below and it sounded like laughter.

'Is it…?' she managed.

Aiden straightened and met her gaze. 'It is if you find the person you want to spend the rest of your life with.' He caught her hands and gripped them tightly. 'I don't want to go on any more dates with you, Soph. I want…I want us just to be together. For ever. I want to marry you.'

'Oh…'

This was the last thing Sophia had expected to happen on this—the final—date. Had she really thought her heart had been breaking earlier? It had only been a crack. This was what it felt like to really break. To shatter into a million little pieces.

'I love you,' she whispered. 'Please, know that.' She had to close her eyes. 'But I could never marry you.'

* * *

Oh…*God*…

How devastating was this?

Aiden had planned this date knowing that his future was on the line here. That the stupid three-dates rule he'd not only invented but had given to Sophia meant that this was his last chance.

And he'd blown it.

The silence around them was deafening. Excruciating. Had Jim heard him putting his heart on the line and being turned down?

His dating rule wasn't the only stupid idea he'd ever had either. He'd chosen what seemed to be the most romantic place in the world to propose but he hadn't given any thought to failure. To being trapped in a floating box in the sky with nowhere to go. Nowhere to hide.

He would just have to grit his teeth and ride it out. To look as if he wasn't dying inside. Surely there was something out there he could focus on. Those other balloons, maybe, dotted in the sky at various levels. Yeah…there was one that had rainbow stripes. Pretty.

'It's not about the three-dates rule,' Sophia said quietly. 'It's about why you made it. About the responsibility you feel for Nate and…and how you feel about having a family.'

'I—' He had to tell her that his brother's world had changed. That his level of responsibility had been downgraded, but she didn't let him continue.

'I understand,' she told him. 'Honestly, I do. And I know that me not being able to have my own babies should make us perfect for each other but…'

He could see the way she took a deep breath. Could see the soft light that came into her eyes. 'But I *want* a family,' she said. 'And there are lots of ways of doing that without giving birth yourself.'

Aiden hadn't expected that. How arrogant had he been, assuming that Sophia had embraced the idea of limited relationships because she had no reason to want something long term when she couldn't have her own children? He had no idea what he could say to that but he didn't need to say anything yet.

Sophia's smile was poignant. 'You should know,' she said. 'Nathan is your brother, not your son, but you pretty much raised him. I love that you love him so much and it says a lot about what an amazing person you are that you've kept up that caring for him.' She scrubbed at her face with her glove as if she was wiping away a tear. Sure enough, her next words sounded choked. 'And I know it was tough. I understand why you wouldn't want to do it again.'

'I've just never considered it as an option,' Aiden put in. He needed a minute to get his head around this. Was this why Sophia couldn't marry him? Because he'd said he never wanted kids?

'I look at Emily,' Sophia said, 'and I know that that's what I want. A family. And I know it can be easier to adopt kids that aren't quite perfect and I'd be okay with that. But you've already spent your life caring for someone who needed extra help.'

'So doesn't that make me an expert?'

That surprised her into silence and it gave Aiden a moment to clear his head. To let the pieces fall into place.

Maybe it was the mention of Emily that did it. The memory of what it had been like in the Evanses' house that night. The way Sophia had looked when she'd been cuddling Toby in his fluffy sleepsuit. The laughter and warmth in that kitchen. The dog under the table.

Family.

He wanted that too, dammit.

The burst of the burner was the longest yet and it ignited something inside Aiden. Determination?

Jim's voice added a sense of urgency.

'Sorry, guys, but we're on the way down now. You'll see our chase vehicles parked up near that lake.'

Aiden didn't even look.

'The "not wanting kids" was just another stupid rule,' he told Sophia. 'Like the three-dates one. I convinced myself that's what worked because I didn't think I had the option of anything else. I felt guilty about Nate and I stuck to the promise I'd made when the accident happened. That I would look after him for ever.'

'Of course you did. Your loyalty is up there with all the other amazing things I love about you.'

'I was wrong,' Aiden insisted. 'Not about being loyal. About believing it was my fault. Nate told me but it wasn't until *you* told me that I started believing it. And now I really do. Nate and I made a deal. I'd stop feeling guilty about him and he wouldn't have to feel guilty about me.'

'He feels guilty about you?'

'He thinks I'm throwing away my own life because I think I need to look after him. He's made it very clear he's going to live his own life. He's getting married. Sam's going to have his baby.'

'Really?' Sophia sounded delighted. 'You're going to be an uncle? That's perfect for you.'

'No it's not,' Aiden growled. 'It's not enough.' He shook his head to emphasise his words. 'Yeah, I convinced myself that I didn't want anything that got in the way of putting Nate first but I did that for too long and it's a good thing that I'm not allowed to do it any more. And it means that for the first time in my life I'm going to be able to choose what *I* want. Just for myself.'

They were getting close to landing now. He could see the shadow of their balloon and its basket clearly outlined on the ground below. There was a truck parked that would carry the balloon back to its base. A car with support crew to help pack up.

Sophia wasn't looking at their shadow getting larger as the land rose to meet them. She was staring at him.

'What *do* you want?' she asked softly.

There was no hesitation on his part. 'You. Us. A family. A dog even.'

There were tears in Sophia's eyes but she was smiling. Laughing, in fact.

The bump of the basket touching the ground knocked them both off balance. A perfect excuse to take the woman he loved in his arms. To kiss her with all the joy of knowing there was hope that nothing was left to get in the way of them being together.

'That's it, folks.' Jim's voice came over what sounded like applause from the ground crew surrounding them. 'The ride's over.'

But it wasn't. Aiden couldn't keep a grin off his face as he helped Sophia from the basket and then pulled her close for another kiss.

The real ride was only just beginning.

'What happens now?' Sophia asked when he finally let her go.

The basket was on the back of the truck now and people were squashing air out of the balloon so it could be rolled up and put in its bag.

'A champagne breakfast,' he told her.

Her smile lit up the world. 'Is that a date?'

He grinned. 'Only if we have a new rule.'

'What's that? A thirty-dates rule?'

'I'm thinking more like a three-hundred-dates rule. And if that runs out, we'll make a new rule.'

Laughing, with their arms around each other, they made their way to the car that would take them to the vineyard restaurant.

'Or maybe we should make a rule about never having another date,' Aiden suggested.

'No.' Sophia tugged him to a halt and peered up at him, her bottom lip caught between her teeth as if she was trying not to smile. 'It's good that you've had so much practice because there's one date that's going to need quite a bit of planning.'

'What's that?'

'Our wedding?' Yes. The smile escaped.

Aiden's smile was coming but not quite yet. After a kiss, maybe. When that tight feeling in his chest of too much joy to handle had had a chance to subside a little.

It might need to be a long kiss, he realised as his lips captured hers.

Just as well Sophia didn't seem to mind.

* * * * *

HEALED BY THE
MIDWIFE'S KISS

FIONA McARTHUR

Dedicated to Finn, author Kelly Hunter's legend
of a four-legged friend,

who went to doggy heaven while I was
writing this book.

It just seemed right to say there are
Finn heroes everywhere.

Vale Finn.

PROLOGUE

AT SIX A.M. on a Thursday, Lighthouse Bay's maternity ward held its breath. Midwife Catrina Thomas leaned forward and rubbed the newborn firmly with a warmed towel. The limp infant flexed and wriggled his purple limbs and finally took a gasping indignant lungful.

The baby curled his hands into fists as his now tense body suffused with pink. 'Yours now, Craig. Take him.' She gestured to the nervous dad beside her and mimed what to do as she encouraged Craig's big callused hands to gently lift the precious bundle. One huge splashing silver tear dropped to the sheet from his stubbled cheek as he placed his new son on his wife's warm bare stomach.

Craig released a strangled sob and his wife, leaning back on the bed in relief, half laughed in triumph, then closed her hands over her child and her husband's hands and pulled both upwards to lie between her breasts.

For Catrina, it was this moment. This snapshot in time she identified as her driver, the reason she felt she could be a midwife for ever—this and every other birth moment that had come before. It gave her piercing joy when she'd thought she'd lost all gladness, and it gave her bittersweet regret for the dreams she'd lost. But mostly, definitely, it gave her joy.

An hour later Catrina hugged her boss awkwardly, because Ellie's big pregnant belly bulged in the way as they came together, but no less enthusiastically because she would miss seeing her friend in the morning before she finished her shift. 'I can't believe it's your last day.' She rolled her eyes. 'Or my last night shift tomorrow.'

'Neither can I.' Ellie's brilliant smile lit the room even more than the sunlight streaming in through the maternity ward windows.

Trina marvelled at the pure happiness that radiated from a woman who had blossomed, and not just in belly size but in every way in just one year of marriage. Another reason Trina needed to change her life and move on. She wanted what Ellie had.

A family and a life outside work. She would have the latter next week when she took on Ellie's job as Midwifery Unit Manager for Ellie's year of maternity leave.

She'd have daylight hours to see the world and evenings to think about going out for dinner with the not infrequent men who had asked her. The excuse of night shift would be taken out of her grasp. Which was a good thing. She'd hidden for two years and the time to be brave had arrived.

She stepped back from Ellie, picked up her bag and blew her a kiss. 'Happy last day. I'll see you at your lunch tomorrow.' Then she lifted her chin and stepped out of the door into the cool morning.

The tangy morning breeze promised a shower later, and pattering rain on the roof on a cool day made diving into bed in the daylight hours oh, so much more attractive than the usual sunny weather of Lighthouse Bay.

Summer turning to autumn was her favourite time of year. Trina turned her face into the salty spray from the sea as she walked down towards the beach.

She slept better if she walked before going up the hill to her croft cottage, even if just a quick dash along the breakwall path that ran at right angles to the beach.

Especially after a birth. Her teeth clenched as she sucked in the salty air and tried not to dwell on the resting mother lying snug and content in the ward with her brand-new pink-faced baby.

Trina looked ahead to the curved crescent of the beach as she swung down the path from the hospital. The sapphire blue of the ocean stretching out to the horizon where the water met the sky, her favourite contemplation, and, closer, the rolling waves crashing and turning into fur-like foam edges that raced across the footprint-free sand to sink in and disappear.

Every day the small creek flowing into the ocean changed, the sandbars shifting and melding with the tides. The granite boulders like big seals set into the creek bed, lying lazily and oblivious to the shifting sand around them. Like life, Trina thought whimsically. You could fight against life until you realised that the past was gone and you needed to wait to see what the next tide brought. If only you could let go.

Ahead she saw that solitary dad. The one with his little girl in the backpack, striding along the beach with those long powerful strides as he covered the distance from headland to headland. Just like he had every morning she'd walked for the last four weeks. A tall, broad-shouldered, dark-haired man with a swift stride.

Sometimes the two were draped in raincoats, sometimes his daughter wore a cheery little hat with pompoms. Sometimes, like today, they both wore beanies and a scarf.

Trina shivered. She could have done with a scarf. When she was tired it was easy to feel the cold. It would be good to move to day shifts after almost two bleak years on nights, but falling into bed exhausted in the daytime had been preferable to the dread of lying lonely and alone in the small dark hours.

She focused on the couple coming towards her. The little girl must have been around twelve months old, and seemed to be always gurgling with laughter, her crinkled eyes, waving fists and gap-toothed smile a delight to start the day with. The father, on the other hand, smiled with his mouth only when he barely lifted his hand but his storm-blue eyes glittered distant and broken beneath the dark brows. Trina didn't need to soak in anyone else's grief.

They all guessed about his story because, for once, nobody had gleaned any information and shared it with the inhabitants of Lighthouse Bay.

They drew closer and passed. 'Morning.' Trina inclined her head and waved at the little girl who, delightfully, waved back with a toothy chuckle.

'Morning,' the father said and lifted the corner of his lips before he passed.

And that was that for another day. Trina guessed she knew exactly how he felt. But she was changing.

CHAPTER ONE

Finn

AT SEVEN-THIRTY A.M. on the golden sands of Lighthouse Bay Beach Finlay Foley grimaced at the girl as she went past. Always in the purple scrubs so he knew she was one of the midwives from the hospital. A midwife. Last person he wanted to talk to.

It had been a midwife, one who put her face close to his and stared at him suspiciously, who told him his wife had left their baby and him behind, and ran away.

But the dark-haired girl with golden glints in her hair never invaded his space. She exuded a gentle warmth and empathy that had begun to brush over him lightly like a consistent warm beam of sunlight through leaves. Or like that soft shaft of light that reached into a corner of his cottage from the lighthouse on the cliff by some bizarre refraction. And always that feather-stroke of compassion without pity in her brown-eyed glance that thawed his frozen soul a little more each day when they passed.

She always smiled and so did he. But neither of them stopped. Thank goodness.

Piper gurgled behind his ear and he tilted his head to catch her words. 'Did you say something, Piper?'

'Mum, Mum, Mum, Mum.'

Finn felt the tightness crunch his sternum as if someone had grabbed his shirt and dug their nails into his chest. Guilt. Because he hadn't found her. He closed his eyes for a second. Nothing should be this hard. 'Try Dad, Dad, Dad, Dad,' he said past the tightness in his throat.

Obediently Piper chanted in her musical little voice, 'Dad, Dad, Dad, Dad.'

'Clever girl.' His mouth lifted this time and he felt a brief piercing of warmth from another beam of light in his cave-like existence.

Which was why he'd moved here. To make himself shift into the light. For Piper. And it did seem to be working. Something about this place, this haven of ocean and sand and cliffs and smiling people like the morning midwife soothed his ragged nerves and restored his faith in finding a way into the future.

A future he needed to create for Piper. Always the jolliest baby, now giggling toddler and all-round ray of puppy-like delight, Piper had kept him sane mainly because he had to greet each day to meet her needs.

His sister had said Piper had begun to look sad. Suspected she wasn't happy in the busy day care. Didn't see enough of her dad when he worked long hours. And he'd lifted his head and seen what his sister had seen.

Piper had been clingy. Harder to leave when he dropped her off at the busy centre. Drooping as he dressed her for 'school' in the morning. Quiet when he picked her up ten hours later.

Of course he needed to get a life and smile for his

daughter. So he'd listened when his sister suggested he take a break from the paediatric practice where he'd continued as if on autopilot. Maybe escape to a place one of her friends had visited recently, where he knew no one, and heal for a week or two, or even a month for his daughter's sake. Maybe go back part-time for a while and spend more time with Piper. So he'd come. Here. To Lighthouse Bay.

Even on the first day it had felt right, just a glimmer of a breakthrough in the darkness, and he'd known it had been a good move.

The first morning in the guesthouse, when he'd walked the beach with Piper on his back, he'd felt a stirring of the peace he had found so elusive in his empty, echoing, accusing house. Saw the girl with the smile. Said, 'Good morning.'

After a few days he'd rented a cottage just above the beach for a week to avoid the other boisterous guests— happy families and young lovers he didn't need to talk to at breakfast—and moved to a place more private and offering solitude, but the inactivity of a rented house had been the exact opposite to what he needed.

Serendipitously, the cottage next door to that had come up for sale—*Would suit handyman*—which he'd never been. He was not even close to handy. Impulsively, after he'd discussed it with Piper, who had smiled and nodded and gurgled away his lack of handyman skills with great enthusiasm, he'd bought it. Then and there. The bonus of vacant possession meant an immediate move in even before the papers were signed.

He had a holiday house at the very least and a home if he never moved back to his old life. Radical stuff for a single parent, escaped paediatrician, failed husband,

and one who had been used to the conveniences of a large town.

The first part of the one big room he'd clumsily beautified was Piper's corner and she didn't mind the smudges here and there and the chaos of spackle and paint tins and drip sheets and brushes.

Finally, he'd stood back with his daughter in his arms and considered he might survive the next week and maybe even the one after that. The first truly positive achievement he'd accomplished since Clancy left.

Clancy left.

How many times had he tried to grasp that fact? His wife of less than a year had walked away. Run, really. Left him, left her day-old daughter, and disappeared. With another man, if the private investigator had been correct. But still a missing person. Someone who in almost twelve months had never turned up in a hospital, or a morgue, or on her credit card. He had even had the PI check if she was working somewhere but that answer had come back as a no. And his sister, who had introduced them, couldn't find her either.

Because of the note she'd given the midwives, the police had only been mildly interested. Hence the PI.

Look after Piper. She's yours. Don't try to find me. I'm never coming back.

That was what the note had said. The gossip had been less direct. He suspected what the questions had been. Imagined what the midwives had thought. *Why did his wife leave him? What did he do to her? It must have been bad if she left her baby behind...*

The ones who knew him well shook their heads and said, *She'd liked her freedom too much, that one.*

At first he'd been in deep shock. Then denial. She'd come back. A moment's madness. She'd done it before. Left for days. With the reality of a demanding newborn and his worry making it hard for him to sleep at all, his work had suffered. But his largest concern had been the spectre of Clancy with an undiagnosed postnatal depression. Or, worse, the peril of a postnatal psychosis. What other reason could she have for leaving so suddenly so soon after the birth?

Hence he'd paid the private investigator, because there were no forensic leads—the police were inundated with more important affairs than flighty wives. But still no word. All he could do was pray she was safe, at least.

So life had gone on. One painful questioning new morning after another. Day after day with no relief. He hadn't been able to do his job as well as he should have and he'd needed a break from it all.

Buying the cottage had been a good move. Piper stood and cheered him on in her cot when he was doing something tricky, something that didn't need to have a lively little octopus climb all over him while he did it, and she waved her fists and gurgled and encouraged him as he learnt to be a painter. Or a carpenter. Or a tiler.

Or a cook. Or a cleaner. Or a dad.

He was doing okay.

He threw a last look out over the beach towards the grey sea and turned for home. 'That's our walk done for this morning, chicken. Let's go in and have breakfast. Then you can have a sleep and Daddy will grout those tiles in the shower so we can stop having bird baths in the sink.'

Piper loved the shower. Finn did too. When he held her soft, squirming satin baby skin against his chest, the water making her belly laugh as she ducked her head in and out of the stream always made him smile. Sometimes even made him laugh.

So he'd spent extra time on the shower. Adding tiles with animals, starfish, moon shapes and flowers, things they could talk about and keep it a happy place for Piper. And he'd made a square-tiled base with a plug. Soon she could have a little bath. One she could splash in even though it was only the size of the shower.

Doing things for Piper kept him sane. He didn't need the psychologist his sister said he did, or the medication his brother-in-law recommended. Just until he'd climbed out of the hole he'd dug himself to hide in, he would stay here. In Lighthouse Bay. Where nobody pointed or pitied him and every corner didn't hold a memory that scraped like fingernails on the chalkboard of his heavy heart.

Except that around the next corner his heart froze for a millisecond to see the morning midwife crouched on the path in front of him.

He quickened his pace. 'Are you okay?'

She turned to look up at him, cradling something brightly coloured against her chest, and with the shift of her shoulders he saw the bird cupped in her hands. 'She flew into that window and knocked herself out.'

The lorikeet, blue-headed with a red and yellow chest, lay limp with lime-green wings folded back in her hands. A most flaccid bird.

Still, the red beak and chest shuddered gently so it

wasn't dead. 'How do you know it's a girl?' He couldn't believe he'd just said that. But he'd actually thought it was her that had been hurt and relief had made him stupid.

She must have thought he was stupid too. 'I didn't actually lift her legs and look. Not really of major importance, is it?'

Just a little bit of impatience and, surprisingly, it was good to be at the receiving end of a bit of healthy sarcasm. So much better than unending sympathy.

He held up his hands in surrender and Piper's voice floated over both of them from his back. 'Dad, Dad, Dad!'

The girl sucked in her breath and he could see her swan-like neck was tinged with pink. 'Sorry. Night duty ill temper.'

'My bad. All mine. Stupid thing to say. Can you stand up? It's tricky to crouch down with Piper on my back. Let's have a look at her.'

The morning midwife rose fluidly, calves of steel obviously; even he was impressed with her grace—must be all those uphill walks she did. 'She's not fluttering her wings,' she said, empathy lacing a voice that, had it not been agitated, would have soothed the bird. He shook himself. She was just being a typical midwife. That was how most of them had spoken to him when Clancy had disappeared.

'Still breathing.' He stroked the soft feathers as the bird lay in her small hands. 'She's limp, but I think if you put her in a box for a couple of hours in the dark, she'll rouse when she's had a sleep to get over the shock.'

'Do you think so?'

'I do. She's not bleeding. Just cover the box with a light cloth so she can let you know she can fly away when she's ready.'

'Do I have to put food or water in there?'

'Not food. A little water as long as she doesn't fall into it and drown.' He grimaced at another stupid comment.

She grinned at him and suddenly the day was much brighter than it had been. 'Are you a vet?'

'No.'

'Just a bird wrangler?'

She was a stunner. He stepped back. 'One of my many talents. I'll leave you to it.'

'Thank you.'

'Bye.'

She looked at him oddly. Not surprising. He was odd. He walked on up the hill.

Her voice followed him. 'Bye, Piper.' He heard Piper chuckle.

CHAPTER TWO

Trina

TRINA FINISHED HER night shift at seven a.m. on Friday and picked up her mini-tote to sling it on her shoulder. Her last night done, except for emergencies, and she did a little skip as she came out of the door. At first, she'd been reluctant to take the night shift to day shift change that Ellie had offered her because change could be scary, but it had started the whole paradigm inversion that her life had needed. Look out daylight. Here she comes.

Yes. She'd come a long way in almost two years since Ed had died.

Not just because on Monday morning she'd return as acting Midwifery Unit Manager, an unexpected positive career move for Trina at Lighthouse Bay Maternity.

But things had changed.

Her grief stayed internal, or only rarely escaped under her pillow when she was alone in her croft on the cliff.

And since Ellie's wedding last year she'd begun to think that maybe, some time in the future, she too could look at being friends with a man. If the right one came along.

Not a relationship yet. That idea had been so terrifying, almost like PTSD—the fear of imagining what if history repeated itself; what if that immense pain of loss and grief hit her again? What then?

She'd been catatonic with that thought and to divert herself she'd begun to think of all the other things that terrified her. She'd decided to strengthen her Be Brave muscle.

Last week she'd had her first scuba lesson. Something that had fascinated but petrified her since she'd watched the movie *Finding Nemo* with the daughter of a friend. And in the sparkling cove around the corner from Lighthouse Bay the kindly instructor had been so reassuring, so patient, well… Maybe she'd go back on Saturday for another lesson.

And when she'd mastered that she was going out on a day of deep-sea fishing. The captain's wife had not long delivered a late-in-life baby and Trina had been the midwife. Even though he'd fainted again, he'd promised her a day of deep-sea fishing when he felt better. She'd bought seasickness bands and stored them in her drawer just in case.

She wasn't sure about the parachuting. The girls at work had all joined the idea factory and brochures and social media tags of extreme sports and adventure holidays appeared like magic in her pigeonhole and on her private page. Parachuting? She didn't think so but she'd worry about that later.

Her aim to do one challenge a month seemed possible to allay the fear that she was relying on work to be her whole world. Though not too adventurous—she didn't want to kill herself. Not now.

Her friends were cheering. Thinking of the mid-wives of Lighthouse Bay...well, that made her whole world warm into a rosy glow. A fiercely loyal flotsam of women tossed here by the fickle cruelty of life, forging into a circle of hands supporting birthing women and each other. All acutely aware of how fortunate they were to have found the magic of the bay.

There was something healing about that crescent of sand that led to the cliffs.

A mystical benevolence about the soaring white lighthouse on the tallest point that looked benignly over the tiny hamlet of coloured houses and shone reassuring light.

And the pretty pastel abodes like a quaint European seaside town were a delight, a new trend that had taken off with the gentle crayon façades dipping in colour like playful toes into the sea.

Crazy coloured houses, and if she could do all those crazy-coloured feats of bravery then just maybe she could be brave enough to begin a real conversation with a man. Like yesterday. She'd almost forgotten the handsome dad was a man when she'd snapped at him. They'd almost had a whole conversation. She wouldn't mind another one so he didn't think she was a short-tempered shrew but she had been concerned about the bird. The one that had flown away two hours later, just like he said it would.

If she could talk to a man she could try again to go out with one. At least once. She'd been turning them down for six months now. None of them had been Ed.

Now there were more midwives around to lessen the

on-call restrictions. Four new midwives had come on
board to swell their ranks with the shift to a midwife-
led unit. They still had old Dr Southwell in the hospital
for non-maternity patients and maternity emergencies,
but all the midwives had moved to four days of ten-hour
shifts and caring for a caseload of women, so suddenly
there was more time for life with an extra day free and
people to cover you if needed. And she'd scored the
admin side Monday to Thursday, daylight hours, for a
year. Starting Monday. Imagine.

So she'd better get out there and grab that exciting life before it drifted past in a haze of regrets. She
lifted her head and sucked in a pure lungful of gorgeous sea air.

Without realising it her feet had followed the well-
beaten path down to the beach and just as she turned
to start her morning breakwall walk she saw the dad
and his little girl come up off the beach.

He looked happier today. Nice. It made her smile
warmer. 'Beautiful morning.'

He looked startled for a minute. 'Yes, it is.' Almost as
if he was surprised. 'Good morning—how is your bird?'

'Flew away two hours later. Didn't look any worse
for wear.'

He gave her the first real smile she'd seen. 'That's
good.'

Then he was past. Trina turned her head to glance
back and the little fair-haired girl waved.

Trina smiled and yawned. She should go to bed and
get a couple of hours' sleep before Ellie's farewell lunch.
Just a quick walk.

CHAPTER THREE

Finn

THE EARLY-MORNING BREEZE off the ocean seemed cooler. The water had taken till now to shine like a jewel. She'd been late this morning. Finn had waited a minute, hoping she wouldn't see him do it, and strangely the minute seemed to take for ever, then he'd looked back. He'd been thinking of her last night. Wondering if she were sad about a dead bird or happy when it flew away.

He thought back to her response. Now that was a smile. He could see it in his retina like a glance at the sun. Warm and glowing. Saw her walking quite a way in the distance—she'd moved fast. He'd noticed that before, that her pace ran to brisk rather than dawdling. Nurses often did walk briskly. Couldn't seem to slow themselves enough to meander even on a seaside walk. He tore his eyes away.

He'd done the breakwall walk she did a couple of times when he'd first come here but he liked the effort of walking through the sand with Piper on his back. If nothing else he'd become fit and tanned and physically healthier here in a month. And Piper too had sun-kissed limbs and sparkling eyes that exuded health.

His sister would be pleased when she came today. His first visitor. He shied away from that intrusion into his safe world and thought again of the young midwife. Maybe not so young because he'd seen the signs of loss and life in her big coffee eyes—even in those brief glances they'd shot at each other. For the first time he wondered if other people had suffered as much as he had? Well, that at least seemed a positive sign that he could reconnect with his inherent compassion that he'd seemed to have lost.

The thought made him wonder what it would be like to talk to someone who could actually begin to understand his hell, and then called himself crazy for making up a past about someone he didn't know. Poor woman probably had never had a sad day in her life. But something told him otherwise.

Just before one p.m. his sister stepped out of her red convertible and through his front gate. 'It's beautiful, Finn. I can't believe you've done all this yourself!' Her perfectly pencilled brows were raised as she gazed at the pale pink external walls of the house and the rose-red door.

He'd been a little surprised himself. And the front path bordered by pansies and baby's breath looked as if it belonged to some older lady with a green thumb—not a guilt-deranged paediatrician running from life.

She rocked her head slowly. He'd expected disbelief but not this patent incredulity. He felt strangely offended. 'I didn't even know you like to garden!'

He shrugged, urging her towards the door. 'Neither did I. But Piper loves being outside and we needed to do something while we're out here.'

Frances rubbernecked her way up the path, nice and slow for the neighbours, he thought dryly, and sighed while she gushed. She gushed when she didn't know what to say, though what the problem was he had no idea.

'And the house. Freshly painted? You actually painted?' She glanced around. 'Pastel like the others in the street. It's gorgeous.'

Finn looked at the stucco walls. They'd been a pain to paint. 'Piper chose the colour. I would have preferred a blue but, given the choice, she went for pink every time. Never thought I'd have a stereotypical daughter.'

Frances laughed and waved her hand dismissively. 'Piper's too young to choose.'

'No, she's not,' he said mildly. 'How can you say it's not her choice if I give her four colours and she keeps choosing pink?'

Frances looked at him as if he needed a big dose of sympathy for his feeble brain. 'You didn't pretend she was choosing?'

'Who else was I going to ask?' He heard the edge in his voice. And his sister shut up. So then he felt mean.

It was always like this. On and on until he shut her down. She meant well, but for heaven's sake. He wanted her gone already.

They finally made it to the front door.

In an attempt to lighten the mood he stopped to show her something else. 'Piper helped everywhere.' He kissed the top of his daughter's head as she perched on his hip. Quiet for a change because she hadn't quite found her ease with her aunt. Or maybe she was picking up Finn's nervous vibes. Either way she leaned into him, unusually subdued.

He pointed to a handprint on the front step that he'd finished with instant cement. Using a layer of cling wrap over the wet surface, he'd pressed her starfish hand into the step on each side while holding her clamped to his side. The little palm prints made him smile every time he opened the door.

'Come in.' He heard the pride in his voice and mocked himself. Finn the decorator. 'There's still the kitchen and laundry, but I've finished Piper's corner, the bathroom and the floating boards on the floor because she'll need a solid surface to learn to walk on.'

Frances rotated her neck, as if stuck to the step and that was the only part of her body she could move. 'It's tiny.'

He frowned. 'Yes. It's a beach cottage. Not a mansion.'

She blinked. Shifted uneasily. 'Oh, yes. Of course. But your other beautiful house...'

'Is on the market.'

Now the shock was real. Frances had approved mightily of his imposing residence on top of the hill. Two hills over from her imposing residence. He'd only liked it because Clancy, his missing wife, had loved it.

Frances spluttered, 'You're buying a new house?'

'I've bought a new house.' He put out one hand and gestured. 'This house. I'm staying here.'

'I... I thought you'd done this for the owners. That you rented?'

'I am the owner.' *A little too fierce, Finn*, he chided himself.

Frances leaned towards him pleadingly. 'But your work?'

'Will be here too when I'm ready. One of the GPs

here has offered me a place in his practice when I'm ready. I'll specialise in children but do all the GP stuff I've almost forgotten. It'll be good.' He wasn't sure who he was convincing, Frances or himself. 'It won't be yet because I'm in no hurry.'

'But…'

'But what?'

His sister turned worried eyes on his. 'You were only supposed to come here for a few weeks and then come back. Come home.'

'Home to where, Frances? To what? To an empty castle on a hill full of ghosts and pain. To a clinic with not enough hours in the day so I had to keep my daughter in long day care?'

Frances looked stricken and he leaned in and shared a hug with her, Piper still a limpet on his other hip. Frances meant well and she truly loved him. And now that Mum was gone she was all the family he had. Of course she'd never understood him with the ten-year age difference. Frances hadn't understood Mum either, if they were being honest. 'It's okay. This is a magic place to live and for Piper and me this is the right place at the right time. We're staying.'

Frances almost wrung her hands. 'You won't meet any eligible women here.'

He could feel his mood slip further. His irritation rise. His disappointment deepen. His sister didn't understand his guilt couldn't be fixed by an eligible woman. 'Eligible for what, Frances? I'm no good for any woman at the moment and won't be…' he didn't say *ever* '… for a very long time.'

He decided not to demonstrate the shower. Or point

anything else out. Ditched the plans to take a picnic to the beach.

Instead he took Frances to the most expensive restaurant in town, where Piper slept in her stroller beside the table despite the noise of conversations and laughter all around, and listened to her stories of droll people and dire events in her husband's practice.

In the corner of the restaurant he noticed a very attractive brunette. She nodded at him and he realised it was his morning midwife, elegantly dressed—*sans* scrubs—and made-up like a model, her brown hair blow-dried and shining, the glints catching the sun. Looking like a million bucks. Other men were looking at her. He preferred the windblown version.

She sat, a little isolated, in a lively group of people, all chinking champagne flutes to celebrate. Frances would approve of the clientele, he thought dryly, but recognised the older doctor he'd mentioned to his sister, and noted the stylish older woman next to him who leant into his shoulder, probably his wife. Another young woman he hadn't seen around was chatting to the vibrantly glowing woman in the latter stages of pregnancy who drank water, and next to her a man hovered protectively, obviously the doting father-to-be.

He wished him better luck than he'd had. Finn felt his heart twist in self-disgust. He'd tried that. A lot of good that had done him.

'Finn?'

His sister's voice called him back to the present and he jerked his face away from them. 'Sorry. You were telling me about Gerry's partner?'

Frances hovered over being cross for a moment and

thankfully decided to forgive graciously. 'I was saying she has no idea how a doctor's wife should dress.'

The lunch dragged on until finally Piper woke up
and gave him an excuse to pay the bill.

They waved Frances goodbye after lunch with much
relief. 'Seriously, Piper. Your aunt is getting worse.
We're lucky to be so far away.'

They took the sand buckets and spade back down to
the beach in the afternoon because Piper's routine had
been disrupted and she needed to get some play time
in and wear herself out before bedtime.

To his surprise, and with a seagull-like swoop of
uplifting spirits, the morning midwife sat there on the
breakwall, back in beach clothes and mussed by the
wind. He smiled at her like a long-lost friend. After the
visit from his sister he felt as if he needed a pal.

CHAPTER FOUR

Trina

TRINA SAT SWINGING her legs on the breakwall down on the beach and breathed in the salt. The sea air blew strands into her eyes but it felt too good to worry about that. She saw him before he saw her and a deep, slashing frown marred his forehead. Different to this morning. Then his expression changed as he saw her, the etched lines disappeared and an unexpected, ridiculously sexy, warmly welcoming smile curved in a big sweep. *Goodness.* What had she done to deserve that?

'Lovely afternoon,' he said and the little girl waved.

Trina's mouth twitched as she waved back. 'Beautiful. I saw you at lunch. That's three times in a day.'

'A new world record,' he agreed and she blushed. No idea why.

He paused beside her, another world record, and looked down from far too high. Up close and stationary, told herself again, he would be a very good-looking man—to other women. She studied him almost dispassionately. Long lashes framed those brilliant blue eyes and his dark brown wavy hair curled a tad too long over his ears. His chin was set firm and his cheekbones bordered on harsh in the bright light. She could see his effort to be social cost him. She knew the feeling.

'I'm Catrina Thomas.' She didn't enlarge. He could ask if he was interested, but something told her he wasn't so much interested as in need of a friend. Which suited her perfectly.

'Finlay Foley. And you've met Piper. My daughter.' The little girl bounced in the backpack.

You could do nothing but smile at Piper. 'Piper looks like she wants to get down amongst the sand.'

'Piper is happiest when she's caked in sand.' His hand lifted to stroke the wiggling little leg at his chest. Strong brown fingers tickling a plump golden baby ankle. 'We're going to build sandcastles. Piper is going to play hard and long and get extremely tired so she will sleep all night.' Trina wasn't sure if he was telling her or telling Piper. She suspected the latter.

'Nice theory,' Trina agreed judiciously. 'I see you have it all worked out.'

He began to fiddle with the straps as he extricated his daughter from the backpack and clinically she watched the muscle play as man power pulled his loose white shirt tight. His thick dark hair tousled in the wind and drew her eyes until she was distracted again by the wriggling child. Finlay popped her down in the sand on her bottom and put a spade and bucket beside her.

'There, miss.' He glanced up at Trina. 'Her aunt came today and she's ruined our sleep routine.' He paused at that. 'Speaking of routines, this is late in the day for you to be on the beach.'

'Nice of you to notice.' She wasn't sure if it was. There had been a suspicious lift of her spirits when she'd realised the woman he'd shared lunch with was his sister. What was that? She didn't have expectations and he wouldn't either—not that she supposed he would have. She wasn't ready for that. 'Don't get ideas or I'll have to leave.' Almost a joke. But she explained.

'Today is my first official Friday off for a long time. I'm off nights and on day shifts for the next year. Monday to Thursday.' She looked around at the little groups and families on the beach and under the trees at the park. Pulled a mock frowning face. 'I'll have to talk to people and socialise, I guess.'

'I know. Sucks, doesn't it.' The underlying truth made them both stop and consider. And smile a little sheepishly at each other.

Another urge to be truthful came out of nowhere. 'I'm a widow and not that keen on pretending to be a social butterfly. Hence the last two years on night duty.'

He said more slowly, as if he wasn't sure why he was following suit either, 'My wife left us when Piper was born. A day later. I've morphed into antisocial and now I'm hiding here.'

Died? Or left? How could his wife leave when their daughter was born? She closed her mouth with a snap. Not normal. Something told her Piper's mum hadn't died, though she didn't know why. Postnatal depression then? A chilling thought. Not domestic violence?

As if he read her thoughts, he added, 'I think she left with another man.' He seemed to take a perverse pleasure in her disbelief. 'I need to start thinking about going back to work soon. Learn to stop trying to guess what happened. To have adult conversations.'

He shrugged those impressive shoulders. Glanced around at the white sand and waves. 'I'm talking to Piper's dolls now.'

Still bemused by the first statement, the second took a second to sink in. Surprisingly, Trina giggled. She couldn't remember the last time she'd giggled like a schoolgirl.

He smiled and then sobered. 'Which means Piper and her dolls must go into day care if I go back to work.'

'That's hard,' Trina agreed but wondered what sort of work he could 'start thinking about going back to'. Not that there were screeds of choices around here. 'Maybe part-time?'

'I think so.'

'Are you a builder? The house looks good.'

He laughed at that. 'No. Far from it. Piper's taught me everything I know.'

Trina giggled again. *Stop it.* She sounded like a twit. But he was funny. 'I didn't have you pegged as a comedian.'

His half-laugh held a hint of derision at himself. 'Not usually. Remember? Antisocial.'

She nodded with solemn agreement. 'You're safe with me. If you need a protected space to tell your latest doll story you can find me.' She waited until his eyes met hers. 'But that's all.'

'Handy to know. Where do I find you? You know where I live.' Then he turned away as if he regretted asking.

'Of course I know where you live. It's a small town and single men with babies are rare.' Trina looked at him. 'I meant...find me here. But I'll think about it. I'm happy to have a male friend but not a stalker.'

She felt like an idiot saying that but thankfully he just looked relieved. 'Hallelujah. And I promise I will never, ever turn up uninvited.'

'We have that sorted.' She glanced at Piper, who sat on the sand licking white granules off her fingers, and bit back a grin. 'It's good when children will eat anything.'

Finn focused instantly on his daughter and scooped her up. Trina could see him mentally chastising himself. She imagined something like, *See what happens when you don't concentrate on your daughter*, and she knew he'd forgotten her. Was happy for the breathing space because, speaking of breathing, she was having a little trouble.

She heard his voice from a long way away. 'Sand is for playing—not eating, missy.' He scooped the grains from her mouth and brushed her lips. His quick glance brushed over Trina as well as he began to move away. 'Better go wash her mouth out and concentrate. Nice to meet you, Catrina.'

'You too,' she said, suddenly needing to bolt home and shut her door.

Ten minutes later the lock clunked home solidly and she leant back against the wood. Another scary challenge achieved.

Not that she'd been in danger—just a little more challenged than she'd been ready for. And she had been remarkably loose with her tongue. Told him she was a widow. About her job. The hours she worked. What had got into her? That was a worry. So much so that it did feel incredibly comforting to be home. Though, now that she looked around, it seemed dark inside. She frowned. Didn't just *seem* dark.

Her home was dark.

And just a little dismal. She frowned and then hur-

ried to reassure herself. Not tragically so, more efficiently gloomy for a person who slept through a lot of
the daylight hours. She pulled the cord on the kitchen
blind and it rolled up obediently and light flooded in
from the front, where the little dead-end road finished
next door.

She moved to the side windows and thinned the
bunching of the white curtains so she could see through
them. Maybe she could open those curtains too. Now
that she'd be awake in the daytime. Moving out of the
dark, physically and figuratively.

So, she'd better see to lightening it up. Maybe a few
bright cushions on her grey lounge suite; even a bright
rug on the floor would be nice. She stared down at the
grey and black swirled rug she'd bought in a monotone
furnishing package when she moved in. Decided she
didn't like the lack of colour.

She crossed the room and threw open the heavy curtains that blocked the view. Unlocking the double glass
doors and pushing them slowly open, she stepped out
onto her patio to look out over the glittering expanse
of ocean that lay before her like a big blue shot-thread
quilt as far as the eye could see. She didn't look down
to the beach, though she wanted too. Better not see if
there was the figure of a man and a little girl playing
in the waves.

Instead she glanced at the little croft to her right
where Ellie and Sam lived while Sam built the big house
on the headland for their growing family. She wondered
if they would keep the croft, as they said they would.
It would be strange to have new neighbours on top of
everything else.

The three crofts sat like seabirds perched on a branch

of the headland, the thick walls painted white like the lighthouse across the bay and from the same solid stone blocks. Trina's veranda had a little awning over the deck the others lacked. A thick green evergreen hedge separated the buildings to shoulder height.

On the other side of her house lay Myra's croft. Originally from Paddington in Sydney, stylish Myra ran the coffee shop at the hospital and had recently married the older Dr Southwell—her boss Ellie's father-in-law.

Two brides in two months, living each side of her, and maybe that had jolted her out of her apathy as much as anything else. Surrounded by people jumping bravely into new relationships and new lives had to make a woman think.

She stepped out and crossed to the two-person swing seat she'd tussled with for hours to assemble. Her last purchase as a flat-pack. Last *ever*, she promised herself.

She'd never seen so many screws and bolts and instructions in one flat-pack. Then she'd been left with a contraption that had to be dragged inside when it got too windy here on top of the cliffs because it banged and rattled and made her nervous that it would fly into the ocean on a gust. It wasn't really that she thought about the fact it needed a second person. Not at all.

She stepped back inside, glanced around then picked up the sewing basket and dug in it for the ribbons she'd put away. Went back to the double doors and tied back the curtains so they were right off the windows. Not that she was getting visitors—her mind shied away from the mental picture of a man and his baby daughter.

No. She'd lighten it because now she didn't need to exclude the light to help her sleep. She was a day-shift person. She was brave. And tomorrow she'd scuba again, and maybe talk to Finlay and Piper if she saw them because she was resurrecting her social skills and stepping forward. Carefully.

CHAPTER FIVE

Finn

FINN GLANCED BACK to the rocky breakwall once, to the spot where Catrina—nice name—had disappeared, as he crouched with Piper at the edge of the water to rinse her mouth of sand. It seemed other people did hurt like he did. And were left with scars that impacted hugely on how they lived their lives.

Two years working on night duty. He shuddered but could see the logic. Side-stepping the cold space beside you in the bed at night and avoiding that feeling of loss being the first thing you noticed in the day. Maybe he should have given that a go.

But the way she'd said she hadn't pegged him as a comedian surprised him out of his usual lethargy. He'd made her laugh twice—that was pretty stellar. Apart from his daughter, whose sense of humour ran to very simple slapstick, he hadn't made anyone giggle for a long time. He could almost hear her again. Such a delicious giggle. More of a gurgle really.

So—a widow? Lost like him, for a different reason. He wondered how her husband had died but in the end it didn't really change her pain. He was gone. For ever. Unlike the uncertainty he lived with.

Would Clancy ever come back? In a year. In ten years? Was she even alive? But, most of all, what would he tell Piper when she grew up? How could he say her mother loved her when she'd walked away and never asked about her again? The pain for Piper's future angst had grown larger than his own loss and he had no desire to rush the explanations.

Milestones with Piper never passed without him singeing himself with bitterness that Clancy wasn't there to see them. First tooth. First word. First step last week—though she still spent most of her time on her bottom. And on Sunday—first birthday. He felt his jaw stiffen. That would be the day he said *enough*. Enough holding his breath, expecting Clancy to walk through the door.

A milestone he'd never thought he'd get to. He hadn't decided whether to stay in Lighthouse Bay for the day with their usual routine; he was leaning towards taking Piper shopping, something he loathed, so that the logistics of strollers and car parking and crowd managing with a toddler drowned out the reminders of the best day of his life twelve months ago that had changed so soon after.

He wondered suddenly if he could ask Catrina to come. As a diversion, a pseudo-mother for the day, and then found himself swamped by such intense anger at Clancy for leaving their daughter he almost moaned. Piper clutched his hand and he looked down to see his daughter's eyes staring up at him as if she could sense his pain.

He scooped her up and hugged her, felt the lump

in his chest and willed it away. Whatever they did, he needed to remember it was a celebration of this angel in his arms, not of the woman who'd left them.

'I'll always love you, darling.' The words came out thickly. 'What would you like to do on Sunday, Piper?'

'Mum, Mum, Mum, Mum.'

He groaned and buried his face in her shimmering golden cloud of hair. Fine mist-like hair that floated in the breeze and tangled if he didn't tie it back but he couldn't bring himself to get it cut. His gorgeous little buttercup with her fine-spun headache of hair.

'Mum, Mum, Mum,' Piper chirped.

The last thing he needed to hear at this moment. 'Oh, baby, don't. Please.'

She squirmed and the baby voice drifted up to him. Uncertain. 'Dad, Dad, Dad, Dad?'

Pull yourself together. He lifted his head and looked into the soft dimpled face so close to his. 'Yes. Dad, Dad, Dad, Dad.' He carried her into the waves to dangle her feet and she wriggled happily. He concentrated on his fingers holding her as he swept her ankles through the waves and the foam ran up her knees as she squealed in delight. Guilt swamped him all over again. 'You can say *Mum, Mum, Mum* any time, my darling. Of course you can. Daddy's being silly.' *Stupid!*

Piper gurgled with laughter. 'Dad, Dad, Dad, Dad.' Finn could feel his heart shattering into a million pieces again and any lingering thoughts of Catrina the midwife washed into the sea with the grains of sand stuck to Piper's feet.

CHAPTER SIX

Trina

THE EARLY-MORNING SUNBEAM poked Trina in the eye with an unfamiliar exuberance and she groaned and threw her hand up to cover her face. *Who left the curtains open?* Only one answer to that. The twinge of morning memory and loss made her breath hitch and she forced herself to breathe calmly.

Saturday morning. Scuba lesson. She groaned again and all the doubts and fears from last week came rushing back to twist her stomach. Why had she said she wanted to do this again? Why the need to push herself to extremes she didn't feel comfortable with?

She flung the bedclothes back and swung her legs. The floor was warmed a little under her feet from the sun. That too seemed different.

Okay. Why was she fighting this? This was a new chapter in her life. Same book. She wasn't removing any of the pages—just going forward.

She squinted at the morning beams painting the inside of her one-room croft in golden stripes and decided they were quite lovely. Not worth groaning about at all.

She padded across to the uncurtained double doors

looking out over the ocean and decided the light streaming in shone still a little too bright until she'd made an
Earl Grey to start the day and turned her back.

As she busied herself in the tiny kitchen nook, she
pondered on yesterday and the advances she'd made
towards holding a sensible conversation with an eligible male. Though technically she guessed he wasn't
eligible. But probably safe to practise on, as long as he
was okay with it.

Not that she had any long-term intentions but she'd
done all right. Beaten the bogeyman, and so had he.
That made it a little easier. And no doubt different for
him, as his wife had chosen to go. How on earth could
a woman leave her baby? And why would she leave
Finlay? That too was a teensy worry.

Trina thought back to where she'd been a year ago.
Still in a black fog with a bright shiny mask on her
face for work.

She didn't believe that time healed all wounds, but
maybe it scabbed over some of the deeper lacerations.
The problem with losing your true love was they were
never really gone, always hovering, a comfort, and an
ache that flared into pain that burned right through you.

Boy, did she recognise the symptoms of reluctantly
dipping a toe into the real world after the misty haze
of deep grief. There were some aspects of her loss of
Ed that would never disappear but in other ways she
could, and would, live a happy life. She didn't think
that Finlay Foley had reached that stage yet. Which
was a tiny shame.

But she'd better get on and prepare for her scuba lesson. She'd eat when she came back.

By the time Trina left her croft on the cliff she knew

she'd be late if she didn't hurry and her steps skipped as she descended to the beach with her towel and specially fitted snorkelling mask. That was one good thing about living right on the beach—she didn't need to carry much because home was always a few steps away.

The path stopped at the sand and Trina began walking quickly around the headland. She'd glanced once towards the curve of the bay but no Finlay and Piper there, no sign of him, so tall and broad and unmistakable, so no golden-haired Piper on his back either, and fancifully it felt strange to be hurrying away without seeing them.

She forced herself to look forward again and concentrated on the scuba lessons she'd learnt last week from old Tom, running through the procedures.

'Nice even breathing through the mouthpiece; no holding your breath. This is how to replace a regulator in your mouth if it gets knocked out. This is how to control the speed of your ascent and descent by letting air in and out via the buoyancy control, so your ears don't hurt. Nothing to be nervous about. We'll go as slow as you need.'

Two hours later as she walked home in a much more desultory fashion a glow of pride warmed her as she remembered old Tom's quiet pleasure in her. 'You're a natural,' he'd told her.

A natural scuba diver? Who would have known? But today he'd taken her to the little island just off the beach and they'd dived slowly around the tiny inlets and rocks and seen colourful fish, delicate submarine plant life that swayed with the rhythm of the ocean, once a small stingray and one slightly larger shark, and it had all been Technicolor brilliant. Exciting. And, to her absolute delight, she'd loved it.

Her mind danced with snapshots of the morning and she didn't see the man and little girl sitting in a shallow rock pool under the cliff until she was almost upon them.

'Oh. You. Hello,' she stammered as she was jerked out of her happy reveries.

'Good morning, Catrina,' Finlay said. Though how on earth he could remain nonchalant while sitting in a sandy-bottom indent in the rock where the water barely covered his outstretched legs, she had no idea. 'You look very pleased with yourself.'

She regarded them. She liked the way they looked—so calm and happy, Piper dressed in her frilly pink swimsuit that covered her arms and legs. And she liked the way he called her Catrina. Ed had always called her Trina and she wasn't ready for another man to shorten her name. 'Good morning to you, Finlay.'

'Finn. Please. I'm usually Finn. Don't know why I was so formal yesterday.'

'Finn.' She nodded and smiled down at Piper. 'Hello, Piper. What can you see in the rock pool?'

The little girl turned her big green eyes back to the water. Pointed one plump finger. 'Fiss,' Piper said and Finn's eyes widened.

His mouth opened and closed just like the word his daughter had almost mouthed.

'She said fish!' His eyes were alight with wonder and the huge smile on his face made Trina want to hug him to celebrate the moment of pure joy untinged by bitterness. 'I can't believe she said fish.'

'Clever girl,' Trina said and battled not to laugh out

loud. She'd thought it had been more like a mumbled *fiss*. But she was sure her father knew better. Her mouth struggled to remain serious. In the end she giggled. Giggled? Again? *What the heck?*

She'd never been a giggler but this guy made her smiles turn into noises she cringed at.

To hide her idiotic response she said, 'I've seen fish too, Piper.'

Finn glanced at her mask. 'You've been snorkelling?'

Trina spread her arms and said with solemn pride, almost dramatically, 'I have been scuba diving.'

'Have you? Go you. I used to love to scuba.' He glanced around. 'Would you like to join us in our pool? There's no lifeguard except me but if you promise not to run or dive we'll let you share.'

Trina scanned the area too. Nobody she knew. She'd look ridiculous, though a voice inside her head said he looked anything but ridiculous in his skin-tight blue rash shirt and board shorts that left not one gorgeous muscle top or bottom unaccounted for.

She put down her mask and the sandals she carried, folded her towel to sit on, hiked up her sundress so it didn't drag in the water and eased herself down at the edge of the pool and put her feet in. The water felt deliciously cool against her suddenly warmer skin.

Finn watched her and she tried not to be aware of that. Then Piper splashed him and the mood broke into something more relaxed. 'So where did you go to scuba?'

She glanced the way she'd come. 'Have you been around the headland?'

He nodded. 'Around the next two until Piper started to feel like a bag of cement on my back.'

Trina laughed. She could so imagine that. She smiled at him. 'The next bay is called Island Bay and the little rocky island that's about four hundred metres out is called Bay Island.'

He laughed. 'Creative people around here.'

She pretended to frown at him. 'I like to think of it as being whimsical.'

'Whimsical. Right.'

She nodded at him. 'Thank you. So, Bay Island is where I did this morning's lesson. Old Tom takes beginners out.'

Piper sat between Finn's legs and he had his big brown long-fingered hands around her tiny waist so she couldn't slip. She was splashing with her starfish hands and silver droplets of water dripped in chasing drops down her father's chest. An unexpected melancholy overwhelmed Trina because the picture made her ache for lost opportunities she should have had with Ed. Opportunities Finn should have had with his wife. She wondered when these thoughts would stop colouring her every experience.

Finn smiled. 'Let me guess. His business is called Old Tom's Dive Shop.'

She jerked back to the present. Her brows crinkled in mock disbelief and she drew the sentence out slowly. 'How did you know that?'

'I'm psychic.' His expression remained serious.

'Really?' She tried for serious too but he was doing it again and her mouth twitched.

'Mmm-hmm. True story.'

'Wow.' She noted the little girl had found a treasure. 'So you can see your daughter is about to put a shell in her mouth?'

Without taking his eyes off Trina's face, his hand came up gently and directed Piper's hand away from her lips. Brushed her fingers open until she dropped the shell and bent down and kissed the little fingers. 'Absolutely.'

'That's fascinating.' And it was. Watching this big bronzed man being so gentle and connected to this tiny girl-child. The bond between them made tears sting Trina's eyes and she pretended she'd splashed water in them. Until she felt, and heard, her tummy rumble with sullen emptiness and seized on the excuse.

'Well, as lovely as your private ocean pool is, I need to have food. I missed breakfast and I'm starving.'

'Ah. So that's what the noise was,' he teased. 'I thought it was an outboard motor.'

She flicked tiny droplets from her damp fingers at him. 'Too rude.'

He rolled his eyes at her, then shifted Piper from between his legs to sit in the shallow pool and stood up easily. He leant down to offer her his hand. 'Piper's hungry. I should feed her too.'

She barely heard him. His so casually offered fingers were a stumbling block and she hesitated. Piper splashed and she knew she was holding them up. Reluctantly she put out her hand to his and his strong brown fingers closed over hers to lift her smoothly. Way too easily. But the touch of his fingers on hers created such a vibration between them that their eyes met. One pair as startled as the other.

When she was standing he let go quickly and bent down to hoist his daughter into his arms. His face stayed hidden as he tickled her and Trina straightened

her own shocked features into a mask of politeness as
Piper giggled.

'Well,' she said awkwardly, still rocked by the frisson of awareness that had warmed her whole hand. Her
whole arm really. 'Thanks for the swim.'

'Can we walk back with you?'

No, she thought. 'Of course,' she said. And resisted
the urge to hold her tingling hand in the other. She bent
down and picked up her sandals and mask, slung her
towel over her shoulder and resolutely faced the bay
until they began walking beside her.

'Would you like to have lunch with us?'

No, she thought. *I can't. I don't know what I'm feeling
and it's making me more nervous than scuba diving ever
did.* But that was the idea of these new challenges. To
challenge things that seemed daunting. And Finn was
safe. It took her a long time to answer but strangely she
didn't feel pressured to make that snap decision. So she
thought about it some more. It was just an impromptu
lunch. And Piper made it much easier than if there were
just the two of them. 'Okay. Where?'

'How about the beach shop? They have a closed-in
play area that Piper loves to crawl around. It's shady
and the breeze is always good there.'

'Sounds easy. But how about I meet you there? I
didn't bring my purse. I can just run up to the croft
and get it.'

He looked a little crestfallen. 'Piper may not last that
long. She's nearly ready for her sleep. I could shout you.
You could pay for ice creams or something next time?'

Next time? They hadn't tried this time yet. This was
all happening way too fast. And wasn't he having as
much trouble as she was, putting a toe in the water of

opposite sex conversation? Panic built like a wave rising from the ocean to her left. She tried to ride it and not be dumped.

He must have seen the indecision on her face because his features softened in understanding. 'It's okay. We can do a rain-check for another day.'

Disappointment dipped in her stomach. Did she want that? Why was everything so hard? 'No. Let's not. Thank you. I'll just buy the next one, if that's okay. A quick bite would be nice with company.'

They sat under the umbrellas and watched Piper play with a stand of coloured balls, then crawl importantly to steer a pretend ship with a bright blue Captain's wheel. Every time the conversation flagged, Piper sparked a new discussion with some cute little parody of life in her determination to experience all that the colourful play area offered.

Trina could do with her enthusiasm. Considered that fact. 'Babies should be compulsory on all outings. You could watch her all day.'

Finn laughed. Then, more seriously, said, 'I do. She keeps me sane. Makes me get out of bed in the morning.'

Trina knew that feeling. 'Well, you've certainly been busy since you got here. Your cottage is pretty in pink.'

'Piper chose the colour,' he said and then looked at her as if expecting her to laugh.

'So she's a pink girl. I can believe that. It looks good on her.' Trina rested her cheek on her hand to watch his face, trying to understand why he should be so wary. 'How did you get her to choose?'

'I gave her swatches. I was hoping for blue but she took the pink every time.'

Too funny. Trina laughed. 'Great idea. I can see that too.' She looked at his face and his beautiful smile. She shook her head. 'Her decision. You were stuck with it. Nothing you can do about that, then.'

He shrugged, his expression light and relaxed. It made her warm that he could be that way around her. 'I'm used to it now. I've been learning to be a handyman. And quite enjoying the challenge.'

Handyman. Or woman. The bane of her life. She rolled her eyes. 'Boy, have I had some repair challenges in the last two years? I've had to learn that too. Maybe I should paint my croft. Just yesterday I was thinking it looks very dark inside.' She shut her mouth. Now, why did she say that? Almost an invitation for help.

Finn's voice was light—lighter than her thoughts. 'I can send Piper up if you like. To talk colours with you.'

Trina felt herself relax. He got it. Her expression had probably telegraphed the message that she'd regretted being so open. 'I might take you up on that one day.' She could hear the relief in her voice. Hoped he couldn't.

They'd finished their roast beef sandwiches and iced coffee and Trina desperately needed some distance to think about the morning with Finn but the moment passed.

A commotion at the next table made them both turn. A woman had overturned her chair and the crash turned every head her way. She shook a small child hysterically. 'Spit it out. Come on.' She glanced around wildly. 'He swallowed a button.'

The child gasped weakly, tried to cry and couldn't find enough air to do so as he gulped and coughed. His face was tinged an alarming shade of blue as his mouth quivered.

Finn rose from their table and crossed the space in two strides. 'May I? I'm a doctor.' He didn't wait long.

The woman sagged, nodded and, sobbing in panic, watched as Finn took the child from her. Trina had followed him and righted the woman's chair and urged her back into it. Finn was a doctor. *Wow.* He'd said he wasn't a vet.

Finn sank into the nearest seat and lay the little boy, head down, across his knees and patted his mid back firmly in slow pats.

Trina leaned towards him. 'Can I help?'

Finn shook his head and concentrated on the boy. He patted again, then tipped him further. 'Come on now, mate. Everything is fine. Cough it up.'

To Trina's relief a sudden plop heralded the arrival of the button as it flew out onto the floor, initiating a collective sigh of relief from the entire café. And her. *Wow. Calmness is us.*

Finn righted the little boy and gave him a reassuring squeeze. Then he stood up with the exhausted child in his arms and passed him to his mother as if nothing had happened.

'He'll be fine. Just needs a minute to get his breath back.' He rested his hand on her shoulder and spoke quietly into her ear. Trina couldn't hear what he said but the woman nodded. Once. Twice. Glanced at the boy in her arms and squeezed him tighter. Then looked back at Finn with a vehement nod. 'Thank you.' The words were heartfelt.

Trina felt her eyes sting. Her heart still thudded from the spectre of a child choking to death in front of them all. She had no doubt everyone there had felt for the fear of the mother, though Trina would have liked to have given her a few pointers about first aid manoeuvres.

She glanced to where Piper played contentedly, oblivious to the drama she'd missed, and oblivious to the fact her daddy had quite possibly just saved a little boy's life. Trina wanted to go home. She felt too emotional to be out in public. Though she suspected she would still be thinking about Finn even if she was away from him.

When Finn sat back down and the conversations around them had begun again she nodded towards the woman, who was paying her bill and leaving with her little boy hugging her leg as he waited.

'Good job. What did you say to her?' She didn't mention he'd said he was a doctor. It didn't matter what he was.

'I asked if she'd seen what I did and, if there was a next time, to try that instead. That shaking didn't help and was actually dangerous. That calm speaking would relax the oesophagus as well.'

'I'm impressed. Discreet and direct.' The guy did everything right. But she still needed to get away from the emotionally charged atmosphere. She collected her mask and towel from the ground beside her and pushed her chair back. 'Before all the excitement I was about to leave. So thank you for lunch.' She glanced at his daughter, who had apparently wrung every conceivable amusement out of the play area and looked to be ready to depart as well.

'Maybe next weekend I could repay the favour.' Piper wailed. 'As long as Piper is free?'

Finn stood up to rescue his daughter. 'I'll look in her calendar and let you know.'

Their eyes connected for a moment, both a little bemused by the ease of their conversation. 'That would be lovely. Thank you, Finn.'

'Thank you, Catrina.' He watched her again and she knew he didn't want her to go. His approval circled her like a whisper of flame crackling and warming her around the base of her lost confidence. But the lure of time away from this new and challenging situation beckoned enticingly.

She stood and waved to the tiny girl. 'Bye, Piper.'

CHAPTER SEVEN

Finn

FINN WATCHED HER walk swiftly across the car park to the path. Almost hurrying away from him. Was it the incident with the little boy? That had turned out okay. Poor terrified little kid and mum—but all right now.

His eyes followed Catrina as Piper leaned into his neck. Maybe she'd left because she felt he was pushing for her company? He was. Why was he pressuring her? If someone had pushed him like he was pushing her he'd have run for the hills. Or a croft. Which she did.

Maybe he was sabotaging himself and hoping she'd stop it before he did? But there was no getting over the fact he'd been a little desperate for Catrina to stay.

And then there had been that jolt when he'd helped her stand at the rock pool. Unconsciously his hands came together to replicate the action, as if to see if he could still feel that vibration that had taken them both by surprise. It had been bizarre, and he'd seen the shock in her face—apparently he hadn't been the only one to feel it—before he'd picked up Piper to give himself a moment to recover.

He wished he'd told her it was Piper's birthday tomorrow. Because at lunch, after an initial stiffness, conversation had felt so easy. It had been strangely healing to have her sitting opposite him as they both watched his baby playing. When Catrina was there it was easier not to think about where Piper's mother would be tomorrow.

The guilt hit him like a fist in the chest and he sucked in his breath. What was he doing? How could he think that? He was a coward and tomorrow he'd celebrate Piper—he needed to be man enough not to cower in a corner feeling sorry for himself. He paid the bill and gathered Piper up in his arms.

Tomorrow he'd survive and Monday he'd see about getting a job.

Sunday morning Finn woke with a headache. Unusually, Piper had been unsettled most of the night and he wondered if they were both coming down with a cold. Or if the emotion of the coming anniversary of Clancy's desertion was rubbing off him and onto Piper.

He took two paracetamol and a vitamin tablet, and hand-squeezed an orange to give Piper with her breakfast. Because she was still asleep, he decided they wouldn't go out for the day if they were both unwell. He looked at the two wrapped presents he had for Piper. One was a tiny gardening set in a flower-decorated garden basket and the other a push-along block set for inside or out.

The cupboard above the sink drew his eyes and he crossed the room and searched for the packet cake mix he'd thrown in there a month ago in case he needed to make Piper's birthday cake. The packet mix came with little blue cupcake wrappers, pink frosting and fairy princess stickers to press into the icing after they'd been cooked.

The instructions seemed basic and he set it all out, with the candle, for later when he could make some noise. He glanced across at Piper but she snored gently and he wandered to the front of the beach house and stared out at the waves across the bay.

He could see Catrina walking along the breakwall and watched her brisk walk as she strode further away, the wind whipping her hair across her face. He wanted to wave and call her and share the burden and the blessing of this day with her, but knew he wouldn't.

'Last thing she needs,' he told himself out loud, keeping his voice quiet.

'Boo,' said a little voice from behind him and he turned to see Piper standing in her cot with her bunny cuddle blanket over her face.

Despite his aching heart, he smiled. 'Where's Piper?'

Piper pulled the blanket off her head and appeared like magic. Her eyes crinkled with delight at her own cleverness. 'Boo.'

'There she is.' He crossed the room to her but before he arrived he put his hands over his face and then pulled them away. 'Boo to you too, missy. Happy birthday, Piper!' He lifted her up out of her cot and hugged her. She gurgled with squirming delight and he had to force himself not to squeeze her too tight.

He began to sing 'Happy birthday' but faltered halfway through when he thought of Clancy and all she was missing. Forcing himself to finish the song, he carried Piper over to the window. 'It's a breezy sunny day for your birthday. What would you like to do?'

Piper put her head on his shoulder and snuggled in.

Suddenly it was okay again. They could do this. 'You feeling a little fragile today, poppet? Me too. But I'm making you a cake this morning. You can help by pushing on the stickers. It will be our first cake but your daddy is a doctor and supposed to be very smart. I'm sure we can manage little pink cakes for our birthday girl.' She bounced with a little more enthusiasm in his arms.

'Then we can sit outside and let the sunshine and fresh air kill all the germs, if there are any. No work today. Lazy day.'

He put Piper down on the floor and she crawled away from him to her box of toys in the corner with just a little less than her usual surprising speed.

He watched her go and thought about looking for childcare tomorrow. If he couldn't find anything then they'd leave it all for a while longer. That thought brought comfort. Surely it would be hard to find someone in a small town like this at such short notice.

He glanced out of the window again down to the beach and saw Catrina was on her way back. She didn't pass his house, or hadn't in the past or he would have noticed, and he leaned towards the window and saw her moving up the hill towards the cliff opposite the lighthouse. She'd said 'croft' yesterday. Maybe she was in one of those three little cottages on the cliffs that matched the lighthouse. All white stone.

He'd liked the look of them but the real estate agent had said they weren't for sale. He'd never actually gone up that way towards the hospital along the cliff path. Maybe it would be a nice place to go for a change when he went walking with Piper. Just in case he was missing out on a good walk, he reassured himself. But not today. He had promised he'd never drop in uninvited and had no intention of doing so.

Except the morning dragged. They went to the beach but the wind was a little cool to get wet and if Piper was coming down with a cold he didn't want to make it worse. Before long they went home and played inside. But he felt closed in staying indoors. Piper seemed to have recovered and before lunch she'd become unusually bored.

So after lunch, full from eating little pink cakes and with a sealed bag holding an extra one, he hefted Piper onto his back and went for a walk up the hill.

Yes, he nodded to himself dryly, towards the cliff path, not totally directed to one of the crofts that he wondered might belong to Catrina, but certainly it felt good to be outside, with a fresh breeze blowing the cobwebs and fingers of darkness from his lowered mood.

'Dad, Dad, Dad,' Piper burbled from behind his ear—so Piper liked being outside too, and it was her birthday. He was supposed to be doing what she wanted. Each of his steps up the hill lightened his mood and the hill path was well maintained and solid under his feet. He could feel the exertion and decided Catrina could probably run up this hill if she did it a couple of times a day. He wasn't quite up to that yet.

The path forked towards the cottages one way and down onto a cliff edge path on the other and he realised the crofts had hedges around them for privacy from below.

That was good. He wouldn't want anybody to be able

to peek into Catrina's house just by walking along the path, but it was a tiny bit disappointing that he couldn't see any of the buildings up close. Then he rounded a bend and the path snaked up again and as he trekked up the hill he realised they'd come out past the cottages.

Quite ingenious really. At the top they came out onto a little open area with a bench and an ancient telescope that had been cemented into the footpath to look out to sea.

He paused and bent down to peer through it, which was hard with Piper suddenly excited and bouncing on his back, when a voice spoke behind him.

'I bet Piper is heavier going uphill.'

He could feel the smile on his face as he turned— he hadn't imagined her.

'Hello there, Catrina.'

'Hello, you two, and what are you doing up here in the clouds?'

'We've never been here before. And it's Piper's birthday.'

Her face broke into a shining sunbeam of a smile and she stepped closer to drop a kiss on Piper's cheek. 'Happy birthday, sweetheart. I hope Daddy made you a cake.'

Piper bounced and crowed.

'Of course. Though really we made cupcakes with pink princess stickers.'

This time the smile was for him. 'I wish I could have seen them.'

It felt good to know he'd thought ahead. 'By a stroke of luck, we do have a spare one in our bag which I'm sure Piper would love to share with you?' He looked around and considered the logistics of Piper and a cliff edge. Maybe not.

It seemed that Catrina got it in one. 'It's too tricky here for a birthday girl. Come back and I'll show you the croft. We can sit on the balcony; it's well fenced and safe.'

CHAPTER EIGHT

Trina

TRINA TURNED ON the path and directed them along the
other fork back towards her house, beckoning them to
follow. Thankfully, facing the other way, Finn couldn't
see the expression on her face. She still couldn't believe
she'd invited them into her home. So blithely. Since
when had her bravery suddenly known no bounds?

Well, she could hear Finn's springing footsteps behind her as she led the way around the loop that led to
the cottages again and within seconds they'd popped
out onto the road outside the last croft, where Myra and
Dr Southwell lived. As they passed the door opened and
the older gentleman stepped out.

He smiled when he saw her, and then his face lit up
further when he saw who followed her. 'Trina. And
Finn. And Piper. Hello. Delightful. So, you've met.'

Trina could feel herself blush. 'Hello. Yes. At the
beach.' Glancing around for inspiration to change the
subject, she added, 'Lovely day.' Not only had she invited a man back to her house but she'd been caught
in the act. Everyone would know. Dr Southwell wasn't

a gossip but, seriously, Ellie's father-in-law? *Small blinkin' towns.*

Trina blushed again under Dr Southwell's pleased smile.

'The weather is super. Love to stay and chat but I'm off to the hospital.' He waved and strode off.

Trina shrugged off the awkwardness with determination. 'So that's who lives next door on this side and my boss, Ellie, and her husband, who happens to be an obstetrician, Dr Southwell's son, live on the other side.'

He looked around at the three crofts as they came to hers, and paused. 'You're well covered for medical help then.' He smiled a little awkwardly.

'Never too many in an emergency.' She smiled back, too concerned with whether she'd left the house tidy before he arrived to worry about trying to read his reaction to her neighbours. She indicated her own front path. 'Come in. It's small but compact, much like yours is, I imagine.'

'Yes. Tiny, but I like it. You'll have to come and see my renovations.'

Not your etchings? She thought it and smiled to herself. Didn't risk saying anything in case he heard the amusement in her voice. At least she could be amused by something that she would have run a mile from a month ago. In fact, she could have rubbed her knuckles on her chest. Darn proud of herself, really.

She pushed open the door and was glad she'd opened all the blinds this morning. With everything open the sea seemed to be a part of the room, with all eyes being drawn to the open French windows out onto the little terrace. She gestured him to walk that way.

'Great view,' Finn said after a low whistle. 'That's

really magic.' He walked slowly to the French windows and absently began to undo Piper's straps.

Trina came up behind him and undid the other one. 'Here, let me help.' She lifted Piper out of the straps and set her down. 'There's nothing to climb on. I only keep the swing chair out there and it's against the house wall. It has to come in when it's windy.'

Piper crawled straight for the rails and her little hands grabbed on as she pulled herself up. She bounced on the balls of her feet. Finn followed her out and Trina stood back a little and admired them both.

A bouncy, healthy little girl and her gorgeous dad. She wasn't sure when he'd graduated from attractive to other women to gorgeous for her, but she had to admit he made an admirable picture with his big shoulders and strong back silhouetted against the ocean. His long fingers rested lightly and then the curved muscles in his arms bunched as he gripped the rail for a minute. She wondered what he was thinking about as he stood guard over his daughter, his powerful thighs either side of her as one hand left the rail and brushed her small head.

Then the penny dropped. Piper's birthday. And his wife had left soon after Piper's birth. That made this time of year a distressing anniversary as well as a day for celebration for Piper. Tough call. She hadn't even crawled out of bed on the anniversary of losing Ed.

Why hadn't he said something yesterday? Then she chastised herself. Why would he share that with a stranger?

She swallowed past the lump that had suddenly formed in her throat. 'Would you two like a cold drink?' She managed to even her voice. 'I have a spill-proof cup I use for one of my friend's daughters.'

'Piper has her water here, thanks.' He came back in and bent down to Piper's pack. Pulled out a little pink pop-top bottle. 'She'll use hers.' Then he pulled out a Ziploc bag. 'Aha! Here's your part of Piper's birthday cake.'

He glanced back at his daughter. 'Probably best she doesn't see it as I had no idea she could gobble as many as she did and she'll be sick if she eats any more.'

Trina nodded and swiped the bag, turning her back to the veranda and opening the seal. She lifted out the little blue-papered cake and admired the rough pink icing and slightly off-centre sticker. 'It's magnificent.'

'Piper put the stickers on herself.'

'Clever girl.' She looked at him. 'Clever Daddy for the rest.'

He looked at her. Maybe saw the lingering distress in her eyes and he closed his own for a minute and then looked at her again. Nodded. 'So you've guessed it's a tough day?'

'You have a different set of triggers but I was just thinking I didn't even get out of bed when mine went past.' They needed to get out and fill the day with something. 'How about we go for a walk along the cliffs further? There's a really cool cave overlooking the ocean about a kilometre north I could show you. And there's a sweet little dip of green grass Piper would love.' She smiled at the thought. 'She could probably log roll down the tiny hill. I watched some kids do that one day and it looked fun.'

She saw relief lift the creases from his brow. 'That does sound good. Is there somewhere you'd prefer me to change Piper before we go? I have a change mat.'

'You have everything!' And wasn't that true. 'Change

mats are great. You can use my bed and save you bending down. I'll make a little snack for the meadow.' She turned away. Excited for the first time in a long while with a task she couldn't wait to play with.

She slipped in two small cans of mixer cordial that she'd bought on a whim. A packet of dates and apricots for Piper. She even had arrowroot biscuits, perfect for a little girl to make a mess with. Threw in some crisps, two apples and a banana. It all fitted in her little cool bag she carried to work each day, along with the tiny checked throw she had never had the opportunity to use for a picnic.

They set off ten minutes later, Piper bouncing on her daddy's back and Trina swinging along beside them as if she was a part of the little family. She winced at her instinctive comparison. No. Like a party of friends. Looking out for each other.

The sun shone clear and warm on their backs as they strode along the path. The sea breeze blew Piper's bright golden mist of hair around her chubby face as she chattered away. Trina decided Finn looked so much more relaxed out in the open. It made her feel good that she'd helped.

A cruise ship hugged the horizon and she pointed it out to Finn. Piper saw a seabird dive into the water far below and they had to stop and watch for a minute until it came out again with a fish in its beak.

Trina admired the skill of the surfers, bobbing and swooping like brilliant supple-bodied flying fish on the curling waves.

When she commented, Finn shared, 'I love surfing.'

'I've never tried.' Maybe she could add that to her adventure list.

Finn said, 'When Piper is old enough I'll teach her to surf. This looks a great place to do that.'

'Dr Southwell used to surf every morning before he was married. Though I have to admit he did come a cropper when he was washed off the shelf last year.'

He looked back the way they'd come. 'Really? Ouch. Which shelf?'

She pointed. 'The ones under the cliffs, with the rock pools we were in yesterday.'

Finn frowned. 'It doesn't look dangerous there.'

'It is on a king tide. And his timing was off if you ask him. They lifted him out with a chopper but the good news was his son met Ellie, my boss, when he came to locum while his father was away, and they married and are having a baby. That's why I'm doing Ellie's job for the next year—hence the change from night duty.'

'Happy ending.' His voice held only a trace of bitterness. She got that. But she'd moved on herself, thankfully.

She wondered if he'd heard his own subtext because his voice came out warmer than before. 'So were they all the people in the restaurant on Friday?'

She'd forgotten. 'Yes, that's right—you were there. With Piper and your sister.' She thought back over those present. 'They were celebrating Ellie's leave and my promotion.'

'Congratulations.'

She laughed. 'Thanks. First day tomorrow. We'll see.'

She thought back to Friday and the pleasant lunch. Her own surprise to see Finn there. With another woman. Felt just a little embarrassed now she knew it was his sister. Hurried on in case it showed on her face.

'The other older lady at the table is the one who makes the most divine cakes—Dr Southwell's wife, Myra.'

'I guess I'll get to know them all. Dr Southwell's offered me a place in his practice. I'll start as soon as I can find day care for Piper.'

She raised her brows. 'Do you have a specialty?'

'I started in general practice. Then I went on and studied paediatrics. I thought everyone knew?' Then he shook his head. 'I guess I haven't really spoken to many people. I have my Diploma of Obstetrics from my GP days, but no real experience in that. Just the antenatal side of it. Not the delivery part.'

He didn't look old enough to have done all that. Catrina smiled at him, decided she wouldn't share that thought and shook her head mockingly. 'We don't say delivery any more. Especially in Lighthouse Bay. We're Midwifery Group Practice.'

He put his hands up. 'Midwifery Group Practice. And I said *delivery*. My bad.'

'Very.' She smiled at him. 'Everything is midwifery-led and woman-centred. The antenatal clinic is drop-in and popular. When the mother births, we support her choice to stay or go, and she's visited at home within the day after if that's what she wants or she can stay for a few days in the hospital. Either way, we don't call a doctor unless someone is sick.'

He put out his hands helplessly and pretended to sigh. 'I'm defunct and I haven't even started.'

She laughed. 'You'll get used to it. You should meet Ellie and her husband. Sam's the Director of Obstetrics at the base hospital and fell in love with Lighthouse Bay too. And Ellie, of course.' She smiled at the thought. 'Sam moved here from a big Brisbane Hospital so we're lucky to have him as an unofficial back-up in real emergencies when he's not on-call at the base hospital.'

She looked at him thoughtfully. 'I've thought of someone who could mind Piper, if you're interested.'

His face went blank and she hesitated. Maybe he wasn't ready yet.

'I'll need to find someone eventually,' he managed but she could see it cost him. She wished she hadn't mentioned it now.

Then he said more firmly, 'Sure. That would be great. I need to start looking.'

Trina thought about Marni. She didn't regret mentioning her, though. 'She's a doll. A natural mother. Her twins are six months old and she's just registered for day care status.'

CHAPTER NINE

Finn

FINN FELT HIS stomach drop. He wasn't seeing the path or the ocean or the sky overhead. He shouldn't have asked about day care. But something inside had dared him to. Something that wanted him to move on, as if he'd known he'd be catapulted into a decision if he put it out there. All his instincts wanted to draw back. Stop her telling him. Say he'd ask if he decided it was time. She'd understand. Not sure how he knew that but he believed in the truth of it.

Instead he said, 'Would you recommend her?'

She looked at him thoughtfully. Kindly. 'That's tough because it's not about me,' she said gently, as if she could read his distress. Then she looked at Piper. 'Marni could mind my child, if I had one.' The tone was almost joking. He saw something that looked like pain flit across her face and remembered again there were people out there who did suffer as much as he did. People like Catrina. Left alone by the love of their life—without choice and unintentionally. Loss of love and no baby to hold like he did. Imagine life without Piper.

Catrina's voice wasn't quite steady but he could hear

the struggle to make it so. It had been a very brave thing to say and he wanted to tell her that. Wanted to tell her that he understood. But still the coward inside him shied away from so much emotion.

Catrina said, 'Maybe you could see if Piper likes her before you commit to work and see how she goes? Just an hour or two?'

'That's a good idea. Tell me about her.'

He saw her gaze into the distance, a soft smile on her face and a glimmer of distress, though this time he didn't think it was for herself. 'She's a younger mum. Early twenties. She and her husband own the dry-cleaners in town but she's a stay-at-home mum. Marni's Mother Earth and the boys are six months old. Bundles of energy, healthy as all get-out, which is great because she nearly lost them at twenty-three weeks, and she spent a lot of time in hospital. As far as the midwives of Lighthouse Bay think, she's a hero to us.'

He had to smile at that. '*The Midwives of Lighthouse Bay*. Sounds like a serial on TV.'

She laughed a little self-consciously and he regretted making light of the one stable thing she had in her life, hadn't meant to embarrass her. 'Don't get me wrong. It's another good ending to a story.'

Catrina seemed to relax. 'It really was. Ellie's husband, Sam, had been involved in research into preventing extreme premature birth in Brisbane, and thankfully he was here when she went into labour. Marni and Bob are a lovely couple who'd already lost an extremely premature baby daughter.'

Finn wasn't so sure. She already had twins and he wanted someone who could concentrate on Piper. 'How could she care for Piper as well?' Finn was more uncertain now. 'Sounds a bit hectic. She has twins and she's doing day care?'

He caught Trina's encouraging smile and suddenly saw how she could be a good midwife. Her empathy shone warm—he felt she understood and was reassuring him that he would conquer his fear of letting Piper out of his sight. All without putting on pressure. Encouraging him to test his own strength without expectations. Treating him like a woman in labour battling her own fear. *Wow.* She had it down pat.

Then she said, 'She loves minding babies. And babies love her. Usually she's minding them for free. We keep telling her she should become a midwife and I wouldn't be surprised when the boys go to school if she'll look at it. But, for now, she's just starting up official day care.'

Absently he bent and stroked Piper's leg at his side. 'Maybe I could meet her before I talk to Dr Southwell? It's a good idea to see if Piper likes her before I commit to work, though. You'll have to give me her number.'

'Or we could visit her. Meet her and her husband. See their house. They're a lovely couple and live only a few doors up from you. In the blue pastel cottage.'

It was all happening too quickly. He could feel the panic build and squashed it down again. He could do this. Just not today.

Catrina touched his arm—the first time she had physically connected with him of her own volition—and again that frisson of awareness hummed where they touched. He glanced at her but her expression still showed only compassionate support. 'It's something to think about. Marni is just the one I know. There will be others when you're ready.'

His relief made his shoulders sag. She must have seen it on his face. Was he that transparent? He'd have to work on his game face before he went back to work or his patients' parents would run a mile.

He tried to make light of it. 'I imagine every parent must feel like this when they have to go back to work. Torn.'

'Absolutely. We see mums that can't stay in hospital for one night after birth because they hate leaving the other child or children too much.' She looked towards Piper and smiled. 'I'd find it hard to leave Piper if she were mine.'

His face tightened. He could feel it. Some women could. Piper's mother had no problem. And he'd be the one who had to break his daughter's heart when the time came to tell the truth.

Catrina opened her mouth—he didn't want to talk about Clancy—but all she said was, 'The cave's just around this next headland.' He was glad she'd changed the subject.

The cave, when they arrived, curved back into the cliff and created an overhang half the size of his house. A few round boulders acted as seats for looking out over the ocean out of the sun. Or rain. Plenty of evidence suggested people had camped and made campfires there but on the whole it had stayed clean and cool, and dim towards the back. The sort of place young boys would love to go with their mates.

He could stand up in the cave easily and they stomped around in it for a few minutes before Catrina suggested they go the small distance further to the glade so Piper could be released from the backpack.

The glade, when they arrived, had a park bench and

table at the edge of the slope down into the bowl-shaped dip of grass. The bright sunshine made the grass lime cordial-coloured and the thick bed of kikuyu and daisies felt softer and springier than he expected when he put Piper down to crawl. Because of the sloping sides of the bowl Piper tended to end up back in the lowest point in the middle even when she climbed the sides and he could feel his mouth twitching as she furrowed her brows and tried to work out what was happening.

He pulled a bright saucer-sized ball from her backpack and tossed it in the centre of the glade while Catrina set their picnic bag on the table and spread the cloth. Piper crawled to the ball and batted it. Of course it rolled back down the side to her again. She pushed it again and crowed when it rolled back again.

'Clever girl,' he said to his daughter, and 'Clever girl,' to Catrina, who grinned at him as she finished laying out their treats and came to sit next to him on the side of the grass hill. 'I can't remember when I last had a picnic,' he said as he passed an arrowroot biscuit to Piper and took one of the apples for himself.

'I know. Me either.' She handed him the can of drink and took a sip of her own. Then he heard her sigh blissfully.

'We couldn't have had more beautiful weather this afternoon.'

'A bit different to this morning.'

'That's the beauty of Lighthouse Bay. We're temperate. Not too hot for long or too cold for long. Always leaning towards perfect weather.'

'Always?'

Catrina laughed. 'Well, no. We do have wild storms

sometimes. That's why I have shutters on my windows and doors. But not often.'

The afternoon passed in a desultory fashion and once, when Piper dozed off in his arms, he and Catrina lay side by side watching the clouds pass overhead in companionable silence. He'd never met anyone as restful as she was. It would have been so simple to slide closer and take her hand but the man who could have done that had broken a year ago.

An hour later, on the way home from their walk, he asked again about the exact location of the day care mum.

'I could come with you to knock on the door? Maybe meeting the family would help?'

'Just drop in?' Despite his initial reluctance, he could see that an impromptu visit could be less orchestrated than one when they expected him. And he had Catrina to come with him to break the ice.

It made sense. Not fair perhaps, but this was his baby he was considering leaving in their care, and he wanted a true representation of the feeling of the household.

When the door opened to answer his knock, a smiling red-haired man answered. Past him they could hear the sound of a child squealing and the smell of a roast dinner drifted out to tantalise his nose. He hadn't had an old-fashioned roast for years. His mouth watered.

'Can I help you?' Then the man saw Catrina and smiled beatifically. 'Trina!'

'Hello, Bob. How are you?' The man stepped forward and hugged her and Finn was surprised.

When they stepped back from each other she said, 'Something smells divine. Lucky you—Sunday roast.'

'You're welcome any time, Trina.' He grinned and looked at her companion.

'This is Finn Foley. He's a friend and I told him about Marni offering childcare and—' she indicated Piper '—he and Piper have just started looking.' Finn glanced at Catrina. Took a second to savour that she'd claimed friendship. She really was his only friend here.

She still spoke to Bob. 'I wondered if he could have a chat with Marni?'

'Absolutely. Any friend of yours and all that.' Bob grinned at Finn. 'Come in. Marni? There's a dad here looking for information about childcare.'

Finn liked the way he said that. To his wife, with deference, and that he wasn't committing to anything. Just asking. His nerves settled a fraction as he followed Catrina, with Piper on his back, in the door.

The room had been divided into two, with a kitchen and lounge on one side and a wall with doors on the other. Bedrooms, he guessed, unlike his one-room cottage. An extension had been built out the back with a big play room that overlooked the tiny fenced garden. Everything sparkled; even the toys strewn on the floor in the play room caught the sunlight and looked new and well cared for. The family warmth in the little abode made the tension drop from his shoulders and his eyes met Trina's in acknowledgement.

A young woman crossed to them, drying her hands on a tea towel. She too hugged Catrina, and her shy smile eased the tension in Finn's stomach like magic. 'Trina. Great to see you.'

'This is Finn, Marni.' She turned to help Finn extricate Piper from the backpack—which he was pretty darn good at, but he had to admit it was quicker with help. And he liked her touching him.

'Nice to meet you, Finn. You live a few doors down, don't you?' she said as she held out her hand. They shook briefly and he liked that her fingers were cool and dry, her grip confident.

'Welcome.' She smiled at Piper, who now sat on his hip, then turned around and pointed to two boys as if introducing her to them not Finn. 'The one on the left is Olly, and the cheekier one is Mikey.' She looked at Piper. 'And what is your name, beautiful?'

Previously fascinated by the smaller humans, Piper looked back at the lady's face, realised everyone was looking at her and then she clutched at his neck and buried her face.

Finn rubbed her back. 'Piper can be shy.'

'Of course she can.' Marni indicated the rear of the cottage. 'Come and sit out on the deck at the back and we'll show you the play area and I can answer your questions.

'So Catrina told you I've started doing childcare?' The smile Marni gave Catrina lit up her face. 'The midwives are my cheer squad. They're all champions up there. If it wasn't for them and the younger Dr Southwell, we wouldn't have our gorgeous boys.'

Finn looked at the two chubby-faced little boys, one sitting in a blue tub of a chair kicking his feet and the other lying on his back on the patterned play carpet with a red spiral rattle. The little boy—Finn thought it was Olly—began to screw his face up, dropped the rattle and began to rock until he rolled over and lay on his stomach. The mischievous chortle he let out at the feat made Finn smile.

'Clever boy, Mikey,' his dad said. So he'd got that wrong, Finn thought. And then Bob gestured to his wife. 'I'll finish the potatoes. You take our guests and Piper out and have a chat.'

Finn liked that too. He could see they were a team and, despite having two babies, the air of serenity as Marni smiled made his trepidations settle. This sort of calm atmosphere looked perfect for Piper to learn about other babies and new adults.

A heck of a lot different to the busy, efficient child-care he'd had her in before. But Piper still clung to him like one of the stripy shells on the side of a rock pool and he remembered the hard times at the big kindergarten when he'd tried to leave.

Marni pointed to a scrubbed wooden table and four sturdy chairs. Two highchairs took up the other spaces. They all sat down and Marni put a soft-sided squeaky farm book on the table in front of Piper without making a fuss of it.

'I am looking for two more toddlers. That will give me enough to cover the wage of the girl working with my husband at the dry-cleaners and then there's no rush for me to go back to work. I'm hoping to stay home for the next year at least. In a perfect world, I won't go back to work until the boys go to school.'

She smiled calmly at Finn. 'But we'll see what happens.'

So a stable place, Finn was thinking, and he wondered, if he offered to pay twice the rate, would Marni consider having Piper by herself, at least at the beginning so the young mum wasn't pushed by the demands of four children? Piper would benefit and money wasn't a problem. Finding someone caring and kind for Piper would be priceless.

He tried to think of a question. 'Catrina said you've just been registered. Having two babies seems intense to me. Piper can keep me busy and there's only one of her.'

She glanced lovingly towards the two gurgling on the floor and then across at her husband. 'I mind lots of children. Have always loved them and thought for a while we'd never be able to have any. But then the boys came along, though I spent a couple of months in hospital hanging onto them, so they are beyond precious.'

She shrugged ruefully. 'I'm worried I might spoil them and want them to learn to share, not just with each other but with other children. Some extra income would help and my husband and I are both the eldest from big families. Our families are in Western Australia so we miss having lots of kids around.'

'I guess childminding makes sense in that case.'

Piper reached out and picked up the book. Scrunched it with her inquisitive fingers. Barely audible squeaks erupted when she squeezed and a crooked smile tipped her mouth as she battled between shyness and delight.

All the adults looked at her fondly. 'So, information-wise, what sort of minding were you looking for?'

'I've been offered a position three days a week, Monday, Tuesday and Wednesday.'

Marni nodded. 'Three is better than five for Piper. Especially in the beginning. Has she been in care before?'

'Yes, poor baby, most of her life, when I worked. About fifty hours a week. But not for the last six weeks and she was becoming unhappy before that. I was thinking to start a half-day, as a trial, just until Piper gets used to it. If she gets too upset I'd probably not go back to work for a while.' He shrugged his apology.

Apparently she didn't need it. That serene smile drifted across her face. 'Being adaptable is good around kids. One of the secrets. She'll miss you if she's had you to herself for six weeks.' A quirked brow made that question.

'I'm not even sure it's what I'm ready to do.'

'That's fine. You're fact-finding, which is very sensible.'

Well, he'd better glean some facts. This was harder than he'd thought it would be. He glanced at Catrina and she sat tranquilly beside him, lending moral support, not interrupting. Just there. It felt good not to be on his own through this. 'What hours do you have available?'

Marni laughed. 'As I haven't started yet it's hard to say. Big picture—Monday to Friday, no more than forty hours, but the hours are flexible. And I get to keep the weekends for the boys and Bob.'

'Where would she sleep in the daytime?'

'We've a little room next to the boys' room. Bob put two new folding cots in there and I think it'll work well. And I'll supply all the food. No hardship to make for one more and that way nobody wants what others have.'

It all sounded too good to be true. Plus they lived a few doors away from his own house. Even in this short time Piper seemed relaxed here. He gently swung her off his lap, book still in her hands, and rested her bottom on the floor. Just to see if she'd go.

As soon as she hit the floor she dropped the book and crawled curiously towards the two little boys. Stopped about a body's length away and sat up. The three tiny people all looked at each other.

The adults smiled and Finn felt the tension leave his shoulders. The gods, or Catrina, had saved him again.

'What about if I go and talk to my prospective employer tomorrow? Perhaps leave Piper here just for an hour and see how she goes while I negotiate? Then we'll all know more.'

'Why don't you make it two hours? That will be a quarter of the time of her next visit, if you decide to go ahead. Just to give her time to settle. And take the rush out of your appointment. She'll be fine. It will give us all a chance to trial the fit.'

'I think that sounds like a plan. Yes, please.' Finn stood up. Blew out a breath. 'Phew. Thank you. I do feel better for asking and talking to you. That would be great.' He glanced at Catrina, who stood as well. She smiled at him as if he'd just done an excellent job. It felt good. Reassuring.

Marni went across to the dresser and picked up a business card. 'Here's our phone number, and it's got my mobile on it as well. You can ring or drop in when you know your time. The sheet has information about my business.' She handed him a sheet of paper with her numbers and the payment rates. Easy.

'That's great.' He picked up Piper, who had crawled over to him as soon as he stood up. She didn't cling, more curious than panicked he'd leave her. 'I'll leave one of my own cards when I bring Piper. Then you can contact me any time.'

'Give yourself ten extra minutes before you leave her tomorrow. To help her settle.'

He nodded. Then Bob came and shook his hand. Then they were outside and the door closed.

He felt like sagging against it. He'd done it. Another step towards a new life.

'You didn't say much.'

Catrina laughed. 'I didn't have to. You're all made for each other.'

CHAPTER TEN

Trina

TRINA'S FIRST MORNING as Midwifery Unit Manager, and her first day shift for a long time, proved too busy to worry about a man she'd met on the beach and declared her friend. Though she had spent a fair time mulling over all the things she'd learnt about Finn the night before.

This morning, in her new world, the midwife coming off shift had celebrated a birth at five a.m., so still lots of settling of mother and baby for Trina to help with before mother left at lunchtime to go home. Another mother who preferred to rest at home, not separated from her toddler, and it made her think of her conversation with Finn yesterday. Finn again. She pushed those thoughts away and concentrated on the new tasks.

There were Monday pharmacy orders and sterile stock orders, and a hospital meeting and a visit from Myra, her neighbour, which lightened a busy time with a quick break.

'Hello there, new midwife in charge.' Myra's serene face peered around the corner of the nurses' station, where Trina typed efficiently into the discharged mother's electronic medical records.

'Hello, Mrs Southwell, what have you got there?' Myra had a steaming cup and a white paper bag tucked under her arm. Ellie had said that Myra always brought something when the place got busy.

'A long black with extra water, the way you like it.' She smiled mischievously. 'And a savoury tart with spring onion in case you haven't had lunch.'

Trina glanced at the clock, the hour hand resting on the two. 'An angel. That's what you are.' Though she would pack lunch tomorrow to make sure she had something. She hadn't realised how hard it could be to get away from the ward to the cafeteria. She'd expected that on night duty but not through the day.

Myra tilted her head to scrutinise her. 'Have you had time to stop for a few minutes?'

Trina sat back and gestured to the chair beside her. 'Not yet. But I do now. And I will.' She took the china mug Myra carried and took a sip before she put it down on the desk beside her. 'Ah!' She smiled at the older lady. 'I seriously needed that.' She looked at the mug again and picked it up. Took another sip and closed her eyes. 'The world won't stop turning if I don't achieve everything today.'

Myra laughed. 'Something I've learnt since I came here. So how is it going? Is it strange to be on the ward in the daytime?'

Trina glanced around the sunlit reception area. The windows that showed the gardens. The sunlight slanting across the polished wooden floors. 'It is. And there are so many people I need to talk to.' She pretended to shudder. 'Business requirements have given me inter-action overload. Present company excluded, of course.'

'I won't be offended.' Myra looked at her with concern. 'Are you sure you wouldn't prefer sitting in the tea room and I could answer the phone for you while you finish your tart?'

Trina laughed. 'No. This is a social conversation. Much more fun. Besides, I haven't seen you for days. How are you? How is married life? Any adventurous plans?'

'I'm well. Ridiculously content, and I'm trying to talk Reg into coming away with me on a cruising holiday. There's a last-minute deal that's breaking my heart not to take.'

Trina could see Myra at a Captain's Cocktail Party, dressed to the nines in those stunning vintage outfits she seemed to source at will. Trina could never find anything when she looked in the pre-loved section. Or if she did she looked ridiculous. But Myra looked soft and elegant and stunningly stylish. She sighed and let the envy go. She hadn't really thought much of clothes since Ed. 'That sounds fun. Does he like the idea?'

'More than I thought he would. But it all depends if he finds locum relief for the practice. I'm a little keen for him to scale right back but he's become immersed in the bay and the hospital.'

Trina could see why Myra wanted to play. 'I haven't seen him out on his surfboard lately.'

'He still goes out every Sunday with his son. It's lovely to see. Says he doesn't have the need to get out of bed at the crack of dawn now—especially with me in it.' Myra smiled with just a hint of pink in her cheeks and Trina smiled back.

'Understandable.' She thought of Finn. Her own cheeks heated and she dipped her head and took a sip from her mug to hide it. Of course he was the locum Myra hoped for, and of course she wasn't blushing just because of Myra's mention of mornings in bed. 'Is he hopeful of the locum situation?'

Myra sighed. 'There's a young doctor in town he's had a chat with. Some family issue that's keeping him from starting, but hopefully that will sort soon. If not, I think he should advertise.'

'I met the one I think he's talking about. Finlay Foley. He's a single dad. Has a delightful little one-year-old.'

Myra unwrapped the tart from its white paper bag and pushed it towards Trina. 'That's the one. That's right—Reg said he had a daughter. What's he like?'

'He's an amazing dad. Anyone can see that. It's a wonder you haven't seen him walking along the beach with his little girl on his back.'

Myra's eyes brightened. She lifted her head in delight and glanced towards the general direction of the beach way below, though she wouldn't be able to see it. 'Oh. I have seen him. Younger than I expected. I didn't think of him as a doctor. Looks too young.' She lowered her voice and said suggestively, 'And handsome.'

Trina laughed. 'I used to see them in the mornings after work when I walked. Been here for a month but I've only really talked to him this weekend.' Funny how it felt as if she'd known Finn for ages. What was that? 'His little girl turned one yesterday. And I did mention Marni as a suggestion for childminding. He's thinking about it.'

'Oh, that's marvellous news. And a really good idea. Marni is the perfect mother to those tiny boys. I might get Reg to give him a nudge—not a big nudger is my Reg. But I would like to catch that sailing if possible.'

Trina laughed. 'You might have a surprise when you get home, then.' She picked up the tart and bit into the buttery pastry with slow enjoyment. The tang of Parmesan cheese, fresh spring onions and cream made her eyes roll. She took another bite and savoured. Before she knew, the tart was gone. 'Goodness, Myra. I should have a standing order for those.'

Myra laughed. 'My man is a bit pleased with my cooking.'

Trina picked up her coffee and then paused as a thought intruded. If Finn took over Dr Southwell's practice while he was away, he'd be working in the hospital. And he'd probably walk through Maternity. Might even seek her out as a friendly face. Not that everyone wasn't friendly at Lighthouse Bay. Maybe he'd even come over if they needed a third for a tricky birth. Their own personal paediatrician.

Her belly seemed to warm and it had nothing to do with food and hot coffee, though they had been good. She finished the last of the coffee not quite in the present moment. It was all positive because he was a paediatrician. Good for those babies that didn't breathe as well as you expected them to. *Oh, my.*

'You look much better for stopping and eating,' Myra said with some satisfaction. She stood up. 'I won't bother you any longer and let you get on before your afternoon midwives come on.'

'You're never a bother. More of a life-saver. Thank you.' She glanced down at the empty crumpled white bag. 'You've made my day.' In more ways than one.

* * *

Trina finished work at five-thirty that evening and decided to walk quickly down the breakwall and blow the stress of the day away. The administration side of the maternity unit would take a little time to get used to but she'd mastered most of the things that had slowed her up. The joy of finishing work and not having to worry about sleep until it was dark felt like a sweet novelty. Especially when, on her way back, she saw that Finn and Piper, wrapped in scarves, were walking too. Finn swung along effortlessly, the bundle on his back wriggling when she saw Catrina.

Finn raised his hand and changed direction and she sat on the breakwall and waited for him to reach her. As they approached she couldn't help watching his stride as his strong thighs closed the distance between them. His broad shoulders were silhouetted against the ocean and his eyes crinkled with delight as he came up to her.

The smile he gave her made the waiting even more worth it. She realised she'd been staring and spoke first. 'Hello. How did Piper go today?'

He patted Piper's leg. 'She didn't want to leave when I went to pick her up.'

Trina tried to hide her smile behind a sympathetic look but it didn't stick.

He pretended to scowl at her. 'You think that's amusing?'

She straightened her face. 'I'm pretty sure you were relieved too.'

He dropped his mock-injured façade. 'Absolutely. It felt good to see her so comfortable in another setting. And I owe that to you.' A genuine heartfelt smile which she might just snapshot and pull out later when she got home. 'Thank you, Catrina.'

She'd done nothing. He seemed so serious. And he seemed to expect some comment. 'For the little I did you're very welcome, Finn.'

'I'm serious.' Had he read her mind? 'In fact, Piper and I would like to invite you to our house to share dinner on Thursday night. In celebration of her finding childcare and me starting work next Monday. If you don't have a previous engagement?' There was a tiny hesitation at the last comment and she wondered why he thought she would.

'No previous engagement.'

Was that relief on his face? 'Just our usual slap-up meal. So you don't have to cook when you get home.' He hurried on. 'It will be early and if you needed to you could still be home by dark.'

She laughed. It would certainly be an early dinner as night fell about seven. 'I finish at five-thirty so can be there by six. Though sometimes the wheels fall off at work and that could slow me down or make me cancel.'

He shrugged. 'Been there. We'll take that as we have to.'

Trina smiled. Of course. A paed would know that. 'In that case, lovely. Thank you.' She tweaked the baby toes at Finn's chest. 'Thank you for the invitation, Piper.' The little girl gurgled and said, 'Mum, Mum, Mum.'

Trina pretended she didn't see Finn's wince. 'I bet she was saying that all the time at Marni's house. The boys will come ahead on their speaking with her there.'

He still looked subdued so she went on. 'Soon they'll be able to say *fiss.*'

Finn seemed to shake himself. She saw him cast his

mind back and his smile grew. Could see when he remembered the rock pool. Saw the relief for the change of focus.

His smile dipped to rueful. 'You're right.' Then he straightened and gave her his full attention again. 'How was your first day as the boss?'

'Administrative. Hats off to Ellie for never complaining about all the paperwork and ordering. But it's well worth it to have finished work at this time and still get a full night's sleep. It will be amazing when Daylight Saving comes back in and it doesn't get dark till after eight at night.'

CHAPTER ELEVEN

Finn

FINN SHIFTED ON the hard boardwalk, listened, but inside he thought, *Yes, she's coming on Thursday.* He felt like dancing a jig. Didn't want to think about why. The tension that had been building slowly released. She made him feel like a teenager which, though disconcerting, made a good change from feeling like an old man most of the time.

He'd considered the invitation from every angle because it had become increasingly important he didn't scare Catrina away and he still remembered her warnings when they'd first met. Enjoying her company had lifted his life from survival to anticipation. And he anticipated that Catrina could be great company for the foreseeable future if he stayed careful.

But she'd said she didn't want a relationship. It suited him fine, he kept telling himself that, and it had nothing to do with the fact that every time he saw her he noticed something new about her.

Like that especially golden strand of hair that fell across her forehead and made him want to move it out of her eyes. Or the way the soft skin on the curve of her long neck made him want to stroke that vulnerable spot with one finger. Just to assess if it felt like the velvet it resembled.

Of course it was all about Piper—she needed to have a female figure in her life who didn't demand anything—but Catrina gave so much warmth he could feel himself thawing more each day. Or maybe it was the fact he'd told himself he'd change now that Piper's first birthday had passed.

He tamped down the suspicion it could be selfish to blow so persistently on the flame of their friendship when he didn't have much to offer, was still married in fact, but he could feel the restoration of his soul and sensibilities. And the better he was in himself the better he was for Piper.

So he'd considered all the barriers she might have had to agreeing to a first dinner date and had methodically worked on arranging for them to disappear. To make it easy for both of them.

It would be a celebration—Piper's care with Marni and his new job.

She started work early the first four days of the week—so he'd invited her on Thursday—she had to eat, so no reason not to grab a free meal from him on the way home.

Plus he was hoping to set up some connections with her over the coming weekend and that would seem more impromptu if he mentioned those on Thursday.

And the big card—Catrina had to be curious to see his house. It had all paid off.

'Did you like the Southwells' surgery?' Her voice startled him back into the present moment. He thought

back to earlier in the day. To the white cottage that held
Dr Southwell's medical rooms.

'It's quaint. Not as strange as it could have been. A
small practice, one receptionist, and I'd have my own
room to settle into, which is always better than using
someone else's. I'll have all my equipment sent ASAP.'
Or he could drive back and get it, but the idea made
him shudder.

Catrina's voice grounded him. 'That's good. Did you
see any patients?'

'You mean behave like a real doctor?' He smiled
at her. 'Not yet. But I will start with those with urgent
needs and Reg seems to think I could concentrate on
children, which would suit me very well, and meet a
need for the community.'

Catrina nodded slowly as she thought about it. 'I
know at the base hospital it takes a few weeks for the
paediatrician to see new patients. Perhaps you would
even have some of those mums driving their children
over this way, like the Lighthouse Bay mums go to the
base for the service. Certainly easier for people like
Marni to take the boys for their premmie check-ups.'

'Plus I'd be available for general patients when it was
busy, but it seemed pretty sleepy today. Perfect hours of
work for a dad with a little girl to consider.'

'Did he talk about you covering the general patients
in the hospital when he goes away?'

'He did say that. Which is fine with me. It's not a
big hospital and I can read up on who's in there when
the time comes.'

Catrina stifled a laugh and he glanced at her. 'Dr
Southwell's wife is keen on a cruise that leaves soon.
Don't be surprised if it happens faster than you think.'

He raised his brows in question. 'Inside information?'

'I saw Myra today and she did mention she hoped Reg would find someone soon and that she had a boat she didn't want to miss.'

'Thanks for the heads-up. I'm sure I'd manage. That's what locums do, after all.' But everything seemed to be happening very fast. 'Do they get called out at night much?'

'Rarely. And it's shared call. So no more than three nights a week as a twenty-four-hour cover.' He watched her expression change as she realised that leaving Piper could be a problem on those nights.

'Hmm.' He could tell they were both thinking of Marni's flexibility as a day care mum.

'Something to think about,' Catrina said with massive understatement. 'And it won't be a problem unless Dr Southwell takes Myra away.'

'Which apparently might be sooner rather than later.' Had he started work too soon? Would his boss have an idea? Was it too much to ask the babysitter for Piper to sleep over those nights? As long as he didn't go over the forty hours, maybe it would be okay? His feeling that everything had fallen into place shifted again and he sighed. He wondered, not for the first time, how single parents managed to work at all.

Thursday arrived and Finn had been cooking, creating and carving in the kitchen. Something his mother had tried to instil in his sister but she'd found more fertile ground with Finn. He'd loved the times he and his mother had spent cooking, and in his short marriage the kitchen had been his domain at the weekend. It felt good to make something apart from nutritious finger food for Piper.

So, tonight a roast dinner. Something his wife had scoffed at but something he loved and missed—possibly because when they'd called at Marni's house the smell had reminded him how much he'd enjoyed a roast dinner as a child. And when Catrina had shared their lunch that first weekend they'd started talking—was it only a week ago?—she'd chosen a roast beef sandwich so she must like meat.

He'd slow roasted the beef and it lay, carved and foil-covered, in the oven with a veggie dish of potatoes, sweet potato, pumpkin and whole small onions. A side of fresh beans, carrots and broccoli would have Piper in seventh heaven. His jug of gravy was reheating and fresh bread rolls were on the table with real butter waiting.

He glanced around. The house remained a little spartan in his areas and cluttered in Piper's. She lay on her side in the playpen talking to her bunny. She'd had her bath and was dressed in her pyjamas, now looking a little sleepy, and he wondered if he should give her dinner early in case Catrina was late.

But it would be hard to dish up Piper's and not pick for himself. His belly rumbled. Just then a knock sounded on the door and he put the oven mitt back on the bench. He felt an unaccustomed eagerness as he crossed the room and tried to damp it down. They were just friends.

Then he opened the door and there she stood, the afternoon sunlight a glow around her and an almost shy smile on her beautiful lips. Her eyes were clear and bright and her lovely dark auburn hair swung loose in the sea breeze with glints of gold dancing like ribbons.

She'd changed out of her work clothes. Stood calmly clad in a pretty sundress and a cream cardigan, her bare legs brown and long with painted toes peeping out of coral-coloured sandals. Finn admonished himself not to feel too special because she'd taken the time to change for him.

He couldn't believe how good she looked. Needed to remind himself he barely knew this woman, but it was as if he'd been waiting a long time for this moment. Found himself saying softly, 'You truly are a picture.'

Catrina blushed but lifted her head. He liked the way she did that. No false modesty that she hadn't put in any effort. 'Thank you.' She lifted her chin higher and sniffed slowly. 'And you have a divine aroma floating out of your house.'

He laughed. 'I'll be glad when we can eat. It's been teasing me for hours now.' Not the only sensation that had been teasing him but he was trying not to think about Catrina's mouth.

She laughed then, her lips curving enticingly, but, unlike another woman, this one held no expectations to use her beauty and the tension stayed behind in the swirl of salt and sunshine outside as he invited her in and shut the door.

CHAPTER TWELVE

Trina

TRINA STEPPED INTO Finn's house, still feeling a little mentally fragile at the tiny handprints she'd seen on the step. There was something so heart-wrenchingly adorable about a dad doing cement prints with his baby daughter. If she wasn't careful she'd end up falling for this guy so hard she'd be vulnerable again to loss.

It was a sobering thought.

Then, to make matters more serious, when Finn had opened the door her heart had lifted at the sight of him. Two steps up, he'd towered over her, but his quick movement sideways as if he couldn't wait for her to come in had softened the impression of feeling small into a feeling of being very much appreciated.

She couldn't miss the approval and delight on his face as his gaze had run over her. So, yes, she was glad she'd spent the extra fifteen minutes changing and refreshing her make-up. Brushing her hair loose—not something she did often but it did feel freeing, and apparently it met with Finn's approval.

She felt the warmth of his body as she squeezed past him into the bright and airy room, and more warmth when she saw the way Piper pulled herself up and smiled at her. She bent down and blew a kiss at the little girl, who clutched her bunny and smiled back. Then to be enveloped in the warmth of expectation with a table set and meal prepared for her—well, it did seem a little too good to be true.

She turned back to look at Finn—Dr Finn—lounging against the closed door as if savouring the sight of her. His strong arms were crossed against his chest as if taking the time to watch her reaction. She was getting a little heady here. She licked unexpectedly dry lips. 'I'm feeling special.'

'Good. You are special. Piper and I can thank you for the help you've given us.'

She hadn't done much. But her grandmother had said, *Always answer a compliment with gratitude and don't correct the giver.* 'Thank you.' But she could change the subject. 'It looks great in here. So light and airy and fresh. I love the wood grain in the floor.'

He crossed said floorboards towards her and pulled out her chair. 'Silky oak. It was under the carpet. Feels nice underfoot and I can hear Piper coming up behind me when I'm not looking. Though I had a polisher come and help me rub it back and polish it by hand. Hardest day's work I'd done all year.' He grinned at her and she could see he'd enjoyed the challenge.

'And what did Miss Piper do while you were playing around on the floor?'

'Luckily it was a typical Lighthouse Bay day—sunny—and we put up a little pergola. She stayed just outside the door in her playpen and kept us hard at it.'

Lucky her. To watch two men rubbing polish into wood for a few hours. Something very nice about that thought, Trina mused as she took the seat he held out for her.

Finn crossed to pick up Piper and poked her toes into her high chair and she snaked her way in like a little otter. Then he clipped a pink rubber bib around her neck. Piper did look excited at the thought of food.

'Can I help?' Trina asked, feeling a tad useless.

'It's a tiny kitchen nook, so you girls sit here while I produce my masterpiece and wait on you.' Then he glanced at his fidgety daughter. 'But you could hand Piper that crust on the plastic plate. She can chew on that while she waits for her veggies to cool.' He cast a sideways glance at Trina. 'I learnt it's better to give her something to chew on when she's in the chair or she starts to climb around when I'm not looking.'

'Ah—' Trina hurriedly passed the crust to Piper '—there you go, madam. Diversion tactics.'

Piper held out her hand and gleefully accepted the morsel and Finn strode the few steps to the kitchen bench and back across with the first plate and a jug of gravy.

'Roast veggies. Gravy.' He deposited his load and spun away, then was back in moments with a heaped plate of carved roast beef, the barest hint of pink at the centre of each slice. 'If you don't like it rare the more well-done pieces are at the edge.'

Trina's mouth had begun watering as the food began to arrive. 'I think I'm in heaven. It was busy today and I missed lunch. Plus I haven't had a roast for two years.' Not since before Ed's illness. Guilt and regret swamped her and she tried to keep it from her face.

Finn took a swift glance at her and said smoothly, 'It's all Marni's fault. That first day we visited. The

way her house smelled of roast dinner did me in.' She
decided he was very determined that they would enjoy
the meal. Good thing too.

Trina pulled herself together and asked, 'So is this
Piper's first roast dinner?'

'Indeed. More cause for celebration.' He leaned and
poured them both a glass of cold water from the carafe
on the table. The water glasses looked like crystal to
Trina. 'Let's drink to that.' Then he raised his hand to
hers and they touched glasses with a tell-tale perfect
ching and her melancholy fell away as they sipped. Life
was pretty darn good.

He indicated the food. 'You serve yours and I'll fix
Piper.' Finn dished some veggies and meat onto Piper's
cartoon-illustrated plastic plate and swiftly cut them
into bite-sized pieces.

This was all done so efficiently that Trina found herself smiling. Such a maternal thing to do but this dad
had it covered.

She arranged her own plate, finishing with a generous serve of gravy, and sat back to wait for Finn.

He wasn't far behind. He topped his meal off with
his gravy and then looked up to meet her eyes. '*Bon
appétit.*'

They didn't talk much as they ate, neither did they
rush, and Trina glanced around as she savoured the
subtle and not so subtle flavours of a well-cooked roast
dinner. Marvelled at the decorating touches that showed
this man's love for his daughter. A mobile of seashells
over the cot, a run of circus animals in a wallpaper
panel behind her bed. An alphabet mat on the floor
with a Piper-sized chair on it. A row of small dolls in
bright dresses.

She indicated the dolls with her fork. 'So these are the ladies you talk to?'

'All the time. Especially the brunette on the end. Remarkable conversationalist, really.'

'I can imagine.' She smiled at the dark-haired doll which, at a stretch, could look a little like Trina herself.

'Do you like our home?' Needy? Keen for her approval? But there was something endearing about that.

She nodded sagely. 'I think Piper will be a famous decorator one day.'

She was teasing him but it must have been the right thing to say because his pleasure was almost palpable. 'Remind me to show you the shower. We have very nice tiles.'

'I'll make sure I do that.' And she allowed herself to consider the possibility of a future here. With this man and his daughter. At the very least as friends and with a potential for more…but she wouldn't rush. Couldn't rush. And neither could he.

The thought crashed in. Who knew where his wife was? The thought brought a deluge of dampness to her sunny spirits and she looked down at her food, which suddenly didn't taste as good as it had.

'So tell me about the rest of your week. Did Piper still want to stay at Marni's when you went to pick her up after a full day or did she miss you?'

'Both. Marni is wonderful with her. And your Myra has booked her drop-and-go cruise. A five-nighter to Tasmania. They leave Sunday. So call and three-day rosters at the hospital. Piper will have to stay over when I'm on call. Though they've managed to give me only the one night call, which I appreciate.'

'Wow. You've dived into work with a vengeance.'

'I should have done it earlier. I'm feeling more connected to humanity every day.' He glanced up at her with definite warmth. 'Though that could have been you.'

Glad he thought she was human. But that wasn't what he meant and she knew it. Her face heated and she looked down at her almost empty plate. 'Thank you, kind sir.' She lifted her head and shook the hair away from her face. It was getting hot in here. 'One night seems like the perfect answer. That's not too bad as a start. When did you say that night was?'

'Next Thursday. We'll see how she goes. Marni's not worried.'

She could have offered for a Thursday night but she was glad he hadn't asked. She wasn't ready for that much commitment. 'Well, good luck.' She lifted her glass of water. 'And here's to your first week at the hospital. I'll look forward to your smiling face.'

'I'll try to remember to smile.'

CHAPTER THIRTEEN

Finn

By MONDAY MORNING, his first day in the hospital, Catrina continued to seep into Finn's thoughts with alarming regularity and he was feeling just as strange about that as he was about the new work model he'd slipped into. A general GP, admittedly with extra specialist paediatric consults on the side, and a rural hospital generalist as well. With maternity cover? Never thought he'd see the day.

Over the weekend he and Catrina had met a lot, each meeting better than the last, plus they'd talked about the hospital and the patients he'd probably find come Monday. About how the medical input had changed since the new midwifery model had started, even some of the times that Dr Southwell had been called away from the main hospital to provide back-up in Maternity.

He could see Catrina enjoyed their discussions and, to be truthful, he was a little curious to see how it all worked. They'd bumped into each other often. Intentionally on his part and, he suspected glumly, unintentionally on hers.

He'd managed the Friday morning beach bump into

when, after his own walk, he'd offered to share the breakwall with Catrina, Piper on his back, and they'd spent more than an hour together talking non-stop.

Saturday morning, after Catrina's scuba lesson, he and Piper had been back in their rock pool at just the right time for her to walk past them again and fortuitously share an early lunch as Catrina offered to return last week's lunch shout at the beach café.

Saturday night he and Piper had been invited to a barbecue dinner at Ellie and Sam's and, of course, Catrina had been there as she lived next door.

Naturally he'd spoken to other people but they'd spent most of the time standing together. He'd had an excellent conversation with Sam on the strangeness of working in a cottage hospital after coming from a tertiary health facility and Myra had shaken his hand and thanked him for making it possible to drag her husband away on a cruise. But the stand-out moments were those watching Catrina's quiet rapport with the other dinner guests.

His eyes had drifted in her direction way too often.

The best had been on Sunday when Catrina had asked if Piper—and Finn—could come and help her choose colours for her new carpet and cushions and they'd had a hilarious day at the nearest large town choosing colours via a one-year-old in a stroller.

A huge weekend, in fact, but one that had passed without kissing her once. And that also was something he couldn't get out of his mind.

Her mouth. So mobile, always smiling and doing that soft chortling thing when he said something to amuse her—a new skill he seemed to have acquired that did more to heal his soul than anything else.

Or that unconscious, but luscious, lip-pursing she did when she seriously considered something he said. Or just her mouth looking downright kissable when he didn't expect it, and he was having a hard time not drifting off and staring at the lift of a corner or the flash of white teeth.

He didn't remember being this fixated on Piper's mother when he'd met her. There had certainly been attraction, almost a forest fire of heat and lust culminating in a headlong rush into marriage when their contraception had failed. More his idea than hers and he had certainly paid the price for that.

But he was coming to the conclusion that he must have been meant to be Piper's daddy because he couldn't imagine life without his baby girl so he thanked Clancy for that. There was a bit of healing in there somewhere and he wasn't sure he didn't owe Catrina for that thought too.

But Catrina? Well? He needed to slow down and not lose the plot, but Catrina made him want to be better at being himself, a better person, even a better partner since he'd obviously fallen short on that last time.

His attraction to Catrina had been exquisitely stoked by want and need, and he feared—or was that dared to hope?—she might be coming to care for him too.

This morning, as he climbed the hill to the little white hospital sitting on a cliff, he hoped that very much. He glanced at the cottage garden as he approached for his first day as visiting medical officer and could feel his spirits soar as he strode towards a new perspective of Catrina at work.

The ocean glittered a sapphire blue today, brighter and more jewel-like than he could remember seeing.

Piper had been as lively as a grig being handed over to Marni and the boys. And he, well, he was back at work, feeling almost comfortable already in Reg's practice, like a normal human being. It had taken a year of shadow. And a week. And Catrina.

Except for the colour of the ocean, Catrina had a lot to do with most of his forward progress. Though maybe all the colours were appearing brighter this week because of her as well.

Reg had suggested he call into Maternity first—'Around eight, my boy!'—to see if any women were in labour—'Just so you can be aware.' And then attend to his hospital round on the other side of the small white building.

He suspected that the midwives didn't need the visit but Reg clearly felt paternal in his concern for them. Finn thought it prudent not to share that insight with Catrina.

But what a gift of an excuse, he thought as he stepped through the automatic front door to Maternity and glanced around for her.

Instead, a nurse he'd met on his orientation round with Reg on Friday came in through the side door from the main hospital at a run and her relief at seeing him alerted his instincts faster than her voice. 'Dr Foley—please follow me through to the birthing suite. Urgently!'

The smile slipped from Finn's face and he nodded and followed.

When he entered, he saw Catrina standing over a neonatal resuscitation trolley, her fingers encircling the little chest with her thumb pressing cardiac massage over the baby's sternum in a rhythmic count.

Another nurse held the tiny face mask over the baby's face, inflating the chest with intermittent positive pressure ventilations after every third compression.

Finn stopped beside them, glanced at the seconds ticking past on the trolley clock that indicated time since birth. It showed ninety seconds.

Catrina looked up and the concentrated expression on her face faltered for the briefest moment and he saw the concern and the relief on her face. Then she looked at the clock as well. Her voice remained calm but crisp.

'Rhiannon's baby was born two minutes ago, short cord snapped during delivery so probable neonatal blood loss. Baby is just not getting the hang of this breathing business.' Her voice came out remarkably steady and he filed that away to tell her later.

'Heart rate less than sixty for the last thirty seconds so we added cardiac compression to the IPPV and it's just come back to eighty.' She loosened her fingers around the baby's chest and turned down the oxygen to keep the levels similar to where a two-minute-old baby would normally be. Too much oxygen held as many risks as not enough oxygen for babies.

'This is the paediatrician, Dr Foley, Rhiannon,' she called across to the mum, who was holding the hand of an older woman, concern etched on their faces.

Finn lifted his hand and smiled reassuringly. Because the fact the baby had picked up his heartbeat was an excellent sign. 'Give us a few minutes and I'll come across and explain.'

He glanced at the pulse oximeter someone had strapped to the flaccid pale wrist. 'You're keeping the oxygen levels perfect. Umbilical catheter then,' Finn said calmly. 'I'll top up the fluids and the rest should stabilise.'

'The set-up is in the second drawer. There's a diagram on the lid because we don't use it often.'

He retrieved the transparent plastic box and put it on the nearby bench, squirted antiseptic on his hands and began to assemble the intravenous line that would be inserted a little way into the baby's umbilical cord stump and give a ready-made large bore venous entry point to replace the fluids lost.

He glanced at Catrina. 'Warmed fluids?'

'Cupboard outside the door.' The nurse he'd arrived with handed Catrina the clipboard she'd taken to jot observations on and slipped out to get the fluids. By the time he had all the syringes and tubing set she was back and they primed the line with the warmed fluids and set it aside.

Finn squirted the antiseptic on his hands again and donned the sterile gloves to wipe the baby's belly around the cord with an antiseptic swab, and wiped the cord stump liberally with the solution.

After placing a towel on the baby's belly to give himself a sterile field he could work from, he tied the soft sterile tape around the base of the finger-thick umbilical cord. The tape was a safety measure, so that when they removed the cord clamp Catrina had fastened at birth, he could pull the tape tight around the umbilical cord to control any further blood loss.

Once the tape was in place and fastened firmly, Catrina looked at Finn, who smiled reassuringly because he doubted it was something she did on a newly cut cord very often, and watched her remove the cord clamp with only a trace of anxiety.

Finn nodded to himself, satisfied—no bleeding—
then sliced off the nerveless ragged edge of the snapped
cord closer to the baby's belly with a scalpel blade, the
white tape preventing any further blood loss. Now he
could easily see the vessels inside where he wanted to
put the tubing.

Using fine artery forceps, he captured one edge of
the cord and then offered the forceps to Catrina to hold
to free up his other hand.

With the cord now pulled upright, Finn lifted the
catheter and another pair of forceps to insert the end
into the gaping vessel of the vein in the umbilical cord.
He glimpsed the nurse from the main hospital looking
wide-eyed and said quietly, 'It's easy to tell which is the
vein, being the largest and softest vessel of the three in
the cord. That's the one that leads to the heart.'

Catrina asked, 'Do you have to turn the catheter to
insert it? Aren't the vessels spiral?'

'Yes, spiral so when the cord is pulled in utero there's
give and spring, the longer the cut cord the more spiral
you have to traverse until you get to the bloodstream.
That's why I cut this fairly short. Not too short that you
don't leave yourself a back-up plan, though.'

The fine clear intravenous tubing disappeared just
below the baby's abdominal skin. A sudden swirl of
blood mixed with the warmed fluid Finn had primed
the tubing with.

'And we're in,' Finn said with satisfaction. He adjusted the three-way tap on the line with one hand and
slowly injected the warmed saline fluid with a fat syringe into the baby's bloodstream. 'Ten mils per kilo
will do it, and I'd say this little tyke is about three kilos.'

He glanced at Catrina, who watched the monitor to

see the baby's heart rate slowly increasing. She nodded. He then glanced at her colleague, still calmly applying intermittent puffs of air into the baby's lungs, and then watched as the tiny flaccid hand slowly clenched as tone returned to the baby's body and he began to flex and twitch.

Finn looked over at the mum. 'Not long now.'

'Get ready to tighten the cord again, Catrina,' he said softly and, once the full amount of fluid had been injected and Catrina was ready, he turned the tap on the infusion and removed the syringe.

'We'll just wait a few minutes before we remove it in case we need to give any drugs, but I think that will do the trick.'

CHAPTER FOURTEEN

Trina

TRINA'S GALLOPING PULSE slowed as the baby's heart rate began to rise above eighty. Her hand loosened on the resuscitation trolley she seemed to have gripped as Finn did his thing. After what had seemed like forever the baby's heart rate hit a hundred and ten and finally the baby blinked and struggled, grimaced against the mask and, in the most beautiful screech in the world, he began to cry. The tension in the room fluttered and fell like a diving bird and she watched Finn slowly withdraw the tubing from the vein. She tightened the cord as it came clear and then snapped on a new umbilical clamp close to the end of the stump. Done.

Baby threw his hands and kicked his feet and they pushed the resuscitation trolley closer to the mum's bed so he could be handed across with the pulse oximeter still strapped to his wrist.

Trina considered removing it as he'd become so vigorous with the replacement of fluid but it would be easier to monitor instead of listening with a stethoscope so, despite the tangle of wires, she left him connected and pressed his bare skin to his mother's naked breasts.

Once baby was settled on his mother, his breathing clear and unobstructed, she could relax a little more. A blanket covered them both, and she glanced at Finn, standing at the side of the trolley, his beautiful mouth soft as he watched the baby and mother finally together. His eyes shone with pleasure and he gave a little nod just before he saw Trina looking at him.

The smile he gave her, one of warmth and pride and appreciation, made her clutch her throat and heat surged into her cheeks. She'd done nothing.

When she looked back at him he was watching the mum again, his eyes still soft as he spoke to her.

'Hello there. Congratulations. As Trina said, I'm Dr Foley, the paediatrician, and your little boy looks great now. Snapped cords are fairly rare, but if a baby grows in utero with a short umbilical cord...' he smiled that warm and reassuring smile that seemed to seep right down to the soles of Trina's feet and he wasn't even looking at her '...which he is perfectly entitled to do.' He shrugged. 'Not surprisingly, though it *is* always a surprise, they can run out of stretch at birth and the cord can pull too tight.'

Rhiannon nodded and her own mother sat back with relief to see her grandchild safely snuggled into Rhiannon's arms.

Finn went on. 'Babies don't have a lot of blood to spare so some extra fluid through that intravenous line allowed his heart to get back into the faster rhythm it needs. As you saw, it's usually a fairly dramatic improvement. We'll do some blood tests and if we need to we'll talk about a blood transfusion. But he looks good.'

'Too much drama for me,' Rhiannon said, as she cuddled her baby close to her chest. Trina could agree with that. Now that she had time to think about it, she had to admit that Finn's appearance had been a miracle she'd very much needed. But there wasn't time for that yet as she began to attend to all the things that needed doing in the immediate time after a baby had been born.

Two and a half hours later Trina had settled Rhiannon and baby Jackson into their room, and the myriad of paperwork, forms and data entry had been sorted. The nurse from the hospital had stayed to help Trina tidy the ward because Faith, the midwife from night duty, had already stayed later than normal. Trina glanced at the clock, just ten-thirty, so, on top of the tasks still waiting to be done, she did need a moment to sit back in the chair and consider the excitement of the morning.

It had been a little too exciting but thankfully Finn had appeared at exactly the right moment without needing to be called. An opportune thing.

Like he did at that moment. Striding through the doors from the main hospital as if he owned the place.

She felt a smile stretch her face. 'I was just thinking about you.'

His laughing eyes made her belly flip-flop and caution flooded her. He had a wife. Somewhere.

'Good things, I hope?' he said.

She shook her head. Pretended to think about it. 'How I didn't need you this morning and you just pushed in.' Teasing him.

His face froze for a second and she slid her hand over her mouth in horror, saying quickly, 'Joke. A very mean joke. Especially when you were so good. I'm sorry.' But she could feel the creases in her cheeks as she smiled because his shock had been palpable when the statement had been totally ridiculous. He must have known she'd needed him desperately. She had no idea why she'd said such a crazy thing except to startle him. Or maybe because she'd been trying to hide how absolutely thrilled she was that he'd come back to see her when she'd thought he would have been long gone from the hospital.

This man brought out very strange urges in her. At least she wasn't giggling like a twit. She was saying bizarre things instead.

He laughed a little sheepishly. 'I was worried for a minute there.'

She looked up at him. Seriously? 'Don't be. Sorry. I was never so glad to see anybody in my life. My pulse was about a hundred and sixty.' And it wasn't far from that now with him standing so close, which would not do.

He studied her. That didn't help the galloping heart rate. 'Well, you looked as cool as a cucumber.'

'On the outside. Good to know.' Hopefully she looked that way now as well—especially with her brain telling her to do stupid things in fight and flight mode. 'But, seriously, you were very slick with inserting that umbi line. Most impressive.'

And she had no doubt her eyes were telling him a tad more than she was saying because he smiled back at her with a lot more warmth than she deserved after what she'd just done to him. He sat down beside her at the desk.

To hide the heat in her cheeks she looked past his shoulder towards Rhiannon's room and murmured, 'It would have been very tense to keep resuscitating a baby who didn't improve as we expected. He really needed that fluid in his system to get him circulating properly.'

He didn't say anything so she looked at him. He was studying her intently again and her face grew hotter. 'What?'

'We were lucky. That was all it was. I'm wondering if you could call me for the next couple of births through the day while Piper is in care, just so I can sneak in a refresher course on normal birth. It's a long time since my term in Obstetrics working towards my OB Diploma and I want to be up to speed if an emergency occurs.'

His diffidence surprised her. 'Of course, you're welcome. I call in a nurse from the hospital as my second but I can easily call you instead if we have time. Or as well. I don't mind. And I can run a simulation through the latest changes in post-partum haemorrhage and prem labour if you like.'

'Excellent. I've been doing some reading but things aren't always the same when you get to the different hospital sites.'

'We're a birth centre not a hospital, even though we're joined by an external corridor. So all of our women are low risk.' But things still happened. Not with the regularity you saw in a major hospital but they did deal with first line emergencies until a woman or her baby could be transferred to higher care.

He nodded. 'Is that your first snapped cord?'

'My first here.' She shook her head, still a little shocked. 'We've had them tear and bleed but to actually just break like that was a shock.'

'It's rare. Had probably torn already and when the last stretch happened at birth it broke—but you handled it well, getting the clamp on so quickly. I've seen some much worse situations.'

'I kept expecting him to get better, like nearly all babies do when you give them a puff or two, but by the time you arrived I was getting worried.'

He nodded. 'Hypovolemia will do that. How's Mum?'

'Taken it in her stride. Said her angels were looking after her and baby Jackson.' She thought he'd laugh.

'Useful things, angels.' Then, in an aside, 'My mother was a medium. I should have listened to her.'

He shrugged and Trina tried not to gape. His turn to say something off the wall, maybe, or he could be pulling her leg because he grinned at her surprise.

He changed the subject before she could ask. 'Today Jackson also had the midwives and doctor.' He grinned. 'Shall I go down and see if she has any more questions now she's had a chance to think about it?'

Trina stood up as well. Off balance by his throwaway comment about his mother…and his proximity. Moving to a new location sounded like a great idea, she thought, still mentally shaking her head to clear it. That had been the last thing she'd expected him to say. But she'd ask more later. This moment, here at work, wasn't the time. Angel medium? Seriously, she was dying to find out.

'Great idea. Thank you.' She stood up and followed him. Finn was thoughtful, kind and darn slick as a paediatrician. Lighthouse Bay might just have to count its blessings to have another fabulous doctor in the wings when they needed him. Speaking of wings… Angels? Her head spun as she followed him down the hallway.

Over the next four days while Finn covered the hospital, he shared three births with Trina between breakfast and morning tea. It was almost as if the mothers were on a timetable of morning births to make it easy for him to be able to watch and even catch one.

She could tell he was enjoying himself. Basking in the magic that was birth. But the busyness meant she didn't get a chance to ask about him. About his mother's angels. About his childhood. About his marriage— not that she would! The woman who had given birth to Piper and what had happened to her.

Trina hoped they were at the stage of friendship where she could ask about at least some of those things soon. But then again, she hadn't shared anything of her past either. Maybe they should just leave it all in the past and keep talking about Lighthouse Bay nineteen to the dozen like they had been. Share the past slowly because she was probably reading too much into his interest.

Lighthouse Bay Maternity must have decided to draw in the babies for Dr Finn, because they just kept coming. The overdue ones arrived, the early ones came early, and the more time they spent together with new babies and new families the more her curiosity about Finn's world before he came here grew.

He left soon after each birth to continue his appointments at the surgery but returned at late lunchtime with his sandwiches to talk about the morning's events.

On Thursday, his last hospital shift before Dr Southwell returned, Finn entered the birthing room quietly after the soft knock Trina had trained him in. She'd left a message with his secretary to say they were having a water birth, and even though he'd not long gone he'd been very keen to see the way water and birth 'mixed'.

Trina had given him a scolding glance at his wording, but she had immense faith that once he'd seen the beauty of the way the bath environment welcomed babies into the world he'd be converted. She was glad he could make it.

Sara, the birthing mum, was having her second baby and had come in late in the labour. She'd phoned ahead to ensure the bath had been filled, mentioned she wanted lots of photos of her daughter's birth because she had lots from her son's birth.

They arrived almost ready for second stage and Trina had the bath prepared. At Finn's knock her head lifted and Sara frowned at the sound.

Trina worried. Maybe things had changed. 'Are you still okay if the doctor sits in on your birth, Sara?'

'As long as he stays out of the bath, I'm fine,' Sara said with unexpected humour considering the glare at the door and the contraction that had begun to swell and widen her eyes.

Trina turned to hide her grin and motioned for Finn to enter the room. She liked the way he always waited for permission. Though she might have mentioned it a few times and she had no doubt her eyes betrayed her amusement at his docility. No, not docility—respect. Her amusement faded. As he should.

Finn said a brief thanks to Sara and her husband and settled back into the corner on the porcelain throne, making himself as inconspicuous as a six foot tank could be. Once he was seated Trina tried to forget about him.

She suspected by the way Sara was breathing out deeply and slowly that she'd felt the urge to bear down. Second stage. Time to up the monitoring. When the final louder breath had been released Sara lay back with her eyes closed.

Trina murmured, 'Is baby moving down and through, Sara?'

'Yes.'

'Can I listen to the heartbeat between those outward breaths?'

'Yes.' Bare minimum. She had more important things to concentrate on than answering questions and Trina understood that.

Sara arched her belly up until it broke the surface of the bath water and Trina leaned forward and slid the Doppler low on Sara's belly. The sound of a happy clopping heartbeat filled the room. With her eyes closed, Sara smiled.

After a minute Trina moved the Doppler away and Sara sank back below the water, causing ripples to splash the edge of the bath. She didn't open her eyes when another minute passed and her heavy outward sighs started again.

It took fifteen minutes, and five cycles of breathing, listening, smiling and sinking below the surface of the water and then they could see the baby's head below the surface.

Sara's breathing didn't change, nobody spoke. Below, in the water, the small shoulders appeared. Trina hovered, but Sara reached down, waiting, as an expelled breath larger than the rest released a flurry of movement. The movement heralded the rest of the baby's body had been born. Sara clasped her baby firmly between her hands below the water level and lifted her smoothly to the surface to rest on her belly. The little face rose above the water, blue and gaping, and then the baby's eyes opened and she began to breathe in as the air hit her face.

Everyone else breathed out. The father photograph-
ing constantly and the glance the couple shared between
clicks made tears sting Trina's eyes. So beautiful.

The birth left Finn sitting thoughtfully at her desk as
he replayed the scene.

Finally, he said, 'That was amazing. The mum was
so in control, lifting the baby after birth out of the water
like that.' He quirked one brow at her. 'How could you
stop yourself reaching in to do it for her?'

Trina smiled. 'If she'd hesitated or if she'd needed
me to, I would have. But Sara had it covered. That's her
second water birth so she knew what she wanted and
what would happen.'

He rolled a pen between his fingers thoughtfully. 'I
have to admit to scepticism. Why add water to the list
of things that could go wrong for a baby at birth?' He
tapped the pen on the desk. 'I could see Mum looked
super-relaxed—baby just appeared with the breathing,
not even pushing, and slowly birthed. Hands off. A
very relaxed baby though a little bluer than normal in
the first few minutes.'

That was true, Trina thought. 'We find the colour
can take a minute or two longer to pink up, mainly because the babies may not cry.'

She shrugged. 'People need to remember no analge-
sia was needed for Mum because of the thirty-seven-
degree heat and relaxation of the bath, so babies aren't
affected by drugs for the next twenty-four hours like
some are. That helps breastfeeding and bonding. She
didn't have an epidural so no drip or urinary catheter
either.' And no stitches. Trina always felt relieved when
that happened—and it was usually when a mother ad-

vanced second stage at her own pace. Something they prided themselves on at Lighthouse Bay—but then they had all the well mums and babies to start with.

It had been a beautiful birth and Trina still glowed from the experience, even after all the tidying up and paperwork had been done.

She glanced at the clock. Finn would go soon. Lunch-time seemed to fly when he came to talk about the births and she could feel their rapport and their friend-ship, the ease she fell into with their conversations, had all grown this week with his shifts.

Finn stroked the cover of the book Trina had lent him to read on water birth. 'I'm intrigued how you managed to sell the idea here to the board of directors. I know water birth was vetoed at my last hospital.'

It had been easier than expected. One of the board member's daughter had had a water birth at another hos-pital. But they'd covered their bases. 'Our statistics are meticulous. Ellie has always been firm on keeping good records and it shows we have excellent outcomes on land and water birth. I'm doing the same.' She thought about how smoothly their transition to a midwife-led unit had been in the end. 'Of course it helped with Sam as back-up. Ellie's husband has such high standing in the area now. The local authorities consider us backed by experts even though Sam's not technically here. So water birth with the midwives at Mum's request is the norm here and proved to be very safe. Just remember we start with well mums and well babies.'

'Good job. Everyone.' He stood up. Looking down at her with that crooked smile that seemed to make ev-erything shine so bright it fuddled her brain. 'Well, you've converted me. Which is lucky as tonight is my all-night on-call.'

He gathered up his lunch wrap from the kiosk meal he'd bought. 'I'd better get back to the surgery; my afternoon patients will start to arrive at two. Then my first night without Piper for a year.'

She knew plenty of mums who would love to have a night where their babies slept overnight with someone else. 'How does that make you feel?'

He shrugged. Apparently not overjoyed. 'Very strange, I have to admit. I think I'm going to be lonely. Don't suppose you'd like to join me?'

'If you get forlorn give me a call.' As soon as she said it Trina began to blush. What on earth had got into her? Practically throwing herself at the man at the first opportunity. But she'd been thinking he'd looked sad when he'd said it.

She soldiered on. 'What I meant was, unlike Piper, I can go home if you get called out.' That sounded even worse.

His blue eyes sparkled. Mischievously. Suddenly he looked less like an assured paediatrician and more like a little boy offered a treat. 'Now that's an offer I'd like to take you up on. We could get takeaway.'

'Now I feel like I've invited myself.'

He laughed. 'Thank goodness. We could both die of old age before I had the nerve to ask you properly and I've been wanting to since Marni agreed to have Piper overnight.'

He flashed her a smile. 'It's a date. You can't back out now. I'll see you at mine at six p.m.'

She couldn't have him cooking for her after work. 'I finish at five. So why don't you come to my house?

I can make us dinner or order in and your mobile will go off anywhere. Do on-call from there.'

'If that's okay, then great. I'll appear at six.' He waved and smiled and…left.

Good grief. He'd been wanting to ask her. Then reason marched in. Wanted what? What could happen if she wasn't careful? It was a small town and she needed her reputation and her just healing, skin-grafted heart needed protection. Was she getting too close to this guy—a guy with a cloud of unresolved questions that even he didn't know the answers to?

Well, yes. She was getting too close.

Did it feel right?

Um, yes. So why couldn't she spend the evening, or the night if that came up, with a man she was very, very attracted to?

Because he was married. His wife was missing, alive or dead, he was still married—and she didn't sleep with married men.

CHAPTER FIFTEEN

Finn

FINN KNOCKED ON Catrina's solid timber door and his heart thumped almost as loudly as his knuckles on the wood. He couldn't believe he was back in the game. Taking risks. Making a play. With his twelve-month-old daughter asleep at a babysitter's and his wife still missing.

He wasn't a villain to do this. He was on-call. Calling on Catrina beat the heck out of sitting at home alone, waiting for his mobile phone to ring for work. And Catrina made his world a more rounded place. A warm and wonderful place.

Different to the walls he normally pulled around himself and Piper. Guilt from the past had become less cloying over the last few weeks, the cloud still there but it had gone from dense and choking to thin and drifting away like ocean mist. Like a new day awakening. Thanks to Catrina.

The door opened and she stood there, with that gorgeous smile of hers that lifted his heart and made him want to reach forward and, quite naturally, kiss her. Which, to the surprise of both of them, he did. As if he'd done it every time she opened the door to him—when in fact it hadn't happened before—and, despite the widening of her eyes in surprise, she kissed him back. *Ah, so good.*

So he moved closer and savoured that her mouth melded soft and tentative against his. Luscious and sweet and…

He stepped right in, pulled the door shut behind him, locking the world away from them, because he needed her in his arms, hidden from prying eyes.

She didn't push him away—far from it, her hands crept up to his neck and encircled him as she leaned into his chest. The kiss deepening into a question from him, an answering need from her that made his heart pound again and he tightened his arms even more around her. Their lips pressed, tongues tangled, hands gripping each other until his head swam with the scent and the taste of her. Time passed but, as in all things, slowly reality returned.

He lifted her briefly off her feet and spun her, suddenly exuberant from all the promise in that kiss, then put her down as their mouths broke apart. Both of them were flushed and laughing. He raised his fingers to draw her hold from his neck and kissed the backs of them. 'Such beautiful hands.' He kissed them again.

In turn, she created some sensible space in the heat between them and turned away.

But not before he saw the glow in her eyes that he had no doubt was reflected in his. They could take their time. The first barrier had passed—they'd kissed, and what a kiss. The first since heartache and they'd both survived. Not just survived—they'd thrived! Finn felt like a drooping plant, desperate for water, and he'd just had the first sip. You could tell a lot from a first kiss, and Catrina had blown his socks off.

Finn slowed to watch her cross the room, mostly because she fascinated him—she walked, brisk and swinging, out through the open door of the veranda overlooking the sea, the backdrop of sapphire blue a perfect foil for her dark hair as distance widened between them.

He tried hard not to look at the bed in the corner of the big room as he passed but his quick glance imprinted cushions and the floral quilt they'd bought on Sunday which she said she'd needed to brighten the place. He pulled his eyes away but he could feel the tightening in his groin he couldn't help and imagined carrying Catrina to that corner.

'Come on,' she called from the little covered porch and he quickened his step. Almost guilty now his body had leapt ahead after one kiss but the cheeky smile she'd flung over her shoulder at him eased that dilemma. She was thinking about the bed too. But not today. He needed to make sure she knew it all. Before he tarnished something beautiful and new with ghosts from the past.

He'd never seen her so bubbly—as if she were glowing from the inside—and he watched her, a little dazed, that he'd done this to her. Lit her up. With a kiss as if she were a sleeping princess. But he was no prince. And it was a long time since he'd lit anyone up like this—just Clancy in the beginning—and look how that ended. He pushed that thought away.

She'd set the table with bright place mats and put out salad and pasta and cheese. Orange juice in a pitcher stood beside glasses and the sunlight bathed it all in golden lights and reflections as the day drew to a jewelled close above the sea.

Like a moth to the light, he closed in on her where she'd paused against the rail overlooking the sea. Her silhouette was willowy yet curved in all the right places, her dark hair, sun-kissed in streaks, blowing in the ocean breeze. He came up behind her and put his hands on the rail each side, capturing her. Leant ever so lightly against her curved back, the length of his body warming against her softness, feeling the give against his thighs.

Then he leant down and kissed the soft pearly skin under her ear and she shivered beneath him; her breath caught as she pushed back, into him. His hands left the rail and encircled her hips from behind, spreading low across her stomach and pelvis. 'You're like a sea sprite up here.' His voice came out low and deeper than normal. 'A siren high on her vantage point overlooking the sea.'

She turned her head and, with a slow wicked smile, tilted her face to look at him. 'Does that make you a pirate?'

He lifted his brows. 'I could be?'

'Not today, me hearty,' she said and pushed him back more firmly with her bottom to suggest he give her space and he let his hands slide down the outer curve of her thighs, savouring the feminine shape of her, and then away.

'Right then,' he said and stepped back. 'Do your hostess thing, sea sprite.'

She spun and pulled out a chair at the table. 'Yes, you should eat in case you get called away. It's Thursday and I know there's a buck's party on tonight before the wedding on Saturday. You might be needed if things get silly.'

She indicated the food in bowls. 'Start now, please. Don't wait for me.' She avoided his eyes and he saw the exuberance had passed. There was no rush and this wasn't just about him—it was about this brave, beautiful widow finding her way to exposing her heart again. He reminded himself he knew how that felt though his circumstances were far different. He wanted to do this right. Right for Catrina. Right for him. And right for Piper. He needed to remember Piper. And try not to forget he had Clancy in the wings.

Though how could he do this right with a missing wife God knew where and this woman bruised from her own past? He forced a smile to his mouth. 'The pasta looks amazing.'

He saw the relief as he changed the subject and knew he'd been right to give her space.

She gestured vaguely to the hedge that separated her house from the one next door. 'Herbs make the difference. We share a herb garden. Myra does the tending and Ellie and I share the eating.'

She smiled with her mouth but not her eyes and he wondered what she was thinking while she was talking trivia about herb gardens. Had he been too full-on? Yes, he had—they both had—but that had been some kiss. Like a steam train carrying them both along at great speed and only just finding the brakes.

'But it works for us.'

What works for us? Then he realised she was still talking about the herb garden. He had it bad. Just wasn't so sure about her. He stuffed some pasta in his mouth.

A taste explosion rioted there and he groaned in delight. And she could cook. His gaze strayed to her.

Time. *It all takes time*, he reassured himself. Took another scrumptious bite and prayed the phone wouldn't ring at least until he finished his food. Preferably not at all.

She poured him some juice, then sat opposite him, her hair falling to hide her face, but something about the hesitant way she tilted her face as if she were weighing her words before she spoke. He swallowed more divine food and slowed down. Then asked, 'Question?'

'I'm wondering if it's too early to ask you about your mother. You said something on Monday that's been driving me a little wild with curiosity.'

His head came up. More because the idea of her being driven a little wild stirred his interest rather than any concern about her prying into his past. 'A little wild, eh?' He speared a pasta curl.

She looked at him and shook her head. 'You're a dark horse, Dr Foley. One bit of encouragement and I can see where that leads you.'

He grinned at her. Spread his fork hand innocently. 'I'm just happy.'

She laughed. 'I'm happy too. So, now that I've made you happy, can I ask you about your mother?'

'Go ahead.'

'What did you mean she was a medium? It's the last thing I expected.'

He'd come to terms with it years ago. Funny how women harped on about it. His sister. And Clancy. Both had hated it. Funny he hadn't thought Catrina would be like that. He'd always thought of his mum's beliefs like a choice. Believe in angels or not. Be a vegetarian or not. Take up ballroom dancing or tarot cards.

'What's to expect? She was a psychologist then became fascinated by the cards and became a medium. I loved her. My sister couldn't have been more horrified if my mother had taken six lovers instead of a sudden attraction to talking to the angels.'

Catrina leaned forward earnestly. 'It doesn't repel me. I'm not sure what fascinates me about it. It's just different. That's all. And a bit out there for a paediatrician to have a medium in his family.'

He'd heard that before. 'That's what my sister said. But it made Mum happy and when she went she went with peace. She died not long after I fell for Clancy.' He shrugged but heard the grief shadowed in his voice. Tried to lighten the tone. 'She said that Clancy had sadness wrapped around her like a cloak and she worried about me.'

Catrina opened her eyes wide.

He sighed. 'I didn't listen.'

CHAPTER SIXTEEN

Trina

TRINA GLANCED OVER the rail to the wide ocean in front of them. Sought the point where the ocean met the sky and sighed too. Of all the things she wanted to ask Finn, she wasn't sure why she'd chosen to ask about his mother. And now that she knew she'd never meet her it made her sad. Another mother gone. It had been a ridiculous question.

Or maybe it was about her because she couldn't remember her own mum, could only remember an ethereal figure tucking her in and singing a lullaby she couldn't remember the words to. But she knew mothers were special. She'd always wanted one and Finn's had sounded magical. Someone who talked to angels.

For Trina there'd been a succession of foster homes in her childhood, the quiet child, the plain one with her hair pulled back tightly, the one people were briskly kind to but nobody became interested in, except the younger children she seemed to gather around her every time she ended back in the home.

Many kids had it a lot worse, and she'd come to a stage where she'd asked not to be fostered, not to raise her hopes that she'd find a mother to love, and she'd stayed and helped in the home until she could leave. Had worked for a scholarship, always determined to do her nursing.

A nice sensible profession followed by her glimpse into midwifery—and that was when she'd seen it.

The families. Starting from the glory of birth, the connection to the child, the true beginning of a mother's love. The journey she'd make one day because she knew in her bones this was her destiny and then she'd be home. She had so much love to give.

'I'm sorry your mother died. I would have liked to meet her.'

He looked at her thoughtfully and then nodded. 'She would have liked you too.'

The thought warmed her melancholy and she appreciated his kindness. 'Thank you.'

He was the one with the questioning look now. Weighing the difference of needing to know and being too forward. 'Where did you meet your husband?'

So they'd reached that stage. She'd started it. Gingerly she began to unpack it a little. 'Edward was a nurse like me. At uni. We both worked at a restaurant waiting on tables and we laughed a lot. Then we both graduated and went to work at the same Sydney hospital. We married just before I started my transition to midwifery year. He was my knight in shining armour, my soulmate, an orphan like me and a man who understood my need for family.'

She had to admit Finn looked less happy. 'He sounds a great guy.'

She breathed in slowly. To control the tickle of sadness in her throat. 'He was.' Gone now. They'd been so full of plans. 'We were saving up for our family that never came. Because Ed died. Killed by a fast brain tumour that robbed him of speech before we could say much, and his life before we could properly say good-bye.'

She saw the empathy for her sudden loss. Not as sudden as his. But worse.

Finn said, 'That must have been devastating.'

'It was. I sold our flat and came here. Watching the sea helped.' She'd been adrift, swamped by the withdrawal of a future again, the loss of her love and her husband. She'd sworn she would not risk broken dreams again. But then she'd stumbled into Lighthouse Bay and the warmth of her midwifery family had helped her begin the long, slow journey to heal.

'But it seems I'm resilient. Maybe all those foster families in the past made me tough. Because now I'm scuba diving and I've even had lunch and dinner with a man and his daughter. It took two years but I'm becoming braver.' She looked at him. 'But I'm still wary.'

'I understand that.' He grimaced. 'I'm a little wary myself.'

One more question then, Trina thought as Finn put the last of the pasta into his mouth. She waited for him to swallow. 'So how did you meet Clancy?'

CHAPTER SEVENTEEN

Finn

FINN GUESSED HE owed Catrina that. He remembered the day vividly. Puffy white clouds. Brilliant blue sky. Painted ponies and unicorns. 'At a fairground, of all places. She was riding the merry-go-round with a little girl my sister had taken there. A distant relative she'd asked my help to mind for the day. We were introduced by a five-year-old. Clancy knocked me sideways. Her hair—' he shook his head '—just like Piper's, a daffodil cloud around her head.'

He saw Catrina's wince and mentally smacked himself up-side the head. *Idiot. Don't tell one woman another is beautiful.* He moved on quickly. 'I should never have married her. She wasn't that young but she was a child, not a wife.'

'Do you think Clancy knew what she was doing when she ran away? That she planned to stay hidden?'

'I hope so. That has kept me sane. She ran away for a couple of days twice during the pregnancy. I was frantic. Then she reappeared as if she'd never been away and I told myself to stop making a big deal of it. That nobody owns anybody. But to leave straight after the birth?' He shrugged. 'It was a quick labour, but physically it was still a labour. So why would she leave her recovery time and make life hard on herself?'

'What happened?' He heard the gentleness in her voice, the understanding, and, despite his reluctance to talk about a time he wanted to forget, Catrina was a midwife and understood women, plus—he'd kissed her. Planned on doing more. She needed to know.

'Clancy stayed very focused during the birth. Distant, when I look back on it. As if she'd already pulled back from me. Even when Piper was born Clancy pushed her to me and of course I was over the moon. I scooped her up whenever she wanted. Clancy said no to breastfeeding so I gave Piper her first bottle.'

He remembered those first precious moments with his daughter in his arms. 'I've wondered how long she'd known that she was leaving.' He shook his head. Felt Catrina's eyes on him and was glad she didn't interrupt. He just wanted it out. 'So I changed the first nappy, gave Piper her first bath. And when I came back in on the second day to take them home she'd already gone. She'd left Piper with the nurses.'

He saw Catrina's hand cover her mouth but now he was there—in the past—remembered the incomprehension and disbelief. The beginnings of anger and how he'd expected her to walk back in at any moment.

How could Clancy possibly leave her day-old baby? How could she leave him when they were just starting as a family? And the worst. Selfish really. The innuendo that he had been impossible to live with and for what dark reason had she left?

Finn found himself opening his mouth to let those words out too. Ones he'd never shared with anyone else.

'I could feel the sidelong glances from the midwives—domestic violence must have run through their minds. Why would a new mother leave her baby? Was I the sort of man who looked loving on the outside yet was evil on the inside? What had I done to her to make her do this?'

'I don't think so,' Catrina said softly. 'If that were the case, I imagine the mother would take the baby and not leave a child at risk. The staff would have seen how you cared for Piper.' She reached out and laid her fingers on his arm. 'I see how you care for Piper.'

He appreciated that. He really did. But maybe he had done something Clancy couldn't live with. He'd re-hashed their short marriage but couldn't see anything. If only he knew why she'd left. 'I don't want the guilt if something happened to her. But I'm well over waiting for her to turn up every morning. My biggest regret, and it still rips out my heart thinking about it—is how am I going to explain to Piper that her mother walked away from her? That's what makes me angry. I can survive but how does a young girl understand her mother doesn't care enough to at least ask how she is going?'

'Every child needs a mother. But Piper has you. I guess Clancy knew you would make Piper your world. You're a paediatrician so you must love kids. Could keep her safe.'

'Maybe. But to have no contact? Just disappear?'

'You don't know why?'

He shook his head.

'Then you may never know. And it's no wonder you wanted to hide and start again.'

Start again. The words repeated in his head. Yes. He wanted to start again with Catrina. Instead he said, 'Moving here helped with that. Living in our house was pure hell. She wanted the big house, but it wasn't as much fun as she thought it would be. She didn't want a baby, just wanted to enjoy life without worries. She didn't want to be a doctor's wife or a stay-at-home mum. She wanted to be seen with a man on her arm. And I was busy. I guess I did let her down.'

CHAPTER EIGHTEEN

Trina

TRINA LISTENED TO Finn and tried not to judge Piper's mother. Tried not to hear the reverence in his voice when he spoke of her hair. He was right. Of course people would ask why she had left. Would wonder if he'd been the monster to force her into such a desperate act. Would harbour suspicions that somehow he had harmed her. She wondered if Finn knew how lucky he was she'd left the hospital and not when she'd got home, when the innuendos could have been worse. At least he hadn't been the last person to see her.

She tried to comprehend a mental imbalance, or a strange delusion, or just plain selfishness that had made it possible for a woman to leave her day-old baby. To leave without warning, or explanation except for a brief note, but no assurance of her well-being and expect her husband not to suffer with doubts and worry and loss of the family dream all under a cloud of suspicion. It proved difficult to imagine. Poor Finn.

'You said you tried to find her. The police?'

'The police agreed the note was real, didn't find anything and then other cases took precedence. They didn't have the resources for runaway wives.'

'You said you hired a detective?'

Finn waved his hand. 'The detective finally tracked down her last known contact before I met her, an older man, an uncle, but he'd gone overseas recently. The trail stopped there.'

Trina couldn't imagine how hard that must have been. 'She never wrote? Or phoned you?'

'Her phone went straight to message bank and eventually even message bank disconnected. Her credit cards or bank accounts that I knew she had were never touched. She didn't drive so they couldn't trace her through her driver's licence.'

Poor Finn. 'How can someone just disappear?'

'I've asked myself that question many times.'

'Do you think she went with her uncle? Overseas?'

He grimaced. 'It's possible. Or he set her up somewhere. I never met him. Didn't know of his existence until the detective told me.'

'What about your wedding?'

'She wanted the register office. My mother was in her last month and very ill. Half a dozen people came on my side. None on hers.'

It all sounded very sterile and unromantic. Quite horrible really. Not in keeping with this man who adored his daughter and made cupcakes and sandcastles.

She wanted to ask if Finn still loved Clancy. Started to. 'Can I ask…'

Finn's phone rang and they both looked at it vaguely and then reality hit. He was on call.

Finn dug it from his shirt pocket and said, 'I did not

plan that.' Then he stood up to listen. Trina tried not to strain her own ears.

Finn left a minute later. 'One of your buck's night boys has cut himself on oysters.' He kissed her cheek. 'Thanks for dinner. And for listening. My turn next time.'

He said *next time*. So she hadn't scared him away. And, despite that harrowing story of his wife's disappearance, he hadn't scared her away either. And he kissed her before he left. Trina hugged herself briefly and began to clear the dishes away. There were lots of reasons not to rush this.

Friday morning Finn met her on her walk and invited her down to his cottage backyard for a barbecue. Despite her need to prepare for the next week of work—washing, sorting, a little shopping—the day dragged until it was time to go over, and her stomach was knotted with excitement when she arrived. This was not being wary.

He looked so good when he opened the door.

He bowed her in. Then he kissed her. Twice. Piper was toddling across the room stark naked and put her arms up to Trina. *Wow.* She scooped her up and hugged her.

'Well, that's a hello anyone would be happy to get.' She met Finn's eyes over the top of Piper's head and her cheeks warmed at the smile Finn sent her. She hoped he didn't think she wanted him naked to greet her at the door. Her face grew warmer.

'Welcome,' Finn said softly. Then changed the subject away from the charged atmosphere of how fast this was all going. 'It's fresh-caught fish tonight. As soon as I bath Piper.'

'Let me.' Trina laughed as the little girl played peek-a-boo around her neck at her father. 'You go ahead. I'll bath her.'

Piper wriggled to be free and Trina put her down. The little girl toddled towards the bathroom. Finn laughed. 'She's getting smarter and faster.' Then he gestured with his hand. 'Her clothes are on my bed.'

So Trina bathed Piper in the little shower tub Finn had made. The enchantment of ceramic tiles with starfish, animals, moon and flowers around the walls of the shower cubicle, a mishmash of words that Piper tried to say when Trina pointed them out.

She loved that Finn had created the novelty for his daughter. Loved the way Piper watched her father with sometimes wise eyes. Loved them both. She sighed.

She was in trouble and she knew it. She'd fallen for him and he was still married. Fallen for the idea of joining their family as pseudo mother and she had no right.

Somewhere there was a woman who did have the right and until that dilemma was sorted she should be spending less time with him, not more—but she couldn't seem to say no. She didn't even want to ask if he still loved Clancy. She didn't want to know.

On Saturday morning she met Piper and Finn at the rock pools on her way back from her scuba lesson. 'What a surprise!'

Finn laughed when she teased him about being predictable and they bickered pleasantly about who was paying for lunch this week after a pleasant half an hour splashing.

After lunch Finn took Piper home for her sleep and Trina went home to make a cheesecake.

She'd been invited to Myra and Reg's for another barbecue; they'd arrived home from their cruise excited about the fun they'd had and eager to talk about the adventure.

Reg was impressed when Trina told him of Finn's assistance during Rhiannon's baby's birth and patted himself on the back for finding such a useful fellow. He rubbed his hands and winked at Myra and then Finn arrived and the story was repeated.

Finn came to stand beside Trina with Piper on his hip. Piper leaned towards Trina so naturally she put her hands out and took her from Finn.

'It's a great unit. I was glad to help,' Finn said as Piper's soft little hands reached up and touched Trina's hair on her cheek. Pulled it experimentally. Absently Trina lifted her fingers to free herself and caught Ellie's raised brows as she adjusted the child on her hip more comfortably. It was clear Piper felt at home with Trina and, judging by Ellie's expression, she was wondering why.

Finn went on, oblivious to the unspoken conversation between the two women. 'Catrina was as calm as a cucumber, as was Faith, of course.' She saw him glance around and was glad he'd mentioned Faith. Faith, Trina and Ellie had been the original three midwives and Faith wasn't there to hear. But it was nice to be mentioned. His gaze settled on Ellie. 'You have great midwives.'

Ellie's questioning gaze finally shifted off Trina, who gave a little sigh of relief. 'I know. Though it's the first time we've actually had to give fluids by a UVC in our unit.'

'Happens a couple of times a year where I worked,'

Finn said and took a ginger ale from Ellie's husband. 'What about you, Sam? Seen many babies need IV fluids at birth?'

'Nope. And don't want to. That's one of the benefits of working at the base hospital. Paeds do all that stuff. Give me a nice straightforward obstetric emergency every time and leave babies for the paeds.'

Finn laughed. 'Each to their own. I'm the opposite. Though Catrina's been letting me sit in on births for the week as a refresher and we even had a water birth.' He smiled at her and she felt her cheeks heat. Ellie winked at her and she tried unsuccessfully not to blush.

Quickly she decided she might as well join the conversation and try to look normal. 'He's converted. It was Sara and you know how calm she is.'

Ellie nodded. 'I was there for her last baby. Gorgeous. I'm hoping to have a water birth,' she told Finn. Then glanced at Sam, who pretended to sigh.

'I'm just the father. But, as an obstetrician, I'd like to go to the base hospital and feel like I have every conceivable back-up plan in place—but I've been outvoted.' He didn't look too worried.

'When's your baby due?' Finn asked Sam and, seeing the expression on his face, Trina wondered if he was remembering the feeling of being a father and knowing too much—but not wanting to say it.

'Three weeks.' Sam grimaced. 'I'm more nervous than Ellie.'

His wife took his hand and kissed it. 'You're excited, dear, not nervous, and it could take five weeks if I go overdue.'

Sam looked at her, his face softened and he squeezed her hand back. 'I'm very excited.'

Trina decided he was manfully suppressing the *and nervous* addition to that sentence and she remembered that Sam's first wife had miscarried many times. Everyone had their past and their crosses to bear. She should be thankful that she had good friends, wonderful support around her, and now she had Finn. *Be thankful. And stop worrying.*

The night held lots of laughs, tall stories and excitement from Myra and Reg about their cruise. And a few hints that they'd go again soon if Finn was happy to take Reg's on-call roster.

Myra and Trina had shared a bottle of lovely champagne they'd brought back from Tasmania and Trina glowed with good food, good wine and the joy of having a male dinner partner who fancied her for the first time in two years and didn't mind letting others know.

Finn and Trina left the party at the same time. Trina ignored the arch looks. As they stopped at Trina's gate she pointed to her door. 'You're welcome to come in if you like and have coffee.'

'I'd like that but Piper is drooping and she'll go to sleep soon.'

Trina's previous reservations were muted by the delightful fizz of the pleasant evening and she didn't want the night to end. She could sleep in tomorrow. 'I do have a folding cot in the cupboard. Sometimes Faith's daughter sleeps over if her aunt has to go away. She could sleep in there until you go.'

Finn looked surprised. 'I didn't realise Faith had a daughter.'

'We all have life stories. Her daughter's a real doll. We should introduce her to Piper.'

He looked down at his dozing daughter. Pretended to panic. 'I don't think I'm ready to cope with play dates.'

Trina laughed. 'You're funny.' Then glanced at the door. 'Come in or go?'

'If you have a cot, I'll come in. Thank you.'

Trina led the way, pushed open the door and gestured to her bed in an airy fashion. 'You could change her there and I'll make up the cot.'

Finn nodded and carried his daughter across the room and undid the nappy bag while Trina happily poked around in the cupboard and pulled out the bag with the folding cot in it. She had it out in minutes, grinning a little when it proved difficult to stand upright and kept sagging in the middle.

'I think you're tipsy,' Finn said, laughing. 'Here.' He reached forward with one hand and clicked the last lever into place to make the folding cot stand straight.

'Who, me?' Trina laughed. 'Maybe slightly but this cot is tricky.' She smiled at him a little dreamily. 'It was a lovely night.'

Trina laid the two quilts she'd taken from the bag down on the cot mattress—one as a bottom quilt and one to put over Piper as Finn laid her down in the cot. He put her cuddle bunny beside her head and Piper took it, rolled over and put her thumb in her mouth. She closed her eyes, secure that she was safe, even though the bed was different.

Trina gazed at the little girl for a moment and then sighed softly as she turned away. 'I'll put the kettle on.'

'Wait.' Finn's voice was low, gentle. His hand on her arm stopped her. 'What was that sigh for?'

'Just because.'

'Because what?'

She sighed again. 'Because you're a great dad. Because you have a beautiful daughter who doesn't seem to give you a moment's bother.' She paused, then finished the thought. 'And I want that too.' Trina felt herself sobering fast when she realised that she'd actually said that out loud.

She pulled away. 'Must be tipsy. Sorry.'

'Don't be sorry. I wish Piper had a loving mummy like you would be. But that's for the future.' Then he turned her and drew her into his arms. 'It was a lovely night. You looked beautiful and happy and I'd really like to just sit and talk and maybe canoodle a bit. What do you think?'

'Define canoodle?'

He stroked her cheek. 'I really, really want to kiss you.'

And she melted. He drew her to the sofa and as he sat he pulled her towards his lap. She wasn't fighting him. In fact she did a bit of climbing on herself. They both laughed. 'So beautiful. So sweet,' he said and then his mouth touched hers and she lost herself in the joy of being cherished.

CHAPTER NINETEEN

Finn

FINN WOKE TO moonbeams spilling across the bed and despite the silver threads of light a feeling of foreboding crept over him. He didn't like it. Splashes of brightness fell on the gently rounded form of a naked Catrina in his arms and he could hear the little snuffles of Piper asleep in the cot they'd moved close to his side of the bed.

They should have waited. His fault. They should have talked about worst-case scenarios if Clancy came back. Should have put in a plan to protect Catrina, but his resistance had been tempted beyond sense once Catrina had climbed onto his lap.

He thought about waking her. Telling her that he would start looking again so he could end his marriage. Protect Catrina from gossip. Gossip that if he stayed would follow her from tomorrow morning when he was seen leaving her croft.

He whispered, 'It might not happen but there's a chance…' But she was asleep. Sound asleep.

Finn slid his arm out gently from beneath Catrina and paused to look down at her in the moonlight. How had he been so lucky to have found this woman—how could he have been so careless to fall in love when he didn't have the right?

He should never have slept with her, should never have let her fall in love with him, with everything still unsettled, and he knew she did love him enough to be vulnerable to hurt, knew she trusted him now, knew he had to fix this if she was ever to forgive him for such carelessness.

He considered waking her then. He'd always intended warning her there was still a chance but the time had never been right to say it again. What they had nurtured between them had seemed so fragile, so new, had happened so fast, he'd feared to destroy it before it began.

Impossible. Fraught with danger. To lose what they'd just found was unthinkable. He needed to work out tonight how they could move forward with Clancy still out there. But for the moment he could prevent some of the gossip. He'd come back tomorrow.

He wrote a quick note on the back of one of his business cards, then gathered up his sleeping baby, felt her snuggle into his shoulder with complete trust. Like Catrina had. He winced. Slung the nappy bag over his other shoulder and let himself out.

The moon was up, full and bright like daylight, which was lucky as he had no hand free for a torch. Suitable really—he'd been baying at the moon like an idiot, following the siren's lure. Impulsive fool, risking Catrina's happiness.

In minutes he was home, had tucked his daughter

into her cot and sat on his own empty bed to stare at his feet.

He should never have slept with Catrina with his wife still out there somewhere.

CHAPTER TWENTY

Trina

SUNLIGHT PEEPED AROUND the curtains in Trina's croft as she stretched her toes luxuriously and remembered Finn's arms. She could almost feel the warmth and strength around her that she'd missed so much and couldn't believe she'd found again. Found again but different. Fairy tales did come true.

It was as if she'd turned into someone other than the broken-hearted woman she'd been for the last two years; she even had a new name. She was Finn's Catrina. Not Ed's Trina. Or maybe both.

She squashed down the piercing guilt and sent love to her departed husband. Yes, she would always love him, but now, after these last few weeks, she knew she loved Finn too. Needed to love Finn. In a different way. But in a real way. Not the ethereal way she loved and always would love Ed. And then there was Piper. Sweet, motherless Piper. She loved Piper too. And, my goodness, she loved life!

How had she been so lucky? She stretched again and wondered what Finn was thinking this morning. She'd found his note.

Spare the gossips—we need to get this sorted.
Finn Xx

Her thoughts took a sensuous turn down the hill to-wards his house and she was tempted to sneak down there and snuggle into his bed. And him. But apparently, until they told people, they should be discreet. For her sake, he said. But he was the new doctor. For his sake as well. She got that. But what a whirlwind these last two weeks had been.

Maybe a six a.m. break and enter wasn't discreet.

She took her time. Showered in a leisurely fash-ion. Washed and dried her hair. Applied light make-up though—she stared into the glass with a small curve of her mouth—her well-kissed lips needed no colour this morning. The heat surged into her cheeks. Nor did her face need blusher either. She smiled at herself—a cat-that-ate-the-cream smile—and turned away from the blushing woman in the mirror.

She'd never been that uninhibited with Ed. Their lovemaking had been wonderful but there was some-thing about Finn that drove her a little wild. Or a lot wild. Apparently, she did the same to him. She smiled again.

Her chin lifted. Life was too damned fickle not to take advantage of that fact and she wouldn't be ashamed, and she never, ever wanted to be cold in the night again.

She could grow used to being driven wild in bed. She drew the gaily coloured scarf that Finn had said he liked from the drawer and flung it around her neck. She looked like an excited schoolgirl.

She tried to think of an excuse to turn up that wasn't purely, *Let me into your bed*.

Maybe she could make a breakfast picnic and they could take it down to the beach and eat it on the break-wall? Piper would like that. She could just knock on his door like a neighbour and invite him to join her. Her stomach flipped at the thought of the light in his eyes. That special smile he seemed to find when she appeared.

She took off the scarf again and made bacon and egg sandwiches, the delicious scent swirling and teasing and making her belly rumble. She was hungry for everything this morning. Even the coffee smelt divine as she made up the Thermos, and extravagantly tucked in a small bottle of orange juice as well. She packed her checked rug and tucked her little picnic bag under her arm as she closed the door.

Then she stopped. Leaned back against the cool wood and sucked in a breath as if someone had thrown a bucket of cold water over her. Finn would be there for her.

For ever? The words trickled through her brain like rivulets of pain on her mind. Questioning. Prodding scarred memories. Undermining her belief in their future.

What if he couldn't? It hit her. What if he wasn't there? What if she fell more and more and more in love with Finn until it was too late? What if something happened to Finn and she'd given the last half of her heart, all that was left of her own self, to him and it got smashed and broken and buried in a coffin like the half she'd given to Ed? What if the worst happened and Finn died and left her for ever? She had said she'd never allow herself to feel that pain again. Piper would go to her aunt and Trina would be alone again. Smashed to smithereens like the broken shells pounded by the surf on the beach below.

She sucked in a burning breath and clutched the ball of pain in her chest. It was too easy to remember the ripping pain of loss. Too devastating to imagine her empty bed now tainted with Finn's imprint so it would always be there. *No!* Nobody could be that unlucky!

She reached out to lay her hand against the wood of the door. Seeking support. Felt the hard wood as a solid force and drew strength from it. Drew another deep breath as if she were one of her mothers and she needed to be coached through a tough contraction. *Okay then.* Breathed again. That wasn't going to happen.

She sagged against the door. Beat it. She'd beaten it. But the voice inside her mind wasn't finished yet.

So, you don't want to imagine that? The voice in her head tried another tack. What if the almost as bad happened and his wife came back and Finn chose her as Piper's mother over Trina? She'd never asked if he still loved Clancy. Had she?

Of course Piper's needs would outweigh hers, maybe even outweigh Finn's, to be fair to him. Either way, she would lose.

Of course Piper needed her mother. If Finn had Clancy he wouldn't need Trina either.

No! They were going to talk about that. Make plans. She straightened her spine. Thought back to the gentle way Finn had cradled her through the night. The whispered promises. The closeness. Finn was a worthy man and she trusted him. And she needed to trust in the future.

Catrina tweaked her scarf reassuringly, lifted her head and a little less jauntily set off down the hill. Felt the promise of the day fill the void. She stopped and closed her eyes and welcomed the sunshine in. Felt it flooding through her body, healing the fear that had gripped her moments before. Opened her eyes and began walking again. A panic attack. She'd had a panic attack. That was what it was. *Silly girl.* Everything would be fine. She clutched the picnic bag and lifted her face again. Smiled.

The sun seemed to be shining with extra brightness today—what was that? Overhead, gulls soared and swooped and she could feel the rocks scatter and pop with exuberance under her every step. The salty breeze brushed her hair across her cheek and it tickled, making her smile. Like Piper had tickled her cheek with her hair. It began to seep back into her. The joy she'd woken with, the excited thrum of blood in her veins. It had been so long since she'd felt this way—excited, alive and happy, yes, happy. Too long. She'd just been frightened for a moment but she was fine now. One night in Finn's arms and she was a goner. But what a night!

Life had certainly taken a turn for the good. New job, new man friend—she shied away from the word *lover* as she glanced down through the trees to where she could see Finn's front door.

There was an unfamiliar car in the driveway and she slowed her steps. Then she remembered Finn telling her about his sister's new car. A red convertible. That was who it would be. *Darn it.* She couldn't be neighbourly when he had a visitor.

Her footsteps slowed. The door opened and Trina stopped in the lee of a telegraph pole, not wanting to intrude on goodbyes. Three people stepped out. One was Finn with Piper on his hip, clinging like a limpet. Trina smiled fondly.

One was the woman Trina had seen at the restaurant that day that seemed so long ago but was only weeks—Finn's sister. She'd been right. She had a look of Finn.

And the other… Well, the other had a mist of fine flyaway hair the colour of sun-kissed corn, the exact hue of daffodils, just like Piper's. Finn and the woman stood together and only Finn's sister got into the car. Trina felt as if her heart stopped when Finn's sister was the only one who drove away.

Finn and the golden-haired woman turned and went back into the house. The door closed slowly, like the happiness draining from Trina's heart. An icy wind swirled around her shoulders as she stared at the closed door. *Who was that?* But she knew with a cold certainty who it was. Felt the knowledge excising the joy from her day like an assassin's knife. A killing blow. She turned around and climbed the hill like an old woman to her lonely croft.

Once inside she closed the door and locked it. Before she could shut the curtains and climb into bed the phone rang.

It wasn't Finn.

They needed her at work.

CHAPTER TWENTY-ONE

Finn

IN THE MORNING someone knocked on Finn's door. Surely only minutes after he'd fallen asleep just before daybreak. Groggily he sat up, pushed the covers away and automatically glanced at Piper.

Bright inquisitive eyes sparkled at him and she bounced up and down on the balls of her feet, holding onto the top of the cot rail. 'Mum, Mum, Mum,' Piper said gleefully.

'It better not be,' he muttered for the first time but he had to smile. It probably was Catrina. It was good she was here. Though he smiled to himself at her lack of discretion. To think he'd sneaked away to stop the gossips and she'd come at sparrow call anyway. Today he would throw himself on the mercy of the court and find out how to file for divorce. He wanted that new beginning.

Except when he opened the door it wasn't Catrina. It was his sister. Looking shell-shocked and pale. She opened her mouth and closed it again.

'Frances? What's wrong?' Finn reached out to draw her inside but she pulled back. Glanced at her car.

'She's here.'

'Who's here?' He looked at the car. Saw the cloud of floating golden hair and knew. Felt the world slam into him with the weight of a sledgehammer, driving the breath from his body. He leant his hand on the door frame to support himself for a second and then straightened.

Licked his dry lips and managed to say, 'Where did you find her?'

'She found me. Saw your house was for sale in the paper and recognised it. The real estate agent rang me.'

Finn's mind had shut down. He couldn't think. Piper was clinging to him and the door was closing his wife and his daughter inside his house.

One year late.

And—absolute worst—one day late.

Finn shut the front door and turned around to lean against it, the weight of Piper on his hip grounding him like she had done so many times before, and he stared unbelievingly at the woman he'd given up on seeing again.

And, after last night, hadn't wanted to see again. Or not like this.

She was talking. He could see her lips move, though she was looking at the ground as she spoke, so that didn't help the comprehension. Her hair was that floating cloud of daffodil yellow that he'd noticed when they'd first met. Beautiful, he thought clinically, as if he had nothing to do with the scene about to unfold, but too fine; her hair was a golden mist around her head, like Piper's.

She was still talking but his ears were ringing and

seemed to echo with the weight of his emotion. She wasn't dead. That was a good thing. That was good for Piper. For the future. Maybe they would have some connection in the future. Not so good for him. He was married. And he'd just slept with another woman. Her timing could not have been worse.

He cut across her long-winded explanations that he hadn't heard a word of. 'Wait. Sit down. I can't understand you when you talk to the floor like that.'

She glanced around a little wildly, her hair a drift of golden cotton in the breeze of her movement, so fine and light it swayed with her like yellow seaweed under the ocean.

He sat down too. Piper stayed stuck to his hip with her head buried into his shoulder. He wished he could bury his head too. 'Why are you here?'

She spoke softly. Hesitantly. 'To talk to you. Talk to Piper.'

He could feel the scowl on his face. Tried to smooth it out. To listen with empathy as if she were a tiresome patient who refused to take necessary advice. But she wasn't. She was his wife who had abandoned them. Remember his oath to treat the ill to the best of his ability. He'd always known she wasn't one hundred per cent well. It didn't help a lot. 'You're a year late.'

'I'm sorry.'

Well, that didn't cut it, but he hadn't heard the reasons yet. He fought the panic that engulfed him. His brain had seized. His chest felt tight. And he had to keep from squeezing Piper too tightly against him. How could she be here? And—the most frightening of all—was he even glad?

He stood again. Turned his back on his wife and

moved across to put Piper down in her playpen, but she clung to him. He kissed the top of her head and reached for the fruit sticks he kept in a jar in the fridge.

'Here you go, sweetheart. A bit cold but you don't mind, do you?' Then he put her in the playpen and she sat quietly with her big eyes watching him as she began to chew the fruity sticks.

He heard Clancy's soft voice. 'You're very good with her.'

He stamped down the anger. 'We are family. Plus...' he looked at her steadily '...someone had to be.'

She flushed. 'I made a mistake.'

Really? he thought. *Just one?* But didn't say it. *And it took a year for you to tell us that?* Instead he tried to make his voice neutral and said, 'I don't understand why you would drop out of nowhere like this. What are you hoping to get out of this?'

'Just to talk. At first.'

He winced at 'at first'.

She went on hesitantly. 'See what happens. If what happens is good then maybe—' she drew a long breath and squared her shoulders for a second '—I'm hoping that we could start again.'

Finn sucked in a breath, stunned she could even contemplate that, but then he was in shock. His thought processes were not good. He needed to be calm.

Her shoulders drooped again. 'I could learn to be a mother.' She looked up at him and her eyes were shiny with tears. 'Maybe even a wife.'

CHAPTER TWENTY-TWO

Trina

TRINA PUSHED OPEN the door to Maternity and from down the hallway she could hear quiet moans from the closed doors of the birthing units. Someone sounded very close to having a baby.

In the other birthing room it sounded as if someone else was also very close to having a baby. It happened sometimes. Not often, but when it did at change of shift a third midwife was needed. Technically she didn't start her Sunday call until after eight a.m. but the other midwife had plans for today and Trina was pathetically grateful to be doing something.

She tucked her bag into her locker and washed her hands. The fine tremor of distress was barely noticeable but still she glared at her quivering digits. *Stop it.* She liked and trusted Finn. She would just have to leave it there, parked, until she finished work.

But, deep inside, a crack of loss began to tear and rip and widen. Too soon for loss. She should have stayed safe from pain for a lot longer. Healed more solidly before ripping at the wound.

The woman down the hall moaned louder and Trina

drew a deep breath and shut the world outside the doors far away. This was her world. Inside this unit. This was where she needed to concentrate.

The called-in midwife appeared beside her and spoke very quietly. 'I'm in room one with Bonnie. She won't be long. All going well and I have a nurse with me. Jill has Jemma. It's been a long hard labour and slow second stage. Will you take her?'

Catrina was one hundred per cent there. 'Absolutely.'

She turned and knocked gently and pushed open the door.

Jill, the midwife on night shift, looked up with wordless relief. 'Here's Trina, come in to help,' she said to the woman with a brightness that didn't quite ring true. 'You know Jemma and Pierce, don't you, Trina?'

'Yes, I do. Hello there, Jemma.' She nodded to the usually jolly Pierce as well, but his face had strained into taut lines. Some dynamic wasn't working or there was a problem. 'You both look to be doing an amazing job here.'

Then she looked back to Jill as she reached for the handheld Doppler to check the baby's heart rate. 'I always like to say good morning to babies too, so is it okay if I have a listen to yours, please, Jemma?'

'Sure,' Jemma sighed as the last of the contraction ebbed away, and Trina put the dome-shaped Doppler on Jemma's large rounded stomach. Instantly the clop-clop of the foetal heart-rate filled the room. The contraction ended and no slowing of beats indicated the baby had become tired or stressed, and the rate sat jauntily around one-forty. There was even a small acceleration of rate as baby shifted under Trina's pressure, which told her that baby still had reserves of energy, despite what she guessed had been a long labour.

She stared at the large shiny belly and guessed the baby's size to be larger than average. Acknowledged that position for birth would be important to optimise pelvic size.

'He/she sounds great,' she said after a minute of staring at the clock. 'Magnificent belly there, Jemma.' The tension in the room eased another fraction.

'Can I check the position, please?' Jemma nodded and Trina ran her hands quickly over Jemma's abdomen. Confirmed the baby was in a good position and head too far down to palpate. That was good. 'So, catch me up on Jemma's progress, Jill?'

Jill glanced at the couple and smiled wearily. 'It's been a long night and they've been amazing. Jemma's due tomorrow; this is her first baby and her waters broke about four p.m. yesterday. The contractions started pretty much straight away and they came in here about five p.m.'

She glanced at the clock that now pointed to almost seven a.m. 'The contractions have been strong and regular since six p.m. so she's been working all night to get to this point. Her observations have stayed normal, and she's been in the shower and the bath, has tried the gas but didn't like it much. We've walked a fair way and at five she felt the urge to push. I checked and she'd reached that stage already.'

Two hours of pushing and head well down. *Good, not great*, Trina thought. 'Wow, that's a hard and long labour,' she said gently and Pierce nodded worriedly.

'So,' Jill went on, 'Jemma's been pushing for just under two hours now; she's tired and we almost have head on view but it hasn't been easy for the last few pushes. We've been in the bathroom for most of that time, but she wanted to lie down so she's just come back to the bed.'

Trina looked at the night midwife and nodded. In bed on her back was the last place any midwife wanted Jemma if she had a big baby on board. Jill wasn't happy with the progress which, on the surface, seemed timely and acceptable so there must be more.

Jemma moaned as the next wave of contraction began to build and Trina tuned to see why Jill would be worried as the team went to work to support Jemma in the expulsive stage.

Tantalisingly close, the baby's head seemed to be hovering but not advancing that last little bit to birth and Trina kept the smile on her face as she suspected Jill's concern.

Trina moved in with the Doppler again to listen to the baby after each contraction. 'How about you give the doctor a ring and he can be here at the birth? Then he can do his round early and leave early. He'll like that. I'll stay with Jemma and Pierce for this last little bit. You can write up your handover notes here in the room, and that way you'll be ready to go as soon as we have this determined little passenger in his mother's arms.'

Gratefully, Jill nodded and they changed places. When Jill had finished the phone call, she settled herself on the stool in the corner at the side desk and they all rested as they waited for the next contraction.

Trina looked into Jemma's tired face. 'After this next one, I'd like you to think about changing position.'

Jemma sighed and Trina smiled. 'I know.'

Jemma grumbled, 'I just want this over.'

Trina nodded and glanced at Pierce. 'I'm thinking Pierce wants to see this baby snuggled up between you both too. Your baby probably has his father's shoulders, so I'm suggesting turning around and kneeling on the bed or even down on the floor, because that position gives you an extra centimetre of room in your pelvis. That tiny amount can make all the difference at this stage when it feels hard to budge.' She smiled at them both. 'It's a good position for making even more room if we need it after baby's head is born.'

'Is there a problem?' Pierce had straightened and looked down at his wife.

'No. But sometimes when second stage slows this much it means there might be less room than expected. We have set body positions a mum can go into that create extra space in her pelvis. I'd rather have Jemma ready to do that, even if we don't need it, than try to awkwardly scramble into position if we have a more urgent need.'

Pierce nodded. 'What do you think, Jem?'

'I think I'd do anything to get this baby here.'

After the next long contraction a weary Jemma rolled over in the bed onto her knees and rested her head on her forearms on the high pillows that had been behind her. Trina settled the thin top sheet over her and gently rubbed the small of her back. Pierce offered her a sip of water from the straw at Trina's silent prompting.

In the new position baby made progress and the first of the head began to appear on view. There was a soft noise at the door and, instead of old Dr Southwell, it was his son, Sam, and Trina could have kissed him.

Reg was good, but there was nothing like an obstetrician when you needed one. 'This is Dr Southwell, Jemma. Pierce, this is Sam.'

The men shook hands quickly as Trina went on. 'We've some second stage progress since Jill spoke to you, after moving to all fours. There's better descent with the last contraction.'

She moved her hand and placed the ultrasound Doppler awkwardly upwards against Jemma's now hanging belly. It wasn't as clear as before in this position but they could hear the steady clopping from the baby on board.

Sam nodded at the sound. 'Baby sounds good. I'm here as extra hands if position changes are needed.' He went to the sink, washed and put gloves on.

Pierce looked at him. He glanced at his wife and seemed to change his mind about asking more. The next contraction rolled over Jemma and she groaned and strained and very slowly the baby's forehead, eyes and nose birthed. But that was all.

'Keep pushing through,' Trina said with a touch of urgency and Sam nodded. But no further descent of baby occurred. Trina found the foetal heart again with the Doppler and it was marginally slower but still okay.

'We'll try putting your head down. Move the pillows, Trina,' Sam said quietly. Jill appeared at their side and Sam said, 'Phone Finn. Tell him I want him up here to stand by.'

Trina looked up as Jill disappeared and her heart sank. Sam must think it was going to be more difficult than expected.

She removed the pillows and encouraged Jemma to put her head on the bed and stretch her knees up towards her chest with her bottom in the air. It would straighten out her sacrum and, hopefully, give them a tiny bit more room in her pelvis.

The head came down another centimetre and the face cleared the birth canal but then the chin seemed to squeeze back inside like a frightened turtle's head against his shell.

Trina listened to the heart rate again and this time they all heard the difference in rate. Much slower. The cord must be squeezed up between the body and the mother's pelvis. That would dramatically reduce the oxygen the baby was getting.

'It looks like your little one has jammed his anterior shoulder against your pubic bone, Jemma. Not letting his body come down, even though his head is out. I'm going to have to try to sweep baby's arm out so the shoulder collapses to make room.'

'Do it,' Jemma panted.

'Try not to push as I slide my hand in.' From where she stood, Trina saw Pierce fall back in his chair and put his hand over his face.

Jemma stared at the ceiling and breathed slowly, striving for the calm that was so important, and Trina felt her eyes prickle with admiration for the mother in crisis as she squeezed her shoulder and spoke reassuring words in Jemma's ear.

She watched Sam's eyes narrow as mentally he followed his hand past the baby's head and reached deeply to slide along the upper arm to the elbow. Trina saw the moment he found the baby's elbow and swept it slowly past the baby's chest and face; she saw the relief and determination and wished Ellie was here to see her amazing husband, saw the muscles on Sam's arm contract and watched the slow easing of the limp arm out of the jammed space and suddenly there was movement.

The arm was out, the head shifted. 'Push, Jemma,' Trina urged, and then the baby's flaccid body slid slowly into Sam's hands.

'I'll take him,' a voice said behind Sam and Trina looked up to see Finn there. The relief that swamped her was so great she didn't care that his wife had arrived. Didn't care her heart was broken. No space for that. She wanted this baby with the best paediatric care and she didn't doubt that was Finn.

Sam cut the cord quickly. Trina saw Jill's worried eyes and knew she'd be better at the resus than Jill without sleep.

'Swap, Jill.'

Jill looked up, relief clear on her face. She nodded and hurried over to change places with Trina beside the mother.

CHAPTER TWENTY-THREE

Finn

FINN HEARD CATRINA say, 'Swap, Jill…' as he carried the silent and limp baby to the resuscitation trolley that Jill had set up. The lights and heater were on and Finn rubbed the wet baby firmly. Catrina handed him the next warmed dry towel and he did it again.

She spun the dial on the air and handed the tiny mask to Finn, who started the intermittent positive pressure breaths while she placed the pulse oximeter lead on the lifeless white wrist.

After thirty seconds, the heart rate was still too slow. 'Cardiac massage.' Finn said briefly.

Catrina circled the baby's chest and Finn wondered if this had happened twice in a fortnight before for her. It was unusual. For a low-risk unit this was too much.

He watched as she began compressing the baby's chest by a third in depth. He intoned, 'One, two, three, breathe. One, two, three, breathe.' For another thirty seconds.

Catrina said, very calmly—too calmly, 'Still heart rate below sixty.'

He glanced at her face and saw the fear she held

back. 'Thinking about adrenaline after the next thirty seconds,' Finn said quietly, and then Sam appeared.

'I'll take over the cardiac massage, Trina.' He'd be thinking that, as the midwife, she could find their equipment faster.

Trina nodded and Sam slipped in with barely a pause in the rhythm. She reached down and pulled open the drawer, removed the umbilical catheter set he recognised and pulled out the adrenaline. Once you needed adrenaline things didn't look so good.

Good idea about the umbi catheter. He prayed it wouldn't get to that. Finn hoped this baby would breathe before then. Then the big adrenaline ampoule appeared in his vision; the sound of her snapping off the glass top was reassuring. She was slick and he heard her muttering as she began to draw it up. 'The new guidelines say point five of a mil standard; is that what you want, Finn?'

'Yes, thanks. ARC Guidelines.'

He glanced at the clock. 'Next thirty seconds. Heart rate still fifty. Slightly better. Keep going.' He looked at Catrina and nodded at the box.

Thirty seconds later and Catrina had dashed out for the warmed fluid for the umbilical catheter box.

'Seventy.' He saw her sag with relief. He felt a bit that way himself. *Thank goodness.* No adrenaline needed. No umbi catheter needed. If the heart rate kept going up.

Sam stopped compression and Finn continued on with the breathing. The baby wasn't white any more. Streaks of pinkish blue were coming. The blue on the face stayed but that would be compression of the head causing congestion and that might take hours to go. The body was pink. *Excellent.*

He heard Trina breathe out as the baby's hands flexed, as did his little blue feet. Then the neonate struggled and gasped. And cried. Finn sighed and let the mask lift off his face for a second to see what he did. The baby roared.

He glanced at Trina, saw the tears she was trying to hold back. He didn't blame her. That had been a little too close.

'Good job,' Sam said quietly and Finn looked at him. All in all, it had been an emotional day.

'You too.'

Catrina had gone. Over to the mother to explain her baby was coming over soon. Reassure, like she always did. Being the midwife. To help Jill with settling the woman more comfortably when her baby came across. The baby that was crying vigorously now. Finn felt the muscles in his shoulders release.

Sam said, 'It was in good condition before the cord was occluded by the body. So he had some reserves.'

'They'll have to keep an eye on his blood sugars after that resus.'

'Does he need transfer?'

'See what the glucometer says. Not if his sugars stay good.'

They both knew it wasn't good if a baby had no reserves and got into that kind of bother. Shoulder dystocia was a mongrel. Not common, but fifty per cent of the time there were no risk factors when it happened. At least this baby had been strong enough to come back with a little help.

Sam had lived up to the glowing praise he'd heard. Catrina had been amazing again. They all were. He could grow to be a part of this team.

Then the real world crashed in. If his wife went away and left him to it. And he still hadn't told Catrina that Clancy had arrived.

He stepped back as Catrina lifted the baby to take across to the mum.

Sam was leaving; he'd go too, as soon as he'd spoken to the parents, explained what had happened, that baby had been fine by five-minute Apgar and he didn't expect any sequelae. Then he'd go, but he cast one glance at Catrina. She was busy. Too busy for his drama. It would have to wait. He just hoped he got to her before she found out.

CHAPTER TWENTY-FOUR

Trina

TRINA SAW FINN leave the room after he'd spoken to the parents. *Good.* She didn't have the head space. He'd come to help when he'd been needed. And gone as well. She'd needed him to go.

She didn't think Finn had known his sister would bring his wife. She wasn't that blindly jealous. She even still had faith that he'd come eventually to explain and thanked him mentally for not attempting that now in the midst of the birthing centre drama. But then again, he didn't know that she had seen his visitor. Guest. Whatever.

Her heart cracked a little more and she forced a smile onto her face. 'Let's get you into the shower, Jemma. Then into bed with your little man for a well-earned rest.'

Jemma had physically fared well. Apart from some grazes, she hadn't needed stitches, her bleeding had been normal not excessive, which could happen after a shoulder dystocia, and her baby had recovered to the stage where he'd fed very calmly, had excellent blood sugar readings and gone to sleep in his father's arms after an hour on his mother's skin.

Finn had explained everything very slowly and calmly and both Jemma and Pierce seemed to have come to an understanding of what had happened. And, without being told, what could have happened. They kept thanking everyone. It was after such a harrowing experience that things replayed in a mother's mind— and a father's. So it was very important the information was given and the chance to ask questions was given.

Trina reassured her again. 'It's one of those things that we practice for. Do drills and prepare for because when it happens we need to have a plan.' *We also had two very experienced doctors available*, Trina thought and thanked her lucky stars they hadn't had a tragedy. For a minute she thought how good it would be to talk to Finn about what had happened, then remembered she couldn't. Maybe never would be able to. Pain sliced through her and she hugged it to herself to stop the heartbreak showing on her face. He'd probably leave now and she'd never see him again.

Four hours later the second birthing mother had gone home with her baby and the morning midwife could take over the care of Jemma and baby. Trina could go home. Not that she wanted to but she wasn't needed here now.

She had time to think. Maybe that was for the best. But damned if she was going to regret the fact she had shown Finn she cared. A lot. And he'd cared about her. There was nothing sleazy in their making love last night. Not a lot of sense either. But mostly the fact they hadn't waited showed a whole lot of bad timing.

It would probably be better if she didn't see him again.

Except that when she got home he was leaning against her front door.

Her heart rate thumped into overdrive and suddenly she felt like crying. She forced the words past the thickness in her throat, looking at a spot beyond his left shoulder. 'I didn't expect to see you here.' Understatement of the year.

'I asked the morning midwife to ring me when you left,' he said. His voice came to her low and strained. 'Clancy turned up.'

'I know.' When she glanced at his face she saw his shock. And, if she wasn't mistaken, his distress that she had found out on her own. The thought brought some comfort. At least he cared about that.

'When did you find out?'

She sighed and shrugged. Pushed past him to open her door. 'I saw your sister drive away. Saw a woman with the same hair as Piper go back inside with you. It wasn't hard.' She felt him come in behind her and didn't know if she wanted that or not. Might as well get the whole embarrassing mistake out in the open. But in private. Her face heated a little and she hoped her hair hid it. She'd let it down when she left the ward, needing the screen of it blowing around her face. Even more now. 'I was bringing breakfast.'

His hand touched her shoulder, the barest skim of his fingers, as if he thought she might shy away from him. 'I'm sorry, Catrina. I wouldn't have had you find out like that.'

What was the optimal way to find out your lover's wife had moved back in? She turned to face him. Saw the sincerity in his face, the pain, and spared a moment to think about just how much his world had been turned upside down by the unexpected return of his wife into his house. If she was Superwoman she'd feel sorry for him. Couldn't quite achieve that yet. 'Where's Piper?'

His face twisted. 'With her mother. Who has no idea what to do with her. Thinks she's a doll to play with.'

And that hurt too. And there was the crux of the matter. Trina had grown up without her mother and, even if Clancy was ditzy, like Finn had given her the impression she was, she was still Piper's real mother. Trina would have given anything to have an imperfect mother over no mother. One who was her very own. There was no way she could go anywhere near taking Piper's mother away from her or Piper away from the woman who'd given birth to her.

She forced the words out. 'I'm glad for Piper. Every little girl needs her mother.'

He sighed. Pulled his fingers through his hair as if he wanted to yank it out. 'Surprisingly, so am I. And yes, a little girl does need her mother. But don't get me wrong. Or get Piper's mother wrong. This is why I need to be here now. Tell you now. Clancy doesn't want to be a full-time mother. She has that "deer in the headlights" look in her eyes. I can see that already and I can't even stay here long in case she runs.'

If he was worried about that, despite the fact she needed to hear this, he should go. 'Should you even be here?'

He sighed. 'I phoned my sister. When the hospital rang earlier. She turned around and came straight back.

She's with them at the moment. But I had to come. I need to tell you three things.'

She almost laughed. Tried not to let the bitterness out. The loss that she was only just holding back like the little boy with his finger in the dyke. The whole dam was going to swamp her soon and she didn't think she could hold back the disaster from drowning her for much longer. Her voice cracked. 'Only three?'

He stepped closer. His voice softened. 'They're important. Because you are important to me. Just listen. That's all I ask.'

She nodded mutely. She could listen. Just don't ask her to talk. She was totally unable to articulate the words through her closed throat.

He lifted his chin. Stared into her eyes. And his voice rang very firm. 'One, I'm sorry that you've been hurt by this.'

Yes, she'd been hurt, but she knew it was partly her own fault for falling in love with a man she knew wasn't free. She'd known right from the beginning and still she'd sailed along blithely, ignoring the impending disaster that had come just like she deserved.

He put up a second finger. 'Two. The good part of Clancy being here is that I can ask her for a divorce. Start all the paperwork that was impossible while she was missing. That is a huge thing for us. For you and me. And arranging when and how and the logistics of Clancy's access to Piper so that she and Piper can find the bonds that work for them. To create a relationship that is wonderful for both of them too. Piper will have two mothers.' He smiled like a man with a huge load lifted off his shoulders. 'You and I and Piper can look to the future. But that's where it is. In the future. It will take time and I may have to leave for a while as I sort it all out.'

She nodded dumbly, her head spinning.

He stroked her cheek. 'When it's sorted I will come back and ask you to be my wife properly. Romantically. Like you deserve and like I want too. Like I need to because you deserve everything to be perfect.' He shrugged those wonderful shoulders ruefully. 'Perfection can take a little while, with me. I'm sorry you have to wait for that.'

Trina sagged a little, relief bringing the dam closer to cracking. But the words swirled in her head, glimmers of light beginning to penetrate the weight of the wall hanging over her. He still wanted a future with her. Wanted her to be a part of the big picture. Part of his and Piper's future. Was it too good to be true?

'Three.' He paused. Stepped closer to her and tipped her chin up with his finger ever so gently. Wiped the tears that she hadn't realised were running down her face. 'I love you, Catrina Thomas. Fell in love with you weeks ago. And it's real love. Not the infatuation I had for Clancy. This is I-will-die-for-you love.' He sucked in a deep breath as if preparing for battle. 'We will conquer all the obstacles, my love.' He pulled back to see her face. 'Will you accept my apology and wait, dearest beautiful Catrina, while I sort this mess I made? Please.'

Trina drew her breath in with a shudder, trying not to sob with the relief of it all. The incredible wonder of Finn declaring his love when she'd thought it all lost. The unbelievable reprieve from having to rebuild her shattered heart. She moistened dry lips with her tongue and whispered very, very softly, 'Yes, Finn. I'll wait.'

His strong arms closed around her and she buried her face in his beautiful chest and sobbed while Finn leaned into her hair and whispered over and over again that he loved her so much.

EPILOGUE

A FULL YEAR later in a little pink cottage on the foreshore of Lighthouse Bay, Finlay Foley woke with anticipation and wonder at the change in his life. His two-year-old daughter, Piper, bounced in her cot. She'd thrown out all her toys and demanded to be allowed up to start this most special day.

'Cat. Want Cat. Where's Cat?' She bounced and searched with her eyes. Finn had to smile as he picked her up and swung her through the air.

'Try Mum, Mum, Mum, Mum, baby. You can't call your new mummy by her first name. And your other mummy wants to be called Clancy.'

'Mum, Mum, Mum, Cat,' Piper chanted and turned her head this way and that as if Catrina would appear from behind a chair in the tiny house.

'She's not here. It's bad luck for Daddy to see his bride on the day of their wedding.'

Her little face crumpled. 'Want Cat. Now!'

'I know, baby. Daddy wants her too. I can't wait either. But the girls will be here soon to pick you up and take you to Cat. Then you can put on your pretty dress and watch your daddy become the happiest man in the world.' He hugged the small body to him, feeling her warmth, and wondered again how he had been so blessed to have Piper and Catrina in his world.

The village church at Lighthouse Bay stood with the open arms of two white-columned verandas overlooking the sea. The slender throat of the small bell tower and the skirts of soft and springy green grass that surrounded it had begun to fill with milling guests who had arrived before the groom.

The day shone clear and bright, freshly washed by an early morning shower as if the extra sparkle of purity was a gift from the sky to help celebrate their day.

Finn drank in the serenity, the warmth of those who smiled at him as he crossed the iridescent grass with his best man, Sam, and the rightness of Catrina's wish to sanctify their union in front of the townspeople and inside the church. He couldn't wait.

The journey of the last few months had taught him to look forward, and that something good—or, in this case, someone amazing—always came out of struggle. He'd learnt to accept that every day held promise, despite the ups and downs, and now his days with Catrina held an ocean of promise that he couldn't wait to venture into.

The minister moved determinedly to greet them as they reached the porch, his kind eyes and outstretched hand reassuring in appreciation of Finn's nerves.

But Finn's nervousness had left—had departed the day Catrina said yes. Eagerness was more the word he was thinking of.

Ten minutes later he was standing at the front of the wooden church in his morning suit, surrounded by smiling townspeople, with row upon row of well-wishers jammed into the little church. All fidgeting and excited and smiling with enthusiasm for the event about to begin. Finn was pretty certain that, despite their enthusiasm, no one was more impatient than he was.

Sam by his side fidgeted too. Probably waiting to see Ellie. He saw Myra, looking particularly stylish in old lace, with Sam and Ellie's one-year-old daughter, Emily, in her arms. He'd been there when Emily was born. Waited outside the birthing room door just in case, to allay Sam's worries, and his own, and been a part of the joy and celebration of their beautiful birth. He couldn't help thinking of that post-birth hour, how such a magic time was one he wanted to share with Catrina when their time came. And Sam would wait outside the door for them. He'd never seen or been a part of such a place that offered so much solid friendship as Lighthouse Bay. And it had all started with the woman who would walk through that door for him any moment now.

The music soared and finally there was movement at the entrance. His eyes strained to see her. Catrina?

Faith, one of the midwives and Catrina's bridesmaid, appeared with his darling Piper in her arms, framed in the doorway. Faith and Piper's deep frangipani pink dresses matched frangipanis in their hair, and Piper was wriggling to be put down. As soon as she was free she toddled swiftly towards him, drawing gasps of delight from the onlookers as she waved a pink sign on a thin stick that read, *Here comes Mummy, Daddy.*

With Faith sedately bringing up the rear, Piper ran full pelt into his legs and he picked her up and hugged her. His throat was tight, his heart thumped, and then Sam's wife Ellie appeared. He heard Sam's apprecia-tive sigh beside him but Finn was waiting, waiting... And then she was there.

Catrina. His Catrina. Shining in the doorway. Rest-ing her hand on Sam's dad's arm, her beautiful coffee-brown eyes looking straight at him with a world of promise and an ocean of love. Finn wanted her beside him now, but he also wanted everyone to see, admire her, as she stood there in her beautiful ivory gown— looking at him with such joy and wonder. Incredibly beautiful. Incredibly his.

Faith reached across and took Piper from him, and everyone turned to savour the sight of the star, Catrina, his beautiful bride, as she stepped firmly towards him with so much happiness in her face he could feel his eyes sting with the emotion of the moment. How had he been so fortunate to win this woman's love? He didn't know if he deserved her but he would hold her and nur-ture her and protect their love and his darling wife for the rest of his life.

Catrina walked on a cloud towards Finn.

Her husband-to-be. Tall, incredibly debonair and handsome in his formal suit, his ivory necktie crisp against his strong throat. Emotion swelled but she lifted her chin and savoured it. She loved Finn so much, had been blessed, finding him when she had never thought she could possibly feel this way again. The music swelled to draw her forward. She needed no coaxing, couldn't wait, couldn't smile enough, feel enough, be thankful enough as she walked towards the man gazing at her with so much love her feet barely touched the ground.

'Cat, Cat, Dad,' Piper said. Then she looked at her father. Frowned and then chortled. 'Mum, Mum, Mum-cat. Mumcat!' she crowed, as if she'd found the perfect word.

The congregation laughed as her parents touched hands and held on.

Much later, in the cavernous surf club hall, the best party Lighthouse Bay had seen for a year had begun winding down. They'd turned the sand-encrusted, silvered-by-the-sun clubhouse into a flower-filled bower of fragrant frangipanis and greenery. Tables and chairs and a small dais for the bride and groom all glowed under ropes of hanging lanterns and people milled and laughed and slapped Finn on the back as he stood surrounded by friends. Waiting.

In a screened alcove at the back of the hall the midwives of Lighthouse Bay gathered to help the bride change from her beautiful ivory wedding gown into her travel clothes, a trousseau created by her friends. The laughter and smiles filled Catrina's heart to bursting as she looked around and soaked in the affection and happiness that radiated from her friends. Her family.

There was Ellie, with Emily on her hip, taking back the reins of the maternity ward full-time for only as long as Catrina and Finn were away. Then the two friends would share the duties, two mothers who had been blessed with a career they loved, and a workplace that could still leave plenty of time for family. It suited them both.

Ellie held out the gorgeous floral skirt found by Myra that had once belonged to a French princess. It felt like a caress against her skin as she drew it on.

Myra held the hand-embroidered cream blouse made by Faith's aunt especially for the occasion, and Faith clapped her hands as she began to slide it on.

She had two families now in her full life. In the main hall she had her new handsome and adoring husband, Finn, and her gorgeous Piper, soon to be her adopted daughter, and Finn's sister Frances and her husband, and, of course, Clancy—her unexpected almost sister.

Catrina had grown to care for flighty Clancy, saw that she had not a mean bone in her body, just a little foolishness and a wanderer's heart, underscored by an adventurer's gleam in her eye. Clancy would never be happy for too long in one place. But now, because of Piper and the growing relationship that made Catrina's orphan's heart swell with joy, Clancy could come and share family time with Piper, where she could have the best of both worlds without the responsibility that made her run. With Finn's new family she had people who loved her and people who waved goodbye and let her go.

Catrina noted that Faith, kind Faith, stood alone as she watched them all, watching her daughter chasing after a determined to escape Piper, a whimsical half-smile on her pretty face as she dreamed.

Catrina took a moment to suggest to Finn's mother's angels that Faith should find her own second family and happiness, like she and Ellie had, in the very near future. *Please!*

But then Ellie straightened her collar and she returned to the moment. She was ready and Ellie spun her slowly to ensure she was perfect and the oohs and ahhs of her friends suggested the outfit lived up to expectations. She felt like a princess herself, the beautiful skirt restored to its former glory by Myra, as she floated out from behind the screens to where her husband waited, his eyes lit up.

Finn's eyes found hers, darkened with approval, and she felt a flutter in her stomach at his expression. A look that said she shone like his princess too.

They stepped towards each other and he took her hand and that frisson of awareness ran all the way to her shoulder with the promise of magic to come. Watching her, his beautiful mouth curved and he raised her hand to his lips and pressed his mouth against her palm.

'I've spent too much time away from you today,' he said quietly as the room swelled with excitement at their impending departure.

'Soon.' She leaned up and kissed him and breathed in the wonderful manly scent of him. She loved him and she couldn't wait until they were alone. 'I wonder how Frances and Clancy will manage with Piper tonight?'

He shrugged. 'One night. They'll be fine. She'll be in her own bed and Marni is on call for them and dropping in tomorrow before we come home, just to check. Then we all go on our honeymoon.'

'We could have taken her.'

'One night isn't too much to ask. I've been talking to Marni. She suggested we should go away every month for one night in the future.' He waggled his brows at her. 'I'm thinking that's a wonderful idea.'

Catrina would take as many nights in her husband's arms as he offered and she had no doubt he felt the same about her. She placed her hand on the crook of his and he captured it there with his other hand.

'Let's go,' he said and, heads high, they walked out into their future.

* * * * *

LET'S TALK
Romance

For exclusive extracts, competitions
and special offers, find us online:

- f facebook.com/millsandboon
- ▾ @MillsandBoon
- ⬛ @MillsandBoonUK

Get in touch on 01413 063232

For all the latest titles coming soon, visit
millsandboon.co.uk/nextmonth

MILLS & BOON
A ROMANCE FOR EVERY READER

- **FREE** delivery direct to your door

- **EXCLUSIVE** offers every month

- **SAVE** up to 25% on pre-paid subscriptions

SUBSCRIBE AND SAVE

millsandboon.co.uk/Subscribe

MILLS & BOON

THE HEART OF ROMANCE

A ROMANCE FOR EVERY READER

MODERN — Prepare to be swept off your feet by sophisticated, sexy and seductive heroes, in some of the world's most glamourous and romantic locations, where power and passion collide.

HISTORICAL — Escape with historical heroes from time gone by. Whether your passion is for wicked Regency Rakes, muscled Vikings or rugged Highlanders, awak the romance of the past.

MEDICAL — Set your pulse racing with dedicated, delectable doctors in the high-pressure world of medicine, where emotions run high and passion, comfort a love are the best medicine.

True Love — Celebrate true love with tender stories of heartfelt romance, from the rush of falling in love to the joy a new baby can bring, and a focus on the emotional heart of a relationship.

Desire — Indulge in secrets and scandal, intense drama and plenty of sizzling hot action with powerful and passionate heroes who have it all: wealth, status, good looks…everything but the right woman.

HEROES — Experience all the excitement of a gripping thriller, with an intense romance at its heart. Resourceful, true-to-life women and strong, fearless m face danger and desire - a killer combination!

To see which titles are coming soon, please visit
millsandboon.co.uk/nextmonth

JOIN US ON SOCIAL MEDIA!

Stay up to date with our latest releases, author news and gossip, special offers and discounts, and all the behind-the-scenes action from Mills & Boon...

 millsandboon

 millsandboonuk

 millsandboon

It might just be true love...

MILLS & BOON
MEDICAL
Pulse-Racing Passion

Set your pulse racing with dedicated, delectable doctors in the high-pressure world of medicine, where emotions run high and passion, comfort and love are the best medicine.

MILLS & BOON

MODERN

Power and Passion

Prepare to be swept off your feet by
sophisticated, sexy and seductive heroes, in
some of the world's most glamourous and
romantic locations, where power and
passion collide.

Julia James

PREGNANCY SCANDAL

Jennie Lucas

SHEIKH'S ROYAL BRIDE

Kim Lawrence

A WEDDING ITALIAN'S DEMAND

Sharon Kendrick

The SHEIKH'S SECRET BABY

Eight Modern stories published every month, find them all at

millsandboon.co.uk/Modern

MILLS & BOON
True Love
Romance from the Heart

Celebrate true love with tender stories of heartfelt romance, from the rush of falling in love to the joy a new baby can bring, and a focus on the emotional heart of a relationship.

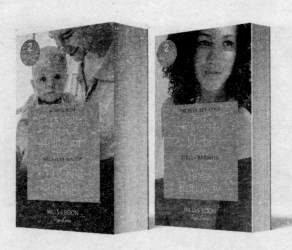